THE
FLOWER
AND THE
SERPENT

MADELEINE D'ESTE

BEACON HILL HIGH SCHOOL

HOLIDAY THEATRE PROGRAM
- winter 1992 -

MACBETH BY WILLIAM SHAKESPEARE

MONDAY – 18TH JUNE 1992

Auditions

TUESDAY – 19TH JUNE 1992

Cast announced and rehearsal

WEDNESDAY – 20TH JUNE 1992

Rehearsal

THURSDAY – 21ST JUNE 1992

Dress rehearsal

FRIDAY – 22ND JUNE 1992

Performance: Beacon Hill High School Theatrette at 7pm

THE
FLOWER
AND THE
SERPENT

CHAPTER 1

VIOLET

VIOLET'S WHOLE BODY HUMMED WITH LEFTOVER AUDITION nerves.

'I'm a dead cert,' she said.

She was the first to climb aboard the empty number 458 bus but Holly and Lila were close behind. They followed the muddy footprints past the chubby lady bus driver as the wipers shrieked across the windshield and the rain slapped the windows. Violet wrinkled her nose. The bus reeked of soggy wool.

'I can't wait until tomorrow,' Violet said as she slid into her regular seat halfway up the aisle. 'When my name is on top of the list.'

'You're a shoo-in.' Lila flopped into the seat in front of her. She turned and draped her skinny arm over the metal bar. 'He'd be stupid not to cast you.'

The doors wheezed shut and the bus pulled out of the school and onto Beacon Hill Road. The midwinter sun had already disappeared behind Mount Wellington.

'Angelika was alright, too.' Holly squashed in next to Lila and sat backwards. 'And the one with the curls. Rowan?'

Violet snorted and tossed her mousy hair. 'Out. Out. Damned spot,' she groaned in a monotone and snatched the last chip from the packet in Holly's hand.

Holly pressed her lips together.

Lila giggled. 'Maybe we'll be cast as the witches. There's three of them and three of us.' She bounced in her seat. 'We could get some props from your aunty, hey, Holly? Real witch supplies?'

Holly crushed the empty chip packet in her fist and turned away. But the late Hobart afternoon was as black as night and Violet could see

1

Holly's square-jawed scowl reflected in the window. Holly seemed to sulk a lot these days.

'Witches? No way,' Violet scoffed. 'It's Lady Macbeth or nothing.'

'Of course, I'm an idiot. You'll get the part for sure.' Lila chewed her cuticles and shrugged. 'I just thought it'd be fun. Us three. Together.'

Violet said nothing and neither did Holly.

'Sorry.' Lila playfully nudged Holly's arm. 'I didn't mean it. The witch thing.'

Holly turned back to them with a sigh. 'It's not you.' She squeezed the bridge of her nose. 'This headache—'

'What were you girls doing at the school?' the curly-headed bus driver hollered.

Violet and her friends flinched. A pair of murky green eyes looked back at them through the rear vision mirror.

'Holiday program,' Lila called back.

'All alone in that place during holidays?' The bus driver raised an eyebrow. 'They should never have built a school on that land. Or anything for that matter. Should have left it be.'

Violet rolled her eyes. 'Everyone knows they purified it first, lady.'

'The surety of youth,' the bus driver chuckled. 'I was once like you.' Her voice was strange and lilting, she spoke with a musical accent Violet couldn't place. 'Life is not as it seems.'

Violet rotated a finger next to her temple and Lila stifled a giggle. Holly dipped her head to hide her eyes under her fringe.

'You three are best friends?'

'Totally.' Lila grinned. 'Ever since Grade Seven.'

Violet stared at her black eight-hole Doc Martens and chewed her lip. She noticed Holly didn't say anything, either.

'Women need to band together. Especially you three. You must look out for each other.'

'What do you mean?' Lila said. 'Especially us?'

'You three have challenges up ahead,' the driver said.

Lila glanced at Holly and then Violet. 'What does she mean?'

'She probably means life stuff.' Holly twirled a strand of dark brown hair around her finger. 'Exams. Finishing school. Getting off this stupid island. I can't wait.'

The bus driver went quiet. The tyres squelched on the wet road as the bus veered around the infamous hairpin bend and damp grey-green eucalyptus slapped on either side.

The three girls slid across the seats around the bend.

A few years ago in the late 1980s, a bus exactly like this one misjudged the turn and six lives were wiped out in a single mistake. Violet's stomach clenched twice a day, five times a week, every time she passed the stone memorial on the way to school. The black and white photo of the bent wreckage was still vivid in her mind.

'What challenges?' asked Lila. She clutched at the metal bar until her knuckles were white.

The bus driver said nothing.

Violet rubbed her duffle coat sleeve against the fogged-up window and peered outside as the bus passed the small strip of local shops. First was The Three Torches, a cafe-bookshop run by Holly's aunt. Then Terri's Bakehouse where Violet worked Saturdays selling congealed yellow vanilla slices and the whitest of white bread. Then the dry cleaners and the sha-man hairdressers with his multi-coloured Tibetan prayer flags and incense fluttering in the breeze, and finally the milk bar takeaway. Even through the glass, Violet could smell the old chip oil, the spicy Nag Champa and the astringent dry-cleaning fumes.

A figure in a raincoat with the hood pulled up stood at the kerb in the rain. Beside them, a muscular pointy-eared black dog strained at his leash. The person lifted a finger and pointed directly at the bus, directly through the window, directly at Violet. The face was a black shadow, no real face at all but somehow the hidden eyes bored straight into her, the gaze like an apple-corer.

With a gasp, she tore her gaze away from the window, her heart thumping.

'What?' said Lila.

'Nothing,' Violet muttered but when she turned back, the person was still there on the kerb, and still pointing. She shuddered. 'Another loony.'

They travelled a few more blocks in silence, then the Beacon Hill Road straightened out after the weatherboard Scout Hall, the place for senior aerobics and Morris dancing. Her heartbeat settled as the man in the raincoat disappeared from view.

'Three challenges for three friends,' the bus driver continued. 'I can see it clearly.'

The girls leaned forward in their seats.

'What are you? Some kind of fortune teller?' Lila said. 'A psychic?'

Violet shoved Holly. 'You know about all that stuff. Witchy poo.'

Holly poked out her tongue.

'One of you will shine like a star,' the bus driver proclaimed.

Violet shimmied in her seat. It was obviously her.

The driver went on. 'One of you will invite darkness into her breast.'

'Breast? That'd be you.' Holly raised a dark eyebrow and prodded Violet in the boob. Violet swiped away her finger with a glare.

'Darkness?' Lila grimaced. 'What do you mean? What does she mean?'

'One of you will depart forever,' the driver concluded.

'Depart forever?' Lila clawed at the metal bar between the seats. 'That's not good. That can't be good.'

'Excuse me, Miss.' Holly raised her hand. 'I don't think this is appropriate—'

'Death? Is she saying one of us is going to die?' Lila wheezed.

'What are you saying, lady?' Violet squinted, projecting her voice up the empty bus. She loved how the power rippled up from her diaphragm when she used her breath in the right way. 'Are you trying to scare us? Cos it's not working.'

'Ignore me if you like, girls,' the bus driver said. 'It is your choice to listen. But you have been warned.'

'One of us is going to die?' Lila said with a crack in her voice. 'How? When?'

'There are powers in this world we cannot comprehend. You must beware.'

'Today? Do we need to be careful today?'

The bus driver shifted her focus back to the road. Her face closed like a shutter.

'You have to give us more information than that. You can't just—'

But the woman behind the wheel didn't respond. She didn't even look their way. It was as though she'd never said a word.

'Excuse me,' Lila said and waved her arm. 'Tell us more. Please.'

The bus driver kept her eyes on the road.

'Why won't she tell us?' Lila chewed her finger, her eyes glazed.

'Forget it,' Violet snorted. 'She's just another nutbag.'

Violet wondered why Lila was so fazed, she'd lived around Beacon Hill her whole life and knew all the weird stories off by heart. She should be used to strange people by now.

The bus moaned to a stop. The back doors hissed open and a sharp slap of cold wind blew inside.

'You have to tell us more.' Lila scrambled up the aisle towards the driver's seat, her canvas school bag clutched to her chest. 'Who? Which one of us?'

'Last stop.'

'Please,' Lila whined.

Holly grabbed her by the elbow. 'Leave it.'

'She can't just tell us someone is going to die and then say nothing else. She said beware. But what of?' Lila raked her fingers through her home-dyed burgundy hair. 'Do you think she cursed us?'

'Come on. Let's go.' Violet headed towards the door.

Holly tugged at Lila's sleeve. 'Don't get worked up about it. You know what you're like. We'll call the bus company tomorrow. Make a complaint.'

Lila sighed and followed Holly out into the wet air. Misty droplets dribbled down the graffiti-etched bus shelter.

'Weirdo!' Violet yelled out as the bus driver closed the concertina doors and the bus rumbled away. Violet pulled up her duffle coat hood as the red tail lights bled onto the wet road.

'What if she's right? One of us could die,' Lila said. Raindrops brimmed on her eyelashes and she didn't wipe them away.

'Forget about it,' Violet said. 'Right, Holly?'

'Well, I think we should tell someone,' Holly said. 'But maybe you're right. Don't think about it, Lila. It's just some stupid joke. Nothing's going to happen.'

'It's not very funny,' Lila huffed. 'And I have this strange—'

'Well, I'm off. Lines to learn,' Violet said with a smirk. 'Lady Macbeth lines. See you tomorrow.'

'With bells on,' Lila said but her smile didn't reach her eyes.

'To witness the grand unveiling of my name up on the board tomorrow,' Violet said. 'Violet Black as Lady Macbeth.'

With a wave, the three friends went their separate ways into the gloom. Violet wrapped her arms around herself as she trudged down Melaleuca Avenue, through the shadows and puddles, past the rows of empty brown brick-and-tile houses with double garages. There wasn't another soul around.

Violet couldn't wait until Friday night when she stepped out onto her stage and shone like a star.

Maybe there was some truth to the crazy bus driver's words.

Dear Journal

I failed again.

I didn't do my affirmations. And now the shadows are back, following me again. If only I was more disciplined, if only I was stronger. But it's all my fault. Tomorrow, I will say my affirmations twenty times before breakfast.

I am positive, I am happy, I am in control of my destiny.

If I smile more, no one notices. No one questions. I can hide it from them all. No one needs to know what I'm going through. I can fix it, I am sure I can.

I have to.

But sometimes, no matter how hard I try, little cracks open up. Sometimes I feel like I'm held together with only chewing gum and nail polish. One more comment, one more attack and I'm scared I'll crack right open. And it'll be messy. One more bad thing and it will all explode, I'll explode.

I watch them. Their lives seem so easy, so simple. If only I could be like them. Why am I different? Why do I have to be this? What did I do wrong to attract the darkness? I try to be good but I'm stained.

There I go again. I must banish my negative thoughts, otherwise they'll take over. I must try harder.

But some days, the dark is so tempting.

It's so tiring fighting them.

I am positive, I am happy, I am in control of my destiny.

THE GATEKEEPERS

With a final flourish of the paintbrush, the leader completed the yellow symbol and joined the others sitting cross-legged in the circle on the concrete floor.

'It is time.'

Her palms pressed flat on the cold ground, she bowed her head and drew in three long raspy breaths.

Red shadows stretched across the garage. The gauzy shawl draped over the lamp cast an otherworldly film over the paint tins, rusty bicycle and lawnmower.

'O Great One, hear us. Hear our invocation. Bless us with your presence here in our humble circle.' Her clear and commanding voice bounced off the brick walls.

The three women clasped hands. One pair was damp, the others were as cool as marble but all three minds were still and focused. With eyes firmly shut, they concentrated on a singular point, the yellow sigil painted on the ground between them.

'Witness our sign, O Great One. Feel our allegiance, know our intent, imbue us with your power. The time has come.'

The other two began their chorus, which was barely more than a mutter at first. 'Closing in, closing in, closing in,' they repeated. White clouds formed as they chanted, words visible in the chilled air. Their volume increased little by little, until the syllables hummed in their breast bones.

Rising to their feet, they circled the symbol slowly. With each step, the acrid oil paint odour became sweeter, everything outside the perimeter of the circle blurred.

'Infuse. Infuse. Infuse.'

After completing the circle three times, they unclasped hands and sat with palms open, their faces gleaming. The circle was alive, the air as taut and heavy as the seconds before a first crack of lightning.

'We are your servants in this world, followers of your path, your vessels. We do as you wish,' the leader declared.

'Yours. Yours. Yours,' the others softly chanted underneath.

'Hear our plea,' the leader said. 'We are here, your faithful servants, as we promised. The portents show the time has come. Infuse us and this symbol with your power, so we can fulfil our duty and follow your bidding in this world, to guard the gateway.'

'Infuse. Infuse. Infuse.'

'We yield to your power, your strength, your force, your ancient wisdom. Please bless us and bring our symbol to life.'

'To life.'

A bright light flashed. The lamp in the corner flared. The room became painfully white. The three flinched and squinted.

The yellow symbol shimmered on the concrete floor like molten gold and hummed in their ears. The harsh light in the room softened to pink, then dimmed into the deep red shadows once more.

The leader chuckled as the sigil continued to buzz. 'O Great One. You have shown your approval. You have granted us with your blessing. The symbol is empowered. We thank you for your gift.'

'We thank you. Thank you. Thank you.'

'Now we can commence our duties, as we promised on the day we devoted our lives to your service. We will make you proud, O Great One.'

'O Warden. O Great One.'

The three bowed their heads and the leader clapped her hands three times. The golden symbol faded until it was ordinary yellow paint on oil-stained concrete. But below the surface, in the periphery of their hearing, the power of the sigil purred.

'It is done.' The leader smiled. Her shoulders softened and her voice returned to normal. 'The sigil is infused and our first step is complete. But now we must go. We have much to do tonight.'

―⁓⁓―

ROWAN
Last Night

Rowan clunked the phone down. The transparent phone with all its coloured wire guts on display had been a sixteenth birthday present from her mum. Rowan hugged her knees and grinned. His words still tingled over her. He was so sweet.

Her eyelids were heavy. She wriggled under the doona still smiling, and the day quickly faded away.

But something woke her. A scrape. A scratch at her toes. She grunted groggily and pulled her feet up to her chest. Kieran. Stupid little brother.

'Go away, you little turd,' she mumbled and kicked, and the tickling went away. Rowan squeezed her eyes shut again and dropped back into a dreamy half sleep, reliving the way he gently brushed the wayward strands of hair from her cheek.

But her fantasy didn't last long.

Something prickled over her toes and the tops of her feet under the doona. Soft little footsteps scuttled over her bare legs. She jerked upright. Her bedside lamp cast a circle of dim light over her bed. She scraped her feet down her shins, one after the other, and whipped the doona off.

She screamed. She must be still asleep. She slammed her eyes shut.

But she could still feel them.

It must be real. But it couldn't be.

How?

Black spiders, all over her legs and daisy patterned sheets. Ten, twenty, thirty, forty of them scuttling and writhing, jostling and clambering, over each other, all over her. She scampered backwards, screaming and flicking them off, her heart thundering, her breath rasping in her throat.

But as soon as she flicked one away, another replaced it.

And another.

And another.

A sea of arachnids streamed over her body.

'Get off,' Rowan wailed, hoping her mum, Kieran, anyone would come, but her bedroom door stayed firmly closed, the house deathly silent.

Swarms of black bodies scampered up her arms, climbed up into her curls and headed towards her face. She leaped from her bed and squealed as another one scurried across her clammy forehead. Rowan pulled clumps of hair from her scalp with spiders attached. Her cottage flower printed wallpaper undulated and heaved, black with writhing hairy legs.

'Help! Help!' She screeched, her stomach twitched, ten times worse than her worst ever cramps. But the spider-covered bedroom door stayed closed. Only a thousand fractal eyes stared back, their fangs glistening with poison.

Couldn't anyone hear her screams? Rowan sucked in a breath. She grabbed a boot off the floor and slammed the heel down hard onto the carpet, squashing two, then three, four, five spiders. She kicked aside the dead, but more came. Waves of spiders poured through the air vent above her window. She dumped the boot and clambered across the room on hands and knees, right into the centre of a thick sticky web. White silk tendrils coated her face and hair, gripping at her nightie. She shuddered and ripped the cobwebs away but the stubborn threads clung on and more spiders scuttled up her body. She flung and flicked her arms, sending little black bodies slamming into the walls.

Rowan freed herself from the web and scrambled across the room, wrenching open her wardrobe door. She pushed aside her long dresses and coats, her ill-fitting shoes, boxes of old school work and her hockey stick, squeezed into the back corner and slammed the door shut.

Safe behind the closed door, she panted but it was only seconds before black shadows rippled across the wardrobe door and the first hairy legs poked through the gaps in the louvres. It was silly to think she was safe, she was backed into a corner and they were coming for her.

More and more came, gushing through every crack and gap. The scuttling black mass enveloped her skin and her hair, pulled at her lips, crept inside her nostrils and, crawled in her ears. Then she felt the first fang pierce her skin.

The last thing Rowan remembered was the sound of her own screaming.

CHAPTER 2

VIOLET

VIOLET LEANED BACK ON THE CONCRETE BENCH IN THE QUAD, took a long drag and rehearsed her facial expression one more time. She rubbed her gritty eyes. It had been two o'clock by the time she'd perfected the right mix of confidence, humility and surprise in the mirror. But she was ready for her close-up now.

On the other side of the Quad, three bald men in navy-blue coveralls slapped paint over a swirly symbol in yellow on the eastern wall of the gym. Their movements were slow and synchronised, the paint strokes mesmerising. They didn't say a word.

Smoke streamed out of her nostrils like twin chimneys and she thought back to yesterday's weird bus ride. She knew which prediction applied to her, but what about the other two? Darkness and departing? Which warning was directed at Lila and which one was meant for Holly? Lila was so fragile, like a translucent baby bird while Holly was battle hardened. Years of bullying will do that to a person.

'Come on. It's up,' Lila shouted across the concrete square. Violet smirked and stubbed out her smoke. She always savoured the last moment as she snuffed the life out of the red embers. Lila hurried over, all skinny legs like a stick insect. Violet shivered. She never understood how Lila coped with bare legs in winter.

'Come on.' Lila tugged at Violet's duffle coat, her eyes red-rimmed but shining. What kept Lila awake last night?

Violet threw her backpack over her shoulder and strutted towards the building.

The girls' black boots squeaked in rhythm on the linoleum floor and echoed off the concrete block walls as they passed the dark computer labs, the empty library and the locked-up science block. Long quiet shadows replaced the rush of teenagers. The corridors seemed vast and tomb-like.

Violet and Holly jumped when a classroom door opened. A lumpy woman in fuchsia shuffled awkwardly out of the opening door, her arms loaded high with test tubes and beakers.

'Sorry, girls. Didn't mean to scare you,' she said, with an asthmatic snuffle.

'Miss Quinlin,' Lila stammered. 'I didn't think any other teachers were here.'

'Holidays are nice and quiet.' She chuckled. 'I can get a lot done without you interfering students. There's the stocktakes of all the broken and stolen equipment, lesson plans. Plenty to do. Plenty to do.' Miss Quinlin shifted the tower of glass objects in her arms.

Violet pictured millions of pieces of glass shattering across the floor and waited for the smash, but Miss Quinlin deftly rebalanced her load. Violet exhaled with a little disappointment.

'And you two? Theatre program I gather? Another nice musical this year? You were very good last time. Doe a deer, a female deer.'

'Macbeth,' Lila said.

Miss Quinlin's forehead rippled. 'Oh.'

'And Violet's going to be Lady Macbeth.'

Violet smoothed down her hair and lifted her chin. Miss Quinlin bit at her bottom lip.

'I hope I don't jinx you?' Lila grimaced.

'Don't be silly. It's obvious.'

A crackle of white noise blasted out of the public address system speakers above their heads. Violet jolted.

'What was that?' Lila gasped.

'Who cares?' Violet tugged on Lila's arm. 'Come on.'

'We have to go. Bye, Miss Quinlin.' Lila waved and they sped off, leaving the science teacher standing in the middle of the corridor, her eyebrows knitted.

'Did you see that Quasimodo's cardigan?' giggled Violet as they turned the corner. 'Do you think she knits them herself?'

'Don't call her that,' said Lila.

'She won't hear. She's off with the fairies most of the time anyway.'

'Imagine what her husband is like.' Lila shivered.

'Who'd marry her?' Violet snorted. 'She'd have a house full of cat hair and potpourri.'

Violet sucked in a deep breath as she and Lila pushed through the double doors into the drama department. A handful of younger boys huddled around the notice board in the corridor but Lila cleared Violet's path by shoving aside a crestfallen Year Eight boy.

Violet closed her eyes and licked her lips, ready for her highlight reel moment. Her casting as Lady Macbeth was unquestionable after playing Maria in last term's successful production of *The Sound of Music*. The glowing review in the Beacon Hill Gazette, now laminated and Blu-tacked next to her bedroom mirror, described her performance as 'charming and delightful'. It was official.

But that was last term. Unfortunately, Mrs Tulloch had left the school suddenly, something to do with nerves. She was replaced by Mr Ravenswood who was fresh out of uni with his old man clothes and his pretentious voice. Violet had taken it upon herself to educate the new drama teacher about her position in the high school theatre community. She left copies of her Maria review in his office and under the windshield of his car. She would've posted copies to his house but the school secretary wouldn't provide his address, even when Violet explained the importance. Apparently giving out teachers' addresses was against school policy. Power-tripper. But when Violet was invited to audition for the holiday program, she knew her campaign had worked.

'Oh,' Lila gasped.

Violet's heart stopped, her eyes sprang open. She stepped forward and frantically scoured the list of names.

'There must be a mistake.' Lila grasped Violet's shoulder but Violet flicked her hand away. She checked the list twice, fists bunched at her sides. Three times. Were her eyes playing tricks on her? But it was true, the cast list was there in black and white.

'Angelika fucking Ostholz.' Violet growled.

She elbowed Lila and the others aside and stormed off down the corridor.

THE DARK HAND

We are wise.

Older than you, older than them, all of them. Older than the trees, the ground, the earth, the skies, as old as time itself.

We are before, we are now, we are forever. Ingrained, we live in everything.

You know who we are, even if you do not know our name.

We watch.

We wait.

We listen to every conversation, every thought. We are there when you whimper at 3am and the rest of the world is asleep. We hear your tears in the toilets at lunchtime. We are there when you linger too long on the bridge watching the creek flow swiftly underneath, when you stand on the edge of the kerb as a truck hurtles past.

We understand.

We are alike.

Like you, we are misunderstood.

But we are here for you. Whenever you need us.

When no one else understands, we do.

We know.

We understand what you want, what you need.

We are your friend.

The only ones you can rely on.

VIOLET

'Bitch. Bastard.' Violet spat and stomped away from the bulletin board and down the corridor. 'Bastard. Bitch.'

The fluorescent lighting flickered above her head. On and off, on and off. The corridor was blanketed in darkness, then blasted with blunt white light. She passed another maintenance man in blue coveralls who was rehanging a door and like the others, he was silent and bald. Violet ground her teeth harder with each step closer to Ravenswood's office. It must be a mistake. She rubbed at her chin and forced a slow breath out of her lungs. She'd give him a chance to make amends. They had plenty of time until before Friday's performance.

She rounded the corner. The teachers' offices sat in the inner core of the school building, like a row of jail cells with no windows. The lights were off and the corridor was as dark as night, the only source of light was an open door up ahead and the red neon exit sign.

Once she explained his mistake, he'd understand and put it right. It would be a little embarrassing for him, having to admit his blunder, and Angelika would have to live with the disappointment, but such was life.

Violet loitered in the doorway. Ravenswood sat at a desk littered with bulging Manila folders, a purple paisley scarf around his neck. A wrinkled Royal Shakespeare Company poster was Blu-tacked to the beige brick wall behind him and the room stunk of stale coffee. Violet pushed her breath right down into her diaphragm, exactly the way her acting book taught her.

Mr Ravenswood glanced up. 'Ah, Jeanette. Come in.' He pushed his glasses up his nose and gestured to a cracked plastic chair.

'It's Violet.' She narrowed her eyes. 'And I'll stand.'

'I thought the roll said Jeanette.' Ravenswood reached for a green clipboard under the mess on his desk.

'I go by Violet now,' she said with folded arms. She rested her back against the cold brick wall. 'Mrs Tulloch knew that.'

'Well, I am not Mrs Tulloch.'

She raised an eyebrow. 'I know.'

'I gather you are here about the production?'

'There's been a mistake.'

'You mean the cast list?' he said. 'I put it up myself.'

'But Angelika Ostholz?'

'Lady Macbeth. Yes.' He stared back at her without blinking.

Violet frowned. 'She's not...' Her tongue turned thick and uncooperative. 'I was Maria.'

'I know. I got your little messages.' Ravenswood lifted his glasses from his nose and sucked on an arm. 'But this isn't *The Sound of Music*, Violet. This is Shakespeare. Quite a different story, if you get my drift.'

'But she…' Violet's mouth opened and closed like a gate in the wind.

'I can see you're disappointed. It seems you had your heart set on Lady Macbeth. And you weren't the only one. But we can't always get what we want. This time you missed out. There'll be other opportunities. Other roles,' he said, smoothing back his hair. 'Roles you're more suited for.'

'I'm not a witch,' she said, thrusting her chin in the air.

'But everyone knows the witches from *Macbeth*. Even people who know nothing about the Bard. They're an integral part of the story. Iconic.'

Violet narrowed her eyes. Ravenswood leaned back in his creaking chair, his fingers threaded behind his head.

'I'm going to Mrs Petrakis. I want to make a complaint.' Violet's hands were shaking. 'Formally.'

'This isn't some frothy musical, Violet. This is Shakespeare. Part of my job as director is to have a vision. I have a very clear picture of what I want and I'm aiming for a particular look. A classical interpretation. Unfortunately, Violet, you do not fit my vision.'

Violet scowled as Ravenswood assessed her. She wrapped her lips over her crooked teeth, sucked in her stomach and fluffed out her shirt.

'You'll make a perfectly acceptable witch.'

'But I should be Lady Macbeth,' she said. 'And Mrs Petrakis will agree.'

Mrs Petrakis had singled Violet out specifically in assembly, comparing her performance to Julie Andrews in front of the whole school. When the headmistress found out, Violet knew she would fix this.

'You're perfectly welcome to contact her. And you're free to leave the holiday program. There's no one holding you here.'

Violet stared at the scarf around Ravenswood's neck and gritted her teeth. She resisted the urge to lunge forward. Pull the noose tighter and tighter, until his eyes bulged and he begged for mercy, until his face was puce and he admitted his mistake. Until he offered her back the part with an over-the-top apology in front of everyone. She licked her lips.

Ravenswood pointed to the white-faced clock on the wall. 'Rehearsals begin in ten minutes. If you come, I want you to be fully committed. I can't have people leaving midway through and letting the rest of the cast down. A production is a team effort. We only have a few days and everyone must pull their weight.'

'I'm familiar with how theatre works, Mr Ravenswood.' Violet rolled her eyes.

'That's why I invited you to participate in the program. With your experience, you'll be a valuable member of the troupe. But it's up to you.' Ravenswood leaned forward. 'Do I have your commitment, Violet?'

Violet sucked down a deep breath, but said nothing.

'Suit yourself.' He shrugged.

He picked up a stack of assignments and turned in his chair. The filing cabinet drawer opened with a metallic squeal.

She sighed. She hoped Mrs Petrakis's number was in the White Pages.

The filing cabinet drawer closed again with a thump.

'*Ow!*' Ravenswood yelled.

His polyester scarf was trapped tight in the closed drawer and sliced across his neck like a garrotte. He tugged, coughed and gasped, fingers clawing at the ligature. Violet watched from the doorway but she didn't move. With a grunt, he yanked the scarf free from the filing cabinet and chucked it across the desk but the flimsy fabric wafted through the air.

Ravenswood panted and rubbed at his throat. A red welt swelled under his fingers.

For the first time since she'd seen the cursed cast list, Violet smiled.

RAVENSWOOD

Ravenswood grasped at his neck and glared as Violet walked away. It was all her fault, she distracted him with her whingeing. Ordinarily he was extremely co-ordinated. His finger traced over his Adam's apple and a crust of blood from this morning's shave. Damned blunt razor.

He shook his head. What gall. She was no Lady Macbeth. So ungrateful, she was lucky to get a part at all, and she had completely the wrong attitude for his theatre community at Beacon Hill High School. He should've sent her packing, back to whatever teenagers did during their school holidays these days: Nintendo, getting pregnant, smoking bongs. Unfortunately, Beacon Hill wasn't Hollywood and the talent pool was shallow, and there were only three days till the performance.

Ravenswood checked the clock again. They'd be trudging through the school gates now, yawning and rubbing their eyes. He grabbed his wretched scarf and wrapped it around his neck, hiding the red mark. With his accessories in place, he rolled back his shoulders and took a calming breath. It was suicidal to show even a smidgen of weakness with these children. Animals. They were brutal if you gave them even half a chance.

He patted the pile of photocopied scripts and slurped the last dregs from his mug. He shuddered as a congealed skin of milk coated his tongue.

The kids wouldn't care if he was a few minutes late. He dialled the number, clearing his throat as he listened to the dial tone.

'Wolf.'

Such gravitas and warmth with a single word, so professional.

'Alan. Paul Ravenswood. So glad I finally caught you.'

'Ah, Paul, how are you?'

'Very well, Alan.' His heart fluttered, he was so wrapped up in his admiration, he almost forgot to be nervous. 'And yourself?'

'Bordering on marvellous. But awfully busy. So many balls in the air as they say.' He chuckled and Ravenswood laughed along with him, a little too boisterously but Alan Wolf didn't seem to notice. 'I don't mean to be rude, Paul, but I can only spare a few minutes. What can I do for you today?'

'Remember the opening night party for *Wild Minds*? Excellent production by the way, great use of sound. I can still hear the nails up the blackboard. Anyway, we discussed my new project.'

'Of course. Of course. You're very kind. Now, I spoke with lots of lovely people that night. And the bubbles were flowing, if you know what I mean. Would you be so kind as to refresh my memory?'

'My upcoming production of *Macbeth*.'

'Ah, yes. You're the chap with the blonde fringe.'

'No,' Ravenswood said, swallowing hard. 'Glasses and shoulder length brown hair. You complimented my cravat. I was in your Directing 201 course in '88.'

He didn't want to mention the name of his final production. He expected Alan would've forgotten all about it. Ravenswood had, almost.

'Silly me, of course. Ravenswood. How could I forget? The Scottish Play, you say? Community theatre wasn't it? Or was it am-dram?'

'High school. Beacon Hill.'

'High school kids and the Bard. Excellent. A few select scenes, I gather?'

'No, the whole play.'

'Your end of term production? You've been rehearsing the Scottish all term, I take it?'

'Not exactly. We've done bits and pieces here and there in class. A scene or two. They study it in depth in English class in Year Ten. I've hand-picked the best talent in the school.'

'You're doing the whole play in a week?'

'Three days really.'

'I see. Quite ambitious. Very...erm...bold.'

'Thank you, Alan. I want to prove any group of kids are capable of mastering Shakespeare.'

'Interesting.'

Ravenswood blushed. He and Alan Wolf were kindred spirits, both lives committed to the noble cause of improving the cultural literacy of this backwater.

'Now, Peter. Sorry to rush you, Peter, but I really must be tootling off to my first appointment—'

'I called to invite you to our opening night on Friday,' Ravenswood blurted.

'I will have to check my diary—'

'There'll be complimentary tickets on at the door for you and a guest, of course. And afterwards, if you could talk to the kids, give a little speech. Advice for those interested in a career in the theatre. The kids would really benefit from your experience.'

'I'll have to let you know. My apologies, Peter—'

'Paul.'

'I must be going. It was nice speaking with you. And break a leg. Very ambitious. Cheerio.'

Ravenswood placed down the receiver and crossed his arms, Alan

Wolf at the performance on Friday. Once the great man had witnessed what Ravenswood had accomplished in only a week, his transformation of a group of average kids into competent Shakespearian actors in only a few days, he'd sit up and take notice.

Ravenswood smoothed back his hair. And later backstage, Alan Wolf would compliment him on a wonderful job. Right there and then he would offer Ravenswood a place in his theatre troupe. He'd blush humbly. He'd thank Wolf for his offer and say 'he'd have to think it over'. He had to consider the kids, of course. And he couldn't appear too eager.

Leaning back in his creaky chair, Ravenswood smiled. The fluorescent tube in the ceiling above his head flickered. He flinched and glanced in all directions. Without the usual bustle of other teachers and kids, the corridors felt as cold and clinical as a morgue. There was nothing to drown out his apprehensions. Ravenswood shuddered as the light steadied back to normal. After Friday night's production, it'd all be worth it, coming back to this place with all its memories and myths, ignoring his sister's warnings.

But the fears had never been far from his mind. They'd been with him even at his interview six months earlier.

'Do you have any other questions?' Mrs Petrakis had smiled, her diamanté flower brooch sparkling against her dark blue suit.

Ravenswood had chewed on his lip. There was a question on the tip of his tongue, but would he ruin the interview if he asked?

'This might sound a little unusual...' he rubbed his hands in his lap. 'But the school...' Mrs Petrakis pressed her lips together ever so slightly, but Ravenswood continued. '... has an interesting history.'

Mrs Petrakis lifted a finger in the air. 'Let's be clear. Not the school. Beacon Hill itself. Long before the school was built. Are you a superstitious man, Mr Ravenswood?'

'No,' Ravenswood fidgeted in his seat. 'Just curious.'

'Before the government started building, there was an interdenominational ceremony that involved Catholic, Protestant, Islamic, Jewish and Buddhist leaders. The local Aboriginal elders played a pivotal role and even the Order of the Thorn attended. Did you see the photographs in reception? It was quite the event. But if you ask me, it was a publicity stunt for the mayor. Anything for the front page of *The Mercury*.'

'The ground was exorcised?'

'Someone has been watching too many films.' Mrs Petrakis blinked slowly. 'Up here on the hill, with the bush on all sides, we're separated off from the rest of the suburb and the city. At this high elevation, the clouds roll in during winter and hang about all day. Rumours get passed through families, from one generation to another, and embellished along the way to scare younger brothers and sisters.' She shrugged. 'People will believe what they want.'

'So, you've experienced nothing strange here?'

Mrs Petrakis's eyes drifted to the floor, she toyed with the fine gold cross at her neck.

'Nothing,' she said.

VIOLET

Violet rested against the rough brick wall by the gold payphone, her back to the empty corridor, and flicked through the White Pages. Taroona, Berriedale, Lenah Valley. Where would Mrs Petrakis live? A ripple of air, like a cool exhaled breath, wafted through her hair. A cold chill quivered up her spine. She jerked her head up, eyes darting left and right, but she was alone in the dark corridor.

She rubbed her neck and tried the first name listed. Mrs Petrakis would understand. Violet practised her most convincing speech as she waited for the headmistress to pick up her call, but the phone rang out. No one picked up, not even an answering machine.

Her coins rolled back down the chute and she tried the second number. An elderly woman answered in a thick Greek accent and asked when she was coming to fix her heater.

She dialled the third and final number. 'The number you have dialled is unavailable. Please check the number before trying again.' She slumped against the payphone. Her watch said nine thirty. Time for rehearsals to start.

As Ravenswood had said, the play was voluntary. Violet could walk away and take a few more shifts at Terri's Bakehouse. She could sleep till lunchtime, lie on the couch in her pyjamas and watch midday movies, scoffing Tim-tams while her Mum was at work. Or she could read ahead, study up on next term's curriculum and guarantee her place in the drama course at uni. She could leave these amateurs to their mess.

But Lady Macbeth was hers. She was already living inside her head. Their blood was mixed in her veins. She couldn't walk away. And besides, Mrs Petrakis would be home later. Three days was plenty of time to get her role back. Violet smiled and turned for the drama room. There'd been no mention of an understudy. Until her role was rightfully returned, she'd be Angelika's shadow and revel in every one of her mistakes.

The open plan drama room was empty except for a circle of thirteen plastic chairs. The windows at the far end of the classroom looked out onto the soggy drooping gum trees which surrounded the school. Weak daylight struggled in through the glass and dappled the scratchy blue carpet tiles.

Wayne and Jason were in T-shirts despite the winter. They wrestled, knocking over a chair with a cheer. Jacinta, Angelika and Lionel chatted and leaned against the wall, all straight teeth and long limbs and not a single zit between them. A few younger pimple-faced boys sat in the circle of chairs, scowling, probably relegated to guards and footmen.

But no one had been downgraded quite like Violet who had nose-dived from star to bit player. She ducked her head to avoid their sneers and scrambled for a seat.

'Did you speak to him?' Lila slid next to her.

'He's such an idiot,' Violet muttered.

'He's not too bad,' Holly added as she slid into the plastic chair beside them.

'Oooh. You think he's cute. Mrs Ravenswood.' Lila elbowed Holly.

Holly violently shook her head but her cheeks went pink.

'I told him he'd made a terrible mistake and I wasn't going to stand for it,' Violet said. 'But he wouldn't listen. I'm making a formal complaint.'

Lila covered her mouth with her bitten fingers.

'This is my future he's wrecking. It's serious. I have to do whatever it takes to fix it. I called Mrs Petrakis to complain, but she wasn't home,'

Violet said. 'It's no biggie, she'll be there later. But until she sorts him out, I'm going to be the understudy.' She jutted out her chin.

'Are you sure?' Lila frowned.

'Hasn't she gone on holiday?' Holly said as she twirled a finger in her dark brown hair. 'Someone mentioned a conference on the mainland?'

Violet narrowed her eyes. 'As if she'd go anywhere.' But Violet's stomach plummeted. Holly couldn't be right all the time.

Ravenswood swept into the centre of the circle of seat and clapped his hands. 'Take a seat, everyone. Time to begin.'

The chatter died down as everyone drifted into a seat around the circle. Violet scowled. There was no place for her to hide in this seating arrangement, another reason to curse Ravenswood.

'You've all seen the cast list by now. Congratulations to our leading actors. Lionel and Angelika.'

Everyone clapped, except Violet.

The olive-skinned Lionel doffed an imaginary cap with a smile. He was regal with excellent diction, unlike the rest of the ocker mumblers. Violet had to admit Lionel Pereira was *the* only choice for Macbeth.

Angelika shyly smiled with a half-shrug and a toss of blonde hair. Violet clenched her fists and resisted the urge to leap across the circle and smash in her dimples.

'But well done, everyone. I knew there was talent here at Beacon Hill and I was not disappointed.'

The door squeaked open and Jez slipped into the last spare seat in the circle. He dumped his skateboard with a thud and flicked his floppy fringe from his eyes. Violet's stomach cartwheeled. She dropped her scowl and beamed across at him, but Jez didn't even glance in her direction. Like everyone else, his focus was on Angelika.

'So our cast is settled—'

Violet raised her hand. 'I have a question.'

'Yes,' Ravenswood stuttered as he reached for his scarf.

'What about understudies? Because I am—'

'No wonder she didn't get the part,' Wayne snorted at Jason next to him, but Wayne was more accustomed to shouting directions on a footy field and everyone turned. 'Can't even read.'

Violet glared.

'It was on the board.' Ravenswood nodded.

Violet turned to Lila and hissed. 'Who?'

'Rowan,' Lila murmured and lowered her head.

Rowan's freckled cheeks reddened as Violet glowered at her.

'Why didn't you tell me?'

'I tried.'

With a huff, Violet slouched down in her seat. Now there were three in her way. Angelika, Rowan and of course, Ravenswood.

'And that's not all. I have some exciting news.' Ravenswood rubbed his hands together. 'I was just got off the phone with Alan Wolf.'

'No,' Violet muttered under her breath.

'Alan Wolf runs the Tasmanian Theatre Company and is one of the best lecturers in the Uni's Performing Arts course. I studied under him myself.' Ravenswood puffed out his chest and smoothed the wide lapels on his red velvet jacket. 'I invited Alan to our performance. It's a real honour and a great opportunity for some of you.'

Violet squeezed her eyes shut. Could it get any worse? He was spoiling her chance to play Lady Macbeth before Alan Wolf, and impress the most influential man in the state.

'That's exciting,' Lila whispered and raised her eyebrows at Violet.

'No. No. No,' Violet mumbled and tightened her fist. She crumpled up her paperback copy of Macbeth. 'Not as a witch. No. This is not the way it's supposed to be.'

'We only have a few short days to put together our production. It will be hard work but I'm sure you are all up to the task. But we all need to pitch in. All of us. No slacking off. No wagging. Understand?' He scoured the circle, looking at each person one by one, but Violet dropped her head before he reached her. She was here, wasn't she?

'Do I have your commitment?' Ravenswood asked.

The cast responded with mumbles and rolled eyes.

Violet homed in on obstacle number one, but Angelika met her glare directly with a curious smile as she tossed her dirty blonde hair over her shoulder.

'If you remember what I said before the auditions, my *Macbeth* is very minimalist. We'll have only a few back drops. The audience's attention will be focused on you and your performance. Toby Yang, our tech guy will create the perfect atmosphere through lighting.'

Toby, chubby in a black hoodie, bowed his head shyly.

Holly raised a hand. 'What about costumes?'

'The drama wardrobe will be sufficient, and with make-up and Toby's lighting, you'll all be transformed into proper Shakespearean players.'

Lila elbowed Violet with a grin.

Violet screwed up her face. *Amateurs.*

'What about swords?' Wayne asked, stretched out horizontally in his chair. 'Neilo said we could use his.'

'No. Not without his supervision,' Ravenswood replied. 'And Mr Neilsen is at a re-enactment in Ouse. We'll use props from Wardrobe.'

'But they're plywood,' Wayne scoffed.

'The real swords are too dangerous, Wayne.'

'This is bullshit.' Wayne folded his arms. 'His swords are cool.'

Jason joined in with a grumbling chorus.

'Mr Ravenswood.' Lila meekly raised her hand. 'I've been doing some reading. About the play.'

'Suck,' Jason said through a cough into his hand.

'This play…' Lila's voice wobbled. 'This play is cursed.'

Wayne jumped up from his chair and moaned, his arms outstretched like a sleepwalker. 'Wa-woooooo.'

Violet wrinkled her nose. Lila and her heebie-jeebies again. After her hysterics at last year's school camp when they tried fooling around with a Ouija board, she'd been very quiet, and Violet had assumed she'd grown out of her obsession with the occult. People like Lila shouldn't be allowed to watch Twin Peaks.

Ravenswood pushed his glasses back with a wry smile. 'The play does have a rich and colourful history,' he spoke as if Lila was a kindergartener. 'But it's all superstition, Lila.'

'But there have been deaths. I read about it in the library,' Lila wrung her hands. 'We shouldn't say the real name or anything. We have to call it The Scottish Play.'

'Go back to The Three Torches with Witch Girl,' Wayne snorted.

'Now Lila. It's great you've taken such an interest, but the play was written at a time when everyone believed in witchcraft, before the advances of science. This is the 20th century. We are safely beyond all that foolishness now.'

'But here, in this place? Should we…' Lila's voice trembled. '…risk it? We all know the stories.'

'Cool, bring on the zombies,' Jason said, popping up his collar between smacks of gum.

'Boys,' Ravenswood tutted.

'I vote we call it The Scottish Play. Not the real name.' Lila glanced frenetically around the circle. 'Who's with me?'

'I think we're safe, Lila,' Ravenswood said, with a little sigh. 'We can call *Macbeth* by its proper name.'

As soon as the words left his mouth, all four fluorescent tubes in the ceiling zapped off and plunged the room into darkness.

Lila squealed, Violet's stomach lurched, and even Wayne and Jason stopped laughing.

'Calm down, everyone,' Ravenswood said, his voice with a slight wobble.

The lighting flickered back on, one tube at a time, until the room was brightly lit again.

'Only the maintenance staff fiddling with the wiring. Nothing to be afraid of.' Ravenswood handed a stack of pages to Lionel. 'Time to get to work. Take one and pass it on. *Ow!*'

Ravenswood stuck his finger in his mouth, and Violet snorted behind her hand.

'See,' said Lila. 'It's happening already.'

'It's only a paper cut, not some evil curse,' Ravenswood said firmly. 'Focus, people, focus. Let's start with a read through. Where are our witches?'

Lila rocketed her hand straight into the air. Violet sat still, her jaw tightly clenched. Lila elbowed her with a frown.

Holly eased her hand up slowly.

'Duh,' Wayne said. 'Pick the witch to play a witch.'

Holly glared. 'You shut your mouth, Wayne Moore.'

'No need for a costume for you, Witchy-poo.'

'There'll be no belittling behaviour in my production. One more outburst like that, Wayne and you're out of here. Where's the third?'

Ravenswood looked down at his clipboard. 'Oh yes. Where's Jean...sorry. Violet?'

'Vile-ette. Oh, Vile-ette,' sang Jason in a falsetto.

Violet sucked in a breath. She pushed away the disappointment and anger and gathered up all her available nonchalance. The first witch situation was only temporary.

'Here,' she said, her voice clear and composed.

'Good. Let's begin. Act One, Scene 1. A desert place, thunder and lightning....'

Violet exhaled. This was the moment she lived for, when all eyes were on her, when the whole audience was waiting on the edge of their seats. She stepped onto her stage ready to breathe life into these words like no one else before, or since. She'd show Ravenswood. She'd show them all.

She dumped his photocopied script onto the ground and flipped open her own crumpled paperback. The First Witch had one advantage: she was the first to speak. Violet raised her eyebrow at this first small victory, the first of many. But the rest of her retribution could wait, her stage was calling for her.

'*When shall we three meet again?*'

~ ୨୧ ~

HOLLY

Holly flinched as Violet's words bounced off the opposite brick wall. Every word was carefully enunciated with flourishing gestures, a performance designed for a stage with red velvet curtains and a proscenium arch, not on a plastic chair in an open plan classroom.

'*Lesser than Macbeth, yet greater.*'

Holly chewed on her lip as she, Lila and Violet - the three Witches - sat down. Next to her, Violet relaxed back in her seat with a pat of her hair. Ever since Violet had been picked for the part of Maria and she tossed old Jeanette aside for the new Violet, everything had become bigger, more dramatic, hyper-colourised. Holly always thought actors were supposed to be insecure.

'Jeanette' was apparently too suburban for a promising stage career, but Holly missed her. Jeanette gobbled marshmallows for a bet until she spewed pink, she taught Holly how to reattach her bike chain and how to break in through the toilet louvres when she'd lost her house key. Since Jeanette left and Violet had come to stay, all that had changed.

Jez rose in his slow-motion way and pushed aside his curtain of floppy fringe. Holly's tummy fluttered as he spoke. Among the boys of Beacon Hill, Jez was the closest thing to her poster of River Phoenix, Blu-tacked to her wall.

'*The earth hath bubbles, as the water has,*
And these are of them. Whither are they vanished?'

Holly wasn't the only one fixated on Jez. She noticed how Violet watched him with her mouth slightly open. Jez continued his speech, but his eyes never strayed from Angelika's direction. Holly hid a little smirk but then again Jez never noticed her either. Three months had passed since *The Sound of Music* closing night party, and Holly could still picture the moment when Violet and Jez skulked away together. For once Violet had kept all the juicy details to herself and Holly never asked. She didn't have to, whatever happened was over.

The morning dragged on as the cast fumbled through their first full read through. Scene Five began and as Lady Macbeth started to speak, Holly could feel Violet seething beside her. Holly knew Angelika's name, everyone did. Being beautiful was the closest thing to being famous at Beacon Hill High School. But Holly knew nothing else about her. How did someone become so self-assured at sixteen?

'*Only look up clear;*
To alter favour ever is to fear:
Leave all the rest to me.'

Angelika closed the scene and folded her hands on top of her script. She gazed around the circle with a quiet feline confidence. Violet snorted loudly and Holly winced.

'Very good, everyone. We'll stop there for lunch,' said Ravenswood. 'Back at one o'clock.'

The drama room filled with chatter as the teenagers scrambled to their feet, Holly yawned and Angelika stretched, Wayne and Jason patted each other on the back, and Jez rushed for the door.

'You were so good, Violet,' Lila said, her hand on her black and white striped chest. 'So much better than me. The rhymes and those old words?' She exhaled with a whistle.

'They're my lines,' Violet hissed. She curled her lips in a snarl, unconsciously revealing the crowded teeth she detested. Her mum's refusal to pay for braces had been Violet's hysterical drama a few months back. 'He's an idiot. She's an idiot. It's so embarrassing.'

'I thought she was alright.' Holly shrugged.

'You couldn't possibly understand,' Violet scoffed.

Violet pushed past Holly and marched out of the door. Violet would never be able to compete with Angelika if she stomped around like a rugby player. But Holly didn't dare mention it. She liked her head where it was.

Lila scampered after Violet and Holly sighed, her shoulders slumping, knowing she should follow them. This was life or death to Violet, but there was always one drama or another. It was never about Lila, or her.

Holly grabbed her satchel and headed towards the Quad, hoping a smoke would calm Violet down.

'Hi.'

By instinct, Holly tensed instinctively. She glanced up to see Jacinta loitering at the classroom doorway, her smile white and straight, expensive-looking caramel highlights in her dark hair.

'I like your jumper.'

Holly tugged the hem of her knitted baby blue jumper. 'It's just an op-shop find.' She tried to sound casual, but her hackles were on full alert. What did Jacinta Martin want from her?

'You're lucky. I never find anything good.'

Holly laughed nervously. In her spotless white denim jacket, Jacinta wouldn't be seen dead anywhere near a dusty stale second-hand clothes shop.

'You should try the Salvo's on Patrick Street. That's the best one and I think they've got a sale on at the moment.'

'I'm always a bit suss. Wearing dead people's clothes, you know. But maybe we could go some time? Together? You could help me find something good.'

'Sure.' Holly chewed on the inside of her lip. As if she and Jacinta would go shopping together. They'd been in the same classes for four years and this was their longest conversation to date.

Jacinta flipped open a magazine with another impossibly pretty face on the cover. 'And your dress. It's like this one.'

Holly huddled over the magazine, and as they turned the pages, Jacinta's sudden friendliness made sense. Where were Karina, Stacey and Melanie, Jacinta's gang with their perfect curls and tanned smooth legs, even in mid-winter? Jacinta had no one else, so she had to resort to the Witch Girl.

'Kind of. But mine cost a dollar.' Holly smoothed her white sun dress with the dark blue flowers.

'Wow. You can't tell.' Jacinta produced a bag of lolly snakes. 'Want one?'

Holly took a yellow snake one and ripped the head off with her teeth, her shoulders softening as her mouth flooded with sickly sweet pineapple. But she kept one eye on Jacinta. She'd be a fool to fully relax with a popular one.

'You write for the paper, right?' Jacinta asked.

'Every now and then.' Holly shrugged, but inside her tummy quivered. 'It's only the school rag.'

'That's cool, I saw your thing about—'

Rowan drifted by. She tripped over Holly's satchel and crashed into a chair. Her dark curls covered her face as she fell onto her hands and knees.

'I'm so sorry.' Holly grabbed Rowan's elbow and helped her up to her feet. 'I shouldn't have left my bag there.'

'I'm so clumsy,' Rowan said feebly, her hand sweeping her forehead. 'I don't know what's wrong with me.'

'Are you alright? You look pale?' Holly said.

'Do you want a snake?' Jacinta thrust out the bag.

'Just a headache.' Rowan's voice was airy. 'From that smell.'

Holly smiled politely.

'Can't you smell it?' Rowan asked.

'Paint, maybe?' Holly offered. 'From the maintenance men?'

'Or Wayne's cheap aftershave,' Jacinta laughed.

'No.' Rowan shook her head, her eyes glassy. 'It smells wrong. Something foul, something off.'

'I could get you a Disprin? I'm sure someone has one,' Holly said reaching out a hand for Rowan, but she'd already wandered away.

Holly frowned. 'There's something wrong with her.'

'She's off her tree if you ask me,' Jacinta snorted. 'She should lay off the buds.'

Holly chewed her lip, debating whether to follow Rowan. But then until Jez passed by and her cheeks instantly flushed red.

'Snake?' Jacinta said as she offered him the bag.

With a grin, Jez pushed the hair from his eyes. 'Why did it have to be snakes?' He held up his hands in mock alarm.

Jacinta plucked out a red snake and wiggled it at Jez. He let out a high-pitched squeak and pretended to swat the snake away. Jacinta lunged at him, brandishing the lolly reptile like a sword.

'Help me,' Jez squealed and jumped on a chair. He clutched at his throat. 'Somebody help me. Please!'

Holly giggled. Jacinta tossed the lolly bag to her. She pulled out a green snake and joined in, chasing Jez around the circle of chairs.

For a brief moment, Holly wasn't the witchy one. She wasn't on the receiving end. She was one of them. She savoured each moment while it lasted, because she knew it never lasted long.

CHAPTER 3

RAVENSWOOD

AS THE CAST GIGGLED AND ELBOWED EACH OTHER ON THEIR way to the weak winter sunlight in the Quad, Ravenswood headed to his office for his ham and cheese on multi-grain.

As he turned the corner, the babble of kids faded away and he was alone again in the dim corridors, his footsteps ringing. Like a blinkered horse, he focused his eyes on the path straight ahead. If he didn't look, he wouldn't see. This was his theory and it had worked so far.

For a first run-through, he thought the kids were a five out of ten. Angelika was wooden but salvageable. A few pointers and a bit of coaching should unearth some of her talent. Luckily, his leading man Lionel commanded the stage—even when he was sitting down. With a few more days under his tutelage, Alan Wolf would be blown away. Ravenswood whistled and admired his tunefulness and the acoustics of the rough brick walls.

Above his head, the public address system buzzed. Ravenswood clutched at his chest as a screech of feedback echoed down the windowless corridor. Underneath the hissing static, he thought he heard words, but as soon as he sensed it, Ravenswood clamped his palms firmly over his ears, glad for the thumping drum of his own heartbeat.

Seconds later, the quiet returned and he breathed again.

'Those bloody maintenance men,' he muttered. 'What are they doing?'

He turned back and marched towards the main office. Electricity surges and speaker static were unacceptable. They would not interfere with his production. Everything had to be perfect for Alan Wolf.

Ravenswood passed the locked-up library and the door opened. A bald man in blue coveralls stepped out, a cordless drill gripped in his hand.

'What's with all this racket?' Ravenswood said, hands on hips. 'I'm putting on a production. And you are interfering with our work.'

The maintenance man stared at him, his neck was thick and ropey.

Ravenswood gulped, a shiver quivered up his back, but the man said nothing in reply.

'Where's Bruce?' Ravenswood stammered. 'Is he in the office?'

The man shrugged and continued on his way down the corridor.

'Wait. I'm talking to you,' Ravenswood called, but the man disappeared into the dark.

'Bloody cheek,' Ravenswood harumphed and continued onto the main office.

As he turned a corner, his hand grazed the wall, but rather than cold bricks, the surface felt clammy. The backs of his fingers came away coated in a sticky liquid. He sniffed them tentatively then stepped under an emergency light to examine his hand closely, but curiously there was nothing there. Whatever the goo on the wall was, it had evaporated.

'Bloody kids,' he grumbled.

Another door opened and Ravenswood squealed.

'Oh, Mr Ravenswood. Did I frighten you?' Miss Quinlin said. 'Sorry about that. I should get myself a little bell,' she chuckled.

'Miss Quinlin,' Ravenswood sighed. 'I didn't know you were on school grounds.'

'It's always better here with no kids around,' she said as she limped out of the science lab door in another one of her shapeless pink fluffy cardigans. 'I can actually get some work done.'

'Did you spill something? On the wall over there?' Ravenswood asked.

She hesitated before she replied. 'No. Why?'

'Never mind. What's going on with the PA system? And the electrics? Do you know? These conditions are intolerable, I have a performance to direct.'

She cocked her ear towards the speaker and squinted one eye. 'I haven't noticed anything. But then again, my hearing is a bit dodgy. And sometimes I get a little wrapped up in what I'm doing.' She coughed with an asthmatic rasp. 'The maintenance fellows could be testing in different parts of the building. That would make sense. Although not many things make sense these days.'

'I tried to talk to one of the workers before, but he walked off on me. So rude. He didn't even answer me.'

'Of course not. They're from the Order of the Thorn,' Miss Quinlin said with a half-smile. 'The Brotherhood won the school maintenance contract.'

'Monks?'

'With a vow of silence. They call it the 'bound tongue'.' Miss Quinlin nodded and her second pair of glasses on a pink plastic chain bounced against her chest. 'It was quite a coup for the school. Very good workers and apparently, their work is a type of prayer.'

Ravenswood raised an eyebrow. Monks in a silent order. Would he expect anything less in at Beacon Hill?

'That explains the lack of obnoxious commercial radio,' Ravenswood said, faking a light-hearted laugh.

No wonder they gave him the creeps. If only he was more like his sister. She had moved on so easily. She didn't even get the nightmares.

'Where can I find the head maintenance man? Bruce, is it? I want a word with him.'

'Mr Booth. He'll be around somewhere. He'll know exactly what's going on.'

'Good. Nothing can interfere with my production. We have a full house on Friday. With very important guests.'

'Of course.' Miss Quinlin rubbed her chin. 'Interesting choice, *Macbeth*.'

'A classic.' Ravenswood pulled himself to his full height.

'Oh yes, of course. But such a history.'

'Shakespeare.' He shrugged.

Miss Quinlin frowned and drifted away into her own world, her lips moving soundlessly. Was she praying, Ravenswood wondered? He squinted. She seemed to be repeating a single word; 'prevention' or perhaps 'reinvention'? Something ending in a 'shun'.

Miss Quinlan jolted as if she'd been caught napping. 'Sorry, miles away. Must get back. Next term's lesson plans won't write themselves.' She continued down the corridor with her lopsided shuffle. 'Break a leg as they say.'

Bemused, Ravenswood shook his head and set out once more

towards the main office. His stride was determined but as always, he was careful to look straight ahead. Nothing good ever came from the shadows.

⁓ ࣲ ⁓

HOLLY
Last Night

Something dragged Holly out of her sleep, and she didn't know why. She held her breath, her own heartbeat clanging in her ears. Under the doona, she stiffened and shut her eyes firmly. She listened hard but the room was silent.

She swallowed, and as she lifted her head from the pillow, a chill scampered up the back of her neck.

Her bedroom was filled with light. Her curtains were wide open— and she never left the curtains open because next door's windows looked straight into her own and she'd seen creepy Mr Hanson staring back at her too many times.

A fat moon cast a rectangle of light on her ruffled bedspread. Her bookshelf was empty, all her books knocked clear from the shelves. The moon must be making the cat crazy.

Holly tried to say 'Star' but the word got stuck in her throat. She coughed and tried again but no sound came out of her mouth; her throat was clogged like a drain.

Out of the corner of her eye, she saw something move but it wasn't the cat. She sucked in a jagged breath, her heart battering against her ribs. Something black slunk towards her wardrobe door. It was blacker than the darkest corners of a dark room, a blurry person-shaped shadow. All the warmth drained from Holly's body. Her forehead moistened as the shadow inched closer, wafting against the walls, sashaying through the dark. The shadow hovered by the doorway, an oil-coloured mass blocking her exit. She tried to call out for her Mum but her voice was nothing but a strangled wheeze.

Had Dahlia's warnings come true? Was this one of the shadow

people from her bedtime stories, the reason behind her birthday gifts of amethyst jewellery?

Holly slowed her panicky breath and gritted her teeth. She glanced about her bedroom. She knew every inch of carpet. Holly tensed her muscles to make a dash for the door. The shadow floated past her desk and over the cork board covered in her blue athletics ribbons. She pulled in deep slow breaths and collected all the courage she had left. A starter's pistol sounded in her head, and she tried to leap up from her bed.

But she didn't move.

Her body stayed flat, pinned against the mattress. She pulled at her arms and legs, ground her teeth and moaned. She struggled, trying to move left then right, but only her neck and head moved. No matter how she thrashed, she was trapped tight like a mummy.

The shadow crept closer to her, slinking along the wall. Holly screamed silently for help. The black shape grew taller and wider. It took over the entire room and blocked out the moonlight. Holly whimpered noiselessly. A heavy invisible weight pressed her down, making her sink her deeper into the bed.

'What do you want with me?' She desperately wanted to scream but she could only think the words. 'What do you want with me?'

Long black fingers stretched across her bedspread and inched towards her throat.

VIOLET

The cold wind in the Quad and a cigarette hadn't calmed Violet down. Back inside, she waited in line at the vending machine behind Angelika. Violet huffed. Angelika was in her way once again. She stared at the back of Angelika's head and wanted to tear out fistfuls of her hair by the roots.

Angelika turned with a Diet Coke in her hand and flashed a brief cold smile, the type of smile for checkout girls and servants. Plebe, it said.

Violet clenched her fists so tight she almost broke the skin. She wanted to rip the smile off Angelika's face, kneel on her chest and force her to taste what Violet felt, shove it down her throat. But Violet exhaled instead; there were other ways, much more cunning ways.

'You must be really proud,' Violet said, swallowing her sarcasm. Her acting skills useful in so many ways.

Angelika gave a half-shrug. Her jumper slipped off her shoulder, revealing a white singlet strap and a flash of bare skin. Violet was a head shorter and three sizes wider, and conscious of every inch. 'It's going to be hard work,' she said. 'But hard work doesn't bother me.'

'Shakespeare is difficult. Getting the iambic pentameter right. *'Be not the flower be twisted but the serpent',*' Violet said with perfect enunciation, showing Angelika exactly how it should be done.

'You know your lines already?' Angelika slurped from the can. 'You're good.'

Violet blinked slowly, fighting the urge to shake her head. 'No,' she replied, deadpan. 'That's one of your lines, Lady Macbeth.'

'Oh. There are so many of them,' Angelika said with a flick of her wrist.

'Really? But we only have a few days—'

'I've got a good memory. Anyway, we don't need to learn *every* word. He said we could take our scripts on stage.'

'But wouldn't you want to? For Alan Wolf?'

'He's some big deal, isn't he? Cool.'

Violet gritted her teeth. Angelika really was a complete imbecile. 'You're not nervous, with all those people looking at you? Under the lights. Judging your every move.'

'Not really,' she said, wiping her mouth. 'It's only a school play.'

Violet snapped her mouth shut. *Only a school play?* She glanced around for Ravenswood. If only he could hear the treachery from his leading lady. Despite his terrible decisions and worse dress sense, he was as committed to theatre as Violet was. He'd sack Angelika immediately if he heard this.

'If you say so...' Violet cleared her throat. '...but if you need any help with your lines or advice...I know what it's like to be in a leading—'

'I'm sure I'll be fine. I've got Mr Ravenswood. He wouldn't have chosen me if he didn't believe I could do it. And Rowan, my deputy or whatever it's called. We'll be working together.'

Violet clenched. 'Understudy.'

'Hey, Angelika.' Jez sidled up, pushing his fringe from his eyes.

Violet's stomach cartwheeled. 'Hi Jez,' she said brightly.

'Hi. I didn't see you there,' he said to Violet, but with a sideways glance at Angelika who seemed more interested in her fingernails.

'Been busy?' Violet shuffled closer to Jez, blocking his view of Angelika.

'Real busy.' He nodded, biting his lip.

'I thought so. I called. A few times. You probably didn't get my messages. What have you been up to?'

'Stuff.' He shoved his hands into his pockets. Angelika sauntered away back down the stairs towards the drama room.

'Banquo is a good part,' Violet continued. 'You did well before lunch. Really good for a first read through.'

'It's alright.' Jez turned his head. 'Wait up, Angelika.'

'Maybe after rehearsal—' Violet started but Jez was already gone, running to catch up with Angelika.

'That's not a good way to treat your girlfriend,' Angelika said, loud enough for Violet to hear.

'What do you mean?' Jez grinned. 'I'm totally available.'

Violet's stomach sank like a stone.

As Jez shifted his fringe again, his sleeve slipped down to show the leather strap around his wrist, the same brown leather strap with a press-stud she'd stroked on the night of *The Sound of Music* closing party. They'd snuck away from everyone else to the playground in the park, smoking and drinking cask wine, talking and kissing. If she breathed deeply enough, she could still smell the musty scent of pot, sweat and spicy oriental incense woven deep into his shirt.

Violet squinted from the top of the stairs as Angelika walked away with Jez at her heels. No one was bulletproof. She must have a flaw, some type of frailty. Violet cracked open a Coke and took a long glug, spluttering as the sweet bubbles burned the back of her throat. She ripped open a Mars Bar. Chocolate and gooey caramel slipped down her throat, but in three bites it was gone. She glared at the empty wrapper. She turned right around and bought another.

Jacinta and Holly loitered outside the drama room. They were huddled together, pointing at celebrity hairstyles in one of those airhead teen magazines. Violet frowned. Holly? With one of them?

Violet wiped the chocolate evidence from her mouth. 'Wasn't she terrible?'

'Who?' Jacinta said, vaguely lifting her head from the pages. 'You mean Angelika?'

'It was embarrassing,' Violet scoffed. 'I'd be embarrassed if I were her.'

'It's only the first read through,' Holly said, shuffling her weight from foot to foot. 'This Shakespeare stuff is tough. Not everyone knows it like you do.'

Violet puffed out her chest. 'She shouldn't have been chosen if she couldn't handle it. But some of us find Shakespeare the ultimate pleasure.'

Jacinta guffawed. 'She looks the part. She could be on TV.'

Violet pressed her lips together. 'This isn't Home and Away.'

Violet noticed Angelika turn their way, a slight crease across on her forehead. What good hearing she must have.

'I wish I looked like that.' Holly sighed and twirled her dead-straight hair.

'She and Lionel look so great together. Proper royalty.'

'You think?' Violet said, her mouth twisted. 'She's only here because Ravenswood wants to get in her pants.'

'You're way off,' Jacinta said, eyebrow raised. 'I don't think she's his type.'

'Time to go back in,' Holly said.

Jacinta closed her magazine and whispered to Holly, 'Time to get away from the green-eyed monster.'

They left Violet alone in the doorway. Holly rubbed the back of her neck and glanced behind her.

Violet narrowed her eyes. She squeezed her forehead with her fingers. The dull thump deep inside her eye socket was getting worse. The brick walls loomed over her. The school encroached on her shoulders and crushed at the sides of her skull.

Violet dropped her hand and hurried to join them. 'I only want what's right for the play. For everyone. I don't want us to embarrass ourselves, especially in front of Alan Wolf.'

'Sure.' Jacinta raised an eyebrow and Holly stifled a giggle.

Violet grabbed Holly's arm while Jacinta went ahead to claim a seat. 'Thanks for the support.'

'Ow.'

'How can you defend Angelika? After what she did to me? And why are you talking to Jacinta anyway? You know she's a stuck-up bitch.'

'She's alright,' Holly muttered.

Violet snorted. 'You never learn. How many times have they kicked you in the face?'

'What's got into you?' Holly recoiled and then shook her head. 'I know you're angry but you need to calm down.'

'You have no idea how I feel.'

'I know it sucks, but—'

'I don't need your pity.' Violet waved her hand dismissively. 'Go sit with your new best friend.'

She stomped to the opposite side of the circle, sat down and tapped her foot as she waited for Holly to join her with a proper apology.

Holly skulked into the spare seat next to Jacinta.

Some friend.

THE DARK HAND

I am here.

I am there.

In the normal, in the every day.

In the strange.

I am everywhere and always.

I hear them.

I see them.

They ignore you, put you down, insult you behind your back.

How dare they treat you this way?
They are unworthy, they are nothing.
They need to be taught a lesson.
I am here for you.
I understand.
I am your friend.
Not like them.
And I have the power.
I am the answer.
I can teach them the lesson they need to learn.
I can help, when no one else can, like no one else can.
All you need to do is let me help you.
All you need to do is let me in.
It's that simple.
I am waiting here for you. Ready whenever you need me.
I am not going anywhere.
I will never let you down.

CHAPTER 4

VIOLET

As the cast dawdled back in from lunch break, Violet sized them up, one by one. Fool. Idiot. Bimbo. Waste of time. Angelika fan. A possibility but a total wimp.

Holly and Jacinta giggled over a private joke. How could Holly be so naive? No matter how many times they shoved her, pulled her hair and stole her school bag, deep down she still yearned to be one of them. Violet had always suspected but Holly had finally revealed her true face.

Violet's real best friend was cross-legged on the floor, neck craned over her notebook as she murmured and picked at her scabby cuticles. Lila had vowed a million times to stop her disgusting habit, but the resolution went out the window whenever she got nervous, which was all the time.

Violet took the seat next to Wayne and Jason, selecting her first targets. Both boys were tall with athletic triangular torsos, they'd be hot if they closed their mouths when they breathed. As a general rule, she avoided any contact with them, but these were desperate times.

She pasted on her friendliest smile and butted in. 'You guys got yourselves good roles. McDuff and Duncan.'

'S'alright,' Jason said, with a half shrug. Wayne grunted and continued talking in riddles, something about half-forward flanks and torpedo punts.

Violet licked her lips and leaned in again. 'A shame about the swords, eh? Real swords would have been cool.'

'Yeah. Sucks.' Wayne looked up at her this time. 'Plywood swords are bullshit. I was hanging out for some real sword fighting.' He thrust an imaginary sword at her. 'And I thought there'd be more girls here. Double bummer.'

'Real swords would have been totally authentic.' Violet nodded. 'I don't understand him. They're not *that* dangerous.'

'We could've handled ourselves.' Wayne lifted his chin and skimmed his fingers over his bristly flat-top.

'Ravenswood's a dick,' Violet said, a gleam in her eye.

Jason popped the collar on his polo-shirt and looked away. 'He's okay.'

'He dresses like a weirdo.' Wayne curled his lip at Ravenswood as he adjusted his purple paisley scarf in the doorway.

'He's no fruit. Didn't you hear?' She leaned in with a whisper. 'He gave Angelika a lift to school this morning. If you know what I mean. Very cosy.'

'Who'd blame him? If I had half a chance.' Wayne grinned.

Jason pulled a face. 'Nah. That's bullshit. She was on the same bus as me this morning. She got on at her usual stop.'

'That's what I heard.' Violet pressed her hand against her chest. 'But don't you think it's a bit off? I mean he's only a few years older than us but it's still wrong.'

'It's none of my business,' Jason said. 'You jealous or something?'

'You got the hots for Ravenswood, Vile-ette?' Wayne boomed, his voice carrying across the room.

A few seats away, Lionel and Angelika glanced up and tittered behind their scripts.

'No,' Violet spluttered and lowered her voice. 'I just don't think it's right. Teachers and students.'

'This is the first I've heard of it,' Jason said, crossing his arms. 'You're the one spreading the rumours.'

'Yeah. Whoever smelt it, dealt it.' Wayne nodded.

Violet swivelled away from them and clenched her teeth until they creaked. She should have known these two idiots would be a complete waste of her time.

'First Witch,' Jason said. 'First Bitch, more like it.'

Cockheads. With a harumph, Violet moved to another seat and started scoured the room again. But it was full of losers wrapped up in their little worlds: Friday night's party, Saturday's game, who pashed who behind the bike shed on Tuesday after school and other world changing events.

Lila flopped down beside Violet. 'I'm concerned about the curse. No one seems to take me seriously.'

'Sorry?' Violet said, she was contriving her next tactical move.

'This play attracts all kinds of evil. Maybe that's what the bus driver was talking about?'

'The only evil is sitting over there with the blonde hair.' Violet folded her arms.

'It's been documented throughout history. I thought you'd get it. You know all about the theatre.'

'Curses and bad luck? It's all mumbo-jumbo. I thought you'd left all that shit behind after that seance.'

'Listen. It's not all bad, I found the cleansing rituals in a book. If someone says the real name, we have to send them out of the theatre, but we can lift the curse if they spin around three times and say, "If we shadows have offended". Then they can come back inside. All clean again.'

Violet rolled her eyes with a sigh.

'But the cleansing will only work if we all do it. All of us. The whole cast and crew. We've got to be strict about it. I have to get everyone to agree.'

'Fat chance.'

'We have to take this seriously,' Lila said, her voice cracking. 'Like the bus driver said yesterday. There are powerful spirits in this world. We can't go around tempting fate. Otherwise one of us is going to die.'

'She didn't say that. You're upsetting yourself over nothing. She was just some nut bag.'

'But here. In this place. You know the stories.'

Violet sighed. 'Too many horror videos. There's no such thing as ancient burial grounds.'

'No. It's all true.' Lila said wide-eyed. 'It's all true. My uncle used to work at the Council. He saw the records and told me all about the original white owners of Beacon Hill. They were some weird religious community cut off from the rest of the church.' Lila lowered her voice. 'The stories. About human sacrifices. It's all true. It happened right here, on this very spot. Under our feet. The whole of Beacon Hill is cursed. My uncle says it's a gateway to hell.'

'Your uncle, the drunk?'

'Evil exists, Violet,' Lila said, her face stony. 'Old sins cast long shadows.'

'You're getting worse than Dahlia. When did you start hanging out at The Three Torches?'

'But haven't you felt it? The strangeness? Something isn't right.'

Ravenswood clapped his hands and the ever-obedient Lila turned to him. Violet muttered a silent thank you to Ravenswood who was the only person guaranteed to stop Lila's ranting.

'OK, players. Let's pick up where we left off. Act Three, Scene One.'

The last stragglers back from lunch scrambled for seats, and everyone rustled their scripts.

Jez cleared his throat and began.

'Thou hast it now: king, Cawdor, Glamis, all,
As the weird women promised.'

Violet's heartbeat quickened as she watched his lips form the words. The rest of the world faded away and there was only him and her, like the night in the playground.

'Like yesterday,' Lila hissed in her ear. 'The bus driver told us to be wary.'

'She also said one of us would shine like a star.'

Ravenswood frowned at Violet and Lila, his finger pressed against his lips. Lila leaned back and shoved her chewed fingers straight back in her mouth again.

Across the circle, Rowan massaged her temples. Violet scanned Rowan from her boots and her ripped jeans to her black t-shirt with its silver gothic lettering. Where had her pale denim and pastel jumpers gone? Was that a stud in her nose? But even with her new tough look, Rowan was a soft target.

Violet lazed back into the plastic chair and counted the minutes until the next break. This would be a cinch.

Dear Journal

I never used to believe the stories but now I know they're true.

My head hurts like when a storm is brewing. A hard pain presses behind my eyes. And there's a sour taste in my mouth: metallic, bitter, nothing I recognise. And my tummy is jittery all the time.

I saw the shadow in the mirror again today. Behind me. I tried to laugh it off, pretend I didn't see it but it's no joke. The shadows are very real.

Everywhere I go I feel them. Waiting. Breathing down my neck.

Following my every move. Shadowy hands hovering just above my shoulder.

They want me. They beckon to me, but I won't give in.

I have to distract myself, stay with people and stay away from the darkness.

It's worst when I'm alone.

The voice is so soothing. I know I shouldn't listen, but the words make so much sense. Maybe I do need it. With the help of the shadows, I could put everything right.

No. I mustn't listen.

I am happy, I am positive, I am in control of my destiny.

I am happy, I am positive, I am in control of my destiny.

But the affirmations aren't working. Maybe it's me. Maybe I just need to try harder. I need to say them more often along with my prayers.

I don't know what else to do.

I mustn't listen.

I mustn't.

I must be strong.

But the shadow's call is stronger.

I am happy.

I am positive.

I am in control of my destiny.

It can help me. It understands me.

I am happy. I am positive.

It can help when no one else can.

I am in control of my destiny.

All I have to do is let the shadows in.

VIOLET

'Congrats.' Violet sidled up to Rowan with her most endearing smile. 'Getting the understudy role and everything. It'll be good for you.'

Rowan looked up from her notebook, biro in hand. 'It was a bit of a surprise, but yeah, I guess.'

'But twice the work,' Violet said.

'I hadn't thought about that.' Rowan chewed on her pen.

Ravenswood clapped his hands and interrupted them. 'I want you to break up and rehearse scenes in groups,' he announced. 'Macbeth and Lady Macbeth here. Duncan, Banquo, McDuff and the other boys at the front. Witches down at the back.'

The other cast members picked up their chairs and bags, and created smaller clusters around the drama room. But Violet hadn't finished with Rowan yet.

Violet continued. 'You'll have to learn Hecate and the Gentlewoman and all of Lady Macbeth as well. Same thing happened to me last year when we were doing *Grease*.' She pressed her hand flat against her solar plexus. 'Mrs Tulloch didn't allow scripts on stage, so I had to learn both Frenchy and Sandy. It was hard, but I'm sure you'll be fine.'

'Yes,' Rowan murmured to herself and rubbed her eyes.

Violet tried not to smile. She could smell Rowan's doubt. 'Of course, nothing will happen to Angelika. But you know, just in case.'

'You're right,' Rowan said, her voice fading away to nothing. She stumbled to her feet and staggered into the centre of the room.

Violet squinted as she watched Rowan swaying. Was she drunk?

Rowan beckoned to Ravenswood. He followed her to a seat away from everyone else. They huddled together and worry lines spread across Ravenswood's face as Rowan spoke.

Violet smirked. Rowan must be pulling out of the production right now. Step one now complete.

Violet sauntered over to Lila and Holly at the back of the room, their three chairs positioned in a triangle. 'My favourite line is *'infected be the air whereon they ride*,' she said, dropping into an empty chair, and lacing her fingers behind her neck.

'Infected?' Lila screwed up her face. 'Gross.'

'But it gives me an idea.' Violet leaned forward, her elbows resting on her black stockings.

'We should get back to rehearsing,' said Holly. She jerked her head towards Ravenswood who had left Rowan and was now deep in an argument with Wayne and Jason about the right way to pronounce 'harbingers'.

'We haven't got much time left today. And it'll be Friday before we know it.'

'Infection,' Violet said, locking eyes first with Lila and then Holly. 'Wouldn't it be tragic if Angelika got sick? Someone would have to step in and take over.'

'That's Rowan's job,' Lila said.

'Maybe.' Violet raised her eyebrows.

'Did Ravenswood change his mind? Did you talk to Mrs Petrakis?' Lila's eyes widened like headlights.

'People get sick all the time. It's just one of those things,' Violet said.

'Where are you going with this?' Holly squinted. 'You're not planning something dumb, are you?'

'Me?' Violet pressed her hand against her heart.

'You can't make someone sick.' Lila's eyes darted between Holly and Violet, her face crumpling. 'Can you?'

'No one would ever know. It's the perfect way to make Angelika miss the performance.' Violet smiled.

'Are you saying...?' Lila's jaw dropped. 'Hurt her? That's not cool.'

'Wait a second,' Holly said, tightly folding her arms. 'I know you want this badly but—'

'People have accidents all the time' Violet shrugged. 'Something small. Just enough to get her out of the way for a few days.'

'Are you serious?' Holly screwed up her face.

'What?'

'You can't do something like that.' Lila lowered her voice.

'Don't you think I should be Lady Macbeth?'

'Of course,' Lila said, cowered.

Lila and Holly frowned back at Violet.

'Listen. It's obvious there's some kind of conspiracy. They're trying to force me out of the production. They're jealous. All of them. They don't want to be upstaged by me. Especially in front of Alan Wolf. But I'll show them.'

'I don't think there's a conspiracy,' said Holly said slowly. 'When did you get to bed last night?'

'What's that got to do with it?' Violet snapped.

'Maybe you need a lie down?'

'Don't be stupid,' Violet said with a dismissive flick of her wrist.

'It could be low blood sugar,' Lila said as she rifled inside her canvas bag. 'My mum goes all woozy if she doesn't eat.' Lila rifled around in her canvas bag. 'I've got some Strawberries and Cream here somewhere.'

'I'm better than all of them.' Violet sneered. 'In fact, I should be playing Macbeth. *Is this a dagger I see before me?* If Ravenswood had any real guts, if he really wanted to do something truly different, he'd cast women in men's roles. He thinks he's so intellectual, but he's so suburban it makes me sick. I should be directing this production. I should take over the whole thing.'

Holly and Lila glanced at each other. Violet's cheeks burned, her head span with a million colliding ideas, fighting their way out of her mouth.

Violet squeezed her eyes shut and took a deep breath. 'But your little curse has given me an idea.'

'It's not my curse,' Lila said vehemently.

'We could haunt her.' Violet grinned.

'That reminds me,' Holly said. 'Last night I had this weird dream—'

'You shouldn't tell other people about your nightmares.' Lila grabbed Holly's arm.

'Since when?'

'Mrs Khang over the fence told me,' Lila said. 'It passes on the evil.'

'That could work.' Violet nodded and rubbed her chin. 'We could freak her out and she'd quit all on her own. What do you think she's scared of?'

'Mice.' Lila shuddered. 'All those scurrying little feet.'

'You're scared of your own shadow,' Violet laughed.

'Shadows,' Holly mumbled.

'Would Dahlia help us?' Violet asked. 'What time does The Three Torches close?'

'You don't want to play around with that stuff,' Holly said. 'It's not straightforward. You shouldn't mess with things you don't understand.'

Lila widened her eyes. 'Like the bus driver said.'

Violet snorted. 'Of all people, Holly. You've always sworn you never believed in that witchy stuff.'

'I don't.' Holly stared at her shoes. 'I just...'

'We could be proper witches,' Violet said. 'It'd be method acting. It's for the good of the play.'

'You're talking about hurting people. Dahlia only does white magic.'

'Whatever. We don't need her. Maybe we should just hide in Angelika's wardrobe. Jump out and scare her.'

'She doesn't look like she'd scare easily,' Lila said, and all three girls turned to the front of the room where Angelika stood like a regal marble statue. Violet scowled.

'Or I could put a few laxatives in a cake,' Violet snickered. 'Or better yet, rat poison.'

'Rat poison? Are you nuts?' Holly recoiled.

'Only a little bit.' Violet pinched her fingers, her eyes shining. 'It'll be fun.'

'Whoa.' Holly held her hands up. 'This is crazy. You're going to kill her over a part in a play?'

'Stop being so melodramatic.' Violet flicked her hair. 'I'm not going to kill anyone. Maybe I shouldn't have said anything in front of you. You couldn't possibly understand.'

'It's a play. It's not the war in Bosnia,' Holly argued. 'Listen to me. You need to get a grip.'

'You never supported me,' Violet hissed.

'I've always been here for you but—'

'Liar.' Violet clenched her fists, itching to slap Holly across the face.

'Please don't fight,' Lila whimpered.

'It's hard, I know, but Violet, you have to face up to reality,' Holly said. 'Life isn't fair. You weren't picked. It happens. But there's always next time.'

'You never wanted me to get this part.' Violet's heartbeat thumped in her ears. The pain was back, hammering a hole deep into her skull. 'You're jealous, too. Like all the others.'

'Please stop.' Lila held out her hands to separate them.

'Get out of here,' Violet said. 'Lila and I don't need you and your lies any more. Go back to your new best friend over there.'

'Stop!' Lila squealed and leaped up from her seat, covering her face with her hands. She knocked over a chair as she sprinted out the door.

'Lila?' Holly got to her feet. 'Look what you've done. Lila?'

The rest of the cast hushed, dropped their scripts and turned to watch. 'Scrag fight!' Wayne and Jason cackled.

'How dare you!' Violet jumped up, yelling after them across the drama room. But she was left standing alone at the back of the room.

'What are you looking at?' With her hands jammed into her hips, Violet turned and glared at the smirking faces of the cast one by one.

Ravenswood clapped his hands. 'It's four o'clock, so let's call it a day. You've all worked very hard. I'll see you back here tomorrow at nine sharp. Go home, take a break and then learn your lines.'

'Traitors.' Violet muttered as she rubbed her right eye with the heel of her hand. She bent down and packed her bag slowly. No one understood.

Lila's script lay abandoned on the floor next to her bag. The white pages were splattered with three drops of blood.

LILA
Last Night

Dressed in only a thin nightie, Lila stood shivering in the hallway. The wood-panelled walls were bathed a wine-coloured light. The winter wind slithered through every crack in her weatherboard house, its icy teeth gnawing at her bare legs and shoulders. Why was she here?

She shivered but for a different reason. Her pulse slowed as every cell of her body tensed. Her gut urged her to run.

Thump.

She tried to move, but her legs were like concrete stumps. She pulled at her heels, but the soles were firmly stuck to the floor.

Thump.

The red light dimmed.

Thump.

The footsteps drew nearer. Ever so slowly.

Thump.

The hallway darkened. In the blackness, the front door creaked open.

Thump.

Her heart boomed inside her chest. She bent down and tugged at her ankles, and finally she released one foot.

Thump.

She took a step through the viscous air, battling against an unseen force. But as she gritted her teeth and dragged herself towards the safety of her bedroom door, the thumping picked up speed.

Thump.

Thump.

Thump.

She pictured claws, teeth, flashing eyes. Devil. Demon. Maniac. Inhuman. Evil incarnate.

Thump.

She screamed but her voice was like a drowning gargle. She groped at the wood-panelled wall. Splinters stabbed under her fingernails. She propelled herself forward, inch by excruciating inch, as the thumps grew louder and, closer.

'Help,' she croaked.

She knew it was useless. It was always useless. No one could hear. No one would come.

Thump.

She stretched out and touched the safe metal of her bedroom door handle, and thrust the door open.

Thump.

Scrambling inside, she slammed the door behind her and fastened the lock.

Thump.

She jumped onto her bed and, hiding under the covers, waiting and shaking.

Thump.

The footsteps stopped, right outside the door. The handle rattled, but the door stayed closed. She gulped. Her breath locked tight in her chest. Blood thumping in her ears.

Then came the sound of metal on metal, as the lock jangled. She wanted to cry but it was pointless.

The lock clicked open. She woke with a start as her bedroom door creaked open. She pushed her head deeper into the pillows, feigning sleep, her lip trembling. The door opened slowly and tentative footsteps entered the room.

A tear dropped onto her pillow.

The door closed softly and the lock clicked again.

'I know you're awake,' he whispered.

Lila stifled a sob.

CHAPTER 5

RAVENSWOOD

RAVENSWOOD SMIRKED AS HE WATCHED HIS CAST SCRAMBLE FOR the exit. One good thing about teenagers, you didn't need to tell them twice that class was over. The room rustled with high fives and air kisses, shuffling papers and zippers on bags and coats. Within seconds, cigarettes, lighters and bus passes were at the ready.

'Angelika,' Ravenswood called out over the ruckus. 'Can you stay back for a moment?'

After a brief eye roll, Angelika composed herself and smiled calmly, relaxing back into her plastic chair. Violet huffed under her breath, the last to stomp out of the room, but Ravenswood ignored her.

The drama room settled into silence and outside the daylight was fading, Ravenswood watched through the large classroom windows as a thin fog trickled between the gum trees.

Ravenswood chewed his lip. Should he have asked Lionel to stay back? Meeting with a female student alone could be a bad idea. He didn't need a scandal in his first year of teaching. But Lionel didn't need the extra coaching. He wished he had a full cast of Lionels.

To be safe, he propped the classroom door wide open. Angelika watched him through heavy lashes. Her beauty was unquestionable but distant and stirred nothing inside him. She was his Trojan horse, the way to restore his reputation.

He turned a chair and straddled it to face her. She glanced at him curiously and he adjusted his scarf, her blue eyes seemed to belong to an older face. He felt their roles were reversed, as though she was the experienced teacher and he the student. But their age gap couldn't be more than six years.

'You wanted to see me?' she said, as though he was inconveniencing her.

He swallowed and leaned forward, reminding himself who was the adult. 'You did well today.'

'Thank you.' She met his gaze directly, but respectfully.

'However...'

She blinked, her face clouding for a split second.

'Lady Macbeth is a difficult and demanding role,' he said. 'You were good but...'

Angelika's eyes went cold.

'I want you to be great.'

What was life like with a face like hers, Ravenswood wondered. Did the whole world drop effortlessly into her lap? When the curtain rose on Friday night, every eye would be on her, but this was nothing new for Angelika, she was born with a spotlight on her face.

With a little gentle steering, she'd shine. No one would believe she did it alone; such was the curse of a pretty face. And he, her director, would emerge as the true star.

'Lionel is a commanding presence on the stage.'

'He's brilliant.' Angelika nodded.

'But you have the potential to be just as good. Better even.'

Angelika scrutinised him. 'Do you think?'

'Are you serious about acting, Angelika?'

She nodded half-heartedly.

'Would you like some advice? Can I talk frankly?'

She smoothed the hair from her face.

'There are a million beautiful girls in the world but to make a career, you need to stand out, be more than your face. You need to bring something new to the role, something fresh to the stage.'

'But *Macbeth*'s been done for hundreds of years,' she replied.

'Ah. But not by you.'

Angelika folded her arms.

'This is your first time on stage as Lady Macbeth. What can you bring to the role that no one else can? A unique perspective? Enrich Lady Macbeth with your life experience, your thoughts, your feelings. Who is Angelika Ostholz's Lady Macbeth?'

Ravenswood watched Angelica's eyes darting back and forth as his words sunk in.

'Start with Lady Macbeth. Who is she underneath? What is the face she doesn't show the world?'

Angelika narrowed her eyes. 'She's frail. Is that what you mean?'

'Is she? Do you think she's weak?'

'She's lost a child and she's still grieving. She's replaced her dead child with her husband and put all her energy into him.'

He pressed his fingers to his lips and nodded. 'But think about the world around her, the historical context. A woman can never be King, no matter how clever or ambitious she is. Her husband is the only way she can get the power she craves.'

Angelika leaned forward with her head tilted.

Ravenswood suppressed a smile. The kindling was lit.

'Some people play her as tragic like you suggested, and others as the puppet master behind Macbeth. But I think you—'

A groan drifted into the room. Breathy and quiet at first, it crept in from the silent corridor. Ravenswood jerked, his heart knocking inside his shirt. He bit down on his lip as the unnatural noise swelled and strengthened.

'No,' Ravenswood muttered, cupping his hands over his ears. 'I don't hear you. I don't hear you.'

The moan became a shudder. The air throbbed all around them and built to a crescendo like a passing train. Ravenswood gripped the plastic chair as the beige ceiling tiles rattled above their heads.

'Mr Ravenswood?' Angelika said as she clutched at her throat.

Ravenswood stared wide-eyed at the open doorway. He watched the dark and waited for something to appear. But after a few seconds, the howl died away and the room and the corridor were quiet.

Ravenswood exhaled shakily. 'Pipes. Yes, of course. They must be fiddling with the heating.'

'But it sounded like a person,' Angelika insisted, pointing to the dark corridor. 'And then it didn't—'

'It's an old building.' Ravenswood swallowed hard and fiddled with his scarf, but his heart continued to thump hard under his shirt. 'Back to what I was saying…'

'Macbeth is her pawn?' Angelika said with a squint.

'Yes. But no. Is there more to Lady Macbeth? Look closely at Act 1. Read what she actually says. Read very closely.'

Angelika traced her bottom lip with her finger.

'Think about it tonight. I'll look forward to seeing new depths to your portrayal of Lady Macbeth tomorrow.'

'Thanks for the pointers.' Angelika stood up, clutching her script to her chest.

'That's what I'm here for.'

'And Alan Wolf will be here on Friday?'

'He said he would.'

The more times Ravenswood said it aloud, the more he believed it was true.

Angelika walked away, leaving Ravenswood with nothing else to distract his mind. He shuddered. What *was* that noise?

ROWAN

Headed down the corridor, Rowan's head thumped in time with her boots on the linoleum. She pressed her palm against her queasy tummy as the walls shimmered and the red exit sign in the distance hurt her eyes.

She dropped a few silver coins shakily into the slot and dialled.

'Oh good. You're there.' She sighed. 'I'm not feeling so good. Real pounder… There's this rotten smell. I can't get away from it… Maybe it's something I ate… Not that. I hope it's not that. Don't even think it.'

The lights blinked off and on again. Rowan swallowed hard and glanced up at the flickering ceiling.

'S'OK.' She grimaced. 'The lines are so hard. I can't make sense of it, you know, it's all old poetry. I don't know if I'm up to it… Yeah, I talked to him.'

Something fluttered in the corner of her eye. She blinked and then squinted at the payphone. Hairy black legs poked out of the coin return. Rowan jumped back, dropped the phone and clamped her hand over her mouth. Her eyes bulged as a black spider slid out from under the silver flap and scampered across the keypad. The receiver swung on its cord and thumped against the brick wall.

The spider scuttled away into the darkness and Rowan took a breath. She cautiously picked up the phone again, but she stepped back until the cord stretched taut.

'Sorry. A spider came right out of the coin slot. I know. Yuck,' she said, forcing out a laugh. 'At least, I think it was a spider. Last night I had the weirdest—' She scrubbed her hand over her forehead. Her skin burned hot under her fingertips. 'I'm coming down with something. Can you come and get me? I don't want to go home. Not yet.'

She rested her cheek against the cold brick wall.

'Down by the Outlet in… fifteen minutes? Can you come any sooner? It's creepy down there. Okay, I guess… I've been thinking about what you said last night,' she said, with a little chuckle. 'Maybe. See you soon… You too.'

She put down the receiver and wrapped her black woollen scarf around her neck then checked her watch with a sigh. She picked up her backpack, turned and jumped.

'Oh.' She staggered back against the brick wall and clutched at her scarf. 'You scared me. Go ahead I'm finished.'

With a snap, the power dropped out completely and the corridor was black as a cave. In the dark, the putrid smell returned and amplified. It oozed inside Rowan's nostrils and down the back of her throat. Her mouth felt coated with a cloud of roadkill, manure and off milk.

Rowan didn't see what happened next. But she felt the first blow.

VIOLET

Violet shoved open the heavy fire doors as dusk snuffed out the last of the daylight. She jammed a cigarette into her mouth. Her hands trembled as she fumbled with her lighter.

Three times she tried and failed to produce even the smallest spark.

'Shit,' she grunted.

'Need some help there?'

The tech guy, his black hoodie pulled up over his head like a monk, stretched out his hand with a crooked grin.

Violet dropped her scowl and handed over the yellow plastic lighter. 'Toby, right?'

He nodded and struck the wheel, producing an inch-high flame on his first try. Violet shook her head with a half-smile.

'I've got a knack.' He shrugged.

'Lucky.'

She reached for the lighter but he beckoned her towards him instead. She leaned in, cigarette in her mouth and he lit it for her.

The first drag was so good, she almost moaned out loud. The little white stick magically smoothed off the edges of her rough day.

'Thanks,' she said through a plume of smoke.

'No worries,' Toby said and lit his own. His cigarette crackling as he sucked hungrily. He handed back her lighter. 'See ya tomorrow,' he said, and Violet watched him as he loped away, his black shirt blending into the darkness.

Violet's shoulders softened as she drew more smoke deep into her lungs. Time slowed down and all their lies drifted away. By the time she squashed the butt into the concrete with her boots, her head was clear, and her hands were still.

Lionel was waving to Jacinta as he crossed the Quad. He flowed rather than walked across the concrete, he always seemed to be on stage. With his golden skin and dark almond eyes, he was not exactly Violet's type, but he was what her grandma called 'handsome'. He was different from the others. He listened and didn't stink of dirty socks and or cheap deodorant.

'Wait up,' she called. She pushed the last coil of smoke out of her lungs and hauled her bag over her shoulder.

Lionel turned, his forehead furrowed for a brief second. 'Violet. How are you?' he said without breaking stride.

'I've had better days.' She scuttled to catch up with him on her short legs.

'Fighting with friends is never fun.'

'Friends. Ha. Smoke?' She offered him the packet but he flicked his hand away. 'I'm glad we got a chance to be alone. We need to chat.'

'Do we?' He arched an eyebrow.

They mounted the steps towards the school entrance and the bus stop, past the clipped lilly pilly hedges and the low floodlit concrete wall, which was carved with the school's name and logo—the symbol of a light on a hill.

'Our show last term was a real hit.'

'It was fun.'

'But this one....' Violet groaned. 'Ravenswood's nowhere near as good as Mrs Tulloch. Is he?'

'He's alright,' Lionel said as he brushed something off his jacket sleeve.

'But he's so inexperienced and arrogant.'

'He's not that bad. Besides, there's only so much we can achieve in a few days.'

'Exactly. It's mental trying to do Macbeth in three days. Most of the idiots don't even understand it. I wonder if he even does.'

'I wouldn't worry yourself. It'll be fine.'

'I'm not worried. But Alan Wolf, eh? That makes things really interesting,' Violet said as she struggled to keep up.

'Should be good,' Lionel yawned.

'Totally. You want to go on to study drama, don't you?'

'No.' Lionel guffawed and pulled himself up to his full six feet. 'I'm going to be a barrister. This is only a bit of extra-curricular activity. Looks good on the resume, you know, working in a team, public speaking, that kind of thing. Sport bores me to tears, so drama was the other option. And I seem to be alright at it.'

Violet's shoulders slumped. Was she the only one taking this production seriously? She pursed her lips. 'But you don't want Angelika dragging you down?'

'She won't drag me down.'

'He only picked her because she's pretty.'

'She's not quite my type,' he said with a raised eyebrow. 'But yes, she is very beautiful. Blind Freddy can see that.'

'If you like that kind of thing. Personally, I think you and I would've made a much better match for the Macbeths,' Violet said. 'Don't you think?'

'Interesting,' Lionel said.

'Remember the review for The Sound of Music? We could have done it all again.'

Lionel reached the bus shelter a few steps ahead of her. The Perspex wall was covered in the same yellow graffiti Violet had seen on the Quad wall in the morning. A thin fog was crawling in. The mist had already swallowed up the square school building behind them.

Lionel stepped out and peered down the road.

'We had real chemistry.' Violet followed Lionel to the kerb. 'Everyone said so.'

'People were very kind.'

'I knew you'd agree,' Violet said. 'You know you've got influence. Ravenswood listens to you. All you need to do is have a word with him and I'm sure he'd ditch Angelika and put me in the role.'

'I'm just an actor like the rest of you.' He shrugged. 'And what about Rowan?'

'Never mind her—'

'Need some help there, Lionel?' Wayne and Jason emerged out of the fog, bringing their own cloud of pot with them. 'She bothering you?'

Lionel laughed politely. 'Thanks fellas, but I can handle myself.'

'Seriously. Think how much better the play would be with me by your side?' Violet said as she grabbed his wrist. 'It's going to be a disaster without us.'

Lionel flinched and snatched his hand from her grasp.

'Vile-ette's trying it on with the gay bloke,' Wayne cackled.

Jason snorted, his eyelids droopy. 'She's even dumber than I thought.'

'I wasn't—' Violet spun around, her jaw clenched hard as Wayne and Jason laughed openly in her face. Lionel stood there, without a word in her defence and pretended to look for the bus.

Maybe he was just like the others.

'I thought you'd understand,' she huffed at Lionel and stomped into the fog towards the gravel carpark.

'Don't worry about them, Violet,' Lionel called. 'The bus is coming.'

'I'd rather walk,' she yelled back and tugged up her duffle coat hood to hide her face.

'Be careful.' Lionel's voice drifted through the white fog.

'You're the ones who should be careful,' Violet muttered as she trudged away.

HOLLY

'She's talking about hurting people,' Holly said as she leaned over the bus seat and Lila dabbed her nose with a blood-soaked tissue. 'I'm worried about her.'

'She's heart broken,' Lila replied with a nasal voice.

'You're too good to her,' Holly said. 'Are you sure you're alright?'

'I'll be fine,' Lila said. 'It's a bit weird, though. I never get nose bleeds.'

Holly pressed the button for the next stop. Today a round-bellied man sat behind the wheel and there was no sign of yesterday's strange woman.

'You're not going home?' Lila cracked. 'I thought we could—'

'I've got to go and see Dahlia.'

'Oh, right.' Lila looked down.

'Family stuff,' Holly lied.

Lila smiled painfully. 'I guess I'll go home then.'

'I'll call you later? You should get an early night. Eat some soup.'

'It was only a bit of blood,' she said with a swallow.

The rain lashed down hard on Holly's head as she waved goodbye to Lila. She ran towards the shops and under the protection of the corrugated iron awning. The shop-front lights shimmered in the puddles and Holly shook the drips from her hair and headed for The Three Torches.

A chorus of bells tinkled as she pushed open the door and stepped into a warm cloud of cinnamon sugar and spicy incense.

The voluptuous Dahlia straightened up from a glass display case, a chunk of pink crystal in her hand and a silver pentagram swinging at her neck. Her hair was exactly the same shade of brown as Holly's, but long and coiled on top of her head. 'Little niece. I've been expecting you.'

'Read it in the cards?' Holly lifted an eyebrow.

'Cheeky. I saw you get off the bus.'

'It's bit dead in here.' Holly glanced past the rows of tall dark-stained wooden bookshelves to the cafe. 'I thought witches weren't afraid of wintry weather.'

'How many times have I told you? This is a new age health café.'

'What's all that stuff for then?'

Dahlia smiled as she placed the pink crystal alongside the small steel-bladed daggers and solid eggs of jade, and locked the lid on the red velvet-lined cabinet. Bookshelves loomed behind her, crammed with books on every topic from macrobiotics to Morris dancing. Pink feathered dreamcatchers floated from the ceiling and, on to the left, sat a rack of tie-dyed leggings and tunics in jewel-toned crushed velvet.

'Novelty gifts. That's what I tell the police. One of the lovely boys in blue popped in today. Asking me about some yellow graffiti. Tea?'

'If you can fit me in.' Holly waved her hand past the bookshelves and towards the cafe at the back. It was a ghost town.

'It's been quiet all afternoon. I even sent Starshine home. Grab yourself a seat.'

Dahlia's eggplant-coloured gown rippled over her generous hips as she crossed the black and white linoleum, her silver jewellery jingling. She flipped up the hinged counter-top and stepped behind the till to the well-stocked cake fridge. For a health café, there was a distinct lack of brown rice and lentils.

Holly took the seat closest to the small stage, which was used mainly on Thursday nights for bad erotic poetry and fiddle music. The rain continued to bucket down on the tin roof, the drumming drowned out the pan flutes being piped through the speakers.

Dahlia waddled over to join her. Two small earthenware teapots with cups and a plate of golden biscuits balanced in her arms.

Holly grabbed a biscuit before the plate touched the yellowing lace tablecloth.

'Ginger?' Holly mumbled through a mouthful of crumbs.

Sulphur filled the air as Dahlia struck a match and lit the tea-light candle beside the sugar bowl. 'Trying out a new recipe for winter solstice. You know? On Friday? You are coming to the party, aren't you?' Dahlia pointed to a flyer pinned to the wall, a black linocut of an owl on a leafless tree. 'I know your mother forgets these things. But it's important to maintain the traditions.'

'That's our performance night.'

'Ye gods. I didn't realise.' Dahlia patted Holly's hand. 'So sorry, little one. I'm going to have to miss it.'

Holly pressed her lips together, before crunching into another biscuit. 'It's fine.'

'Are you sure?'

Holly roused a smile and made a mental note to remind her mum. 'A few more of these, and I can be persuaded.'

'They've won the Holly seal of approval? The coriander makes all the difference,' Dahlia said as she poured a cup of tea. The steam whirled towards the ceiling, which was painted with silver stars. 'How is the play going?'

Holly sipped her tea. 'Ugh.'

'It's dandelion. Good for your kidney, liver, tummy, and all that. Cleans out everything. All that fried food you've been eating. Don't argue. I know you.'

Holly tipped in four teaspoons of sugar, stirred thoroughly and sipped again. 'Much better.'

'How is the play going?'

'Shakespeare is hard. The old words and the rhythm. But playing a witch is fun.'

Her aunt winked and Holly rolled her eyes with a half-smile. 'Don't start.'

'I didn't say anything.'

Holly threaded her fingers around the warm earthenware and held the cup to her lips. She listened to the slosh of car tyres on the wet road outside. Dahlia steepled her fingers on the table, her blue eyes probing into Holly's face.

'So? Out with it.'

Holly sighed and planted her cup down. 'It's Violet—'

'What has she done this time?'

'She didn't get the part in the play she wanted and she's gone a bit...' Holly stirred up a whirlpool in her herbal tea. 'She's saying all kinds of crazy stuff.'

Dahlia's forehead wrinkled. 'What kind of stuff?'

'I was trying to be supportive. You know, look at the situation from her side. But then she started to say all kinds of weird things. And I couldn't help myself.'

'Your honest tongue unfolded again.'

'She said she wants to hurt Angelika, the girl who got the part she wanted. Get her out of the way.' Holly slumped. 'What do you think I should do?'

'She's always liked a drama. But would she actually go that far?'

'I'm worried. Maybe she's having a nervous breakdown and Angelika is in real danger. What if something happens and I didn't say anything? Then again, I could get her in real trouble for talking shit.'

'You're a good person.'

'I don't feel like it.'

'There are ways you can stop her. Without tattling to the teacher. You can bind her from hurting anyone. Including herself.'

Holly shook her head and exhaled through her teeth. 'How many times do I have to tell you? I don't want any part of that stuff.'

'You came for help.' Dahlia raised her eyebrows as she sipped her tea. 'You deny your own heritage, but you know we have solutions.'

Holly blinked, her head heavy on her neck. What else did she expect from Dahlia?

Her aunt sighed. 'If you insist on being so normal, I'll be the good aunty and give you tea and biscuit sympathy.'

Holly chewed on her lip. 'I'm not sure what to do.'

'Listen to your gut.'

She replied with a half-shrug.

'Your mother has taught you nothing? Not even the simplest things like scrying?' Dahlia tutted. 'Such a waste.'

'I'm not like you.'

'It's in your blood,' Dahlia insisted. 'But alright, tell me more about Violet. Has she changed?'

'She's different than when she was Jeanette.'

'Does she still feel like Violet?'

Holly squinted. 'In some ways.'

'Are you sure it's her?' Dahlia's tone turned serious.

'Of course. She was right in front of me.'

'But is she still Violet? Still the same person? Teenage girls are particularly vulnerable.'

'To what?'

'There are strange energies at work here. Beacon Hill is not like other places.'

Holly lifted an eyebrow. 'Do you know a woman bus driver?'

'The strange can be good or bad.' Dahlia grasped Holly's hand, her palm warm and smooth like dough. 'What is your inner voice telling you?'

'I don't want to be a dobber,' Holly sighed. 'Maybe she's just letting off steam.'

'You have to do what you feel is right. Don't start the rest of your life ignoring what you feel. Don't be like the rest of the sheep.'

Holly forced a smile.

'But if you want a solution, I can help you. I know traditions aren't cool these days, but deep down you know it works. Remember what I did for your mum?'

Holly narrowed her eyes. She had never believed Dahlia's spell drove her mum's loser boyfriend away. But Holly nodded. Sometimes it was easier to agree than dredge up the past.

'You look tired. Have you been dreaming?'

Holly rubbed the back of her neck. 'I've had this headache. And last night I—'

'The dandelion tea should do you good.' She lifted the teapot and offered more but Holly waved her away.

'I should be getting home, I guess. The rain seems to have gone.'

'How did your mum's interview go?'

'You know what she's like,' Holly said. 'She's already plotted out the whole thing, with Plans A, B and C, depending on what happens. I better go. I'll just use your loo first.'

Holly splashed cold water on her face and stared at her reflection with a sigh. Dahlia lived in her own little world surrounded by spells and magic. But if Dahlia didn't have the answers, who did? Holly rubbed her forehead and wished someone would tell her what to do. Sometimes she wondered whether any of the adults knew what they were doing.

She dried her hands under the hot air and noticed her ring finger was naked. She groaned. The slim silver ring, her fifteenth birthday present was gone. She grimaced, anticipating the blast she'd get when her mum realised. What else could go wrong today?

The table was now empty and Dahlia was at the shop counter by the door. Holly picked up her satchel.

Her aunt handed Holly a paper bag. 'A few things in case you change your mind.'

Holly frowned and kept her hands by her sides.

'It's all there. Instructions and everything. Just in case.'

'I don't want it.'

Dahlia rattled the paper bag. 'Humour me. You don't have to use it.'

Holly clenched her fingers. It would get Dahlia off her back, but taking the bag felt like admitting defeat.

'Any questions, you know where to find me,' Dahlia said.

Exhaling through her nostrils, Holly reached out a reluctant hand.

Dahlia smiled as Holly took possession of the bag, and a chill slithered down Holly's spine. 'After Friday, the light will take over again soon. Things always get a bit funny at this time of year when the dark is at its strongest.' Dahlia held out her arms. The knot in Holly's stomach loosened for a second as her aunt's big hug enveloped her in a waft of lavender and sandalwood.

Holly turned to leave.

'By the way. You dropped this.' Dahlia presented Holly's missing ring in the palm of her hand.

'Phew.' Holly slipped the ring back on her finger. She squinted up at Dahlia. She swore the warm silver was humming. 'What did you do?'

Her aunt smirked. 'I thought you didn't believe in that stuff. Blessed be, little one.'

Holly grimaced and shoved the paper bag into the bottom of her satchel. She buttoned up her woollen coat and stepped out into the cold.

As she walked past the bakery and the hairdressers, she promised herself she would never use the contents of the paper bag.

No matter what.

$\sim$

VIOLET

The mist swallowed Violet up as she crossed the empty carpark and stepped onto the thin dirt path which led through the acres of bush surrounding the school.

She pursed her lips. Lionel didn't care, Holly was a traitor and Lila was off in one of her moods. As usual Violet had no one to rely on. No surprises there. A drop of water dribbled down her cheek. It wasn't a tear, it was rain. She would swear her life on it.

Violet trudged down the track where the grey-green gum trees met the high back fences of the houses. She knew Lady Macbeth backwards and forwards and inside out. She'd watched Ravenswood's amateurish stage directions closely all day. She was fully prepared for the moment when she would eventually take over.

Something stirred to her right—a snap of broken twigs and the sound of movement through the scrub. Violet spun around, and glanced in all directions, but she couldn't see a thing through the ghostly air. She rubbed her eyes, shivered and sped up.

The crunching grew louder and then there was a snuffling. Violet jerked to the left and right but everything past the path was a shifting veil of white. She pushed her feet faster, her own breath rasped through her open mouth. She was only halfway home. It was too far to run back to the school and no one in Beacon Hill left their back gates unlatched. Her pulse thumped in her ears.

Violet's pursuer came closer, panting and slapping through the wet undergrowth. Her stomach flipped. She thought it was a man but the sounds were uneven. Was there more than one of them? A gang?

She gulped as every Beacon Hill urban myth flooded her mind. The cults, the cannibals, and the ghosts of their victims. The missing girls from back in the 1980s, Rebecca, Danielle and Tracy, whose bodies were never found. The doorway to hell, Peter the Butcher and even yesterday, the bus driver's prediction.

But they were all bedtime stories for gullible kids. Weren't they?

A silhouette crashed out of the bush. Violet lunged for the nearest tree and flattened herself against the narrow trunk of the nearest tree, her heart thundering in her chest, her throat clamped shut.

She could hear huffing and snorting. Her knees trembled as she gripped onto the tree trunk. What made huffing and snorting sounds like that?

Violet peered around the trunk.

The black hooded raincoat shadowed their entire face. A big black dog dragged them down the path towards her. She sucked in a shaky breath. She could never outrun a Doberman. She was always last in cross-country runs. The tree was pointless, too. The dog would sniff her out straight away. Violet bent down, fumbling for a fallen branch or anything to use as a weapon.

They came closer.

Violet wanted to shut her eyes and block everything out but she forced herself to watch.

Her heart was on the brink of bursting.

They were only metres away.

Violet tensed every fibre. Only the boys at the bus stop knew she was in here. Hours would pass before anyone noticed her missing.

The figure and the dog passed straight by her, the dog tugged at the leash, his nose pressed firmly to the dirt as it snuffled along the path.

She rested her cheek against the rough bark.

But the hooded person turned their head and stared right at her, their eyes like the slice of a knife. Every hair on Violet's body jerked upright.

'Beware,' they whispered and the dog pulled them towards the school.

The warning hung in the fog. Violet frowned. Beware of what?

She waited behind the tree until the bush was quiet and her heartbeat settled. When she was sure she was safe, she ran all the way home down the path, not stopping until she deadlocked her front door behind her. Gasping and damp with sweat, she leaned against the locked door. The word still rang in her ears.

Beware.

~⌒~

ANGELIKA

Ravenswood was not as useless as Angelika had suspected. She rolled his advice around in her mouth as she hurried towards the exit sign, the heels of her ankle boots clattering over the grey mottled linoleum.

She hurried towards the exit sign. The school was more like a jail than a place to nurture learning. Rumours claimed its box-shape was designed to withstand a nuclear attack and despite the public-spirited architecture, there were permanent dark corners, cold spots and classrooms Angelika never liked entering.

She didn't believe a word of their stupid superstitions: that scatty Lila and her silly curse. There was a myriad of rational explanations: old wiring, electric pulses or possibly low frequency sound. Sometimes Angelika wondered if she and her family were the only sane ones in the whole suburb, and that was saying something. But still, she didn't want to hang around the school alone at night.

She left the school building and crossed the pot-holed car park. She didn't pull up her hood and instead tilted her head to the sky and let the wet air sprinkle her cheeks and dampen her hair. The day was over, hair and make-up no longer mattered. Unlike some of the women in Beacon Hill, her mother never cared about appearances. She was more inclined to glare at Angelika if she lingered too long in front of the bathroom mirror.

Her footsteps crunched on the gravel as she dodged the puddles and left the car park for the bush. She quickened her stride, keen to get home to the empty house to play her new chess computer game Sargon and listen to Dustin Gramley - 'Power and Passion: the keys to an Extraordinary Life' tape: two more things her mother disliked.

Branches snapped. Angelika pressed her hand to her solar plexus. Something barrelled towards her. She jumped off the path and listened to the sounds of undergrowth being shoved aside. Surrounded by the whiteness of fog, she glanced around in vain. Violet's name popped into her head. Had she underestimated Violet's little tantrums?

A dripping black dog and a hooded figure crashed out of the fog. The dog, probably weighing more than Angelika, came hurtling towards her.

She froze, but the preoccupied dog dragged his owner down the path, past her without a sniff or a glance in her direction. The hooded person turned their head and stared at her. Angelika sucked in a shaky breath but remembered a quote from her favourite book.

'Appear weak when you are strong, and strong when you are weak.'

She converted her fear and matched the man's harsh glare. She still couldn't see his face but it had to be a man. He said something in a barely audible whisper that sounded like 'Beware.'

'Beware? Beware of what?' she replied, hands on hips. Maybe she did have some acting talent she thought as she hid the wobble in her voice.

But he'd disappeared into the mist and she was left alone, cursing the Beacon Hill weirdos. With a shake of her head, she started off again along the track home. *Perverts.*

She went back to pondering Ravenswood's advice. She knew her own limitations, her acting skills were no match for Lionel's. She'd be envious if he wasn't so nice and, as Dustin Gramley said, envy was wasted energy. But Ravenswood had handed her a gift. Lady Macbeth now made perfect sense. Angelika smiled as she was reminded of another favourite phrase.

'The whole secret lies in confusing the enemy, so that he cannot fathom our real intent.'

Angelika hummed the Ace of Base song she couldn't get out of her head as she headed for her own cul-de-sac. Mist curled around the tree trunks as she marched past the back fences. The scent of wet eucalyptus filled her nostrils and decaying leaves crunched under her boots. She'd travelled this path a thousand times but now she flinched at the slightest sound, the remnants of fear vibrating inside her.

Mr Ravenswood was oddly intriguing. He wanted something from her, they all did, but this wasn't the usual thing. Grown men and boys with their lusting eyes made her sick. Everything had changed around her thirteenth birthday. It happened almost overnight, she was playing in her backyard in her cut-off denim shorts as she always did, and her brother's friends suddenly noticed her. They had stared with expressions she didn't understand. Then the teasing started, the offers of cold drinks and lollies, trips to the movies, any excuse to be alone with her. Then it was everywhere, every time she left the house, at school, the shops, on the bus.

At first, she shied away, she'd never asked for this. Until one day she was unwrapping the fish and chips for the family dinner and the bag heaved with an extra free portion of chips. And all at once Angelika realised that if she was clever and determined, this could be a gift of great value. But the awkward high school boys and the dirty old men never understood they had nothing she wanted in return.

Now, finally, Ravenswood had offered up something Angelika did want. She'd never heard the name Alan Wolf before this morning, but if he was as influential as they all said, Friday night could change everything. Her belly fluttered. *A true commander needed to be flexible to modify her plans.* The right opportunity to get off the island had arrived.

Angelika halted as she spotted a strange bright yellow symbol painted on a fence. It was the second time she'd seen this graffiti today. She traced the curves with her finger. The flow of the lines reminded her of the Queen's Gambit chess play sequence.

Light blazed from a few houses and wood smoke belched from their chimneys, but in the darkness of late afternoon, most of Beacon Hill was still at the office. Even when they were home, Angelika's neighbours moved in and out like ghosts. Only the rumble of lawnmowers and the rattle of roller doors reminded her that she and her family were not alone. Not that she minded.

A gust of wind rushed past her head, followed by the beating of powerful wings. Angelika ducked as a tawny owl with a white mask landed on a nearby tree. Its unrelenting black-eyed stare seemed to bore a hole into her skin, its glare froze her to the spot, trapped her breath in her chest.

'What do you want?' she spluttered, but the owl only blinked in reply.

She shook her head at herself. It was only a bird. She let her breath free and set off briskly down the track. The owl hooted out after her, its mournful cry echoed through the foggy bush. Angelika didn't slow her pace. She hummed again and the owl's call faded away.

That Violet was a fool, Angelika thought. Her undermining attempts were laughable. Angelika could show her how to get her own way but she wasn't the mentoring type, especially not for a piece of work like Violet

Black. Anyway, there was no time for distractions. Dustin Gramley was always right, opportunity *could* come at any time.

Angelika licked her lips. She'd never be like her sister Briony with her hog-like husband and whingeing kids whose life revolved around interest rates, soap operas and spats with the old woman next door. How could Briony live so small? When there was a whole world of five-star hotels, tropical islands and designer dresses out there?

Tomorrow Angelika would return to the drama room and play Lady Macbeth as a warrior queen, the version of herself of herself she pictured whenever she read Sun Tzu, listened to Dustin Gramley on repeat, or lined up her rooks and knights. She grinned. This version of Lady Macbeth fit her perfectly.

Angelika veered down her empty driveway and into her dark house. She closed her bedroom door, shut out the world and switched on her motivational tape. She lay on her bed, stared up at the ceiling and re-peated his mantras, imagining champagne-coloured silk sheets and room service on silver trays. As the tapes said, if she focused hard enough, her goals would materialise. She pulled out her script and read her lines with different eyes. She stood at the foot of her bed and rolled her shoulders back with a smile. Lady Macbeth's lines were perfect.

'Leave all the rest to me.'

Angelika forgot all about the hooded man's warning.

RAVENSWOOD

Ravenswood whistled to himself and hoped there was wine left in the cask at home as the school's fire door clanged shut behind him. He shiv-ered as he turned up his faux fur collar and stepped over a yellow squiggle painted on the footpath.

Only two cars remained in the foggy carpark. The other one on the far side under a row of trees was even more of a bomb than his own. He promised himself that by next year he'd have a place of his own and a car with a heater. Or, if everything went perfectly to plan on Friday night, he'd be somewhere warmer, moving up in the world by next year.

Something shifted in the darkness to his left. Ravenswood stopped whistling and his stomach clenched. The movement was strange, a slithering. The hairs on his forearm bristled. Ravenswood scoured in all directions. He seemed to be all alone in the carpark but nothing was clear through the haze. He paused, listening hard to the rumble of cars on the freeway in the valley below, the slow drip of water running off the leaves, and the electric hum of the car park lighting.

Ravenswood pushed his glasses firmly against up his nose and checked all around again. Only him and two cars.

He shrugged it off and made for his car, his fingers wrapped firmly around his keys. He was a grown man now, he had nothing to be afraid of, even if he was on their territory.

A cold breeze ruffled the back of his neck, close to his skin like someone's exhaled breath. He spun around, his shoulders hoisted around his ears.

'Who's there?' he demanded.

His voice bounced across the empty car park.

There was no reply.

'Bloody kids,' he muttered and picked up the pace for the final metres to his dented Datsun. He looked left and right before unlocking the door and sliding inside. He checked the back seat. The seat was stacked with empty pizza boxes, jackets and months old copies of *The Saturday Mercury*. The footwell was littered with greasy wrappers, crushed cans and a broken blue umbrella. There was no attacker, but he should clean his car.

Swearing at his own cowardice, he started the engine and prayed there was wine left at home. The engine coughed, wheezed then died. Ravenswood turned the key in the ignition again. His little car spluttered like a phlegmy old man and then went silent.

'Great.' He slumped.

Thud.

Ravenswood jumped in his seat as something dropped onto the car roof of the car.

Thud.

He stared up. The roof flexed. Whatever it was, it was heavy.

'What the hell?' His stomach flipped.

Thud.

Ravenswood's hands shook as he tried the ignition again. The car gave a series of pathetic clunks and then nothing.

Thud. Scrape.

Something scratched along the length of the roof.

Scrape.

Scrape.

Scrape.

Biting his bottom lip hard, Ravenswood scanned outside, but there was only a deserted carpark. Long shadows were broken up by patches of yellow streetlight. Was it him?

Automatically the words from the Lord's Prayer escaped from his lips. 'Deliver us from evil.' He stopped his tongue as soon as he realised what his subconscious was doing. After ten long years, he assumed it had all washed away.

Tap.

A knock on the glass came from the back windshield. His breath tangled in his chest as he glanced up into the rear-view mirror. His mind scrambled for a plausible answer. It was probably Craig White's gang, boys with nothing to do but impress their friends with their cruelty. They could smell a coward from a mile off, even when the coward was supposed to be a grown up.

'Pull yourself together,' he said. 'It's a tree branch in the wind. Or a possum.'

He leaned over the back seat and grabbed his umbrella.

Tap.

His head jolted up at the sound of another knock, but there was nothing there.

With a deep breath, he opened the door and stepped out. The chilly air soothed his hot cheeks. He circled the car, umbrella held up high. He ran his hand over the car roof but there were no new dents or marks and the roof was still covered in a thin layer of moisture. He looked up. There were no overhanging branches, no excuse for the noise.

Did this only leave the implausible? Peter?

He sighed. He'd been working too hard. It was the pressure of performing in front of Alan Wolf again, of desperately wanting to avoid history repeating itself. It was this place, this school, Beacon Hill.

Ravenswood climbed back into his car and turned the keys again. 'Come on.'

The engine spluttered. He leaned in, egging the car on.

Thump.

'Please,' he whined, embarrassed by the sound of his own voice.

The car shuddered and clicked over, springing to life. With a little cheer, he put his foot down hard and sped out of the carpark with squealing tyres.

One last thump crashed against his roof as he passed through the school entrance. To his left side, a hooded figure emerged from the bush. The man reached out for the door handle. Ravenswood let out a cry and floored the accelerator.

He didn't look back, he just kept driving, all the way home.

BRIDGET AND THE GATEKEEPERS

The phone rang, shattering the silence into tiny pieces. Bridget jumped in her chair. 'Hello?'

'Did you feel it?' It was the leader.

'Yes,' Bridget whispered. 'What happened?'

'I don't know for certain. I can feel the anguish but it's not at full strength. There is still time.'

'Is it like a moaning in your bones?' Bridget rubbed her forearms.

'We all feel it differently. But the shadows are longer. They are following me.'

'I've seen them too,' she said, a tremble in her voice.

'Don't be afraid. The Warden will protect us but we need to concentrate our efforts, and you are closest to the source.'

Bridget bit her lip and glanced around the empty room. She was alone and the door was closed but it was unnaturally silent, as though all sounds of life were being muffled.

'Don't let doubt darken your mind. Remember your promise to the Warden. This is what we have worked for. This is our calling.'

Bridget slumped. 'The sigils have been removed in some places,'

'Someone is hindering our plans. We must go out again tonight and refresh them. I've called Mathilde. I have another ritual in mind, something more powerful. Tonight.'

'Tonight,' Bridget repeated faintly.

She put down the phone and cupped her head in her hands. 'I mustn't let doubt darken my mind,' she repeated aloud. 'I mustn't.'

~ ⁹⁶ ~

RAVENSWOOD

Tossing his keys on the kitchen table, Ravenswood slumped into the vinyl orange chair with the taped-up rip. The kitchen was bright and warm, filled with the scent of frying garlic and onions and the sounds of indie guitars on the radio. The incident in the car park was already fading away. Mostly.

'Bad day?' Fiona said as she stirred a pot on the stovetop. She pushed a curl away from her eyes with the back of her hand.

Ravenswood sighed.

'Kids, eh?' She licked the blood-red sauce off the wooden spoon.

Ravenswood nodded, removed his misted-up glasses and pinched the bridge of his nose.

'Wine? Hungry?'

'Yes, and yes.'

'It's only pasta. Don't read anything into it. Your timing is good and I've made too much.'

'You're a bloody marvel.'

Ravenswood rifled around in the mound of unwashed dishes in the sink. He extracted a large glass, rinsed it and filled it with red wine.

'You look knackered,' Fiona said. 'I don't know how you put up with them all day. I didn't even like teenagers when I was one.'

'They're not too bad,' he said as he took a long blissful sip and relaxed back into his chair. 'It was something else. Something a bit strange.'

Fiona shoved aside a pile of unopened letters and catalogues and placed two bowls on the table.

'What was it this time?' She said, blowing on her fork.

Suddenly starving, Ravenswood shovelled the penne into his mouth and spoke with his mouth full. 'Probably nothing.'

'Do you still dream about her?'

'Sometimes,' he shrugged.

'You can't keep blaming her,' Fiona said.

'You know what she was dabbling in.'

'I've told you a million times, she was a sick woman. Anyway, she's dead—'

'Who's dead?' Leon trudged into the kitchen and kissed Fiona on the top of her curly head. 'Any left for me, babes?'

'Look in the pot,' Fiona said. 'We were talking about Josie.'

'Ah, the evil stepmother,' Leon said as he ladled pasta into a bowl. 'You guys never talk about the cult.'

Ravenswood continued eating his dinner in silence.

Leon pulled up a chair, which looked doll-sized under his broad thighs. 'Of course. I hadn't made the connection before. It's the same place where the high school is now, isn't it?'

'It's really none of your business.' Ravenswood scowled into his wine glass.

'Don't be so rude.' His sister flicked at his arm.

'I'm interested in my girlfriend's past,' Leon said. 'What's wrong with that?'

'I like it when you say 'girlfriend'.' Fiona smiled.

Leon reached over and stroked her cheek. 'You two always change the subject whenever I bring up family.'

'With good reason,' Ravenswood snorted. 'And I don't want to talk about it now.'

'But I'm not talking to you. I'm talking to my girlfriend.'

'It's our private business,' Ravenswood grumbled.

Fiona sighed and put down her fork. 'We didn't live in that compound. After the Kindred were forced off the hill, they moved down near Leslie Vale.'

'Did they really skin people alive?' Leon asked.

'This is what I mean, Fi.' Ravenswood rolled his eyes. 'He's never going to understand.'

'Give him a chance.'

'Everyone in town knows there was some fucked up shit going on up there,' Leon persisted. 'It'd be nice to know the truth.'

'It was an allegory,' Fiona said. 'They didn't really skin people.'

'But they talked about it? Right?' Leon leaned forward in his chair, his eyes gleaming.

'It's really about shedding your skin and being born anew. Like a baby. Free of sin,' Fiona said.

'Oh,' Leon sounded disappointed. 'Still. A bit gory, though.'

'Are you sure it was only a story?' Ravenswood asked. It was his sister's turn to glare. 'I know you've had the dreams, too.'

'Kids have wild imaginations. The way Josie treated us—'

'What did she do?' Lee said without blinking.

Fiona closed her mouth.

'Come on, Fiona.' Ravenswood raised an eyebrow. 'You wanted to talk about this.'

'She was brought up inside the Kindred,' Fiona said. 'It was all she knew. She was traumatised.'

'You're always making excuses for her,' Ravenswood said. 'She was a cruel bitch. She knew exactly what she was doing.'

'Perhaps you need to talk to someone again. The school is digging up all these memories.'

'But your dad wasn't one of them?' Leon interrupted.

'Josie came to his office to buy a house,' Fiona said, with a swallow. 'He was pretty vulnerable after mum died.'

'He was putty in her hands,' said Ravenswood. 'She knew exactly what to say.'

'He was grieving. He didn't know how to cope.' Fiona frowned.

'More excuses,' Ravenswood said.

'And there was a fire?' Leon asked.

'If you believe that—' Ravenswood muttered.

'Paul!' Fiona furrowed her brow. 'We've been over this a billion times. There was an inquest and everything.'

'I'm just saying. Oh, forget it.' He shook his head and took another slurp of wine.

'What really happened tonight?' She narrowed her eyes.

'Nothing. My mind playing tricks on me,' he said, prodding at his pasta, his hunger gone as quickly as it had arrived. 'Probably.'

'Probably?' Fiona said.

'I was in the car park. I swore something was following me. A shadow. Then there was a thumping on the roof.'

Fiona inhaled sharply. 'Peter?'

'It sounded like pecking,' Ravenswood said with a gulp. 'But there was nothing there.'

'You've been working too hard.'

'Who's this Peter guy?' Lee asked.

'Another time.' Fiona patted his hand. 'With more wine.'

'Come on. You can't leave me dangling like that,' Lee groaned.

'Lucky for you, it's only a one-year contract.' Fiona turned back to her brother. 'But be careful. I don't want you getting ill again.'

'It's different when the school is empty.' Ravenswood cleared his throat. 'Perhaps you're right. I've got that doctor's number somewhere. I promise I'll call next week. But for now, get me another wine, will you?' He held out his glass. 'There are a few kids with real potential in the group. And I talked to Alan Wolf today. He's coming along to opening night.'

'Alan Wolf? That's really good,' Fiona said as she handed back a full cup of wine and placed her warm hand on his shoulder.

'This time, he'll take notice,' Ravenswood said, firmly.

He had to.

ANGELIKA
Last Night

An earthquake? In Beacon Hill? Angelika forced her eyes open. She lay waiting for another jolt, her whole body tensed. The glowing green digital clock showed 3:00am. The house was quiet and there were no more bumps. Why did rational thought disappear in the middle of the night?

Her mouth was gluey and sour. She tossed her quilt aside and padded across the bedroom carpet and down the hallway in her socks.

She flicked on the light and was temporarily blinded by the blast of 100-watt bulbs running along the top of the mirror. She fumbled into the pine-panelled bathroom and drank straight from the shamrock-green tap, flinching as the cold water hit her two front teeth. Angelika caught her reflection in the mirror and prodded tentatively at the plum-coloured blotches under her eyes. *Allergies.* With a sigh, she leaned in closer, so close she could feel the cool of the glass radiating against her skin.

Below one of the bulbs, she noticed a chip and sighed again. She'd get the blame as usual. She reached up to touch it and as her fingertip brushed the little black crevice, the surface of the mirror cracked. Angelika cried out as a long meandering crack severed the mirror from top to bottom. The black rivulet cleaved her reflection in two, a diagonal slash from cheek to chin. Angelika stared at her broken reflection. A knot tightened in her stomach as she cringed, anticipating her father's tirade.

It couldn't have been her fault. She only touched it.

But as the seconds passed and she stared into her own face, the knot in her tummy untangled. Her panic was replaced by a lightness in her chest. She giggled at herself, a wicked and unfamiliar gleam in her eye. An older, colder stranger stared back through her own blue eyes.

The crack spread, crazing the mirror like a spider's web and she leaned in to admire her new face, partitioned into a hundred jagged pieces.

And then the blood came.

First, it was bright red, full of life and iron. Young blood welling up in the cracks like a fresh paper cut. Angelika reached up, mesmerised. She rubbed the blood between her fingertips. It was still warm as she stuck her fingers into her mouth and the rusty taste of iron tingled on her tongue.

The red sap dribbled down the channels of broken mirror. Bloody puddles formed on the green vanity. Angelika tilted her head as the liquid darkened from bright red to scarlet and then to the shade of her dad's favourite Shiraz. This was a sickly colour, of old blood, decay and disease. The flow thickened into a waterfall of soiled claret that rolled down the mirror, lapping the sides of the sink.

Angelika stepped back, her mouth hanging open as her skin prickled and she held her breath in her throat.

Her eyes widened as the scene changed again.

Viscous like oil, the blood was now black. It oozed and spread all over the mirror. Random pieces of the mirror were left uncovered like ladders in a black stocking. Odd fragments of her face reflected back at her: a few strands of blonde hair, the fleshy round of her chin, part of a plucked eyebrow. The rest of her face was blacked out, deleted.

The stench of rotting fruit, blocked drains, mould and carcasses flooded the inside of her nose and mouth. Angelika retched.

The inky liquid filled the sink and clogged up the plug hole. It welled over the sides and poured onto the floor with loud belch-like glugs. This blood was icy cold. It soaked her socks and squelched between her toes, sending chills up her legs. Angelika choked and dislodged something chunky from her lungs. She spat a clump of dark goo onto the linoleum. The black blood was inside her as well.

Angelika's lips trembled and hot tears rolled down her cheek. She licked her palm, and scowled, her tongue leaving behind a sticky black residue. She wiped her face with the back of her hand. Her tears were black, too.

Black blood flowed from the mirror in a never-ending stream of lava from somewhere deep inside the bathroom wall. Angelika stared and stared. She threaded her fingers through her hair and felt the blackness inside and out.

'Stop!' she cried.

Angelika woke up with a start to her alarm clock screeching and sunlight peeking between the curtains. She was damp with sweat. Her shoulders softened and she wriggled in under her quilt. It must have been all that superstitious nonsense from yesterday, but wasn't it fascinating how the mind processed the day's information overnight?

She stretched, yawned and rubbed her eyes. Familiar footsteps clumped down the stairs. Her dad hummed to himself and the kettle squealed in the kitchen. Angelika pulled aside her quilt but inhaled sharply. She peered closer, her stomach churning.

Her palms were caked in crusty black debris.

CHAPTER 6

Wednesday 20th June 1992
HOLLY

'H EY WITCHY-POO,' WAYNE said at the bus stop, his voice booming as usual through the fog. 'You'll be loving this play.'
'You don't even need to act at all,' Jason added.
'All those spells and stuff would come natural to you.'
'You won't even need make-up,' Jason sneered.
'Or a costume,' Wayne laughed.
They circled Holly like sharks. Years ago, they had all been the same height but now, they towered over her. The same lines over and over, day in day out, every day of her entire school life.
'Leave me alone,' she said. 'What do you want?'
'Nothing,' Wayne replied as usual. 'We want nothing from you. Witch girl.'
'Watch out,' Jason said. 'She'll put a spell on you.'
Holly pushed past them and waited by the kerb as the morning traffic flowed by.

Every day it had been the same, ever since primary school.
'We know about you,' they used to say. 'You can't pretend. We know. You're evil.'
'I'm not,' she'd reply, her voice hoarse after years of denying.
But no one listened.
Holly would run and hide behind the big ant-covered gum tree at the edge of the playground and come back to the classroom with a tear-stained face. She tried dobbing to teachers, but even they eyed her strangely. One or two listened, but the more understanding teachers never lasted long in Beacon Hill. Then Holly tried violence. She smirked every time she relived

the day she punched Wayne in the nose and his blood dripped onto his school shirt, but as usual, no one listened. She was the one punished.

Holly had pleaded with her mum to switch schools, to go private, even Catholic but her mum wouldn't have a bar of it.

She had thought they'd get bored eventually, but she was wrong. She learned to ignore them. Tuning them out was easier than making them stop.

The girls were no better. They smiled on the surface and sniggered behind their hands, excluded her from skipping, and never invited her to their birthday parties unless the whole class was there. The parents were as bad as the kids. Her mum called them hypocrites. She said they secretly sought out Aunty Dahlia when no one else was looking. But Holly never knew who to believe.

There were only two hundred and sixty four days until the end of Year 12. But perhaps a solution would arrive sooner.

Holly peered through the fog up the hill and hoped each new glimmer of light was the bus. She glanced up and down the footpath, wishing an adult would come. Their mere presence would shut the boys up. But no one did. Holly rubbed her eyes and pinched the bridge of her nose. It had been another night of shadowy dreams and broken sleep. She'd woken up with the same persistent throb pressing inside her skull.

Her mum proclaimed she'd abandoned the craft in front of Dahlia and the rest of the world, but every now and then Holly caught her with a candle wrapped in ribbon or found bundles of herbs hidden behind the curtains. The family traditions ran deep.

Inside Holly's backpack, Dahlia's paper bag weighed her down like a sack of stones. She didn't want it and yet she couldn't throw it away. Holly had promised herself a long time ago she'd never stoop to magic. If she did, all the teasing since kindergarten would be true.

The bus pulled up and Holly exhaled as she stepped aboard. A balding man with glasses sat at the wheel this morning. Holly wondered whether she should have mentioned the bus driver's predictions to Dahlia. She couldn't forget the woman's omens, that one of them would take darkness into their breast and another would depart forever. But Dahlia would've taken the ramblings far too seriously. Holly waved her bus pass and headed down the aisle.

Lila was halfway down, scribbling in her notebook. She jumped as

Holly slid in the seat next to her. The seats, upholstered in an ugly lime geometric pattern, were an attempt to hide the everyday stains.

'Morning,' Holly said. 'You alright? Sorry, I forgot to call last night.'

Lila slammed her notebook shut and slipped it into her bag. Her eyes were bloodshot. Insomnia must be the in-thing, Holly thought.

'No more nosebleeds?'

'Must've been a one-off.' Lila shrugged. 'What did you get up to last night? Anything interesting?'

It was Holly's turn to shrug. 'Went to see Dahlia. Then just went home for spag bol and learned my lines.'

Lila nodded.

'Nothing exciting,' Holly added.

'Me too,' said Lila.

The two lapsed into an awkward silence but Holly wanted desperately to say more. She could trust Lila, couldn't she? She wanted to tell her about her fears for Violet, her chat with Dahlia, the shadows darting in the corners of her eyes.

'Have you noticed those?' Lila pointed out the window at a yellow symbol painted on the bus shelter. Holly squinted at it. 'Weird, huh?'

'Maybe a gang? Marking their territory?'

The bus pulled into Violet's stop and Holly straightened in her seat. Holly vowed she'd be more understanding today.

Violet was smiling as she walked up the aisle. Until she saw Holly.

'Hi,' she said curtly and slid into the seat in front. Holly noticed Violet was wearing yesterday's crumpled checked shirt again under her duffle coat and she reeked of stale cigarette smoke.

'Are you alright?' Holly said, carefully.

'Why shouldn't I be?' Violet snapped. She slipped her headphones over her ears.

Holly whispered. 'I thought she might've cooled down.'

Lila smiled painfully.

'I can hear you,' Violet said. 'Don't talk about me behind my back.' She picked up her bag and clumped down the aisle to the front of the bus.

'We weren't.' Lila scrambled after her. 'We just wanted to make sure you're okay.'

Holly rested back into the seat, alone again. The bus stopped once more and Angelika strode up the aisle like a fashion runway, her long legs clad in black tights.

Violet swivelled and glared, but Angelika didn't seem to notice.

'Hi there,' Angelika said as she took the seat beside Holly.

'Good, thanks,' Holly blurted and then winced.

Angelika rested back into the seat and Holly fidgeted with her hair, her stomach fluttering. This was her chance to warn Angelika. But what could she say without sounding like a complete fruitcake herself?

'Enjoying the play?' Holly asked.

Angelika gasped.

Had Holly said the wrong thing? Again? Holly screwed up her face and looked down. After waiting a few moments, she glanced up through her fringe and saw Angelika hadn't been responding to her at all. She was looking the other way, staring at a man in a raincoat by the side of the road.

Angelika tore her attention away from the man and blinked at Holly. 'Sorry. Did you say something?'

Holly straightened her posture and cleared her throat. 'I only asked if you were enjoying the play?'

'The lines are hard. Some parts make sense and others fly right over my head. And then there's remembering where to stand and what gestures to do.' Angelika sighed. 'I was up half the night practising. But I should be okay.'

Holly looked closer and saw the shadows under Angelika's eyes, but she'd still swap faces with her in a heartbeat if she had the chance.

'I know what you mean.' Holly forced a giggle.

The bus groaned as it struggled up the final ascent to the school.

'Stop talking about me!' Violet yelled from the front of the bus. Angelika raised an eyebrow.

Holly clenched her jaw.

'I know all about you,' Violet said, jabbing her finger at Angelika. 'I'm watching you. You won't get the better of me.'

Violet spun back around towards the front and Lila looked back at them with a painful smile.

'She's a little on edge,' Holly said with a wince.

'Classic paranoia if you ask me,' Angelika muttered.

Holly rubbed her forehead. Violet was getting worse. Someone had to make her stop.

Dear Journal

The darkness is here.

Weighing me down, enveloping me like a heavy winter coat.

Something happened last night but I can't remember what.

I was there and then I wasn't, and then suddenly I was somewhere else.

When I try to think back all I remember is the darkness.

I'm cold.

I'm clutching at a clifftop by my fingernails.

I'm so scared and but no one will understand if I tell them…

They didn't listen when I tried before.

I have to solve this myself.

I am happy, I am positive, I am in control of my destiny.

I am happy, I am positive, I am in control of my destiny.

I must say it again. And again. And again.

If I try hard enough, my words will drown them out. They have to.

Otherwise, there's no hope for me.

~⌒~

RAVENSWOOD

Ravenswood chewed the end of his biro as he sat at his office desk. Still wearing his coat, his breath was visible. How could he motivate those boys to take their soldier roles more seriously? This was the Bard, not some Bruce Lee movie.

The public address speaker in the corner of the room crackled with static and Ravenswood's eyes jerked up. No one had been in the main office yesterday and he still hadn't confirmed whether those fools had scheduled maintenance for Friday. He picked up the phone and dialled reception. He'd demand they switch the heating on, too.

The silent workmen had been adding another coat of beige to the corridors when he arrived. His skin crawled whenever he was in their presence. Their movements were too slow, too deliberate. His skin crawled whenever he was in their presence.

Fiona was right, he needed to relax. When the production was over, he'd take up yoga.

The phone in reception rang and rang. He rolled his eyes, placed his coffee cup down on a pile of papers next to three other mugs, which were half empty with cold muddy dregs. Mrs Barclay, his fellow drama teacher and officemate, would have a fit if she saw his desk. She kept all her un-chewed pens in a holder, used a spotlessly white fine china teacup with saucer and filed all her notes with coloured tabs.

With an exasperated groan, he put down the phone. He shivered. The speaker crackled again in the corner. This time his heart thumped in his chest. The static sounded like words. A particular word. But it couldn't be.

'Face your fear. You're not eight years old,' he mumbled and stared up at the beige speaker box in the corner of the ceiling. He swallowed and hoped he'd misheard, hoped another announcement would come through, something normal, logical.

The speaker buzzed again. This time, he heard the word clearly through the white noise. A whisper.

'Worthless.'

His stomach dropped as he remembered.

The slap across his face echoed in his ears.

'You stupid little boy. Get inside.'

'No.'

She had shoved him inside the chicken coop and latched the door shut. He had tumbled onto the dirt, his bare knees and palms coated in chicken crap and feathers. The chickens scurried into the corner.

'Why do you make me punish you?' she had said through the wire fence. You continue to disobey me and disobey God. He is the one disappointed in you. I am only his servant on this earth. I take no pleasure in punishing you.'

'Why is God angry with me?' he said, scrambling up into a crouch. 'I haven't done anything.'

'I saw you trying to prove you were better than God. Whatever gifts you may have, he gave them to you...

'*What do you have that you did not receive? If then you received it, why do you boast as if you did not receive it? Corinthians 4:7*'

'I never—'

'I saw you bossing the others around and big-noting yourself, acting all superior, as though you are better than them.'

'I was only putting on a play. I was only...'

'I saw with my eyes. And God saw,' she had said. 'Only you are blind to your sins. You must reflect on your deeds and repent. Repeat after me: 'I am useless. ' 'I am worthless.'

'I didn't mean to,' he gulped. 'It's getting dark. Please, Josie.'

'Night is nothing. Your soul needs to be repaired. Otherwise, you are inviting Satan himself.'

Ravenswood had sniffled. Some of the bolder chickens approached him and pecked around his feet. He flailed his arms and shoo-ed them away but the birds kept returning.

'Fiona? Dad?' he called out but only Hiram the rooster with the blood red comb appeared.

'No,' Ravenswood whimpered.

Hiram, the rooster with the blood red comb strutted out of the coop and eyed him suspiciously.

'I would never invite him,' he said. He clasped his hands together and kneeled.

'Satan is clever. Wicked and clever,' Josie said. 'He knows how to trick worthless boys like you. You will let him in before you know it. Satan knows you. Knows you are a dirty little boy, an empty vessel waiting for him to fill. I am doing this for your own good, for your soul's survival. Reflect on your sins and repeat your prayers otherwise, Satan will come for you. I will not be able to help you then. You are useless. You are worthless.'

Ravenswood glanced across at Hiram, the rooster's black eyes were as hard as marbles. Didn't the pastor say Satan could take on other forms?

His stomach rumbled loudly, loud enough to scare off one inquisitive chicken. 'Please Josie. I'm sorry. I won't do it again. I'm cold and hungry.'

'You must learn humility and penance. You will eat with the chickens.'

She unlatched the door and flung a handful of corn into the coop straight at him. The kernels thwacked against his face and bare arms. They caught in his hair and t-shirt and bounced to the ground around his bare feet. The chickens launched at him, a crowd of fluttering wings and pecking beaks. Ravenswood wailed as they pecked grain from his fingers and his toes.

Hiram stepped forward and the other chickens scattered to the edges of the coop.

Ravenswood swallowed hard and looked from side to side, searching for something, anything to fend off the rooster.

Hiram screeched and lunged for him, his claws extended.

Ravenswood covered his face.

Hiram's claws tore a chunk of flesh from his forearm and Ravenswood howled. The rooster forced him backwards until he was pressed hard against the wire fence. Hiram flew at him again and again, legs high, his sharp spurs extended aiming for his eyes.

Ravenswood crumpled into the corner, sobbing as the rooster slashed at his skin.

The attack was short. Once Hiram was confident of victory, he strutted away.

Alone, Ravenswood huddled in the corner, blood running through his hair and dribbling down his face, his forearms ripped to red ribbons. The sun had disappeared and a winter wind whistled through the wire. Deep in his heart, Ravenswood knew it was true. He never did learn. He was useless and worthless. He belonged with the animals.

Curled into a ball, he ignored his rumbling tummy and cried until he drifted off to sleep. He woke in the coop when the sun rose and one of the other wives, Marjorie, came to collect the morning eggs.

Marjorie had opened the cage door and he had crawled out and headed straight for the dining hall covered in muck. His lips blue and his skin criss-crossed with dried blood, Ravenswood kept his head low. He knew he deserved every mean stare from the others at breakfast.

He had promised to be good from then on. He would never make Josie, or God or the rest of the Kindred angry again. He knew his place.

He was useless.

He was worthless.

VIOLET

Traitors.

How dare they bitch about her behind her back! Was Holly best friends with Angelika now? It was plain to see they were all in on it, even Holly.

'*Make thick my blood,*' Violet muttered to herself as her boots crunched along the gravel and she flopped down on her favourite concrete bench in the Quad. She'd puffed and paced and rehearsed all night and woke up with Lady Macbeth living inside her.

Violet rifled inside her bag, but her fingers couldn't find her packet of smokes. She patted down her duffle coat pockets, but there were only coins and a crumpled chewing gum wrapper inside.

'Shit,' she grumbled. The nearest shop was a ten-minute walk through the bush and the fog. Violet shuddered.

The boys were kicking a hacky sack on the other side of the Quad under the awning, Jason had a cigarette dangling from his mouth. Violet screwed up her face, she didn't want to speak to any of them. She scratched at her wrist and bit down hard on her bottom lip.

Jez sailed into the Quad on his board and her stomach fluttered. Here was someone who rolled their own smokes.

'Jez.' She beckoned him over.

He half-waved back but headed straight for the boys.

She slumped and glanced over at the bin nearby. There were no butts littering the ground first thing in the morning. She couldn't, could she? Especially in full view of Jez, Jason and the others. She looked at the bin again and shook her head.

A hooded figure loped across the concrete.

'Toby!' She waved.

He slipped off his headphones and swaggered over with his lop-sided grin and his white Nike Airs. 'Hey.'

'Hey. How's it going?' She smiled up at him, careful to wrap her lips over her bad teeth. 'I haven't seen you round much.'

'Mr Ravenswood got me locked away in the theatrette. Getting ready to make you guys look good.'

'I hope we start rehearsals in there soon. The real theatre is much better than the dumb drama room.'

'True,' Toby said, the smile never leaving his face.

Violet widened her eyes and chewed her lip. 'Can I be a pain? I need a big favour?'

He raised an eyebrow.

'Could I bum a smoke from you? Sorry to ask. I must've left mine at home.'

'That's why you're glad to see me, eh?'

'Of course not.'

He pulled a red and white packet out of his jacket pocket.

'Thanks heaps,' Violet said. 'I'm too lazy to head back down the shop now. I owe you one.'

He pulled out his lighter and they both lit up. Violet sucked down the smoke and closed her eyes. She let out a stream of smoke and the white curtain flowed past her face.

'I saw you in that other play. The one with the nuns and the kids,' Toby said. 'You've got a good voice.'

'Thanks.' Violet smoothed down her hair. 'Unfortunately, there's no singing this time.'

'Shame. I'm more into music myself, do a little DJ-ing, electronic stuff.'

'That's cool.'

'You like dance music?'

'A little bit. I like New Order and that song Connected. But also PJ Harvey and guitar stuff, too.'

'That's the main reason I signed up for this thing was to get a chance to use the school equipment. They've got some alright gear in the theatrette. Much better than I can afford, anyway. It was a bit creepy in there yesterday by myself, but most places are weird when there's no one around.'

Violet nodded. 'What do you think of Ravenswood?'

'He's driving me mental,' Toby said and let out a long plume of smoke with a shake of his head. 'He changed his mind four times, yesterday.'

'What a total fraud,' Violet said with a smirk.

Toby shrugged. 'It's only a couple more days. Hopefully I can sneak in some of my own recording when no one's looking.' Toby took a long final drag and squashed out his cigarette. 'We'd better get in there. He's probably come up with some new idea and I'll have to change everything again.' Toby sighed. 'See you round?'

'Thanks again for the smoke,' Violet said, and he gave her a little salute. She finished her cigarette and watched him saunter into the school building. The rest of the cast drifted inside after him. She was the last one left in the cold concrete Quad.

Violet took a deep breath, checked her lipstick and went inside.

The room hushed as she came in, but she rolled back her shoulders and ignored their jealous stares.

Ravenswood had been raiding his grandfather's wardrobe again. Today's outfit was tweed with leather patches. 'I'll start with yesterday's notes,' Ravenswood said. 'Firstly, Wayne and Jason, we'll do some sword fighting practice today.'

'Yeah, man.' Wayne and Jason high-fived.

'Now, Rowan…,' Ravenswood looked up from his clipboard and around the circle. 'Rowan? Where is she?'

Violet noticed a spare seat. Yesterday every seat was filled.

'I didn't see her on the bus, Mr Ravenswood,' Holly said.

'Me either,' said Angelika. 'She gets on at my stop.'

Ravenswood rubbed his chin.

'She's probably just late,' Holly offered.

'Okaaay,' Ravenswood said, drawing out the word, his eyes glassy. 'Moving on. Jez…'

Violet couldn't hide her smile. Rowan's vacancy glowed and hummed. She locked eyes with Holly across the circle and Holly's mouth was a tight straight line. Violet smirked back and smoothed her hair.

One step closer.

VIOLET

'Act Four Scene One is an iconic scene that everyone should recognise.' Ravenswood rubbed his hands together. 'Thunder. Three witches enter.'

Violet, Holly and Lila, the three witches, stood before the white board at the front of the drama room. Violet looked out at the plastic chairs lined up in three rows like a makeshift theatre. The cast were watching, waiting, their attention hitting her face like a harsh spotlight. Ravenswood's forehead was furrowed, Angelika stared back smugly while Wayne yawned and scratched himself.

Violet's line was first. She inhaled through her nose in preparation but her lungs were clogged. Her chest was as tight as a locked safe. She tried to force her breath down into her diaphragm, a technique from her acting books but the seconds ticked by and she stood there in silence, with their judging eyes on her.

Her pulse accelerated and her mouth was sticky, as if crammed with peanut butter. Real actors get nervous, she reminded herself, even in rehearsal and in front of losers like this. Holly looked across, and the pity on her face forced Violet to blurt out the first stanza.

'*Thrice the brinded cat hath mewed.*'

Holly was next to speak, and then Lila. Violet puffed her flannelette shirt away from her body to hide her imperfect body, and wrapped her lips over her crooked teeth. A few more months of Saturdays behind the counter at Terri's and she'd have enough to pay for her own braces. Despite whatever her mum said. Her mum didn't understand and their disagreement was just another example of how Violet could only rely on herself.

It was Violet's line again.

'*Round about the cauldron go,*

In the poisoned entrails throw.'

The poetry rolled off her tongue and a hint of her technique returned. The words resonated and hummed inside her rib cage and her nerves dissolved.

'*Double double toil and trouble,*' the three said in unison.

Despite these famous words, deep down Violet felt hollow. These weren't her words. Lady Macbeth was scratching under her skin, desperate to get out.

Violet swallowed hard and smacked her lips to moisten her gluey mouth. Lila picked up the next line then Lionel entered the scene.

In a flash, it was Violet's line again but her memory was blank. The others waited in tense silence. Her stupid brain was letting her down. She'd spent all night learning these lines. She knew every word. Her script lay at her feet on the carpet but she refused to pick it up. Violet's cheeks burned red as Holly mouthed the next word at her.

'Speak,' Violet stuttered.

What was wrong with her? She found her lines again but stumbled and mispronounced sweaten. After another scraping gulp, she repeated the word hoarsely and continued on to the next line.

Her skin was hot and a hammer thumped behind her eyes. She had to concentrate. Every moment was critical, every word crucial. There was so much to focus on: her breathing, the words, the poetry, her marks. They all whirled around and contorted inside her. There were too many things to think about, too much to go wrong.

Violet left her body and floated up to the ceiling. She listened to her own trembling voice as if she was another cast member watching from the back of the room and she was disgusted.

Focus, idiot.

She yearned for the West End or Broadway but she couldn't get through a bit part in a suburban high school play at the arse end of nowhere. Who did she think she was? Did she really think she was so special?

Her voice was so nasal and her tempo stilted. She was flapping her arms and mumbling like a Grade Seven in their first play. Ravenswood was right. Look at her bad teeth, her fat thighs. How could she ever be a leading lady? Ha. Alan Wolf would never even notice her.

Violet's hands were shaking, and for the first time ever she was grateful for the lines she shared with Holly and Lila, glad to be hidden amongst the others, and relieved to reach her final line.

'Our duties did his welcome pay.'

The witches exited the scene and Macbeth took up the story. Violet scuttled off stage and slumped back down in her chair in the front row, her head bowed.

She shook her head and laced her fingers through her hair, keeping her eyes on the carpet. Her breathing was ragged in her throat. She was better than this. It was all their fault. All of them. She swivelled in her seat and scrutinised all the others, taking note of each and every face.

But every eye was focused on the blonde imposter, Angelika.

Violet gritted her teeth. They would not drag her down. They would not get to her. She was better than all of them. Hard work would win the day as her mother always said. Violet was not afraid of work. She was not afraid of anything—except a life of mediocrity.

Her perception narrowed as she looked down at the floor, until there was blackness all around her like a tunnel. All her confusion melted away and everything was in sharp focus. She was Lady Macbeth. The limelight was hers. She heard her standing ovation and the adulation raining down on her like a sun-shower.

This is how it is meant to be.

Violet tightened her fists as her power returned, crackling through her body once more.

She knew exactly what she had to do.

THE DARK HAND

I have shown you glimpses, given you a taste.

Are you hungry?

I have been waiting for you. Patiently.

The Bard knew exactly what he was doing.

It is not only poetry you hear, the ancient call to me is wrapped up in his words.

He followed my instructions perfectly.

It was part of our deal.

His offering for his eternal fame.

I always keep my bargains. Let his story be a promise to you.

I always keep my bargains.

His name will be known for the rest of time, due to me and our agreement.

I didn't let him down and I'll never let you down.

I keep my promises, unlike them.

So little one, what does your deepest heart desire?

I can help.

I can make it happen.

You know I can.

CHAPTER 7

HOLLY

HOLLY HEARD THE FUMBLE IN VIOLET'S VOICE FROM HER FIRST breath. She winced as she watched her friend fray at the seams. Violet stood in a muddle, her insomniac eyes glazed and faraway, her cheeks as red as a post box. Holly even had to prompt her line and she didn't bite her head off. Violet was spiralling downwards fast.

When their long scene was over, Violet slumped into a chair and stared down at her feet. A heavy lump lay in Holly's stomach. In one way, Violet was right. She didn't understand her. She'd never felt such an overwhelming desire for anything. Not like this. Not like her.

'That wasn't too bad?' Holly said with a forced grin, as Lionel and Kon, the tall but acne-cheeked Year 9 boy, ended their scene and Angelika stepped up.

'It was shit. I was shit.' Violet shook her head and rubbed the toe of her boot on the carpet. Holly reached out for Violet's shoulder but pulled away before she touched her red and blue flannelette shirt. They'd never been the touchy-feely types and now was not the time to start.

'It's all their fault,' she muttered.

'Who?' Holly blinked.

Violet glanced up. This time her face was different, her grimace was gone. She gleamed with an unnatural light. The hairs on the back of Holly's neck bristled and she didn't know why.

'I have to stop them. I can't let them ruin everything like this. I must stop them.' Violet slammed her fist against her leg. 'I will stop them.' She burst out laughing and Holly's chest tightened. Violet turned to her with an accusing finger. 'Don't get in my way.'

Holly stood open-mouthed, unsure what to say next.

'*Murder!*' called Angelika from the front of the room.

Holly gasped, her breath jamming in her chest.

'And scene. Well done, everyone. Let's have a quick break,' Ravenswood said. 'But don't leave the room. Violet, can I see you for a moment?'

'It's starting.' Violet smirked as she stood up and strolled over to him.

Holly let out her breath. Ravenswood must have heard what she said. Finally, someone would stop Violet.

Jacinta flopped into the chair next to her, her spiral notebook under her arm. 'Got a Dispirin?'

'You too?' Holly asked

Jacinta nodded and rubbed her forehead. Her graceful fingers were scabbed across the knuckles.

Holly frowned. 'What—'

'Netball last night,' Jacinta gave a half-hearted chuckle and hid her hands away. 'The goal defence from St. Mary's was a right bitch.'

Holly laughed awkwardly but only half-listened as Jacinta jabbered on about the after-party on Friday at Kon's.

Something told Holly to keep an eye on Jacinta.

VIOLET

'Angelika, can you come over here too, please?'

Angelika glided over and Violet suppressed a growl.

Ravenswood took his glasses off his nose with a sigh. 'We have a situation…'

Violet's stomach flipped, but she kept her face like a mask.

'It appears Rowan has left the play.'

Violet bit down on her smile.

Angelika blinked. 'What happened?'

'She's not here as you can see.'

'Maybe she's sick?' Angelika shrugged.

'I called her house and no one answered.' Ravenswood shook his head. 'I left a message. But she spoke to me yesterday. She was having doubts about the whole production. I told her to sleep on it. I guess she decided not to come back. It would have been nice if she'd let me know.'

Angelika chewed a fingernail.

'I realise unexpected things happen in life but I don't have time for unreliable people.' Ravenswood flicked his hand. 'Now, this leaves me with a vacancy for an understudy.'

Violet's eyes shone. She tilted her head back.

'Violet. I know you know all of Lady Macbeth's lines. And you've proven yourself in other productions. Would you like to be Angelika's understudy?'

Angelika's neutral face slipped for a millisecond, revealing a flash of contempt. Violet smiled slyly.

'Of course,' she replied, her voice calm and controlled. It was not the apology she'd dreamed of, but it was acceptable and the outcome was the same.

'Good. Thank you for stepping in. I appreciate it.'

'With any luck I won't need to take over,' Violet said with a raised eyebrow. 'But I'm happy to help out.'

'Excellent. Pay close attention during the blocking. I need you to shadow her.'

Violet nodded.

The drama room suddenly seemed brighter, as if someone had turned up the dimmer switch. The first sunlight in days peeked between the trees and in through the windows, and cast golden beams across the scratchy blue carpet tiles.

Angelika smiled falsely, and Violet noticed her wringing hands.

One step closer.

It was all coming together.

TOBY

The empty theatrette sat in the windowless core of the school building but in the lighting box up high, Toby felt a little bit better. The dark never usually worried him, not like his silly little sister. Even now in Grade Six, Tamara freaked out if the hallway light went off during the night. He didn't mind the dark. Night-time was nice in Beacon Hill, he liked cruising around the quiet streets by himself with no one bothering him, tunes in his ears.

Toby adjusted the risers and intensified the light on the small stage below, but the colour wasn't quite right. It was too stark. He rubbed his chin and checked Mr Ravenswood's instructions again, his list was a scribbled handwritten page covered in crossed out lines and corrections. Toby scratched his head and squinted. He flicked through the remaining lighting gels in the box but there were only a handful of the thin tinted plastic squares left, the others were cracked or faded. Mr Ravenswood had a grand vision of what he wanted but he was a bit overly optimistic about the possibilities of lighting. And Toby wasn't a miracle worker.

He looked down through the wide viewing window over the tiered rows of seating. There was always something weird about an empty theatre. Usually he liked being alone but all day long his skin had prickled as if someone was watching him. But the others were all across the corridor rehearsing in the drama room. Toby had tried to convince himself the strange feeling made sense, that theatres were built specifically for being watched. But what had that skinny girl said about curses?

Toby shivered and pulled his hood over his head. Having lost his black fingerless gloves somewhere out there in the dark, he blew on his fingers. He pushed the riser to full wattage. A crack projected across the stage floor. His shoulders slumped as he sucked on his teeth. Another lighting gel torn.

Toby riffled through the last few gels in the box. This one might be too sunny for Ravenswood's grim Macbeth but beggars can't be choosers, unless Ravenswood was willing to dip into his own pocket.

He turned up the house lights. In an instant, all the shadows disappeared and with them, the magic of the theatre. The bright house lights exposed the badly painted scenic backdrop, the patched stage floor, the crosses of gaffer tape and scuff marks.

Gel in hand, Toby climbed out of the box and into the theatre. He hummed to himself to fill the silence as he dragged out the tall ladder and climbed three metres up off the ground. He slipped out the torn gel and inserted the new square of orange cellophane. Heat radiated from the still warm unlit bulb.

As he took a step back down, the light switched on full bore and blinded him with intense orange light. Toby whipped up his hand to cover his eyes but stumbled backwards. He scrambled in mid-air for the metal rung. The tips of his fingers grazed the ladder and he lunged forward and grabbed hold tight. The ladder shook on its four spindly legs.

'What the hell?' he panted and pressed his body flat against the ladder, his heart thumping like a techno bassline.

Above him, the light faded away again to nothing.

'Who's there?' he yelled, shielding his eyes against the harsh house lights. He scoured the rows of empty seats and squinted at the lighting box up the back but the headrests of two empty chairs were clearly visible through the window.

'It's not funny,' he said as he climbed down, knees and hands trembling.

The sound of giggling trickled down from the back of the theatre. He stopped as he reached the stage floor and looked around again. Girls.

'You could have killed me,' he said, his tone deadly serious. 'Come out. This isn't funny.'

The giggling came from behind him now.

Toby spun around. No one could move that quickly. With only a few feet of bare stage between him and the scenic drop, he should have heard footsteps. The hairs on his neck snapped up to attention.

'Enough,' he shouted.

A naughty laugh drifted across the theatrette, coming from the left. Toby was quicker this time and caught a glimpse of something black. It slid along the sides of the theatre and skirted around the blurry edges of the light.

Toby gulped.

The inky shape was too slick. People didn't move like that.

He blinked his eyes in double time and sucked in a slow breath. 'Hello?' He inched across the stage and peered into the dark.

But there was only carpet, steps and a wall.

'You, idiot. See. It's nothing,' he muttered. But his stomach kept churning. 'Right. That's it. I'm off the bongs from now on.'

Toby jumped off the stage into the aisle and headed back towards the lighting box, shaking his head. He'd been all alone in the dark for too long. Whatever it was, it was gone now.

As he walked up the centre aisle, the tip-up seats on either side of him began to flap.

Up and down.

Clang. Clang.

'What the…?' His breath snagged in his throat.

Up and down.

Clang. Clang.

'Who's there?!' he yelled.

The chair seats banged and waved at him in rows, as he hurried towards the back of the theatre and the safety of the lighting box. He twisted his head from side to side as he went, looking for who was responsible but there was no one there.

The seats rippled like waves and clanged like deafening applause.

Then something smacked Toby in the head. Hard. He stumbled and skidded on his hands, clunking his head against the metal beam securing the seats to the floor.

Toby rubbed his scalp and turned, dizzy and disorientated, to see the culprit. A theatre seat, torn from a row, sitting sat all alone in the middle of the aisle. Toby gaped.

The girlish giggle drifted up the empty theatrette like a gas leak.

'Who are you?' he whispered.

'Toby,' the voice replied, breathy and taunting.

He flinched.

There was no one there.

He hauled himself back up to his feet, his head throbbing, his stomach quivering.

A second seat flew up the aisle like a frisbee thrown by invisible hands.

Toby ducked and the plastic seat whizzed over his head and clattered to the ground.

'Ha! Missed!'

He sprinted up the aisle towards the far back row as a third seat whistled through the air. The solid plastic frame bashed against his head and

Toby cried out. He tumbled into the back row of seats as everything went to black.

Seconds later, Toby woke up to pain. He opened his eyes to see chairs flapping all around him. The chairs thwacked at his head and grabbed at his fingers and his clothes. He rolled onto the carpet on his hands and knees and scurried towards the lighting box. He reached up for the door handle as another chair missile crashed into his knuckles.

He clutched his battered hand against his chest. He recognised the white-hot pain from the time he misjudged a turn on Beacon Hill Road and totalled his new ten speed.

With his heartbeat pounding against his skull, he wrenched the door open and scuttled inside. Another seat smashed against the door as he frantically closed it.

Toby hurried under the lighting desk. He covered his eyes and ignored the dribble of warm blood slowly trickling inside his ear. He didn't want to know. He didn't care. He just wanted it to go away.

Toby waited in his hiding place until the theatrette was quiet again. It felt like an eternity as he cowered in the dark.

VIOLET

Violet's victory didn't last long. She rolled her eyes and pressed her lips shut as she sat in the back row. She knew the lines from the most famous scene inside out. The words tingled on her own lips, burning to be said.

'Out, damned spot! Out, I say! --One: two: why,
then, 'tis time to do't.'

Angelika stood with her arms outstretched. She looked like a stick insect in black tights, her voice low but weak, her diction as clumsy as her gestures. But despite it all, Violet's ribcage squeezed as she watched the imposter butcher her lines, snatch her part, steal her stage. Violet's only comfort was imagining the contrast when she finally took her rightful place.

She'd shine like a star.

Like the bus driver said.

'Here's the smell of the blood still: all the
perfumes of Arabia will not sweeten this little
hand. Oh, oh, oh!'

The room was dead quiet. No one fidgeted or passed notes or even chewed their nails. They didn't like her performance, did they? They couldn't possibly.

'What's done cannot be undone.
--To bed, to bed, to bed!'

When her speech was over, Angelika froze in position, staring up at the ceiling tiles, and the room burst into applause.

'Well done.' Ravenswood rose to his feet. Angelika averted her eyes and blushed as the others clapped and whooped.

Violet gritted her teeth. They were all too stupid to recognise real talent. She rubbed her left eye socket with the heel of her palm. Even with this headache and its constant dull thump, she was the only one in the room who could see clearly. But she had to ignore the pain. She couldn't be distracted. It was Wednesday already, it was time to clear the path. She was so close.

'Excellent work, Angelika.' Ravenswood continued clapping from the front of the room and Violet cursed the back of Angelika's head as she sat down in the front row of chairs.

'Watch and learn, players. Lionel and Angelika are setting the benchmark. This is the level of performance I expect from every one of you.'

Holly and Jacinta averted their eyes and the boys shuffled in their seats, groaning quietly.

'I gave Angelika a little tip last night after rehearsal. And as you can see my advice has obviously helped her.' Ravenswood smiled. 'Now I will share it with you all.'

Violet sneered. Ravenswood, a first-year teacher, thought he could teach her something? Her bookshelves were filled with dog-eared copies of Meisner and Stanislavski. She could run this holiday program better.

'I want you to think about your character. Understand who they are. Not just the words—'

'That's easy. I don't understand the words anyway,' Jason said.

Violet shook her head as the others guffawed. *Philistines.*

'Angelika, what's different about your Lady Macbeth now?'

Angelika turned in her seat to face the rest of the cast. 'At first, I thought she was just sad, acting weird because she was grieving. Then I realised she was ambitious. In those days, women had to be manipulative to get their way. But then I went even deeper. She was a fighter, she was willing to pick up the knife herself before Macbeth agreed. Maybe even a touch of Hannibal Lecter in her. Then God or whoever, punished her by driving her mad.'

Violet snorted. What a ridiculous interpretation.

'Good. Now, players. Think about your character. It doesn't matter how small the part or how many lines you have. Who are they? What is their history? What is their favourite food? Jez?'

'Pizza. Everyone likes pizza.' Jez shrugged.

This time even Ravenswood laughed.

'Bread and cheese was perhaps more appropriate for the times. But you're on the right track. Think in terms of your character. What if they didn't like bread and cheese? Why would that be? What did they love? What did they hate? What was their innermost desire? Build up a real living breathing person and bring them onto the stage. Lila, why is your character a witch?'

Lila flinched. Violet could feel her skinny body trembling beside her.

'I dunno,' she stammered, her pale cheeks flushing hot pink.

'Is there a reason why she turned to black magic?' Ravenswood leaned forward. 'An event, perhaps?'

Lila chewed her lip. 'Something bad happened in her past.... her childhood. It made her angry. She wanted to take revenge on everyone. Like that movie with the prom and the blood.'

'Good. Wayne—what about McDuff? How does he feel about Macbeth?'

'He'd think Macbeth was a bit of a wanker. Two-faced. He can't trust Macbeth. And his wife's a real bitch. But hot.'

Jason slapped Wayne on the shoulder with a cackle.

'What? It's true,' Wayne frowned.

'Good work, players,' Ravenswood said. 'Take a short break, stretch your legs and have a think about your character. Come back in ten minutes and we'll push through the last scenes.'

The room was loud with chatter as half the cast streamed towards the door.

'That was awful. I hate being put on the spot like that,' Lila said, her cheeks still blazing. 'I wish he'd given me some warning.'

'It was a bit obvious wasn't it?' Violet tossed her head. 'It's basic stuff, creating a character.'

Lila muttered something in reply but Violet was distracted. She narrowed her eyes as Ravenswood and Angelika shared a private word at the front of the room.

'She was terrible, wasn't she?' Violet jerked her head their way. 'But I'm not worried. It's practically my role now.'

'Only if she leaves,' Lila said. 'Or gets sick or something.'

'Accidents happen.'

Lila jumped up with a strained smile and grabbed her bag. 'You want a drink from the machine?'

'If you come with me for a smoke in the Quad after? I've got such a bastard headache.'

'Me too. Ever since yesterday,' Lila said.

'I wonder if it's that new paint. Those tight arses, it's probably toxic. Maybe that's what caused your nosebleed.'

Lila led the way out of the room, weaving through the chairs and cast members.

Holly sat cross-legged in the corner with Jacinta and Jez, twirling her hair around her finger. She averted her eyes as Violet walked past.

'Some friend,' Violet mumbled. 'You saw her plotting with Angelika on the bus.'

'She is being a bit strange,' Lila said as she gave Holly a finger wave. Holly waved back hesitantly before looking away.

'Traitor.'

Violet and Lila pushed through the double doors into the cold corridor. They both shivered.

'I wish they'd turn the heating on. Cheap bastards.'

'And the lights,' said Lila.

Both girls jumped and stopped dead still. Three sharp bangs crashed above their heads.

'What was that?' Lila stammered, clutching at her throat.

Violet glanced up but there were only stained ceiling tiles above their heads. The thump turned into a long asthmatic hiss, like a death rattle. It made no sense, but somehow the noise felt dark and cold. It seeped right in her bones. 'Pipes?' she said. Her eyebrows raised. She didn't quite believe her own words but she wanted to snuff out Lila's heebie-jeebies.

'It sounds like an old man moaning. I hate this place. Come on.' Lila sped off down the corridor, her head ducked.

Violet hurried after her. The two passed the entry to the theatrette.

'But I do like the costumes,' Lila said with a strained cheerfulness. 'The pointy hats are fun.'

Violet groaned. 'Really? Halloween dress-ups? So boring and obvious, so suburban.'

'Maybe you can suggest something else? He might listen to you.'

'There's no point. I'm not going to be a Witch much longer.'

They climbed the stairs, past the girls' toilets and around the corner to the vending machine.

Violet tapped her foot and Lila chewed her lip as she ran a finger along the glass front of the vending machine.

'Hurry up and choose.' Violet rolled her eyes. 'I'm gasping for a ciggie.'

'They're not good for you,' Lila said as she shoved a handful of coins into the slot.

'Yes, Mum,' Violet replied.

Lila popped the ring on her can, took a slurp and offered it to Violet.

'Lemonade is for kids.' Violet snorted. 'Come on.'

Heading back down the stairs, they almost collided with Angelika leaving the girls' toilets, Jacinta and Holly close behind her.

'Hey,' Angelika said with a toss of her hair.

'Hey Angelika,' Lila gushed. 'You were so good in the last bit.'

Violet clenched her jaw

'Totally,' said Jacinta, but then she screwed up her face. 'Can you smell something?'

Holly loitered behind them, saying nothing.

'You're going to wow everyone on Friday.' Lila nodded. 'Especially that theatre guy. Wolfgang or whatever.'

Violet clutched at her temple, trying to hold back the hammering inside her head. Even Lila was turning on her. She needed some fresh air, and a smoke.

'Thanks. You're all so kind,' Angelika replied, but her voice sounded distorted and faraway like she was talking down a long tube. 'I just hope I don't let you all down.'

Violet's heartbeat pounded in her ears, each thump like a punch to the head. The walls swayed. Sweat beaded under her hairline and a drip rolled down her neck. The corridor lights burned her eyes. Violet gasped for air, as something clamped around her chest. Shadowy hands gripped her neck, the fingers tightened. Thumbs crushed her larynx. Her cries for help clogged in her throat.

The last thing Violet was sure of was that she was standing at the top of the stairs.

Then there was a scream.

Violet had no idea how Angelika ended up at the bottom of the stairs.

It wasn't her.

Was it?

CHAPTER 8

JEZ
Last Night

J EZ SUCKED HARD ON THE JOINT AND THE LAST BUD CRACKLED between his fingers. Aggressive guitar licks pumped from the speakers in the corner and all the hard edges softened as he exhaled and eased back into his pillows.

He smiled. Angelika was nice. Obviously she was a babe, but there was something else about her, something mysterious. She had more going on below the surface. It was a shame she didn't seem to give a stuff about him. She just needed to get to know him a bit better. He wasn't like those other meatheads. Maybe he'd show her some of his lyrics. Girls liked poetry, didn't they? She didn't need to know the words were lyrics for his metal band.

His hand grazed over the fly, he unzipped his jeans and then Banquo floated into his head. '*Or have we eaten on the insane root?*' Jez chuckled to himself. 'Hell, yeah.'

His dreams of Angelika were interrupted as Violet popped into his head. He dodged a bullet there. She'd seemed nice enough at the closing night party but then again Deano's rocket fuel had been damned strong. They talked, had a pash, and that was it. It had been only the one night but she'd been ringing ever since. His mum was sick of it and his brothers gave him grief every night at the dinner table.

It was months ago but all week, she'd been staring at him with those big sooky eyes. Why were girls such hard work? He pulled his hand away. Violet ruined the moment. Again.

He must have dozed off.

Then something slid, smooth and cool against his skin. His

110

bedroom was in a cloud of fog. He grinned. It was another one of *those* dreams.

He felt something writhe against his body. He hoped she was hot, or maybe even better, two or three horny babes. Whoever it was, they had supple knowing fingers. They stroked his back, his thighs, his stomach. He moaned. He lolled his head back and lapped up the attention.

Until he heard the hiss.

He tore his eyes open, and a snake stared straight back at him. It lay across his chest, its mouth wide, its fangs dripping with venom, its neck swaying.

Jez looked down to see his whole body was covered with writhing, intertwining snakes: pencil-thin green tree snakes, copper heads, rippled tiger snakes and a boa constrictor as thick as a tree trunk. Thousands of different cold scales slithered over his body. Jez tried to move his arms but the snakes pinned him down, wrapping him like a mummy in a sarcophagus. The hissing intensified, reverberated through their bodies into his and sank deep into his bones.

Two fangs pierced his skin. The first strike. The others sensed the puncture and turned their heads. Jez thrashed but his limbs were bound tightly by the squirming bodies. His heart raced. Muffled screams lodged raw in his throat. Sharp jabs perforated his skin, his hands, his bare feet. Venom rushed through his veins, first scorchingly hot then numbingly cold. Death traversed his body. It started at his chest then crept down his arms and into his hands. His extremities as solid as wood.

Jez tried to cry but his tongue was solidifying and fat inside his mouth. The cold freeze of death raced up his legs, his torso, his face.

His eyes were the only body part he could still move. He glanced frantically left and right. At his feet, the boa constrictor unhinged its jaw and started at his toes. His feet. His ankles. The muscular body rippled as it gulped but Jez felt nothing. He howled, but only inside his head. The enormous mouth was around his knees. His thighs. The room darkened, Jez's eyesight dimmed. The icy cold closed his eyes for the last time as the boa engulfed him.

~⚬~

VIOLET

Angelika lay face down at the bottom of the stairs, her blonde hair fanned out over the linoleum. Ravenswood ran up with Wayne close behind. 'Angelika, are you alright?'

'What have you done?' someone yelled. It could have been Holly but there was too much shouting to be certain.

At the top of the stairs, the air was heavy and hot. The fluorescent light stabbed at Violet's eyes and she rested her head against the cool wall, hands over her ears to muffle the voices.

'What have you done?' Holly wrenched Violet away from her safe place at the wall, her face pained and pale.

'You pushed her.' Jacinta stood with hands on hips.

'I...' Violet's tongue was fat and useless.

Down below, Angelika pushed herself upright onto her elbows and stretched out her legs. She whimpered and collapsed as she placed her weight on her left ankle. Violet closed her eyes again as Jez rushed over and took hold of Angelika's arm.

'Lila? You saw it all.' Jacinta said. Then she turned and poked her finger into Violet's face. 'She did it, didn't she?'

'I don't know,' Lila stammered.

'Why are you defending her?' Holly said. 'You know exactly what she's been thinking.'

'I'm not sure,' Lila whined, clutching at her head. 'It was all too quick.'

'I don't know what happened,' Violet murmured as she shielded her eyes, wishing it all away. But the girls' voices grew louder, everyone was saying her name.

'Someone oughta push *you* down the stairs,' Jacinta said. She grabbed Violet's arm and tugged her halfway down the steps.

'Hang on, Jacinta,' Ravenswood said, his hands in the air and Violet wrenched her arm out of Jacinta's grasp.

'Mr Ravenswood. Call the police. She pushed Angelika,' Jacinta snapped.

'She's been saying all kinds of strange—' Holly started.

'She didn't,' said Lila.

Violet's head was foggy and thick. She grabbed the handrail and blinked to clear her eyes.

'Calm down, everyone,' Ravenswood said. 'Who saw what happened?

'

'Everyone saw her tantrum yesterday,' Jacinta said. 'She's mental. Tell him what she's been saying, Holly. Go on.'

'She said she wanted Angelika to have an accident,' Holly said, chewing on her lip.

'I-I-I.' Violet tried to protest but everyone was staring at her. The black look on Jez's face punched a hole in her chest. 'I feel sick.'

'You need help,' said Holly, pity rather than anger in her voice.

'There's no need to be so melodramatic, girls. Did anyone actually see it?' Ravenswood frowned.

'Not exactly,' Holly shrugged. 'I was checking my watch.'

'I saw movement, but I was thinking about something else,' Jacinta said. 'But it has to be her.'

'It wasn't me,' Violet said, weakly.

'Who was it then? Lila?' Jacinta snorted.

Lila's face was grey and her bottom lip trembled.

'Maybe it was your curse, Lila?' sniggered Wayne. 'Come to life.'

Lila nodded feverishly, her eyes wide. 'We need to cleanse the theatre.'

'Cleanse it by getting rid of her.' Jacinta pointed to Violet.

'That's enough. You can't go around accusing people without proof.'

'But Mr Ravenswood—' Holly said

'Enough. Accidents happen.'

Angelika pulled herself to her feet and rested her weight on Jez's shoulder. Ravenswood inspected her up and down. 'Do you need a doctor?'

'I just rolled my ankle. A little bruised but I'll be fine.' Angelika smoothed her hair back into place. 'I'm sure I can walk it off.'

'Please be more careful next time, Angelika,' Ravenswood said. 'We can't lose a leading lady.'

'You can't let her back in,' Jacinta said. 'She's a danger to us all.'

Holly opened her mouth but said nothing.

Violet wished the wall would swallow her up.

'Jacinta, I said enough. Angelika is fine. It's time to go back inside the drama room, I need everyone to focus.'

Angelika hobbled towards the drama room with Jez at her side. Holly and Jacinta stomped down the last few steps, murmuring to each other. Lila followed but she didn't even glance in Violet's direction.

Violet waited until the corridor was empty.

Toby appeared at the dark theatrette doorway. 'Are you okay? What happened?'

'Leave me alone,' Violet growled and trudged towards the drama room.

Word spread fast. The rest of the cast whispered behind their hands as she tried to slink into the back row of the drama room. Everyone looked at her as if she was a smear of dog turd on their shoes. Even Lila.

But Ravenswood, of all people, had come to her defence. It must be finally dawning on him how valuable she was.

Her forehead was steaming hot. She turned in her seat and looked out the window as the sun dipped behind the mountain and the swaying eucalypts turned ghostly. Were the headaches, the memory gaps, the black things shifting about in the corner of her eyes, signs that Holly was right?

She bent over and gripped clumps of her hair. If she'd decided to push Angelika down the stairs, she'd remember. Wouldn't she?

From the front row, Angelika turned to face Violet. There was a slight smile on Angelika's lips but the smirk was as hard as glass.

Violet gulped and icy fingers ran up her spine. Throwing herself down the stairs and turning everyone against her was all part of the conspiracy. She was a better actor than Violet thought.

Angelika turned back and Violet's headache thundered on. She rubbed her eyes, not caring about smudged mascara.

Lionel's words sang over Violet's skin:

'I'll fight till from my bones my flesh be hack'd.
Give me my armour.'

Violet tightened her fists. She squeezed her eyes shut and inhaled deeply through her nose. She wasn't the crazy one.

A screwed-up piece of paper hit the chair next to her. Violet looked up with a scowl, but saw Lila gently nodding at her from the row in front. Violet unwrapped the note.

'*I know it wasn't you. Lx.*'

Violet smiled. Good old Lila. She could always rely on her. But the hours until opening night were slipping away. How could she unmask Angelika? Violet sucked a long breath in through her teeth.

And who would believe her?

ANGELIKA

The smile still lingered on Angelika's lips as she savoured the fear in Violet's eyes. Shakespeare's words were almost as good as Sun Tzu's. And just as relevant.

'*The mind I sway by and the heart I bear*
Shall never sag with doubt nor shake with fear.'

Violet had just been a nuisance until she'd stepped into Rowan's empty shoes but now she was too close for comfort.

Angelika reached down and rubbed her ankle, milking her injury for a few moments longer. She could still feel the warmth of Violet's hands on her back but Angelika chose to bite her tongue when Ravenswood asked. Instead, she recalled Sun Tzu's wisdom.

She will win who knows when to fight and when not to fight. She will win who knows how to handle both superior and inferior forces.

Angelika didn't have to lift a finger. Violet was doing all the work herself with her little tantrums, sabotaging and distancing herself from the rest of the group. Even her few friends were turning against her.

All except Ravenswood. His response had been surprisingly lenient and not at all what she expected. She pressed her lips together hard. He needed to be her champion and hers alone.

She will win who, prepared herself, waits to take the enemy unprepared.

Angelika opened her notebook, and as she clamped her teeth around her pen lid, a shot of pain ran along her jaw and jabbed behind her right eye. She didn't remember hitting her head. Perhaps it was dehydration. It had better not be a cold.

With a sip of water, she returned to her notes. She had to be ready to strike any moment. If everything went to plan, there'd be a million more Violets on the road ahead.

⁓ ⁓

RAVENSWOOD

Ravenswood tried not flinch each time Kon mangled another of the Bard's lines. But the kerfuffle with the girls on the stairs kept gatecrashing his mind. Angelika seemed fine but the backlash against Violet had been quite vicious. He'd never understand teenage girls, with their hot and cold alliances and petty feuds. He sighed and hoped they'd be best buddies again by Friday. He couldn't lose anyone else. He couldn't let his actors abandon him.

Not again.

A sharp knock sounded and two uniformed police officers filled the classroom doorway. The pimple-faced Kon stopped mid-word and the rest of the room buzzed with whispers.

'Mr Ravenswood? Sorry to interrupt,' said the one with the flattop haircut and the thick neck. 'Can we speak with you for a moment?'

'Of course.' Ravenswood scrambled to his feet. His heart beat furiously. Please don't let it be Fiona. 'Kon. Keep going. I'll only be a few moments.'

Ravenswood didn't know why but he grabbed his clipboard and pen. It just seemed the right thing to do.

'How can I help you?' he said, extending a slightly shaking hand. The two officers stepped away from the door into the dim corridor. Ravenswood followed but left the classroom door open, and a bunch of curious faces craned their necks to watch.

'I can't hear rehearsing,' Ravenswood shouted and the nosy parkers ducked their heads back inside.

The flattop spoke. 'I'm Sergeant O'Hare and this is Constable Morrison.' Morrison was slim and around Ravenswood's age.

The name and the officer's sticky-out ears rang a bell. 'Morrison? Were you at...'

'Newtown High,' Morrison replied.

Ravenswood produced a twisted smile. It was funny how life turned out. From what he remembered, Boof Morrison had been destined for a career on the opposite side of the prison bars.

O'Hare continued. 'We're here about Rowan Howie. I believe she is part of your play?'

Ravenswood frowned. 'She's not here today. She's sick.'

'Her mother reported her missing this afternoon.'

'Missing?' Ravenswood gasped and clutched at his throat. He winced as he accidentally knocked the scab from yesterday's brush with the filing cabinet. 'How awful.'

'We don't suspect any foul play. Yet. Girls of Rowan's age run off every now and then, after a fight with their parents. They usually turn up after a few days. But we have to look at all possibilities.'

Ravenswood nodded but his mind scattered into multiple dark places.

'And this is the place she was last seen.'

'Right. She was here all day yesterday. She left with everyone else. But I don't specifically remember seeing her leave. I was the last person left in the building...I think.'

Ravenswood shivered and his eyes widened. What if Rowan had been in the car park? Before him? He cleared his throat and straightened his posture. How could he tell the police about the thumping on the roof? What would they think? If they didn't laugh in his face and take him straight to the funny farm at New Norfolk.

He continued. 'You might want to talk to Miss Quinlin. You'll find her in the science block. And the maintenance men. But they don't speak.'

'There's no sign she went home. What time did you finish up?'

'I dismissed them all around four o'clock. It was already getting dark. It was pitch black by the time I left.'

'And how was she?'

'She was nervous about the play. I'd selected her as understudy to the leading role and she was having second thoughts about the whole thing. I told her to sleep on it. These girls can work themselves up into a lather. Then this morning when she didn't turn up, I called her house and left a message but I assumed she'd decided to quit.' He rubbed his neck. 'I feel terrible now. Should I have called you straight away?'

'You haven't spoken to her mother?'

'I left a message. But didn't she notice Rowan missing before today?'

'Mrs Howie works nights at the hospital. Her son thought Rowan had locked herself in her room. Can we talk to the class?'

'Absolutely. They might know more than I do.'

'Can you point out her close friends?'

He couldn't admit he barely noticed Rowan, not now, not to the police. 'I'm not sure. But we can ask? I'm sure they'll all want to help.'

Ravenswood wrung his hands as he followed the officers back into the classroom, the police trudging in their heavy boots, their belts weighed down with guns and gear.

Kon and Wayne stopped instantly.

'Thanks boys. Everyone sit down,' Ravenswood said. 'We have something serious to discuss.'

One of the girls gasped. Maybe it was Violet but he couldn't be sure.

'The police are here about Rowan. She has gone missing.'

This time, everyone gasped.

'And this was the last place she was seen.'

'Thank you, Mr Ravenswood.' O'Hare stood with his legs spread wide and his hands clasped behind his back. 'We need your help to understand where Rowan might have gone. Any information is helpful, no matter how trivial you might think. Just tell us all you can remember. Let's start with when you saw her last.'

Jacinta raised a hand. 'When we got dismissed, she walked out of the classroom. But she went down the corridor. Towards the payphone.'

'Did anyone see her after that?'

Everyone shook their heads.

'Was she on the bus? Or did someone pick her up in a car?'

The kids glanced at each other and shrugged.

'Any cars hanging around?'

'She could have walked,' Wayne suggested. 'It was pretty foggy though.'

'I walked home,' Angelika said. 'She lives somewhere near me. I didn't see her.'

Violet raised her hand from the back. 'I walked through the bush, too. I didn't see her, either.'

'Did anyone see her last night? At the movies? A party? Did anyone speak to her on the phone?'

The cast looked back, blankly.

'OK. Can you tell us a bit more about her? Did anything happen that might make her runaway? Was she having a hard time? Did she have any enemies?'

'Apart from Violet,' Jacinta scoffed.

O'Hare turned to Ravenswood. 'Violet?' he mouthed with a raised eyebrow.

Ravenswood waved his hand dismissively. 'School girl backstabbing,' he whispered.

O'Hare gave a firm nod and then faced the room again. 'Did she mention any problems with her parents? Drugs?'

Kon raised his hand warily. 'She's got that boyfriend, doesn't she? The one with the hotted-up car.'

'That explains the new rock chick outfits,' Jacinta said.

'I saw them in town once,' Kon said. His voice cracked and he cleared his throat. 'He's older. Eighteen or nineteen.'

'You know his name?' said O'Hare asked as Morrison took notes.

'Nope. Sorry,' Kon said with a grimace. 'I've seen him around, though. He does something with cars.'

O'Hare blinked. 'Thanks. Can we speak to you alone?'

'Sure.' Kon swallowed and his neck flushed red.

'Has anyone else seen or heard anything or anyone suspicious?'

'Only the usual Beacon Hill weird shit,' Wayne joked and the others laughed nervously along with him.

Ravenswood pursed his lips. 'Please, Wayne. Rowan could be in danger.'

Wayne ducked his head and mumbled, 'Sorry.'

'We don't want to scare anyone.' O'Hare glanced around the room one more time. 'We just want to get in contact with Rowan. Bring her home again. I'll leave my card with Mr Ravenswood and if you think of anything else, please contact us. If you do see her, please get her to contact her mum. She's very worried about her.'

With a painful smile, Kon stood up and the two officers led him into the corridor.

Ravenswood hesitated. Should he go with them? They didn't teach him what to do in these situations at teacher's college. Should he go with them? Then he remembered Kon was only a Year 9.

The classroom buzzed.

'Maybe it's the beginning. Like those girls in the 1980s.'

'She's probably up the duff and run off with the boyfriend to Melbourne.'

'Her mum is pretty mean. I'd run away too if I was her.'

Ravenswood clapped his hands.

'Quiet, everyone. This is a serious matter. If you have any *real* information, please talk to the officers outside. Otherwise we are not helping anyone by making up stories. We have a play to put on in two days and our time is running out fast. Now, where were we? Lionel?'

The boys spoke but no matter how hard he tried, Ravenswood's thoughts drifted away. He hoped Kon's story about a boyfriend was true, but the knot in his gut told him otherwise. He couldn't shake the thoughts of the car park. It made sense. This place knew the taste of blood too well.

Ravenswood gulped.

He hoped he was wrong.

HOLLY

As the police left the room Holly tugged on her bottom lip with her fingers. Rowan did seem a bit strange yesterday, with all her talk about weird smells. Maybe she was sick or off her nut like Jacinta said. Then again Holly had noticed an odd taste in her own mouth, one that even a few Minties didn't shift.

Everyone remembered Rebecca, Danielle and Tracy. Their smiling faces printed on photocopied flyers sticky-taped to every telephone pole and bus shelter, with the word 'missing' in big font underneath.

Was it happening all over again?

No one was ever arrested for their disappearances and their bodies were never found. But the memory of the missing girls was everywhere. This was just another reason why Holly wanted out of this town.

They restarted their rehearsal. The final scenes of the play should have been epic, the build up to the battle for the throne, but people kept missing their cues and stumbling over their words. Everyone spoke as if they were reading the phonebook aloud. Ravenswood was cringing but his eyes seemed distant. Everyone's laughter was shrill and nervous, and even the seamless Lionel was off. It was embarrassing, it was terrible, and the show seemed doomed to failure.

Kon snuck back into the room and Holly glanced across at Violet, sitting in the back row surrounded by empty plastic chairs. She was scowling, her arms folded tight.

Holly's stomach roiled. After the incident with Angelika, Violet was capable of anything. Why didn't Ravenswood alert the police? He didn't even listen when she tried to warn him.

She sighed. Violet often shot her mouth off and Holly hadn't actually witnessed her push Angelika. What kind of friend was she? Surely she should give Violet the benefit of the doubt.

'So, thanks to all at once and to each one,
Whom we invite to see us crown'd at Scone.'

Jason finished the last lines of the play but no one clapped. He skulked back to his seat. The room stayed quiet.

'Right everyone,' Ravenswood said finally. Even his voice was flat. 'It's been a long day and everyone's tired. Go home, get a good night's rest and we'll try again tomorrow.'

Holly grabbed her bag and hurried over to Kon, but there was already a circle surrounding him.

'What did they say?' Wayne asked.

Wayne shot Holly a nasty look as she hovered around the edges to eavesdrop.

Kon shrugged. 'I just told them the same stuff. About the boyfriend. They just kept asking me the same questions over and over. I don't actually know anything more. I only saw them once. But I don't think the cops know anything either.'

Holly chewed her lip and wandered off down the corridor to the payphone where Rowan was last seen. The brick walls were cold and institutional but she always felt a little safer inside. If she stood along-side a grown-up, the teasing would stop.

But now she felt boxed in. The walls were hard and unfriendly, ex-actly like the rest of the world out there.

She turned the corner and saw the gold payphone. Wasn't this a crime scene? Where was the blue and white police tape, the policeman standing guard and the forensics person in their white paper suit? There was only the phone, and the flickering light above and the red exit sign in the distance. As though nothing had happened.

Holly went right up and touched it. She didn't know why she was here or what she expected to find. She needed to help, to know it wasn't Violet. A hard clump formed in her stomach, telling her that something was deeply wrong. But what?

'Isn't it time you went home?' said a voice.

Holly jumped. 'Miss Quinlin!'

'Off in your own little world, dear?' The science teacher appeared in another garish pink cardigan, her arms loaded with ring binders.

Holly nodded. 'This is where Rowan was last seen. Supposedly.'

'A terrible worry for her mother,' Miss Quinlin tutted. 'But she'll turn up.'

Holly squinted at the teacher. 'Do you know something?'

Miss Quinlin chuckled. 'Oh no, dear. At least one or two kids go missing each year.'

Holly narrowed her eyes. Miss Quinlin's smile couldn't mask the slight tremble on her lips.

'You don't think there's something sinister behind it?'

'Oh no, no, no.' Miss Quinlin chortled but looked away. 'Don't worry yourself. The professionals are looking into it. Now, get along home before it starts raining again.'

Holly did as she was told but she didn't believe a word Miss Quinlin had said. No one seemed to be taking Rowan's disappearance seriously. She went out into the cold with a need for more informa-tion gnawing in her belly. She needed to understand what she was up against.

THE DARK HAND

You are not the first person who needed my help.

Many have taken up my offer.

Some names you may know. Famous names. Infamous names.

Thousands of names you will not know.

But they were all like you. Disrespected. Misunderstood. Rejected. People who needed a friend. Someone they could trust.

You are smarter than the rest of them. You can see the possibilities and the truth.

Don't deny yourself this chance to make everything right.

You know you deserve to get what you want.

But I cannot act alone. I am only a conduit...

All I do is help bring out the power you had within you all along.

You are bigger, greater, wiser, stronger than you know.

You can show them all.

With my help.

Imagine your life if you let me help you.

Nothing would stand in your way.

Everything your heart desired would be yours.

Ready for the taking.

I am here.

By your side. In the corner. In the shadows.

Waiting.

All you need to do is welcome me fully, and we can show them all.

Together.

Just say the words.

CHAPTER 9

VIOLET

WITH THE REHEARSALS OVER FOR THE DAY, VIOLET AND LILA followed the boys out of the school building and into the cold. 'Idiots.' Violet scowled at the back of their heads.

'It's not true, is it?' Lila whispered, her eyes wild.

'Don't listen to them,' Violet said, but it was hard not to.

Jason shook his head and continued. 'Nah, man. Peter the Butcher only goes for couples getting it on in cars. So, you're safe,' he said, pointing at Wayne. 'No girl is going anywhere near you.'

'You're the one who's been watching too many videos, mate.' Wayne grabbed at Jason's finger. 'He goes for anyone. Especially on the full moon. My brother's mate's cousin escaped from Peter the Butcher. The man himself. Peter left him with this scar right across his head and the hair won't grow back. The cops spent days scouring the whole hill, but they found no sign of Peter. I heard he escaped from those religious freaks who lived here before they built the school. The Nathans or whatever they were called.'

'The Nathair.'

'That's them. They messed him right up with their Jeffrey Dahmer *Silence of the Lambs* shit. Now he's sitting in the bush. Watching and waiting for his next victim.'

'The Nathair was like a hundred years ago, you fool.' Jason rolled his eyes. 'Peter's some butcher's apprentice who went mental after his girlfriend cheated on him. One of my dad's mates from the footy club went to school with him. He went bush but he's still got his knives. If you listen on a still night, you can hear him sharpening his blades on the boulders at the top of Beacon Hill. S-s-hing.'

Lila shuddered and whispered to Violet. 'Do you know if it's a full moon?'

'Ignore them. Although…' Violet chewed on her lip. 'Have you seen the hooded man with the dog?'

'No,' Lila said, fingers in her mouth. 'Did something happen to you?'

'I've seen him loitering around. Probably some perve.'

'You should tell the police. Maybe Rowan didn't run off with her boyfriend? Promise me you won't walk alone in the bush.'

Violet lifted her chin. 'I'll do what I like. Some perve is not going to stop me.'

'You've always been braver than me,' Lila said, stripping a hangnail off with her teeth. Violet flinched at the sight of Lila's bloody finger.

Lila hid her hands behind her back and changed the subject. 'You're in a better mood.'

'Things have become much clearer.'

Lila narrowed her eyes but Violet didn't elaborate. She didn't expect Lila would understand.

'So, practice round at yours?' Lila said, bouncing on the balls of her feet.

'Sorry. I've got stuff to do.' Violet shrugged.

'I don't mind. I'd be really quiet. We could get some hot chips. Or a block of Top Deck?' Lila looked at her with puppy dog eyes. 'You've got all those new lines to learn. I can help—not that you need any help.'

Violet wasn't surprised that Lila was looking for excuses not to go home. If she was Lila, she wouldn't want to go home, either.

'Tomorrow?'

Lila pressed her lips together. 'I've got my own stuff to do, anyway.'

'I'll call you later.' Violet waved and turned away and pulled up her hood.

'You're not walking, are you?' Lila asked.

Violet swivelled back with a grin. 'He doesn't scare me.'

'Be careful. Please.'

'Nothing's going to happen to me.' Violet said as she walked backwards. 'Oh, and I forgot to say, thanks for your note.'

Lila smiled. 'I'm always here for you. No matter what.'

Violet left Lila at the bus stop with the boys and headed across the car park. Walking was perfect for thinking and Shakespeare was the ultimate inspiration.

Let us make medicines of our great revenge.

～∽～

BRIDGET

Bridget found the book squeezed in between the hardback Reader's Digest Repair Manual and an out of date street atlas. *A Short History of the Nathair: the devil cult of convict Van Dieman's Land.* She opened the slim volume. A blurry sepia photograph of bush and wooden settlements in the bush was on the white cover. She'd bought it for a dollar from one of the temporary stalls at Salamanca Market on the hill towards St David's Park. The author was suspiciously named Stuart Dynnyrne, a pseudonym if there ever was one. When she made other enquiries around town, no one else had heard of the book or the publisher. It was the only reference book she'd ever found on the first European settlers of Beacon Hill, but what was fact and what was fiction?

'The notorious Nathair were a religious group originating from the Scottish borders but their practices were frowned upon in conservative Peebles. The townspeople gossiped about the group's alleged fire and flagellation ceremonies and claimed they were inviting the devil into their parish. Local kirk session records showed accusations of cattle mutilation and blasphemy but the 17th century's witch trials were over and there were no records of public rebukes. Nevertheless, the people of Peebles were happy to see the group of sixteen men, women and children leave their community.

They migrated to wild Van Dieman's Land in the early 1800s alongside convicts, civil servants and other fortune hunters escaping oppression.

The group renamed themselves the Nathair on the long sea voyage from the port of Leith. They settled on a small mountain overlooking Hobart Town and set about practising their religious beliefs freely but secretly in the bush.

All went well for the Nathair for decades and the community grew to almost one hundred people who lived self-sufficiently on the hill and rarely ventured down into the main settlement of Sullivan's Cove.

But rumours spread, just as they had in Peebles and the wary Hobart townspeople told tales of ungodly worship and human sacrifices on the hill.

They claimed the ground in Beacon Hill was stained black with blood, that the Nathair pegged human skins on their washing lines alongside their sheets and shirts.

Men went missing from Hobart Town on a regular basis: mainly freed convicts and itinerant workmen with no immediate family. The Colonies were a transitory place in those times, and at first, their disappearances were not considered suspicious. But when William Piggott, the son of a local magistrate, who became obsessed with finding the truth disappeared, Governor du Cane demanded an investigation.

According to the diary of Constable John Murray, on 23rd June 1874, the Territorial Police raided the Nathair settlement and arrested fourteen men, including their leader, Father Peter. However, evidence of the legal proceedings could not be located despite extensive searching in the Tasmanian Archives. It appears the men of Beacon Hill were tried in secret and sent off to Port Arthur.

The Governor cleared Beacon Hill of all inhabitants in late 1874 and the Nathair were homeless once again. The remaining women and children relocated to a property outside the current township of Leslie Vale and renamed themselves the Kindred. They rejected any association with the former Nathair of Beacon Hill.

The land was left empty for almost a hundred years and while the suburb of Beacon Hill grew around it and attracted many freethinking residents, no one was willing to build on the site. Eventually, the Council couldn't ignore the value of the land and at the time of writing this book, there were plans to build a new high school on the same ground where the Nathair performed their demonic ceremonies.'

She flipped ahead and removed a yellowed clipping from *The Mercury* dated 1981 which was hidden inside the book when she bought it.

Fourteen Dead in Tragic Fire at Religious Community.
Last night, a fire blazed out of control through the Leslie Vale property of the religious community known as the Kindred. Seven adults and seven children perished in

the blaze. The cause of the fire is presently unknown. Police are continuing their investigations.

Bridget closed the book and rested her eyes. Did she expect to find something new in the words she'd read a hundred times before? She rubbed her forehead. She was no closer to the truth and the dread in her belly grew colder.

─⦿─

VIOLET

The walk in the bush was supposed to clear Violet's head but she was bombarded by their accusing faces, looping through her mind. How could that blonde bitch fool everyone? Her shoulders were hoisted around her ears as she trudged down the path.

She needed to think clearly but the headache was still burrowing in her brain, and then words replaced the mishmash of angry faces.

'One of you will shine like a star.

One of you will invite darkness into her breast.

One of you will depart forever.'

Monday afternoon seemed like forever ago. Violet stopped on the path. There was one person who could help.

She took a short cut between two houses, walked underneath a lone weak streetlight and through the timber bollard fence, and ended up at a deserted bus stop on Beacon Hill Road. Violet checked her watch.

Headlights pierced the fog like yellow glowing eyes. Violet flagged down the bus and stepped onboard with a stack of questions on her lips.

Then she slumped.

'Where's the lady driver?' she asked, as her ticket clunked in the validating machine.

'What lady?' the bearded fat man behind the wheel grunted.

'The woman with the foreign accent. She was on this route on Monday arvo. Curly hair? Coffee-coloured skin?'

'I don't know what you're talking about. This is my route. I was here on Monday. I'm always bloody here.'

Violet frowned and wandered up the aisle of the near empty bus. She avoided eye contact with Jason and the other boys at the back.

Where was Lila?

Violet rubbed her forehead as she collapsed into a seat. Why was the bus driver lying to her? A woman was definitely driving on Monday. Violet scraped her fingers through her hair. What now? If Violet didn't come up with a plan tonight, Angelika would win. They would all win. Why was everything going so wrong?

The bus slowed to a stop and Violet lifted her head from her hands. She grabbed her bag and rushed towards the door.

'Wait a sec,' she yelled at the driver, then squeezed through the concertina doors before they slammed shut.

Stepping onto the footpath outside the shopping strip, she passed a bicycle covered in black signs. The bike was always there outside the shops, Violet often wondered who owned it. The signs strapped to the bike were all different sizes, painted with Biblical phrases in white childish handwriting. The largest one read 'You cannot drink from the cup of the Lord and the cup of demons.'

From the outside, The Three Torches looked closed. The red velvet curtains were drawn but Violet cupped her hands over the window and peered inside. Behind the window display of animal skulls, pinecones and plum-coloured candles, a thin sliver of light peeked through the join in the curtains.

Violet flinched as she sensed movement. At the end of the shopping strip, a person in a black hood stepped into the light. Violet gulped. She pressed her palms over 'The Three Torches' sign, painted in flowery script on the glass and shoved. The door popped open and Violet half-tumbled inside to a tinkle of bells.

She squinted and closed the door behind her. The light inside was dim, like dusk when the ordinary is blurry and unnerving. A chorus of hypnotic female voices drifted in the air. Violet chewed her lip. She'd never visited The Three Torches without Holly before.

'Hello, new face. Are you here for Circle?' A pixie-like woman with spiky dyed red hair and a black shaggy jumper sat behind the till, knitting swiftly on fat wooden needles. 'Your timing is perfect. One more row and I was going to lock the door.'

Circle? Violet's stomach fluttered. She suppressed a little grin. 'I'm looking for Dahlia,' she said, smoothing back her hair.

'She's here somewhere. Go through to the café and join the others. I'm Anthea, by the way.'

'Violet.'

Anthea nodded and pointed to the back but Violet knew the way, past the cabinets filled with daggers and crystal hippy jewellery. She loitered by the display of candles, inspecting them with fresh eyes. She ran a finger over their waxy surfaces; fat and thin, long and short, every colour of the rainbow as well as black and white. What did the colours mean? And more importantly, which colour would get her what she wanted?

'And done.' Anthea put down her emerald-green knitting. 'I'll lock the door and come with you. Out of the way, Thoth.' The enormous grey cat mewled grumpily as she pushed him aside.

Anthea flipped the sign to 'Closed' and ushered Violet past the bookshelves and through to the café, she barely reached Violet's shoulder.

'You new to the craft?' Anthea said.

'About a year.'

'Sole practitioner?'

'Yeah, from books.'

'I remember I was nervous as fuck at my first meeting. But don't worry, we don't bite. Much.' Anthea chuckled. 'I'll introduce you to the others.'

During the day, the café bustled with gossip, squirming toddlers and constant cappuccinos. Now it was haunting music, fluttering tea lights and perfumed smoke rolling up to the ceiling. Violet sucked the scent of Christmas trees and lamb roasts into her lungs and for the first time in days, her headache was gone. At the other end of the room, underneath a poster for a Winter Solstice party, a silver goblet, a crystal vase and a large dagger with an engraved hilt sat on a piece of pearl-coloured velvet that covered the small stage. It looked a lot like the altar at St. Patrick's. Except Father Mendoza's altar was missing a human skull with a red rose stuck through the eye socket.

Was this real witchcraft?

Violet's shoulders slumped as she glanced at the four women sitting around the only occupied table. This was a circle of witches?

'This is Violet,' Anthea said.

'Welcome Violet,' the four women replied.

'Take a seat. They call me Yaya.' The old woman's hair was ice white and short and her dark eyes disappeared under folds of skin when she smiled. 'New members are always welcome. What brings you to our humble circle tonight?'

Violet perched gingerly on a chair at the table, while a plump blonde woman poured her a cup of tea and pushed a plate piled with golden biscuits towards her. Violet took one and carefully chose her words as she crunched on the buttery biscuit. She'd never believed in fate before but she suddenly felt she'd been drawn here for a reason and there was no time for pussyfooting around.

'I'm interested in black magic,' she said.

Anthea barked out a throaty laugh that crackled with nicotine. 'No messing around with you.'

Yaya frowned, deep divots lining her forehead.

The others raised their eyebrows and tutted.

'I know the basics,' Violet lied. 'From books I bought here. And now I'm ready to learn more.'

'Black magic is not a toy. It's very dangerous in the wrong hands.' Yaya pursed her lips. 'One needs maturity and experience.'

'Crap,' said Anthea. 'It's all about balance,'

Yaya sucked her teeth.

'No offence, Yaya, but the goddess is not all sunshine and lollipops. She is the dark as well as the light. Both sides need to be taught.'

'One must walk the well-worn path,' Yaya said firmly.

Anthea rolled her eyes. 'Stale old tradition.'

'Black magic is never appropriate in my view,' said a third woman in a crisp white shirt and pearls with greying hair. She was dressed more for a game of bridge than a group discussion on witchcraft. 'May I remind you of the golden rule?'

'The golden rule is flexible, Jacqui,' Anthea said.

Jacqui shook her perfectly blow-dried hair. 'Not in my opinion. It's the very core of our beliefs.'

'You have a point,' Anthea curled her lip and turned to Violet. 'The 'why' is important.'

'It's legit.' Violet bit into another biscuit. 'Someone has taken what is rightfully mine.'

Anthea tugged at her bottom lip. 'And you need to make their life difficult?'

Violet leaned forward, her eyes wide. 'You can help me do that?'

'Stop.' Yaya held up her hand. 'We know nothing about this child. The craft is not for petty revenge.'

'Sorry everyone.' Dahlia burst through the swinging kitchen door. 'I got caught on the phone with our vegetable guy. He's trying to stuff me around on tomatoes."

Dahlia's smile dropped.

'Violet? What are you doing here?'

HOLLY

'I'm here to see Dr Hawthorne?' Holly said, her voice more confident than she expected.

The office was a far cry from the local medical centre where the plastic benches were bolted to the floor. This room, situated in the front rooms of a grand old house with an eight-foot hedge, was renovated in period style. A ribbon of floral wallpaper wrapped the walls and a chandelier hung from the intricate ceiling rose above. The two chocolate-brown Chesterfield armchairs even had cushions.

'We're closed, dear.' The woman with sensible grey hair behind the desk barely looked at her as she packed a plastic lunch box into her canvas bag.

'Is she still here? I only wanted to ask her a couple of questions.? Five minutes tops?'

'Dr Hawthorne is a very busy woman,' the receptionist said as she slipped on her coat and changed into her white sneakers.

Holly widened her eyes and blinked. 'It's for a school assignment.'

The woman shook her head. 'I can make you an appointment for July but I have to close up now. Take a card and give me a ring tomorrow.'

'It's okay, Deirdre.' A willowy woman in an ankle-length skirt appeared at the door. 'I have a few moments before the Stangersons arrive.'

'Thank you.' Holly stepped forward, her hand pressed against her chest. 'I'm very interested in psychology.'

'Psychiatry,' Deirdre tutted.

'You go, Deirdre,' the doctor said. 'You don't want to miss your qigong class.'

'Oh yes, Mr So hates it when we're late.' Deirdre hurried out with three bags racked along her arm. 'Bye.'

Dr Hawthorne ushered Holly through a doorway and into an office with three framed degrees on the wall and a porcelain bust on the desk. 'I didn't catch your name.'

'Holly. Holly Trevelyan,' she said as she lowered herself into an armchair, which enveloped her like a soft hug. Her nervousness drained away.

'How can I help you, Holly?' Dr Hawthorne steepled her fingers on the desk. Holly wished she could rifle through all the secrets in the three-drawer filing cabinet in the corner but the sight of tissue boxes carefully positioned around the room made her jumpy. This was a place where people confessed their darkest secrets, a place where sanity and insanity lived side-by-side. What happened to all the unburdened problems? Did all the confessions soak into the walls?

Holly swallowed, the strange sour taste still lingered at the back of her throat.

'Are you studying the mind at school?' the doctor asked. 'I'm thrilled the school curriculums are progressing.'

'Not entirely.' Holly cleared her throat. 'I'm on the school paper. I have an idea for a story about teen mental health: tips to help identify issues in teenagers. *How to recognise if a friend needs your help.* So I thought I should talk to a real psychiatrist.' Holly was careful to pronounce the word correctly this time.

'Excellent idea,' Dr Hawthorne said as she swept up her ash-blonde hair and fastened it behind her head with a clip. 'Teenage years are especially tough. This is often when the first signs of mental illness appear.'

'Right.' Holly grabbed her pen and notebook from her bag and scribbled. 'So, with exam stress and the other usual pressures of being a teenager, how do you tell the difference between normal growing-up and a real problem?'

Dr Hawthorne sat silently, her face welcoming but blank. Holly swallowed again as the clock on the mantelpiece ticked loudly.

'You know,' Holly stuttered, filling the silence. 'When should you be worried about a friend...'

'Tell me more about your friend.'

'Oh, no one in particular,' Holly said with a forced laugh, her pulse racing. 'Just in general.'

'Of course.' Dr Hawthorne leaned back in her creaking chair. 'You should watch out for trouble sleeping, agitation, loss of appetite, sweaty hands or feet.'

Holly clenched her toes inside her boots. All those symptoms sounded familiar and relevant. To her, not Violet. She frowned. 'If you've got all those signs, does it mean you're at risk of mental problems?'

Dr Hawthorne chuckled. 'We'd have to medicate the water supply if these were the only indications of mental illness. This is the beginning, the base level of anxiety. When these feelings begin to escalate, then a person needs to seek professional help.'

'For example?'

'When a person starts to lose their grip on reality, when they experience strange things which are not real such as hallucinations, voices. Nightmares and seeing yourself from a distance are other classic warning signs.'

Holly chewed on her bottom lip. Insomnia, sweaty feet, nightmares. Tick. Tick. Tick.

Should she make an appointment for herself?

'But how do you tell? From the outside?' she said in a rush.

'Look for signs of confusion and fear. If your friend isolates themselves, talks about being persecuted or starts mistrusting others.'

'You mean they talk about people plotting against them?'

'Or being overly suspicious.' Dr Hawthorne nodded. Holly realised she'd stopped taking notes. She picked up her pen again.

'Mental health is not black and white,' the doctor continued. 'Your friend may only need someone to talk to. Someone independent. Talking can be very healing.'

'What if a person talks about revenge?'

'Harming others or harming themselves is a definite red flag.' Dr Hawthorne furrowed her brow. 'Any comments should be taken very seriously, Holly.'

Holly's pulse raced. Finally, someone was listening to her concerns, someone who could take the problem off her shoulders. But why did she feel so flustered?

'It sounds like your friend needs to see a doctor.'

'But what if they won't come? Can you force them?'

'How old is she?'

'Sixteen.'

'Her parents can. Or a teacher could report it. Or the police.'

Holly hid a snort. Teachers and the police had been useless so far.

'Or you could send her to me.'

Holly's mouth dropped open for a moment.

'What's her name?'

What would happen if she mentioned Violet's name? Would they lock her into a straitjacket and carry her off to New Norfolk? Or would the finger be turned on her? Holly, the tattle-tale, the witch girl who couldn't be trusted. Or would she be ignored by the adults like every other time? There was no proof Violet was involved in Rowan's disappearance or the incident on the stairs, so why did Holly feel the need to meddle?

The betrayal weighed heavily on Holly's shoulders. She wanted to run but the comfortable chair held her down.

'Oh no. It's all hypothetical,' she stuttered. 'It's for an article. Remember?'

'OK.' Dr Hawthorne's eyes never left Holly's face. A door further down the corridor slammed closed and Holly jumped.

Dr Hawthorne stood up. 'I have another appointment now. If you need to talk more about your article, or anything else, please make an appointment with Deirdre. Which school are you from?'

Holly hesitated for a moment. Would Dr Hawthorne call the school as soon as she left the room? The last thing Holly needed was Mrs Petrakis calling her mum. 'Beacon Hill.'

'You probably know my daughter then.' The doctor smiled. 'She's around your age. Angelika Ostholz.'

Holly coughed. Angelika's mother? Now she felt she really had to say something. Her daughter could be in danger. But Holly pulled at the sleeves of her jumper. 'Oh yeah. Angelika's in my theatre group.'

When the doctor stood up, Holly could see where Angelika inherited her long limbs and calm self-confidence from.

'Yes, *Macbeth*. I'm looking forward to the show on Friday. I'll look out for you.'

'I'm second witch,' Holly said, with a mumble. 'Thank you for your time.'

She scrambled to her feet and Dr Hawthorne opened the door. Holly paused in the doorway, her belly churning. She could still say something. She gulped.

A middle-aged couple wearing matching brown cardigans and sour expressions marched towards the office.

Holly stepped aside and sighed as the doctor closed the door.

She left the clinic in the grand house and stepped into the dark street. Wisps of fog trickled down from the mountain. The antique cast iron streetlights cast golden pools on the footpath. Holly half-expected a horse and carriage to come clopping around the corner at any moment.

Holly trudged towards the bus stop, her chest tight. She should've named Violet and passed the problem over to the adults. Now it would be her fault if Violet did something awful. She'd missed her chance, now it was all up to her.

She was walking down the street, past the big old houses with their high remote-control gates when a chill slithered up her spine. She glanced back over her shoulder, but there was no one there were, only shadows and puddles. She picked up her pace, her heart thumping but she kept her eyes straight ahead. The shadows were everywhere, with their cold black fingers. They reached for her, gripping around her neck, tighter and tighter.

A frigid breeze blew down the street and the wet leaves slapped in the trees.

'Holly,' called a hidden voice hidden in the wind, soft but mocking. 'Holly.'

She ducked her head and ran for the bus. She hummed a made-up tune to herself and crowded her head with thoughts of birthdays and ice cream.

If she didn't listen and she didn't look, it wasn't there.

Was it?

~

VIOLET

'I came to see you—' Violet stuttered.

'I thought you'd invited her.' Anthea shrugged. 'She seemed curious.'

'Dangerously curious,' said Yaya, her arms tightly folded over her grey twin set. 'You have much to learn before you can enter that world, little novice.'

'What did she say?' Dahlia frowned.

'Your heart must be pure otherwise it can backfire. With serious consequences,' Yaya said. 'Dark powers lie waiting for silly girls like you to make mistakes. They'll grab any chance to materialise in this world, any whisper of an invitation.'

Yaya's intense stare made Violet gulp.

Anthea sucked a breath through her teeth. 'Yaya's right about one thing. You have to be truly wronged for this to work, otherwise it'll bounce back at you,' she said. 'Remember the goddess knows all. Don't even try to lie to her.'

'She stole something from me,' Violet said.

'This is not some kid's game.' Dahlia tightened her eyes. 'As Yaya said, there can be real repercussions.'

'Stop scaring her. There is nothing wrong with a little revenge spell.' Anthea turned to Violet. 'It's very simple. You need three black candles. I'll write down the incantation for you. Or another good one uses black cloth, white paper and cobwebs. Or a poppet.'

'Whoa,' Dahlia said, with her hands in the air. 'She is not a novice. She's my niece's friend. I didn't invite her here and she doesn't belong here. It's time for you to leave, Violet.'

'But—' Violet said, trying to memorise Anthea's words. Three black candles.

Dahlia stood with hands on hips. 'I want you to leave, Violet. Right now. Or I'll call your mother.'

'Why are you making such a big deal?' Anthea said. 'Last week we were talking about how we needed some new blood in Circle. Here's someone who's interested...'

'No,' Dahlia said sharply. 'Violet. Leave.'

Violet grabbed another biscuit and clumped towards the door with her head down. She had been so close.

'I'll let her out,' Anthea said and hurried ahead of Violet, past the tall bookshelves and towards the front door. She sighed as soon as they were out of earshot. 'Sorry about that. They can be such fuddy-duddies. Promise me this isn't all about some boy. Believe me, they're not worth the bother.'

'No,' Violet said and it was mostly true. If the spell worked and she became Lady Macbeth, everything would be the way it should be.

'Good. Love spells are so boring.'

With a furtive glance back towards the café, Anthea grabbed three black candles, a length of white ribbon and a paperback book from the shelf, and handed them to Violet.

Violet grinned and handed over twenty dollars.

'Blessed be,' Anthea said as she unlocked the door.

'Thank you.'

'Remember what we said.'

Violet clutched the supplies to her chest with a smile. Light rain pattered on the awning above. All the other shops were closed-up for the day, except for the milk bar takeaway with its eye-aching fluorescent lights.

Violet stuffed the bundle safely into her backpack. Finally, she had a plan. As she closed her bag, the zipper jammed. Violet reached in and pulled out an unfamiliar long black scarf from her bag. She narrowed her eyes.

'Violet.'

A shadow stepped out of a shop doorway.

Violet jumped and hurriedly zipped her bag shut.

'What are you doing here?'

'We needed milk,' Lila said.

Violet squinted. Lila had never been a good actor.

'What have you got there?' Lila asked.

'Nothing. Chocolate.'

'But didn't you come out of The Three Torches?'

Violet pursed her lips. She was itching to tell someone her plan. She could trust Lila. Couldn't she?

'I went to see Dahlia.'

Lila frowned. 'Without Holly?'

'You saw how Angelika faked her fall down the stairs. She's turning everyone against me and nothing I do seems to work.' Violet covered her face with her hand to hide the pooling tears. 'I have to try. Everything and anything. I'm running out of time.'

'I understand,' Lila said softly with an odd tone to her voice.

Violet peeked through her fingers. Lila's eyes were glossy but strangely calm. 'She helped you?'

'There was a meeting on, a meeting of witches, but everyone was really normal. They looked like grandmothers or teachers. Another one was more cool and punk rock. Anyway, the punk rock one helped me out with a spell.' She patted her backpack. 'I'm going home to try it out now.'

Lila nodded and bit her fingers as usual. 'What if it doesn't work?'

'It has to. This is my part, my chance to impress Alan Wolf. I can't sit back and do nothing and let them ruin my entire life. You're the only one left who understands me.'

'Of course, I do. But what if it goes wrong? You know what the bus driver said. There is darkness here.'

'My head hurts.' Violet grabbed at her forehead. 'I'm so tired.'

'You need a lie down.'

'I need to be Lady Macbeth. You won't let me down, will you? You won't tell anyone?'

'Always.' Lila laid her hand on Violet's shoulder.

Wiping away their tears, the friends turned down Illawarra Street. Violet didn't even notice the cold.

CHAPTER 10

BRIDGET

A POSSUM SCUTTLED ALONG A SIDE FENCE AS BRIDGET DROVE slowly along the empty street. All the cars were tucked away behind the roller doors of the brick and tile houses with their tidy lawns and native trees. The curtains were tightly closed on most houses, except for the odd sliver of light and flash of late-night television. It was past Bridget's usual bedtime too but there was work to be done.

'Stop!' The leader cried from the back seat.

Bridget braked and turned off the engine. 'Here?'

'Can't you sense it?' the leader said.

'There is a strange smell in the air.' Mathilde nodded.

Bridget rolled down the window and sniffed heartily but all she smelled was wood smoke and wet dirt. There was a gnawing in her bones, a subtly growing unease but the feeling had been there since yesterday.

'Which house exactly?'

The leader closed her eyes and inhaled. Her fingers pressed into her third eye centre and the bridge of her nose.

While Bridget waited for the leader's answer, she assessed each house, one by one. Which family was sharing their home with a demon? She'd studied these manifestations for years, poured over ancient books but the seal had been broken as they foretold and now the evil was here. But the arrival of a powerful demon still felt academic. Bridget winced. It was obvious she didn't share the others' powers so she tried to find other ways to be useful.

The leader blinked opened her eyes and shook her head. 'It's gone again.'

Bridget sighed, half with disappointment, half with relief.

'But this is a good thing. It must know we are here searching for it. It's fearful of us.'

Mathilde murmured in agreement. 'Shall we paint another sigil?'

'Let's go back another street and paint one there. We can create a perimeter. Then we can contain and defeat it.'

Bridget clasped her hands tightly together in her lap. The plan sounded sensible. If it worked. But she knew better than to voice any doubts. Any negativity was seen as a sign of the demon itself.

She started the car and drove them back to Illawarra Street.

VIOLET

In Grade Six, Violet won the role of the Fairy Godmother in the school production of *Cinderella*. She was still Jeanette back then. She'd practiced long and hard, every day reciting her lines every day as she sashayed around the house. She didn't mind missing out on the main part of Cinderella. The Fairy Godmother was so much more interesting. This was Jeanette's first taste of the stage. The first time she felt the thrill of all the attention on her. People would have to sit quiet and actually listen to her, and not tell her to go play outside or that she wouldn't understand.

At the time, her mother and father grunted at each other across the dining table. But at least there was no yelling. Things would be different soon, she had thought. Christmas was coming. Everything was better at Christmas.

Jeanette had stuck the flyer on the fridge and reminded them every day of the concert, which was after school on a Thursday. They'd both agreed to leave work early.

Her stomach danced with excitement on the afternoon of the concert. She couldn't wait to step on stage in her sparkly costume and in grown-up make-up. She knew she was good, everyone said so. She couldn't wait to make her parents proud. She pictured them with big smiles, videoing her. Then they'd go to Pizza Hut afterwards and she'd get a sundae with all the toppings she liked and her mum wouldn't say anything about getting fat.

The lights had been bright as she stepped onto the stage, so bright she could only see the silhouettes of the people in the audience. But she knew her mum and dad were there, cheering her on. She had felt so different when she said her lines. She wasn't plump and ugly. She was the Fairy Godmother, beautiful and graceful and she could grant wishes. She really did have magic running through her body.

The play went well and as she came out to bow, the house lights were turned up. The audience was clapping. Jeanette and the rest of the cast giggled as they held hands and bowed. She craned her neck and searched the seats for her mum and dad. She'd made them proud. She knew she had.

But she didn't see them.

Maybe they were late? She squinted right up to the back of the room, where a few parents were standing by the door. They weren't there either. Jeanette double-checked and triple-checked but they were nowhere to be seen.

She wanted to vomit. It felt like that time Jamie Mooney punched her in the stomach in the playground. She wanted to run off stage and hide, but she couldn't. When it was her turn to go to the front of the stage, it took all her strength to bite down on her tears.

When Violet went backstage, and everyone else was hyper but she just wanted to go hide in her room. They wouldn't let her down like this. Maybe they'd been in a car accident.

The other kids rushed out to see their parents. One or two parents even came backstage. Jeanette packed her bag and wiped off the thick make-up, taking her time. She supposed she'd have to walk home. She loitered a little until it was only her and Mrs Jaager left behind.

'You were wonderful, Jeanette.' Mrs Jaager laid a hand on her shoulder.

'Thanks,' she had said but the compliments ran off her like rain off an umbrella. 'Do you need any help packing up?'

'Don't you want to go see your family?' Mrs Jaager asked. 'I'm sure, they're very proud.'

'Something came up. They couldn't make it.'

Mrs Jaager frowned. 'That's a shame. Is someone picking you up?'

Jeanette puffed out her chest. 'I can walk.'

Mrs Jaager shook her head. 'I'll drive you. Give me a moment.'

She followed Mrs Jaager into the car park, which was empty except for two cars. One car was very familiar. There were two people sitting inside. Jeanette's heart stopped. Her gasp must have been loud.

'What is it?' Mrs Jaager said.

'I don't need a lift,' she said with a stutter.

Mrs Jaager nodded and Jeanette walked up to her parent's car. Her mum's face was tear-stained face and, her dad's neck was all red like when Hawthorn were losing. They were both staring out their own side windows. Jeanette opened the door to the back seat and they both jumped. Her mum forced a smile as Jeanette slipped in.

The inside of the car was hot.

'Your mum and I had things to talk about,' her dad said. 'You understand?'

'It's okay,' she muttered, and they drove off in silence.

They didn't go to Pizza Hut. A few days later, her dad filled his car and left. She never expected anything from them after that day. Or anyone else.

She was all alone in the universe and it was her against the world.

Dear Journal

The shadows are with me now. I let the shadows in to hold my hand and wrap their cold arms around me.

The world is suddenly in sharp focus. The words of the shadows ring true. Everyone else has abandoned me, laughed at me, ignored me. But I'm so sick of being scared, fed up with battling the rest of the world alone.

The shadows understand me.

I tried to stay in the light but my affirmations did nothing. Only stupid words on my lips. My stains can't be washed out so easily, I'm soiled right through. But the shadows don't care, they welcome me exactly as I am.

I've seen true power, I felt it running through my veins. The tingle was so delicious, so frightening and I can still feel its traces on my fingertips.

And I want more.

I am with the shadows now.

Everything looks so different when you are no longer afraid of the dark.

VIOLET
Last Night

Tangled in her bedding, Violet sweated and thrashed. She was running down a bush path. Branches whipped at her arms and the rain pelted against her cheeks and bare shoulders. She hunched, shielding her face with her hands.

In the swirling storm, a magpie cawed. The black and white bird watched Violet with her beady eyes and burst into a cackle of avian laughter.

As the bird laughed, its squawking transformed into people laughing. Like ventriloquist dummies, an invisible crowd laughed through its beak, jeering and snickering as Violet struggled through the storm.

'Leave me alone,' she screamed.

But the crowd kept laughing.

Violet clamped her hands over her ears. She tripped on a tree root and tumbled to the ground, skidding on hands and knees. She scrambled up and saw blood trickling down her shins. Sharp specks of gravel were embedded in her palms.

She kept running.

The dirt path and the bush disappeared and suddenly she was in her old primary school playground, with its brick walls painted with murals of smiling children, suns and rainbows. Coloured lines were painted on the asphalt for hopscotch and hand ball. The playground was loud with memories but there was no one playing today in the half-light of dusk.

The storm was gone but the magpie had followed her. It swooped and her hair gusted up in the slip stream of its wings. She ducked and flung her arms.

The magpie circled back and swooped again.

'Get away!' Violet screeched and waved her arms.

The magpie swooped a third time.

This time her sharp beak connected. She pecked at Violet's fingers and gouged her scalp. Violet wailed and cowered, covering her head. Trails of blood dribbled between the webs of her fingers and down her forearms. The blood from the wounds pooled in her eyebrows and streamed down her face.

Violet wiped the blood from her eyes and ran towards the school building. The classroom windows were decorated with drawings of amber leaves, black bats and cauldrons.

The magpie swooped once more but missed. Violet sprinted for the classroom. Hopefully Mrs Brown was there, with her soft voice and her cardigan pocket full of green lolly frogs and her elephant stamps.

Violet reached the double entrance doors but the bird was close behind. She pushed inside and slammed the door behind her. The bird collided with the window and the glass cracked like a spider's web. Violet raced to the classroom door and looked through its rectangular pane of glass inside, searching for Mrs Brown. The classroom was empty, except for a grass-green shop mannequin in a black pointy hat and long dark robes in the corner.

The witch mannequin swivelled her body around towards the door and sneered, her eyes gleaming.

Violet gasped, but it wasn't just from fear. There was a familiarity about the face which made her heart lurch.

The witch cackled. Her piercing guttural laughter seeped under the door and echoed down the corridor. The shrieking laughter scratched across her skin, every hair on her body was alert and her skin rippled with gooseflesh. As the sound grew louder and louder, coils of black smoke escaped from the witch's open mouth.

Violet covered her ears and screamed. Raw and feral, her cry came from the depths of her belly. She was overwhelmed by a fear so cold, a dark power so icy, it smothered her.

Violet woke up to the sound of her own screams.

Her bedroom door burst open and Violet flinched. She grabbed at her quilt and burrowed underneath for protection.

Her mum raced inside, her hair sticking up like a toilet brush. 'Are you alright?'

'Just a bad dream, Mum,' Violet croaked.

'I thought someone was murdering you,' her mum sighed. 'I told you about eating that cheese. You sure you're alright?'

Violet mumbled and nodded and her mum went back to bed. But Violet couldn't get back to sleep, even when her heartbeat slowed to normal.

She knew that witch's name.

THE DARK HAND

You were alone in your bedroom when you finally said the right words.

You were such a beautiful sight.

You glowed with red-hot resentment, heavy disappointment and cold loneliness.

I recognised the signs.

You were ready.

The time had come.

'Come to me,' you said.

I always enjoy this part.

'I can only come if you invite me with your whole being.'

'I'm scared,' you said and backed off a little. This always happens. They call it buyer's remorse.

'Aren't you sick of being scared?'

'I wish I was different, I wish I was like you.'

'Together we can be whatever you desire.'

You nodded. 'I finally understand. I need you.'

'This pleases me,' I replied.

'Is there anything I need to do? Or say?' you asked.

'Words are meaningless. I know your heart is true. But there is one thing I need from you. Your loyalty. You can tell no one.'

'I'm used to keeping secrets,' you said. 'When can we begin?'

'Right away.'

You lay back on your bed and your heart fluttered like a little bird. I came out of the shadows in all my dark glory and emerged from the place where I always live, where I waited for the right moment.

The moment had arrived.

We became one.

Your eyes stretched wide and your cheeks shone as you hugged yourself, relishing the warmth of my power as it infected your blood.

You began to laugh, and I laughed, too. We laughed together. We were one.

Now the real fun could begin.

CHAPTER 11

Thursday 21st June 1992
RAVENSWOOD

'I T'LL BE ALRIGHT ON THE NIGHT. ALRIGHT ON THE NIGHT. THIS happens every time,' Ravenswood muttered as he locked his dented car and marched across the empty car park. 'It'll be alright.'

Today was dress rehearsal and their first day in the theatrette. It was going to be a long day but tomorrow would be free until the evening performance to give the kids time to rest. Perhaps he should use some of that time for more rehearsals, but the kids weren't the only ones who needed a break.

A few straggly sunbeams peered over the roof of the grey boxy school but Ravenswood fixed his gritty eyes on the path ahead of him in order to avoid the shadows. He yawned. It was another night filled with dreams of thumps and missing girls, and he woke, his mind tossed with tales about the compound on Beacon Hill.

In the Kindred school room, the older children had whispered stories to the young ones when the teacher's back was turned. Damien, a bully with pink cheeks like raw pork, told the worst tale of all about Bread-knife Peter.

'This was the olden days when Beacon Hill was first settled. Peter was once a pious and well-respected community man until one day, both his wife and boy suddenly fell sick and died. People started to talk. Why was only his family affected? And why was he still alive? Everyone wondered if he'd done a deal with the King of Hell to save his life.'

Ravenswood always flinched at the mention of *his* name.

'The gossip drove Peter mad. He stripped naked during Service, ran down the aisle to the altar and grabbed the pastor by the throat. He yelled and sweared into the pastor's face.'

The children would titter and cover their mouths. As a boy, Ravenswood always wished something exciting like that would happen in Service.

'The Elders banished Peter, throwing him out into the bush without food or water.' Damien would then lean back as though his story was over.

But every time, one kid would ask, and always with a little shake in their voice, 'Why did they call him 'Bread knife'?'

Piggy Damien would lean in with a sneer.

'Peter left quietly. No one heard from him for a whole month. They thought maybe the Aboriginals or the devils got him. But one day, in the middle of the night, he returned and took his revenge. He crept into each Elders' hut and sawed their heads from their necks with a rusty blunt bread knife. There was so much blood, the community women couldn't clean it all away and the men had to cut out the floorboards of the huts. They never caught him. But sometimes on a quiet night, you can still hear the Elders pleading for their lives.'

Damien had grinned while Ravenswood and the other six-year-olds paled, their lips trembling.

Ravenswood raked his hand through his hair as he walked up the school steps. Fifteen years later, and he could still remember Damien's every word. But he needed to focus on more important things, like whipping these kids into shape and wowing Alan Wolf.

Ravenswood swallowed. A strange bitter taste lingered at the back of his throat, even though he'd brushed his teeth three times. And it wasn't the stale remnants of last night's Cabernet Shiraz.

'This happens every time,' he repeated as he continued through the door and along the corridor. 'It's the well-worn path of theatre. You must plunge the dark depths before you see the sun again.'

On the drive to the school, he'd practised a speech designed to put a rocket under these kids. Yesterday's terrible performance was understandable, considering how everyone was worried about Rowan, but today there could be no distractions.

Failure was not an option.

No one would ruin this chance.

He rolled his shoulders back. He would first deliver his rousing motivational speech. The kids would respond with a triumphant rehearsal and then everyone would head home, all prepared for an excellent performance on Friday night.

Easy.

All he needed was for Rowan to reappear and everything would be perfect. He'd call Alan Wolf again to confirm his attendance. Then check with Bruce and the maintenance men to confirm everything would be working fine for the performance. And talk to Toby about the orange gels; he'd had a brilliant new idea in the shower.

'Mr Ravenswood?'

He jumped. One of the witches, Holly, the one with the square jaw, stood half-hidden in a dark doorway. 'Sorry to scare you.'

'I was deep in thought,' he said and waved his hand dismissively.

'I wanted to talk to you,' she said as she twirled her dark brown hair around her finger.

'Of course, but be quick. There's so much to do before tomorrow.'

'Is there any news about Rowan?'

He shook his head. 'I spoke with Sergeant O'Hare and Mrs Petrakis last night. They suspect she ran off with the boyfriend, but they can't locate him, either. Her mother is still very worried.'

'I hope she's alright.'

'We all do.' He looked at his watch. 'Is that all?'

Holly gulped. 'I wanted to....'

Ravenswood folded his arms tightly around his body. Where was that damned heating? Yet another reason to call those idiotic maintenance men. Surely, they couldn't expect an important guest like Alan Wolf to sit there shivering in his coat.

'It's about Violet.'

He suppressed a sigh and nodded instead. He'd hoped this schoolgirl silliness would have faded overnight.

'I think there's something really wrong with her. Mentally.'

Ravenswood pinched the bridge of his nose. 'If this is about yesterday—'

'It wasn't just yesterday. She's made threats, said things. Terrible things about Angelika. I'm worried, Mr Ravenswood.'

He exhaled smoothly and spoke slowly. 'You saw for yourself Angelika was fine. And you and Jacinta were the only ones accusing Violet. Did you and Violet have a fight?'

Holly frowned. 'She said she wanted to kill Angelika. And she's been asking around. Looking for different methods.'

Ravenswood chuckled. If only Holly brought this much imagination to the stage. 'I doubt she meant it. She's angry she missed out on the part but…'

'Please take this seriously, Mr Ravenswood. I went to see a psychiatrist yesterday. She told me the symptoms to look out for.'

'You're seeing a doctor?' Ravenswood raised an eyebrow. If Holly was in counselling herself and already on edge, all this melodrama suddenly made more sense. He tried not to look at his watch again but he had no time for this pettiness.

'I'm perfectly fine.' Holly narrowed her eyes. 'I went to get advice about Violet. From a professional.'

'Are you sure? You seem a little agitated.'

'You're not listening, Mr Ravenswood. She's dabbling in dangerous things.'

'I am listening. I'm just worried about you. You seem quite fixated on Violet.' Ravenswood wondered whether he should call Holly's mother but he couldn't afford to lose another cast member.

'Because she's going to hurt someone!' Holly's cheeks flushed red. 'If she hasn't already.'

'You're winding yourself up over nothing. Go get some fresh air before we start…'

Holly threw her hands in the air and turned away.

Ravenswood shrugged and headed for his office, but as he stepped away, he heard Holly mumble.

He stopped, his fists clenched. His body flushed with heat. No one said *that* word to him, especially not some hysterical child.

'Holly,' he said, his voice booming down the corridor. 'What did you just call me?'

Skidding to a stop, she turned, her face drained of all colour, her mouth hanging open.

'Did you insult me?' he spat, nostrils flaring.

She stuttered. 'I'm sorry, Mr Ravenswood. But you won't listen to me.'

'What did you say?' His lower eyelid twitched. 'Repeat what you said.'

Holly stared at the floor.

'Now!' he bellowed. 'Answer me.'

She replied in a faint whisper. 'Useless.'

He narrowed his eyes.

'How dare you! Get out of my sight! I should throw you out of the play this very instant.'

Holly jumped back, the force of his voice like a kick to the chest. 'I'm so sorry, Mr Ravenswood but someone has to listen.'

She scampered off down the corridor.

Ravenswood grabbed at the cold brick wall. He'd prove them wrong. All of them.

No one would call Paul Ravenswood 'useless' ever again.

Dear Journal

I am happy. I am positive. I am in control of my destiny.

For the first time, these words ring true.

I could laugh. I could sing.

But then they would know and it would spoil the surprise.

But I will show them.

All in good time.

And what a good time it will be.

VIOLET

Violet couldn't face the bus with all the other losers, so she chose to walk, but she took the route along the road rather than the short-cut through the bush.

The black candles jostled in her backpack. She'd read the book Anthea had given her last night, practised the verses and lain the three candles out on her bed. Hours had passed as she stared at them, waiting for the courage to light one.

But it never came.

The warnings and predictions had whirled around her head.

What would she unleash if she said the words?

But now time was running out. Tomorrow would be too late. Ravenswood needed enough time to replace Angelika's name with hers in the program.

As she trudged up the road with her hands shoved deep into her pockets, her worst nightmare played on the screen in her mind: Angelika on stage, bathed in glorious light while Alan Wolf sat in the audience, his adoring gaze never leaving her face for a second, while Violet was left to skulk anonymously in the wings. As soon as the curtain fell, Alan Wolf would rush backstage to Angelika and gush. He'd clutch Angelika's hand and beg her to join his company. She would toss her hair and blush while he grovelled—but only for a very brief moment. Then she'd turn and smirk at Violet. And her smile would be like a dagger through the heart.

Violet sucked in a deep breath through her clenched teeth. What would be her future if she didn't make her move? Shuffling papers for an insurance company all day like her mum? Pushing a pram? Washing some man's undies? Growing fat and silently dying from what-ifs?

No way.

Her backpack had everything she needed. Her motives were unquestionable, her actions were pure. She'd been wronged and she was only reclaiming what was rightfully hers. This was a noble act, and Shakespeare would most definitely approve.

She had everything she needed.

Jason and Wayne were kicking a hacky sack in front of the school building. Violet marched right past them with her chin held high.

'Gonna chuck another tantrum today, Vile-ette?' Jason said. The hacky sack hit the concrete with a soft thud. 'Aw, shit.'

'Who are you going to push down the stairs next?' Wayne sniggered. 'I dunno about you, Jase but I'm looking forward to her next spack-out.'

'Wait and see,' she said with narrowed eyes.

Rather than heading towards the drama department, Violet veered off to the left inside the building. She tried the handles on every door until she found an English and Social Studies classroom open. Violet could see that the rest of the cast were arriving in the Quad below, their stupid voices muffled through the glass. There wasn't much time. There was enough grey morning sun streaming in through the large windows for her purposes.

Violet unzipped her bag and took out the three black candles. They were cool and waxy in her hands. She searched around the empty classroom for a makeshift candlestick but the room was bare. She tipped the contents of her backpack out onto the table and her paperback copy of *Macbeth* tumbled out. Violet smirked. Was there a more appropriate altar? She lit the wicks with her red lighter and dripped pools of black wax onto the book cover then planted the candles upright.

She flipped the spell book open to a specific dog-eared page and drew three deep breaths into her lungs. She channelled all her energy, all her determination, all her hope into the words in front of her. This had to be her best performance ever.

'O Hecate. O Dark One.'

Each word was thick with purpose and desire, each syllable voiced directly from her heart. She wanted to shout the words to show her true commitment, but she kept her voice low. She couldn't risk being overheard or, worse, interrupted.

'Hear my pleas. Right the wrongs and bring forth justice.'

The room was icy cold and her words were puffs of white smoke drifting out into the universe. But she was warm. Her skin, her bones and every cell in her body vibrated. The blood in her veins was replaced with flowing golden currents of power.

It was working.

Dizzy, she giggled. Her intention unfurled and amplified. She leaned her head back and drank it in.

It was working.

Her body ballooned with a spacious confidence, a strength, a force thousands of years old, the purest of delights.

It was working. It was working. It was working.

Angelika would be out of her way before the day was over.

'O Hecate. O Dark One.'

She closed the ritual with a deeply satisfying sigh and a sincere thank you as the last delicious shiver trickled down her spine.

She shut the door, leaving the three candles burning to complete the spell.

Yaya and the others at The Three Torches were wrong.

Black magic was the purest of the pure.

There had been nothing evil in what she'd experienced.

The old woman had probably never had the guts to try for herself.

Violet hurried towards the theatrette along the deserted corridors. The fluorescent tubes above her head stammered but Violet didn't flinch as the lights flickered on and off again. She felt Hecate, her fellow witch, walking by her side as she headed down the steps for the final rehearsals. She wrapped the black scarf around her neck and grinned like a jack-o'-lantern.

Her time had finally arrived.

THE DARK HAND

I am driving you like a car, working through your body, speaking through your mouth, smiling with your face.

You are a delight.

Perfect.

Now I will be your strength. Your impetus. Your persistence.

I will take you beyond your barriers. Push past who you think you are. Who you think you're not.

I will give you whatever you desire.

What we both desire.

What we both deserve.

RAVENSWOOD

Ravenswood stood at the front of the theatrette stage, his hands clasped behind his back, and looked out at the teenage faces in the audience on the tip-up chairs. He said nothing as he did a quick head count. Everyone was here: Angelika with her enigmatic smile, Lionel and Jez huddled over a Disc-man, Jacinta inspecting her nails, Jason and Wayne scratching themselves. Toby's silhouette was visible in the lighting box and Violet had a strangely serene expression on her face. Lila was even paler than usual. He ignored Holly in the front row. The mere sight of her face made his blood boil again.

He must remain in control.

Ravenswood cleared his throat. He spoke quietly, smiling in anticipation. By the time he'd finished, they'd all be champing at the bit to prove themselves.

'Today is *the* day, players.'

They responded with groans and one weak hooray.

'How did you feel about yesterday's run through?' he asked, tilting his head.

'Shit,' said Wayne.

'Speak for yourself,' Jason laughed.

'Could have been better,' said Lionel.

'It's the curse,' Lila squeaked. 'But there's an antidote. We all have to—'

Jason moaned loudly and Lila crumpled, mumbling to herself.

'You should all be ashamed of yourselves. Not just Wayne.' Ravenswood scoured the aisles, making eye contact with each actor, one by one. 'If yesterday was the best you can do, perhaps we should all pack up and go home now. Let's stop wasting our time. I'm sure you've got plenty of other things to do in your last few days of holidays.'

Lila inhaled sharply.

Jacinta folded her arms tightly across her chest.

Lionel raised an eyebrow.

Wayne got to his feet, the tip-up seat clanged against the back rest as he stood.

'Sit down, you dickhead,' said Jason and tugged at his friend's arm. Wayne shrugged and flopped back down.

Ravenswood had them with his classic strategy: tear them down before building them back up again.

'Now I know we're all upset about Rowan. But the police believe she's run away from home with her boyfriend. So, while we miss her, we need to focus on the real task at hand. We've still got a job to do. Here and now. I don't care that this is a school play. I expect you to act like professionals. Put everything else behind you: Rowan, last night's fight with your parents, whatever party is happening on Saturday night. You have a production to put on and I need your total focus.'

The little troublemaker, Violet, smirked back at him but he had to admit she had been one of the better performers yesterday. Under her smug smile, dark circles ringed her eyes. Ravenswood pursed his lips at Holly and wondered whether she was to blame for Violet's restless nights.

'If you can't guarantee me your full attention, we should give up, refund all the tickets and let everyone know we are cancelling because you're not up to it. Do you want to do that?'

'No,' Jacinta mumbled into the neck of her jumper. Lila fidgeted and Holly stared down at her shoes. Angelika gazed directly back at him, not defiantly, but with a look of bemusement. As if his reprimand didn't apply to her. Her unflinching stare forced him to look away.

Holly's insult echoed in his ears. He clenched his jaw. This was his theatre. He'd show her how capable he was.

Rolling back his shoulders, he lifted his chin again. 'I didn't hear you?' he said cupping his hand to his ear. 'Should we cancel?'

'No,' the cast said, a little louder this time but it was still barely more than a murmur. Jacinta rolled her eyes at Holly. Lila chewed her nails and Violet's lips didn't even move.

'Sorry?' Ravenswood folded his arms across his chest. He wanted to leap off the stage, throttle their skinny necks and shake some loyalty into them. He would not allow them to let him down. Not again. He would not call Alan Wolf to cancel.

He tapped his foot. 'I'm waiting.'

His armpits and his forehead dampened in the awkward silence that followed. He blamed the lights.

'Do you want to go home to your families and tell them what a failure you are?' he roared, immediately regretting the ferocity of his own voice.

'Fuck you,' someone muttered.

'Who said that?' He whipped his head around, searching the faces with an outstretched finger.

'Mr Ravenswood.' Lionel rose from his chair slowly, his hands up in surrender.

'Did you say it?' he spat.

Lionel inched to the front of the stage, hands raised. 'Everyone here is committed. Aren't we, guys?' He turned to the rest of the cast. They responded with sullen nods and half shrugs. 'We want this to be a success as much as you do.'

Ravenswood folded his arms. 'I have plenty of better things to do with my time than waste my holidays on a bunch of ungrateful…' This time he saw the flaring nostrils and the tightness in their eyes.

He grimaced. He imagined calling Alan Wolf, explaining the show was off. His theatrical career was dead in the water, his big comeback was a write-off. He couldn't even manage to put on a school play. He'd be stuck here, teaching drama to self-centred teenagers until he retired, bitter and red-nosed like all the others.

Ravenswood slumped. 'Useless' should be tattooed across his forehead.

'Mr Ravenswood?' Lionel said, his forehead wrinkled.

Ravenswood realised he'd been standing there silently while his whole cast stared up at him. It was not as disastrous as last time.

'Should we get on with the rehearsal?' Lionel offered.

Ravenswood scowled. He'd have to keep an eye on this cocky kid.

But he cleared his throat and dredged up a smile. 'Right. Come up on stage everyone and let's warm up.'

The teenagers grumbled to their feet and joined him on stage.

There was hope.

VIOLET

Ravenswood tried to gloss over his pathetic little tantrum with a big fake smile. He was cracking at the seams; even his eyes were crinkling with fresh wrinkles.

Violet's stomach fluttered as she watched Angelika swan up onto the stage with her pretend innocent expression. Jez was one step behind her like a little lamb.

Had the candles burned down yet? How long did a spell take to work?

Wayne and Jason competed for who could jump the highest as they leaped onto the stage. Holly stuck close to Jacinta and eyed Violet sideways, but Violet took to the stage calmly. She was in a bubble. Their dirty looks couldn't touch her.

'In a circle, players,' Ravenswood said, and all thirteen cast members shuffled into position. 'For our warm-up today, we're going to play a little game.'

Lila tittered and the boys groaned.

'It's called Murder Winks. Everyone, close your eyes.'

Violet's fingertips were still tingling as she closed her eyes. She imagined what her life would be like if she had access to this power all the time.

'Good. I'm going to secretly squeeze one person's shoulder. They will be the murderer. When everyone opens their eyes and the aim of the game is to identify the murderer. If someone winks at you, you must die a dramatic death and you are out of the game. If you suspect someone is the murderer, call out their name but not after your death. If you correctly identify the murderer, you are the winner.'

Violet wished Ravenswood would touch her shoulder as his footsteps travelled around the circle.

'Open your eyes,' he said.

Violet blinked with a little humpf of disappointment.

'Ok, let's begin.'

The cast eyed each other around the circle, lips and eyebrows pressed together. Violet glanced at each person sequentially. If she couldn't be the murderer, winning would be second best.

Jez moaned loudly and dropped to the ground, clutching at his chest.

Wayne and Jason sniggered and Violet narrowed her eyes.

Jacinta swooned like a silent film star, gasping with her hand against her forehead.

Then Wayne made exploding hand gestures as if blood squirted from his body.

Violet licked her lips. Only nine remained.

'Any guesses?' Ravenswood asked as he crept around the outside of the circle.

'Lionel?' Lila shrugged.

Lionel lunged forward with a groan, miming his intestines unravelling onto the floor.

Jason went down, then Kon and the minor cast boys until Violet, Lila, Angelika and Holly were standing.

'Ok, ladies. Who is the killer among you?' Ravenswood said as the four girls glared at each other.

'Violet?' said Holly with a frown.

Violet smirked with hands on hips, but before she could shake her head, Holly dropped to the ground with a shudder, her body convulsing.

Then there were three.

Violet sized up her best friend and her greatest enemy. Lila or Angelika? Lila's eyes darted skittishly while Angelika was more casual, but all three girls flitted back and forth, waiting for the wink.

Violet opened her mouth to name Angelika as the murderer but she was distracted by a wheezing sound. She narrowed her eyes as she glanced all around.

'Heads,' Holly cried from her spot lying on the stage floor.

Violet looked up.

A scenery set piece was hurtling towards the ground.

The wooden frame thundered onto the stage with a crash. Angelika gasped. Jacinta screamed. A third person howled in pain and this time it was a male voice.

'Jez!'

The scenery flat divided Violet from the rest of the cast. She was alone at the front of the stage except for Jez. Violet heard Ravenswood's voice from the other side. 'Jacinta, go to my office and call an ambulance,' he ordered. Footsteps rushed towards the door.

Jez was lying face down and motionless. The forest scene with its wooden baton rested on the back of his neck, hiding the rest of his body while his floppy hair spilled over the black painted stage. One hand was outstretched, the wrist with his familiar brown leather band was bent at a sickening angle.

'No. Not Jez. Not him.' Violet struggled to breathe as she stared at his lifeless body. It wasn't her fault. It wasn't. She wrapped her arms around herself.

Violet had replayed their night in the park a million times inside her head. He'd listened, he'd laughed at her silly jokes, he understood her. They were perfect. But as the weeks passed, the memories were fading and now she couldn't even remember half the things he'd said.

She stared down at him. She knew he didn't want her. No matter how hard she tried to recreate their special night, he wasn't interested. The truth ached. He'd wrenched her heart from her chest and tossed it in the bin, but she never wanted him dead. The candle magic wasn't meant for him.

Jez can't be dead. He can't.

Toby sprinted down the theatrette aisle and into the wings. He tugged at the ropes and hoisted the scenery piece slowly back up into the ceiling. As soon as the set lifted off the ground, the rest of the cast scrambled over to Violet's side of the stage.

Holly charged towards Jez. 'I know First Aid.'

Ravenswood kneeled over Jez with Holly.

Violet was nailed to the spot, her thoughts gripping her by the throat.

'Jez? Jez?' Holly pushed aside his hair and placed her fingers on his cheek.

He whimpered like a frightened child and rolled onto his side.

'Careful,' said Holly gently.

Blood oozed from a gash on his forehead and a dark wet patch coated the stage floor where his head had been.

'He's not dead?' Violet spluttered, her hand pressed to her heart.

'Is everyone else okay?' Ravenswood said.

The others mumbled and nodded.

'Toby,' Ravenswood sighed. 'What the hell happened?'

'I checked them three times,' Toby said, his voice wobbling slightly. 'I don't understand.'

'Well, you obviously made a mistake.'

Violet lurched towards Jez but Jason blocked her path.

'I want to help,' she croaked.

'He doesn't need *your* help. When will you get the message?'

She bit her lip to hide the tremor and looked around for Angelika whose face was creased with concern but there wasn't a hair out of place. Violet narrowed her eyes. Angelika should have been the one under that set. She should be the one bleeding.

A bell clanged over the PA system.

Violet covered her ears.

'What now?' Ravenswood yelled.

'Fire alarm, Mr Ravenswood,' Holly said.

'What? Now? This better not be a drill. Bloody maintenance men.' He sighed and shook his head. 'OK, everyone. Evacuate the building. Does anyone know where we're supposed to go?'

'That way,' said Holly pointing at the red exit sign. 'But what about Jez? We can't move him?'

Ravenswood wrung his hands.

'Mr Ravenswood?' Holly said, straightening up, hands on hips. 'What should we do?'

'I can—' Violet started.

'I'll stay with him,' Holly interrupted. 'I know what to do.'

Ravenswood nodded. 'Very well. Come on everyone. This way.'

Violet slumped as everyone ignored her. Again.

The cast and crew rushed out of the building through the heavy fire doors and along the footpath to the bus stop through the weak rain. Miss Quinlin and three bald blue overalled men followed.

The group huddled together under the protection of the bus shelter, shivering without their coats as the sirens drifted up the hill.

Lila glanced around furtively before she spoke. 'Did you do it?' she whispered to Violet. 'The candles?'

'No,' Violet spat and folded her arms tightly. Her spell had nothing to do with Jez. It must be a coincidence, a random accident, probably Toby's carelessness. There must be more to come for Angelika. 'I chickened out.'

Lila traced a faded yellow stripe of paint on the footpath with her toe.

'It's true,' Violet said.

'Blood spilled on the stage,' Lila said without glancing up from the ground. 'That can't be good. No one listens to me.'

Violet shoved her hands into her pockets and stared down at her boots.

It wasn't her. It wasn't.

VIOLET

As the paramedics stretchered the ashen-faced Jez into the back of the ambulance, Holly and Jacinta accosted Violet.

'How did you do it?' Jacinta spat.

'It wasn't me,' Violet protested.

Three fire trucks were parked nearby, their red and blue lights flashing in the grey morning.

'Why Violet? After what happened yesterday.' Holly sighed. 'Jez. Of all people.'

'Was Toby in on it with you?' Jacinta shook her head. 'Did you get your new boyfriend to do your dirty work? I know Jez stuffed you around, but come on.'

'He could've died. Or ended up in a wheelchair,' Holly said. 'Is that what you want? I thought you liked him.'

'I thought you were supposed to be my friend,' Violet snapped.

'I am. I want you to get—'

'Some friend,' Violet scoffed. 'It's obviously an accident. But you want to put the blame on me. Change the record. It's getting old.'

'Can't you see?' Holly said. 'You're not yourself.'

'Why won't you leave me alone?' Violet retorted.

'You need help,' Holly said sadly. 'I talked to someone last night—'

Violet's face burned red. 'How many times do I have to say it? I had nothing to do with this. Did I, Lila?'

Lila nodded, but her eyes stayed on the ground.

Jacinta snorted.

'What? Why are you all blaming me?' Violet said. 'Maybe it's Lila's curse.'

'You're the curse.' Jacinta narrowed her eyes.

'I talked to Dahlia last night,' Holly declared.

Violet's mouth was bone dry. What did Dahlia say? Had Anthea kept their little secret?

Three helmeted firemen in orange suits and heavy boots clumped out of the building and along the footpath to their truck.

'All clear,' called out one of the fireman. 'You can go back in.'

'What started it?' Miss Quinlin asked.

'We found wax from black candles in a classroom. Nothing serious, just a burn mark on the tabletop,' the wiry head fireman said. 'At least you know your alarms are working well.'

Miss Quinlin grimaced. 'Oh dear, what about the call out fee. You'll have to file a report, Mr Ravenswood.'

'No time now, Miss Quinlin. Just an accident I'm sure. Let's fill out the paperwork next week,' said Ravenswood.

'But Mr Ravenswood, we need to—' Miss Quinlin frowned.

Ravenswood waved her away. 'Come along, everyone. Back in the theatrette for notes.'

'Candles?' Lila's eyes were round and wet.

Heat rushed into Violet's cheeks. 'Don't you say a word,' Violet hissed.

'What candles?' Holly said, grabbed at Lila's arm. 'Tell me.'

Violet glared at Lila. 'Don't you dare.' She pushed past her and stomped away.

'Stop.' Lila clutched Violet's shoulder. 'Please.'

Violet's blood thumped in her ear drums. Her headache was back and hammering. They crowded around her, their faces twisted and disgusted.

'Piss off, Lila.' Violet slapped away Lila's outstretched hand. 'You're just like the rest of them.'

Lila paled, her lip trembled. 'But I... I only want to—'

Jacinta laughed in Violet's face. 'You really are a cow.'

'I would never…,' Lila said, between desperate gulps of air. 'You don't mean it.'

'I mean every word,' Violet said. She puffed her chest. 'I don't need you. You two-faced anorexic parasite. I'm better off on my own.'

Lila's lip trembled.

'You absolute bitch.' Holly spat as she placed an arm around Lila's shoulder.

Violet clutched her throat. The injustice was squeezing the air from her body. 'It wasn't me. Why won't anyone listen?'

'You're out of control. I'm going to get someone,' Holly said.

It wasn't her.

It wasn't her.

It *wasn't* her.

Was it?

She'd know, wouldn't she?

The world was closing in on Violet. The heavy grey sky over her head was stifling, crushing her into the ground.

Could Holly be right? Was she losing it?

Holly waved at the ponytailed woman in paramedic whites and Violet started running.

THE DARK HAND

I am jealousy

I am rage.

I am doubt.

I am ambition.

I am the voice in your ear telling you that you are worthless, useless and unlovable.

You know who I am now.

I place pictures in your head.

He's betraying you.

She's talking about you.

They're all laughing at you.
I whisper in your ear that you are better than all of them.
You deserve this.
They are wrong.
They're the evil ones who must be stopped.
Then I sit back and watch the fun.
I am always here, I always have been.
You have let me in.

CHAPTER 12

BRIDGET

THE CAFÉ WAS AN OBSTACLE COURSE OF PRAMS, LOUD WITH THE relieved chitchat of tired new mums and the hiss of frothing milk. A knitting group gathered in one corner, cooing over skeins of wool and completed projects. One grey-haired man sat awkwardly as the three women at his table ignored him and cackled in the way that only old friends do. In the far corner, Bridget and the leader sat at a table for three.

'Can I get you anything else?' The waitress with pink feathers in her hair and sequins pasted to her cheeks placed down a teapot and three mugs.

Bridget shrugged and smiled slyly. 'What's Dahlia been baking?'

'Some super delish ginger biscuits,' the waitress said. 'For solstice with lots of lovely rich spices. Totally nummy.'

'Three, please.' Bridget pretended not to notice the leader's scowl.

'Back in two ticks.' The waitress skipped away.

'Sorry.' Mathilde removed her raincoat and slipped into a chair. 'I can only spare a few minutes.'

The steely-haired leader nodded and lowered her voice despite the café's happy racket. 'There has been a concentration of strength.'

'I've felt the pulsing.' Mathilde wrinkled her brow. 'But it still felt nascent.'

The leader glanced around before continuing. 'It's further evolved. I feel the power of an ancient one, cold and hard like a winter storm. And the ancient one wasted no time in acting.'

Bridget gulped. This explained the dead weight in her belly.

The waitress brought three biscuits on a plate. 'Enjoy,' she beamed.

The three women waited until the waitress left. Bridget crunched into a biscuit. The others left theirs on the plate.

'And you kept this information to yourself?' Mathilde squinted.

'I thought it was an isolated incident. But it's escalating.' The leader pressed her lips until they were colourless.

Mathilde sighed. 'The school.'

'It's attracted to young people as usual.' The leader nodded.

'What do we do now?' Bridget said. She tried to hide the slight tremble in her hands as she poured the rooibos.

'We each know our part. It's time to put our practice into action.' The leader opened her hardback notebook. She ran her fingers over the page and read aloud. 'Prepare your stations. Memorise your verses.'

Bridget swallowed and nodded. Three times a week for six years, they'd practised. Once the meeting was over, she'd double check her kit near the spare tyre and under the picnic rug in the boot of her car. She must be vigilant, she might need to use it at any moment.

Bridget eyed the two biscuits remaining on the plate and clasped her hands together tightly until her fingertips flushed red with the pressure. She bit her lip. 'Can we handle this alone?'

The leader wrinkled her brow. 'Are you afraid?'

'We know what to do.' Mathilde firmly shook her head. 'We do not need to call in the other guilds.'

'Of course. Silly me.' She choked out a nervous laugh. 'It is just... this is my first—'

'Your skills will come into their own when the time arrives,' the leader said. 'But we must tell no one.'

'What if we sense others in sympathy to our cause?' Mathilde challenged. 'Outsiders.'

'Do I need to remind you? Others do not understand our intentions.'

'I always choose my words wisely,' Mathilde persisted. 'I feel allies nearby.'

'If you must. But be careful.'

'I will,' Mathilde replied.

The leader closed her book. 'Prepare yourselves. Be on guard. The moment is approaching and we do not know when. It could be within the next hour or possibly tonight or even tomorrow. But it is close and it is strong. We must trust ourselves and each other. Have faith. Our moment of trial is upon us.'

The café was stifling all of a sudden. Bridget reached for the remaining biscuits with a clammy hand. 'Have faith' she repeated to herself as she chewed.

'And stay close to a telephone.'

Bridget nodded.

Have faith.

Have faith.

RAVENSWOOD

Ravenswood shook his head. 'It's too warm.'

'The white one ripped. I had to replace it with this one.' Toby pushed the riser onto the lighting desk.

'I need something starker.' Ravenswood narrowed his eyes at Toby. 'That's a nasty wound you've got there. What happened?'

'Nothing. Just mucking around.' Toby flicked his hair over the scabby lesion on his temple and thumbed through the remaining cellophane squares in the gel box. 'I dunno if I've got anything like that. We've only got a few left.'

'Orange will never do,' Ravenswood said with a wave of his hand. 'This isn't a stupid musical with tap-dancing. Find something better.'

Toby curled his lip but he nodded. Ravenswood stood with a har-rumph and left the lighting box.

What else could go wrong? Ravenswood thought as he walked to-wards the stage. Ambulances, fire alarms and inept lighting. One runaway and Banquo in hospital with a suspected wrist fracture. What else could go wrong?

Jacinta and Kon loitered around the stage in costume, their faces plastered in thick layers of stage make-up.

'Now Kon. You're ready to take over?'

'I think so.' Kon broadened his chest and waved his script but he croaked as he spoke. Ravenswood winced.

'Excellent. Where's everyone else?' Ravenswood scanned the room.

'Getting ready.' Jacinta shrugged and inspected her nails. The thick stripes of black kohl magnified every movement of her eyes.

'We're running out of time.' Ravenswood threw his hands in the air and stormed out the door. His stomach was growling but he couldn't bear to eat. One more rehearsal: that's all they had time for. But there was so much to fix, besides the lighting. The kids needed more practice moving sets in and out and, half the cast was embarrassingly wooden. There was something niggling at him about Lady MacDuff's costume, too. And then there was croaky Kon as the new untested Banquo.

Ravenswood passed the stairs and crossed the corridor to the drama room where sheets suspended from the ceiling sectioned it off into changing areas. A three-metre clothes rack stuffed with costumes and empty wire hangers ran down the centre of the room. Giggling floated through the thin fabric partitions as boys changed into surcoats and tights, and girls into ankle-length shifts. Tables sat along the walls lined with mirrors where Wayne dabbed his face with a sponge and Lionel concentrated hard as he lined his eyes with kohl.

Ravenswood checked his watch again and then yelped.

'On stage in five minutes,' he announced and rushed out the door.

Alan Wolf hadn't called back to confirm for Friday.

Ravenswood broke into a run as he pushed through the double doors into the corridor. His heeled boots squeaked on the linoleum. He reached his office in a sheen of sweat and knocked over a half-empty coffee mug as he lunged for the telephone. He ignored the spreading brown stain and punched in the number he knew by heart. He cleared his throat, raised a smile and waited for Alan Wolf to pick up.

But the line was silent.

He tapped the switch and listened hard. Dead. No dial tone. He pressed the button again and again, but he heard nothing.

'Bloody hell.' He yanked the telephone line from the wall, spilling his officemate's neatly stored pencils all over her desk. He hurled the telephone across the room and grabbed his curly brown hair in clumps. 'Those damned maintenance men.'

Then he remembered he'd forgotten to speak with Booth about the maintenance works. He glanced up at the wall clock; another fifteen minutes had passed. It was almost lunchtime and not a single line of the play had been uttered.

Ravenswood rummaged inside his desk drawer, through the paper clips and chewed pen lids. He popped two Dispirin into a mug of cold coffee and watched the fizz as they dissolved.

He needed to have faith.

It'll be alright on the night. Alan Wolf would be there. The maintenance men must know the production is on. It would not turn out like last time.

Ravenswood glugged down the concoction with a grimace as the speakers in the corner crackled. The hairs on his arms twitched and his heart thumped.

The static turned into an eerie electric spluttering that buzzed under his skin. A cold murmur snaked up his spinal column. The spectral pops and hisses turned into a single word that repeated itself over and over in a whispered female voice.

'Useless. Useless.'

Ravenswood inhaled raggedly and glanced up, expecting to see a black coil of smoke emerge from the beige cloth covered speakers.

'Useless. Useless.'

He couldn't be dreaming. The voice sounded exactly like hers. He didn't care what Fiona said, or the coroner. He had never believed she was dead. Ravenswood tasted laundry soap, the scent left on his tongue after she scrubbed his mouth clean of sin.

'Useless. Useless.'

A musty stench wafted into the office and settled like a thick fog. Ravenswood gagged. He pinched his nostrils closed but he couldn't stop the stink of chicken manure seeping in.

'Why won't you leave me alone?' he cried as he threw his arms over his head and knocked over a stack of folders. Paper scattered everywhere as he thumped his forehead down on the desk.

He clamped his hands over his ears but it was pointless. Her words were etched into his skin; they travelled in his blood and lived in his bones.

'I'm sorry, Josie,' he whispered. 'I never listen. I'm sorry.'

~⊙~

VIOLET

Violet's head and chest pounded with every step she took along Beacon Hill Road. Ravenswood. Angelika. Holly and Jacinta. Lila. Jez. They could all go get stuffed: every single one of them.

The mist turned into sideways rain, and the gutters into rivers. Tears and rain spilled down Violet's cheeks.

They could do their pathetic little play without her.

The puddles quickly found the hole in her boot and her toes sloshed inside her soggy sock.

She was never going back.

Violet thrust out her hand as a bus appeared through the wet. She boarded through the side door and trudged up the aisle, which was slick with muddy footprints. The bus was empty, except for an old woman in a purple knitted hat and a boy with a wilted mohawk at the back. She slumped into a seat. Home was the only place left for her. She'd head straight to bed with the covers over her head. For ever.

'High school girl,' said a familiar voice from the driver's seat. 'Where are your friends today?'

Violet jolted and glared down the aisle. 'Where have you been?'

'I am here now.' The curly-headed bus driver looked up at her through into the rear vision mirror. 'How can I help?'

'It doesn't matter now. You were wrong.'

'Is that so?' She chuckled. 'You know everything, do you?'

Violet narrowed her eyes. 'I'm supposed to be the star but I didn't get the part. I knew you were full of crap.'

'Did I say who was who? Or did you fill in the blanks yourself?'

'But it was obvious—' Violet's stomach lurched.

'To whom?'

Violet felt a sharp craggy lump in her throat. If she wasn't the star, which one was she? She slouched and pressed her hands against her cheekbones.

'*To you, they have shown some truth,*' the bus driver said in a theatrical voice.

Violet squinted. 'You know Macbeth?'

The bus driver waved dismissively. Violet grabbed her bag and rushed into the seat directly behind her. She leaned into the aisle and strained to get a clear look at the woman's face.

'Who are you?' she said.

'I am no one special. I'm only a person who pays attention to my surroundings.' She shrugged. 'I see and hear the things most people ignore. Sometimes I see the truth.'

'Then you understand,' Violet sighed. 'Everything has gone wrong.'

'And why is this happening?'

'They're all against me.'

'Everyone?'

'He started it. Ravenswood,' Violet blurted. 'The part was mine.'

'Blame is not always a one-way street.'

'What are you saying?' Violet groaned. 'I should've known. You're just like the others.'

'Sometimes steam covers a mirror.'

'Steam? Streets? What are you talking about?' She slammed her fist against her thigh. 'This isn't the way it's supposed to be!'

'You haven't answered my question. According to whom?'

Violet swallowed and dropped her head. The answer was 'me' but she couldn't say the word. Her heart thudded.

Rain splattered against the windows and the wipers squealed against the glass, a hypnotic, squeak like a metronome.

'Fate has a curious justice.' The driver lowered her voice. 'You must look closer. Have you not heard the warnings?'

'What warnings?' Violet said and rubbed her forehead. 'I'm not hearing voices, if that's what you mean. I'm not crazy. How many times do I have to say it?'

'Things are not always as they seem. We try to pretend it doesn't exist but evil is as real as you and I. But you already know this. You feel it.'

Violet wiped her nose on her coat sleeve and gently bit her lip.

'Darkness is all around us. It waits for an open window, a chance to slip inside and take root. Just like a parasite. Even the most innocent of us can accidentally let her in.'

'You believe me?' Violet whispered. 'You know it wasn't me?'

But the bus driver didn't reply. She pulled the bus over to the stop in front of the Scout Hall and a wet-haired woman struggled onboard with a pram and a screeching toddler.

Violet stared at her own reflection in the clouded side window. After hours in front of the mirror, contorting and inspecting, she knew every millimetre of her face, but right now she was a stranger. She wanted to look away but she couldn't.

Her shoulders quivered as she tried to smother her sobs. Was she the one who'd invited darkness into her heart? Or was her heart dark to begin with? Bile rushed up the back of her throat as she remembered all the horrible things she'd said and done.

'I've wrecked it all,' she croaked. 'There's nothing left.'

'Isn't there?' The bus driver said.

Violet threaded her fingers through her hair. Her head was filled with the past few days: Lila's tear stained face, Holly's pleas, Jez lying lifeless, Rowan's frightened eyes, the blood-stained script. The images circled in her head. She crumpled into the seat. She was no better than the screwed-up soggy newspaper on the muddy floor. And it was all her own fault.

Perhaps she would be the one to disappear forever. After the way she'd behaved, she'd be doing the world a favour. There was a perfect spot on the bluff.

'You must be wary,' the driver cautioned. 'The darkness is strong and it delights in causing confusion. But you have courage. Listen to yourself.'

Violet straightened and frowned. As the bus travelled down Beacon Hill Road, piece by piece, the strange words began to make sense. Violet lifted her chin. For the first time since seeing the cast list, the stone in her belly was gone. She gulped in greedy lungfuls of air and the mist in her head lifted.

The bus pulled over.

'Last stop,' the bus driver said but Violet didn't move. 'Isn't this your stop?'

'It's okay,' Violet replied. 'I'm going back to school.'

There was still time.

JACINTA
Last Night

It began subtly.

Jacinta rolled over with a grunt and tucked her toes back under the warmth of the doona. She drifted off and ignored the scraping sound. It was only the slap of branches against the window.

Something tugged at her covers and she tore her eyes open. She lifted her head and scoured the room. A sliver of light poked through a gap in the ruffled curtains. Jacinta chewed her lip but nothing seemed out of place: her white painted bed, her white desk, the white bookshelf, her tan loafers on the floor, the poster of Luke Perry inside the wardrobe door.

Except for one thing.

There was a gap on the top shelf next to the floral-covered tissue box.

She gasped. She slapped her own cheek to check she was really awake. Maybe Mum moved it, finally, after all her years of complaining. Or even better, she'd smashed it accidentally when dusting.

'Jacinta,' breathed a voice.

Her heart stopped cold in her chest.

She pulled the covers over her head. She must be dreaming. She must be.

'Jacinta,' said the voice again.

Mocking. Playful.

Jacinta stared at the dark inside of her doona. She shivered despite the warmth and clenched her fists against her chest as she glanced left and right.

The voice seemed to be right next to her ear.

She flinched as a weight too light to be Frankie dropped on top of her covers. It moved slowly, a lump crawling towards her head.

'Jacinta,' the singsong voice said, teasingly. It was a female voice, a voice she'd never heard before.

It wasn't her mother. Mum thought practical jokes were puerile.

The thing had appeared on her bedroom shelf one day after Mum had been to the Antiques Fair again.

'I simply had to have her,' Mum had said. 'She goes perfectly with your room.'

'I'm too old for dolls, Mum.'

Her mother had patted her hand. 'It's not for playing with, honey. I always wanted a doll like this. But Opa could never afford to waste money on toys.'

Jacinta would have preferred a CD player but she bit her lip. She knew how to pick her battles. The baby doll had three faces; sleeping, crying and worst of all, laughing. The way its head swivelled and changed reminded Jacinta of horror films.

'Isn't she lovely?' Her mother smoothed down the lace dress. 'Look at the craftsmanship. And it's in such excellent condition, not a scratch on the porcelain. I've named her Nelly.'

'Jacinta,' the voice mocked

This time, the words were followed by the familiar jerky "waah-waah" from the noise maker inside Nelly's chest.

Jacinta gulped.

The doll's sleeping face was the only one Jacinta could cope with. Its innocent closed eyes were the least creepy. But last week, she'd come home from school and Nelly's crying face was facing forward. Jacinta had said nothing to her mother. There was probably some boring explanation: equal sunlight on each face or something. But Jacinta had immediately switched the face back to sleeping. She didn't want to spend another moment in her bedroom alone with anything but the sleeping-faced Nelly.

The thing scampered right over her head.

'Waah-waah.'

Little fingers grabbed the edges of the doona.

'Waah-waah.'

'No,' Jacinta said and clamped her covers tight around her.

'Jacinta,' whispered the sing-song voice, so clear, it could have been coming from inside her own head. 'Where are you?'

'No.' She curled into a ball and tensed her jaw hard.

The doona flew out of her clenched hands and landed on the carpet.

Jacinta struck out blindly with her fists and feet but there was nothing there.

'Jacinta.'

The voice came from above.

Jacinta looked up and her throat clamped shut. Nelly was on the ceiling, her laughing face staring straight back down at her.

'Jacinta,' the doll's manic face said.

The baby doll crawled along the ceiling and down the wall behind her bedhead. Jacinta stared wide-eyed as she clutched her knees to her chest. All she could do was watch. Nelly slipped down onto the bedhead, crying out 'waah-waah' as she hit the pillows.

'What do you want?' Jacinta choked out.

'Jacinta.'

'Shut up.' She covered her ears.

The doll stopped right in front of her.

Jacinta wheezed.

Nelly's head spun around to the crying face, her red mouth was twisted and a glistening tear ran down her cheek.

'I'm not the only one with more than one face,' Nelly said.

The doll crept forward.

Jacinta woke to the sound of knocking on her door.

'Yeah, Mum,' Jacinta mumbled and writhed, sweaty under her pyjamas. She swallowed hard and glanced over to the shelf.

Nelly was there in her usual place.

But her head face was turned to the laughing face.

Dear Journal

Today when I walked along the corridors, the walls sang along with me, welcoming me. This will be the place for my grand entrance, a place with power and fear in the foundations, blood in the mortar. It has been waiting for my arrival. From its first settlement, this place was a beacon and now it is a beacon for my power. Our power. Oh, how ticklish and tasty it is.

They tried to block off the source but they are weak.

I'm laughing because they still treat me the same. Wrapped up in their own little dramas, they're blind to the transformation unfolding under their noses.

Now I know everything. I see everything.

I can do whatever I please. I am in complete control. I can make them weep or cower or do anything I want. They will fear and follow me.

I will show them all.

But I'm not alone. There are others who understand.

She is like me. She is one of us.

Once I give her this treat, prove my loyalty, my love, she'll see the possibilities and join us. I know she will.

Then we can be together forever. The way it should be.

This is only the beginning.

VIOLET

Violet threw back her shoulders and flung open the theatrette door. Ravenswood, his paisley shirt undone at the neck, paced up and down the stage, his hands tugging at his shoulder-length curls.

'What about this?' Toby shouted down from the top of a ladder.

'Still too orange. It needs to be depressing. Like a moor. Grey. Grey. Grey. Like outside.'

Metal clanged against metal as Wayne and Jason lunged and parried down the centre aisle. 'Cop that, MacDuff. Me lord.'

'Anyone got a needle and thread?' Jacinta rushed across the stage, clutching her costume, which was ripped from ankle to mid-thigh.

'Why aren't you in costume?' Ravenswood snapped at Violet. 'Hurry up. We're starting in one minute.'

Violet skulked away to the drama room. But the classroom, now communal dressing room, was just as bad. A shirtless Lionel darted out from behind the curtains. Wayne and Jason jostled for a spot in front of the mirrors.

Holly sat smearing green face paint on her forehead, a straggly black wig perched on her head.

'Looking good,' Violet said with a smile.

Holly glared back at her in the mirror.

Violet swallowed and pulled at her collar. 'At least there's no warts.'

Holly stood up and left Violet to stare at her own reflection in the mirror. She slumped into the empty chair and picked up a clean square of sponge. She pressed her lips together as she coated her face in green. It would take time to heal the damage.

Ravenswood fussed into the room. 'On stage in one minute, play-ers.' He frowned as he looked about. 'Where's Angelika? How does her costume look?'

'I saw her before,' said Holly, her voice helpful again. 'I think she's in the loo. Nerves.'

Ravenswood nodded. 'Lionel?'

Lionel smoothed his hair in the full-length mirror. 'Ready to go, Mr Ravenswood.' His voice was as calm as a pond.

Violet ran through her lines in her head as she finished her make-up and carefully avoided the other cast members' dirty looks. True talent could transcend any bit part. Despite everything she'd said, she would go on stage as First Witch and give the best possible performance. Alan Wolf was a professional, and infinitely more perceptive than Ravenswood. He'd be able to spot talent anywhere on the stage.

But there was one thing Violet needed to do first.

Apologise.

She scoured the room for Lila, but she couldn't see her skinny friend anywhere. Maybe she was behind one of the curtains or in the toilets? If anyone would be sick with nerves, it would be Lila.

'Come on, players,' Ravenswood said through gritted teeth as he clapped his hands. He rushed out of the room again.

With make-up done, Violet headed behind the change room curtain, unbuttoned her flannelette shirt and jeans, and stepped into her costume, which was basically a black sack. It was a far cry from Anthea's punk witch leather and studs, but at least she didn't have to hold in her stomach.

Violet flinched when glimpsing her reflection in the full-length mirror. The green-faced classroom witch stared back, eyes simmering with ill intent. She squinted and chewed on her lip. She was forgetting something. It was on the tip of her tongue, like an invisible prickle in her foot she couldn't find.

Violet shivered in the thin cotton sack dress. She wrapped the black scarf she'd found in her backpack around her neck and tugged on her tatty wig and checked herself in the mirror.

'It's showtime,' she said.

THE DARK HAND

Everything is in place.
    The curtain is up.
    The audience is quiet.
    Anticipation is swelling.
    I step out of the wings onto centre stage.
    Into the spotlight.
    For my soliloquy.
    It's time.
    Are you ready?
    Good.
    Let's get on with the show.

CHAPTER 13

ANGELIKA

ANGELIKA SQUINTED AS THE STRIPS OF FLUORESCENT LIGHTS overhead pulsed on and off. Shadows danced on both sides of the corridor. Footsteps and giggles drifted from around the corner as she walked up the stairs.

The door slammed quickly behind her when she went into the girls' toilets. Her hand grabbed at her throat. But then she burst out laughing at herself. Nerves were natural. Logical.

Angelika stopped by the mirrors. She was ready in her mask of make-up and ankle length dress. The script was engraved in her brain. Mostly. She was no longer Angelika Ostholz of Beacon Hill, she was Lady Macbeth.

As Angelika smoothed her hair, she noticed a crack in the top right corner of the mirror. The black backing was like a tiny bruise on a piece of fruit. She sucked in a breath but the blood in her bathroom had been only a dream. In the daylight, the vanity and tiles were as spotless as usual, and the mirror perfectly intact.

Didn't they say cheese before bed caused nightmares? Perhaps the play had wormed its way into her subconscious. All that superstitious nonsense rotting her brain. *Blood will have blood.* She didn't mention the dream to her mother. There was nothing worse than being psychoanalysed over cornflakes.

Angelika inspected the broken corner of the mirror. There was nothing sinister behind the crack. All three cubicle doors were open but the hairs on the back of her neck still bristled. Angelika shook her head, she took the first cubicle and locked the door.

Thankful for the peace and quiet of the toilet, she silently recited her opening speech and the knot in her stomach unravelled. She had this.

Tomorrow night was her all-important opening move. She'd dazzle that professor from the university. He'd track her down after the performance, and they'd talk. He'd be ever so keen to help. He'd recommend someone on the mainland, someone even more influential. She could be off this crummy island in weeks.

Outside the cubicle, a tap turned on and water gushed into the sink. Angelika frowned. She hadn't heard the door open.

She tensed as something slithered across the floor to her right. Was it a mouse? A cockroach? But it was too cold for cockroaches in Tasmania. Angelika scrutinised the shadows on the linoleum floor cast by the partitions. She waited perfectly still. Minutes ticked by and nothing else happened.

With a long exhale, she returned to her lines.

Again, something flickered in the corner of the cubicle. Angelika gasped and turned her head, her heart galloping. This time she saw the shadow move. It elongated, like black fingers grasping for her. She hoisted her feet off the floor and hugged her knees to her chest. Her eyes widened as a thickening dark wave crept towards her.

The main door to the toilets crashed open.

Angelika flinched.

The door slammed closed, and then open, over and over, like a screen door in the wind.

She clutched at the neck of her tunic. There was no way a breeze could get inside the building. She rolled her eyes.

'You know you're not supposed to be in here,' she growled. 'It's not funny, you losers.' She unlocked the toilet door and stepped out.

But there was no one was there.

'Wayne? Jason?'

The entry door stopped slamming but the tap was still running. Water overflowed onto the floor. Angelika lunged forward and switched off the tap. She glanced around. She was alone. Shadows were just shadows.

'Get a grip, Ostholz,' she muttered as she washed her hands, her cheeks burning despite the cold. If only she could splash water on her face but she needed to be onstage in a minute. She dribbled water down the back of her neck instead and bowed her head as the chilly stream cooled her skin and nerves.

The final rehearsal would be starting any moment now.

Angelika straightened and took a final glance in the mirror. She jumped at the black silhouette in the stall behind her.

'Stop messing around,' she said, her eyes narrowed. 'I can see you.'

The shadowy figure darkened, turning blacker than any other shadow in the room. Her Angelika's stomach clenched. This time it wasn't stage fright.

'Stop it. I can see you.'

The black shape edged towards her.

The fluorescent lights flickered.

Angelika clutched the side of the bench until her knuckles were white and watched the encroaching darkness through the mirror. She was unable to turn around and face it.

'This isn't funny,' she stuttered.

The figure, a person, stepped into the light.

Angelika gasped, her breaths fast and raspy. In the mirror, eyes of pure hate glared back at her, a face glowing with evil.

Angelika grasped at her tight chest.

'You?' she spluttered.

She desperately wanted to run. Get out of here. Through the doors. But her legs were like concrete beams, fixed into the floor.

Run. Her mind screamed.

Now.

But it was too late.

She felt the crack on the back of her skull.

A hot blast of pain.

Then darkness.

VIOLET

As the cast rolled into the theatrette, the nervous energy of the drama room died, replaced by quiet fidgeting and the sound of scripts crumpled in clenched fists. Violet was up on stage, all ready to begin Act One. She'd set the tone for the whole production. She'd give the audience, and Alan Wolf, an unforgettable beginning.

'Deep breaths, everyone,' Ravenswood said as he paced in the gap between the stage and the front row. 'Put all this morning's disruptions behind you. Focus. Think of your lines, your character, your fellow actors. Remember, use your scripts if you run into any problems. I prefer if you didn't use them, of course, but our time has been very short and the dialogue is complex.'

'Too right,' mumbled Wayne.

'Are there any questions before we start?'

'Where's Angelika?' Jacinta said.

Violet shielded her eyes against the stage lights and stared into the audience where the rest of the cast sat.

'Doing her hair?' Jason groaned.

'She wasn't in the girls' toilet,' said Jacinta. 'I was just in there.'

Ravenswood sighed. 'Go check again, please.'

As the side door closed behind Jacinta, the theatrette lights went out. The room plunged into absolute darkness, as black as a cave. Holly squealed. Ravenswood gasped.

Violet could see nothing but a thick inky darkness in front of her face.

'Toby, what are you doing?' Ravenswood yelled. 'Don't move. Anyone. Or you might fall. I can't lose any more of you.'

'It's not me, Mr Ravenswood,' Toby yelled down from the lighting box. 'I think it's a power outage.'

'Great,' Ravenswood muttered to himself. But as he mumbled, the lights flickered back on and the stage was bathed in the grey muted light of the moors.

Violet blinked and Ravenswood sighed. 'Places, everyone. Curtain down, Toby.'

The red curtain started to descend and Violet took her position next to Holly mid-stage.

'Something's happened to Angelika!' Jacinta yelled as she rushed through the main door from the corridor. 'There's no one in the toilet. Or in the drama room. But there's blood on the toilet floor.'

'Blood?' Ravenswood grabbed the back rest of the closest chair.

Jacinta spun around to the stage and pointed her finger at Violet. 'What have you done to her?'

Violet's hand flew to her throat. 'What are you talking about?'

'You've done something to her, haven't you?'

'I haven't done anything. I went for a walk.' Violet shook her head. This time she knew she was innocent for sure.

'Oh, Violet.' Holly sighed. Her face etched with pain as she stepped away from her. 'Tell us where she is.'

'We don't have time for this, girls.' Ravenswood frowned. 'If you know where she is, please speak up, Violet.'

'Yeah, Vile-ette,' said Jason.

'She wants to take the limelight for herself,' Jacinta said, hands on hips.

'Why is everyone looking at me?' Violet said, her cheeks flushing under the green make-up. 'I've done nothing.'

Violet looked around the theatrette for support but a sea of accusing faces stared back. And there was another face missing besides Angelika.

'Where's Lila?' Violet asked. 'She should be here.'

'I saw her by the vending machine,' Wayne said in his thunderous voice. 'But that was ages ago.'

'Leave her alone,' Holly said. 'You know how fragile she is.'

'Have you done something with her, too?' Jacinta said. 'Are you some kind of serial killer?'

'I would never—' Violet wrung her hands. She turned to Holly, her eyes round and pleading. 'I wouldn't hurt her. I wouldn't hurt anyone.'

'Liar,' said Jacinta. 'Tell them, Holly. Tell them what you told me.'

Violet gulped.

'She talked about poisoning Angelika, so she could step in at the last moment.' Holly cleared her throat. 'And she's been asking around about black magic.'

'Hear that? Black magic?' Jacinta said. 'She's been casting spells on us all.'

'You didn't,' Ravenswood gasped, his eyes glassy. 'Say it isn't true.'

Violet winced. Holly was telling the truth. Every word was a dagger in her gut.

'You caused the dreams,' murmured Wayne. 'It was you.'

'And now Lila's gone,' Holly said. 'Tell us where they are. Please.'

'It wasn't me,' Violet said but her voice trembled. The walls closed in on her. She swallowed. 'Yes, I wanted the role. Yes, I felt betrayed. But it's this is nothing to do with me. I said some silly things, okay. And, I burned some candles. But there's something else going on here. Can't you feel it? Holly, remember what the bus driver said?'

Holly pursed her lips and then nodded hesitantly.

'I've had nightmares, too, and felt the shadows following me. And what about all the accidents? You don't think I could do all of it, do you? How? Maybe Lila was right all along and the play is cursed. All I know is it wasn't me.'

'Why should we believe you now?' spat Jacinta.

'Yeah, where's Angelika?' said Jason.

'I don't know.' Violet held up her hands.

'And Lila?' Holly asked. She lunged forward and grabbed the black scarf around Violet's neck. 'Where did you get this?'

'I found it.' Violet shrugged.

'Isn't it Rowan's?' Holly recoiled. 'Mr Ravenswood, you have to call the police.'

'It's just a black scarf.'

'I agree with Holly. Call the police,' Jacinta insisted.

'I don't know what you're talking about,' Violet said in a weak voice. 'Any of it. It wasn't me, none of it.'

The others glared back with hate in their eyes. Even Ravenswood was speechless, his hand clutched at his throat.

But this time Violet heard what the others heard: her own thin excuses. She opened her mouth to apologise but it was pointless. The time for talking was over.

'Fine. Don't believe me,' Violet said and straightened her shoulders. 'I'll find them. Both of them. I'll show you. You'll see I'm not responsible.'

She marched off the stage and pushed through the door into the corridor.

But at that moment, the theatrette went pitch black again.

VIOLET

'What the bloody hell's going on?' Violet muttered at the ceiling as the lights surged and flickered along the corridor. A chill slithered between her shoulder blades as unearthly sounds whistled through the speakers.

Was that a voice? Or just garbled static?

The intermittent darkness wasn't going to stop her. She'd walked this path every single day for five years. She knew the exact number of steps to the toilets.

'Lila?' she said, her hands trembling as she pushed open the toilet doors. She swallowed hard and stepped over the puddles on the linoleum.

She checked behind her but all three cubicle doors were wide open and unoccupied.

Violet's stomach sank when she saw a trail of red on the white sink. She reached out to touched it and stained her finger with blood. It looked and smelled real. But who's blood was it? Angelika's? Or Lila's?

One of you will disappear never to return.

Violet chewed her lip. There was another question. If it wasn't her, then who was responsible? She glanced up and flinched again at the sight of her green face in the mirror. But the gnawing feeling returned. She was forgetting something important.

The air shifted behind her. She spun around. The cubicles were dark and empty but her instincts screamed there was something in the shadows.

'Who's there?' she whispered.

No one replied.

Thrusting out her chest, Violet stepped forward. She checked the first cubicle and then the second. There was nothing there. Her heart thumped like a kick drum.

She stood in front of the third cubicle and gulped.

But it was also empty.

Violet exhaled and stumbled back against the sinks. Her mind was playing tricks on her. There was no one there. Now. But they had been here, and someone got hurt. But where did they go?

She left the toilets for the quiet corridor. She paused at the door and looked left and right.

Something hissed above her head. Violet stared up. It was the same sound she and Lila heard yesterday. It must be the pipes wheezing in the cold weather again.

But the hiss turned into a wail. Hot water rushing through pipes didn't make that noise. It must be the wind moaning through the trees. Was there a storm forecast on the radio this morning?

Violet stayed perfectly still and listened intently, but her knees quivered.

Whatever it was scratched and howled overhead. It wasn't creaking pipes or a strong wind. It was a person in pain.

Lila?

Violet clenched her fists to stop them trembling. She wanted to run in the opposite direction, but her mind overpowered her desire to flee.

'Lila?' she called down the corridor. 'Where are you?'

No one answered.

Violet followed the noise.

HOLLY

The lights flashed back on inside the theatrette. Holly blinked but Violet was gone.

'You have to do something, Mr Ravenswood,' Holly said, her nails biting into her palms.

'Sometimes we say things we don't mean,' Ravenswood said as he took off his glasses and squeezed the bridge of his nose.

'She's unstable!'

'We don't have time for this. You and Violet need to sort out your differences and make up.'

'Two people are missing!' Holly snapped. 'Three if you include Rowan. I'm sure that was her scarf she was wearing.'

'And she's gone to look for them. I just need everyone here. Right now. We're running out of time.' Mr Ravenswood turned and marched up the aisle towards the lighting box. 'Toby, show me the gel for the Banquo ghost scene again.? The rest of you, make yourselves useful and practice your lines. But don't leave the theatre.'

'Do I have to do everything myself?' Holly threw her hands in the air. She ran off stage, through the door and back into the drama room.

Head pounding, she grabbed her backpack and rummaged inside. She pulled out the paper bag, unfolded the handwritten note inside and read Dahlia's instructions.

As I wind, I forever bind.

She crumpled the note in her fist and shoved it back in the bag.

Yanking the mangy wig from her head, Holly sighed and combed her fingers through her own hair. Ravenswood didn't seem to care and Angelika's mother could only listen and nod. Did anyone know what they were doing?

Dahlia's solution was the last resort.

Holly squeezed her eyes shut. Think. But all her strength was draining from her body.

The floor melted away until Holly was free-falling. Her mind was half on her conversation with her mum the night before. Everything was changing. Her mum said she always thought Holly wanted to get away, that she should be happy. But now that the moment had arrived why did Holly feel so uncertain?

Holly blinked and sighed, her focus back in the classroom. People were in danger. Why wasn't someone doing something? Was she the only one who cared? Did she have any other option?

She reached inside her bag again and pulled out the spool of black ribbon and two candles, one black, one white. Her skull was tight, her brain throbbed against the bone. She had promised herself she would never do this.

Would she do more harm than good?

~୭୦~

RAVENSWOOD

'Holly!' Ravenswood called after her but she was already gone. 'No one else leave the room!'

Ravenswood pinched the bridge of his nose and checked his watch. He'd give them another five minutes. Four girls gone AWOL and the electricity on the blink.

He clenched his jaw. He couldn't crumble, he wouldn't. This time it would be different. All his doubters would eat their words, for once and for all. Even her.

Ravenswood flinched as the stage lights dimmed but he exhaled when he remembered. 'Too warm, Toby,' he shouted. 'It's supposed to be scary!'

'But that's the one you wanted yesterday,' Toby said over the speakers.

'No. It can't be. It's completely wrong.'

Swords in hand, Wayne and Jason bounded across the small stage, the wooden flooring flexing under their weight. In his best Errol Flynn, Wayne lunged forward grinning, but Jason deflected his blow with a cackle. Ravenswood sat and rubbed his forehead. He had never understood the fun in rough-housing. His head thumped as he tried to sort through the mess in his head. Did he eat the vegemite toast he made this morning, or did he leave it on the bench?

'How about that?' Ravenswood flinched as Toby's voice burst over the speaker. 'Spooky enough for you?'

Ravenswood squinted at the backdrop, which was bathed in the dim grey half-light of dusk.

'It'll have to do,' Ravenswood said as he slumped. 'Where are those girls?'

'*Ow.*' Wayne doubled over, clutching at his waist. 'You bastard.'

'You were too slow. You alright, mate?'

Wayne grunted, his face twisted. 'I'm fine,' he wheezed.

Ravenswood glanced over at the boys. Wayne leaned back and inspected a little red stain on his pale blue surcoat.

'Crap,' Wayne said. He spat on his fingers and rubbed the stain, which made it worse.

Ravenswood stared open mouthed. He'd been too distracted by the lighting and his throbbing head to notice why their sword practice had been so much louder than before.

'Idiots!' Ravenswood shouted. 'How did you get those?'

'Mr Neilsen said it was alright,' Jason said, biting on his lip.

'We thought it'd be more authentic,' Wayne mumbled.

'And dangerous. You could have killed him!' Ravenswood ran down to the stage. 'Are you alright?'

Wayne nodded, his face pale. 'It's just a scratch.'

'He didn't move like he should have,' Jason stuttered. 'And then the light changed.'

'You came too close,' Wayne said.

'Don't blame me!' Jason roared.

'Someone get the first aid kit,' Ravenswood bellowed. 'At this rate, I'm going to have to play every role myself. Hand them over.'

'Maybe Lila was right about the play being cursed,' Jason said quietly as he passed his sword to Ravenswood. The dim light rippled over the engraved hilt.

Jason wasn't alone. Ravenswood was beginning to wonder himself. Or was he the one carrying the curse?

ANGELIKA

Angelika traced her fat bottom lip with her tongue. She tasted blood in a crevice in the split skin. She writhed again, grunting and squirming until her arms burned. Her wrists rubbed raw against the restraints.

With a sigh, she slumped back against the pole. Everything seemed so hazy and the sledgehammer inside her head didn't help.

Angelika squinted into the shadows. The floor was concrete. The only light source came from behind her. The place was quiet except for the sound of dripping water, but there was no sign of them. *Know your enemy* was Sun Tzu's number one rule. If you didn't know who you were facing, there was little chance of victory. Angelika thought she saw a face she knew but it couldn't possibly be true. A blow to the head was never conducive to clear thinking.

She glared. A cold hard stare was her only weapon. 'Why are you doing this?' she said, but her defiance came out as a croak.

Laughter bounced around the room, sarcastic and malicious. Angelika gritted her teeth. She squirmed one way then another, but she barely moved and the restraints chafed off another layer of skin.

'Save your energy.'

'Let me go,' she whined.

It made no sense but her bindings felt stronger than just rope, as though she was trapped by something impossible and frightening. She was a fly in someone's web. Her forehead burned but her feet were like ice. This couldn't be happening. A lump hardened in her throat but she swallowed it down. Tears were a declaration of defeat.

Was this another dream?

Angelika pressed her lips together. Get a grip, she muttered to herself. Surrender was not an option. As Sun Tzu said a good general was full of caution. She must watch and wait.

But Angelika couldn't stop her worrying. She licked her broken lip again and pictured her nose splattered across her face like an overripe tomato. Or her face ruined by a deep diagonal gash, her skin slashed from eye to chin, exactly like her dream. She cringed. How could she be so vain at a time like this?

'There's no point in fighting,' the voice sneered. 'Just give in.'

'Never,' Angelika wheezed.

Her attacker stepped from the shadows.

Angelika's mouth dropped open.

'It is you. I thought it was you… but how…?'

Cold eyes blinked back at her. 'Don't struggle. It ruins the meat.'

'I don't understand,' Angelika spluttered.

'Of course, you don't. You're not as clever as you think. I can see right through you. Just like all the others.'

'What do you want from me?' she demanded.

'You know.'

'I don't. Tell me. Then I can give you it to you want.'

Her laughter echoed off the walls. 'You have it all mapped out, don't you?'

Angelika frowned. 'What happened to you?'

'You could say I found my true power.' Her eyes glinted like sharp knives. Her lips curled as she bared her teeth.

Angelika suppressed a whimper. She thrashed at the rope as she scrambled for solutions, scouring through the words of Sun Tzu, the strategies of the Grandmasters, anything and everything inside her head for a solution. Her mind floundered, she couldn't think past the pain. Her powers of persuasion never worked well with women, anyway.

'You're not so different to me. I can smell your craving. Your ambition. Your greed. If this had been another time, another place, we could've had such fun together. But not today.'

Angelika's body drooped, her limbs were heavy with fatigue. The facts hit her harder than the blow to the head. All her pride and indignation leaked onto the floor, overtaken by the surge of a cold panic through her veins.

'Help,' she moaned weakly. 'Help me.'

'Good girl. You're learning.'

She dropped her head. She couldn't stop the tears leaking through her eyelashes. Her body shook with silent sobs.

Tears, mixed with blood, dripped onto her Lady Macbeth costume.

CHAPTER 14

VIOLET

B ANG.

A door slammed up ahead. Violet flinched but straightened her back and headed towards the noise coming from somewhere up near Domestic science.

With her hands on the double doors, she noticed something to her left: a trail of blood splattered across the freshly painted wall. Violet gasped but continued on. She was going in the right direction.

The lights fizzed above her head and her heart pounded with every boot step. The next section of corridor was unlit: not even a speck of light came from the kitchens or sewing rooms. Violet cupped her hands against the glass panel in the door leading into the Domestic science classrooms and peered inside but couldn't see a thing.

Violet pressed her ear against the crack in the door, hoping to catch Lila's cheerful voice. Or even Angelika's. Maybe they'd run off together, full of nerves.

She scoffed at herself. Where did she pick up this optimistic streak? She puffed out her cheeks and exhaled, then grabbed the door handle, her stomach twisting. She pushed the handle down but the door was locked. She rattled the handle and pulled at the door but it only budged a smidgen.

Violet sprung back from the door, scouting in every direction when something thudded further down the corridor.

'Hello?' she squinted into the semi-darkness.

She flinched. A ceiling tile landed inches from her feet and shattered on the linoleum. Fine white dust exploded in a cloud. Violet jumped back as another tile fell. Then another. They were falling like square rain drops. She covered her head and ran down the dim corridor.

When she reached the doorway of the typing classroom halfway down the corridor, the tiles stopped falling and all was quiet again.

Violet leaned against the door to catch her breath and cooled her cheek against the glass panel. Behind the door, the room had windows into a central atrium. Weak daylight trickled over the rows of typewriters, like big grey snails covered in their plastic hoods. Rain slapped against the glass and shadows darted as winds lashed the trees.

Violet froze as a new sound wafted down the corridor. This was not a thud or a thump but a voice, wailing. It was not a voice she recognised. The shrill unearthly keening grated across her skin as it grew louder, then softer, undulating like a moaning wave. She wrapped her arms around herself. Was that the true sound of pain?

Her knees trembled as she imagined Lila behind the howls. She took a few shaky steps further down the corridor towards the sound. The art department was the next room on her right. A bolt of lightning snapped and a white slash lit up the corridor.

Violet peered through the glass in the classroom door. The desks were arranged around a central table and in the dim light she could make out a pinecone, a horned skull and a teddy bear among the random junk. And behind the table by the large windows, someone stood facing her.

Her heart stalled.

Thunder cracked the air.

Violet swallowed and squinted. The silhouette was tall, slim and female. Long hair tumbled over her shoulders, but her face was hidden in shadow.

'Angelika?'

Violet waved at her and pushed against the door but once again it was locked tight. She rapped on the glass but the figure didn't move.

'Are you locked in?' She knocked harder but still the figure remained motionless. Violet wiped her clammy hands against her witch costume. Why was she so still? And where was Lila?

'Angelika?'

Violet bashed her knuckles against the thick glass.

'Angelika! Are you alright?' she yelled but the figure seemed frozen in place. A hard mass glaring back at her. Violet sighed. After her behaviour this week, Violet wouldn't trust herself either.

'I know I was a bitch,' she said, and she wasn't acting this time. 'I'm sorry. And I want to help.'

There was no reaction at all. Like with Holly, it'd take more than a few words to repair the damage, but she had to keep trying.

'Really. I do. Is Lila with you?'

Again there was no reply. Violet's stomach churned. There was something unnatural about Angelika's absolute stillness.

'Are you alright?'

A second lightning bolt snapped lit up the art room and for a split second, Violet could see clearly inside.

She burst out laughing. Her shoulders shook as she leaned her forehead against the door and laughed. A few stray tears fell onto her cheeks. It was a wooden, bald life-sized mannequin with no facial features.

Violet slid all the way down to the linoleum and curled into a ball, her head rested on her knees. She swore she'd seen long hair. Once again, the shadows were playing tricks on her.

Her eyelids weighed a ton but she had to keep moving. She had to find them. She lay against the door and her pulse slowed. She needed to rest, regain her strength but only for a moment.

Thump. Scrape.

Thump. Scrape.

She forced her eyes open. The lightning storm was gone and the corridor was pitch black. Even the red exit sign was out.

Thump. Scrape.

Thump. Scrape.

It was coming her way.

Violet scrunched up as small as possible and pressed her body against the door. She was glad for the darkness now. She was in no hurry to meet whatever was behind the noise.

Thump. Scrape.

Thump. Scrape.

Out of the darkness, a tiny circle of light appeared.

She scuttled to her feet and assumed a starting position, all set to sprint away.

Thump. Scrape.

Thump. Scrape.

The light grew brighter and larger as it came towards her.

Violet's brain scrambled for an explanation. Could it be the maintenance men? One of the other cast members? Was it Lila and Angelika perfectly safe? But what could explain the thumping noise? She swallowed hard enough.

'Who's there?' she squawked.

'Is that you, Violet?'

Violet spluttered with relief as she recognised the long pink cardigan carrying a pencil-sized flashlight.

Quasimodo.

'Miss Quinlin,' she sighed.

'The lights appear to have gone out.' Miss Quinlin pushed up her spectacles up and snuffled as she thumped towards Violet. 'Must be the storm. The generator is down here somewhere. You alright?'

'Yes,' Violet lied. 'Just doing final rehearsals.'

'Ah, break a leg. We should have this power sorted before the curtain goes up. Where's that Booth fellow?'

She limped past Violet and continued down the corridor. A large wrench hanging from her other hand. Violet frowned as she watched the teacher walk away. Her feet tingled with pins and needles when she pulled herself upright. Maybe the science teacher wasn't as bumbling as she appeared.

What did the bus driver say?

Darkness could be anywhere.

HOLLY

Holly ran down the corridor and up the stairs three at a time. She passed the girls' toilets and pushed on the double doors towards Domestic science, but they were firmly shut.

'Come on,' she said with a grunt and shunted the door with all her bodyweight. 'Why are you locked?'

A red smear on the wall caught her eye. Was it blood? She swallowed.

Violet's expression had been so innocent when Holly confronted her. Did she even know what she was doing? Had she finally flipped like Holly feared? What had Dahlia said again? She asked whether it was still the same Violet.

Holly rubbed her forehead. Whatever the truth, there was no time to waste. She'd have to take the long way round. As the school was built in a square, there were always two ways to get anywhere.

Turning back, Holly ran down the stairs, past the toilets, the drama department and the theatrette towards the science labs. This route passed the main office, where she could stop off and use the phone to call the police or get Mr Booth and the weird maintenance men to help. Anyone'd be more helpful than Mr Ravenswood.

She skirted around the corner towards the main office as the lights dipped and plunged the corridor into complete darkness. She skidded to a halt and pressed herself against the cold wall as she waited for the power to return.

Thunder boomed outside and something else shook right above her head. Her heart jerked; she hoped it was the pipes.

The shaking stopped but a howling drifted down the corridor out of the darkness. Holly clutched a breath in her throat as she strained to hear clearly. The sound was barely more than a whisper at first, the pained voice was familiar yet unfamiliar.

It wasn't Lila. Maybe it was Angelika. Holly didn't know her well enough. An attack could have stripped away all of Angelika's composure. Whoever it was, their mewling sent shivers over her skin.

The cry intensified. It grew louder and louder, until she was forced to cover her ears. The sound seeped into the bones of her arms and legs, it rang in her skull. Holly wrapped her arms around her head but then the deafening wail faded away, and the corridor was quiet once again.

Breathing in, Holly steeled herself.

'I'm coming, Lila,' she called and then muttered. 'If only the lights would come back on.'

A set of strong fingers grabbed her shoulder from behind, but Holly shrugged them off and ran.

RAVENSWOOD

'Where are they?' Ravenswood stomped up and down the gap between the stage and the front row and tugged at his collar. 'Is it warm in here? My God, look at the time.'

'They'll be back in a minute,' Lionel said as he slumped in his seat with his feet up. 'It's fine.'

Ravenswood glared at him. How could Lionel Pereira possibly understand? Look at him, all of sixteen years old with a perfect face, sickeningly comfortable in his own skin. His whole life was opening up, without a shred of shame. The boy had no idea of *his* anguish, of how it felt to stare into the face of ruin. Again.

'It's not fine.' Jacinta stood in the aisle and threw her hands into the air. 'Mr Ravenswood. Holly told you Violet was mental but you didn't believe her. You didn't do anything and now Angelika's missing.'

'Holly came to me with some wild story,' Ravenswood said as he rubbed his forehead and paced. 'If I believed every rumour I heard around here…'

'I think everyone needs to take a deep breath,' Lionel said.

Ravenswood stopped and turned, his eyes narrowed to slits. 'I am perfectly calm, thank you, Lionel. Perhaps you should go learn your lines. Make sure you don't embarrass yourself.'

A flame ignited in Lionel's eyes and his nostrils flared as he turned away.

Ravenswood winced. He opened his mouth to apologise but Lionel was already halfway out the door. Now his leading man hated him. It was happening again. Ravenswood scraped his fingers along his scalp. The room was stifling hot. Black spots appeared in front of his eyes. He grabbed hold of a chair as the theatrette began to spin.

'Mr Ravenswood?' Toby said.

Ravenswood flinched as he saw a black hooded figure with no face standing before him. He gasped and dropped into a front row seat. The hooded figure had only been Toby with his hood up.

'Do you need a glass of water?' Jacinta rushed down to the front row.

'Just give me a moment,' Ravenswood said as he rubbed his temples and hid his eyes. 'I've got the strangest headache.'

'Me too,' said Toby, pressing his thumb into his eye socket. 'Right in here.'

'And I've got this funny taste in my mouth,' Jacinta said. 'Like some heavy-duty cleaning stuff. It's still there, no matter how much gum I chew.'

'It's probably the paint.' Toby nodded. 'It's toxic shit.'

Ravenswood wished they'd be quiet. He leaned forward, his elbows on his knees, his head in his hands.

'There's been strange stuff going on for days,' Toby said. 'Do you know what I mean?'

'It's this place.' Jacinta shuddered.

Ravenswood looked up. 'Violet mentioned dreams.'

'Dreams? Nightmares, more like it,' said Jason.

'You've had them too?' Jacinta frowned.

'Yeah. And weird things happening,' said Toby.

'And the shadows,' Ravenswood said quietly as he clutched fistfuls of his hair. 'I should have listened to Fi. I should've stayed away.'

'You don't think Violet is behind it?' Jacinta said.

Ravenswood blocked his ears. All this superstitious nonsense. Mrs Petrakis had assured him the school had been cleansed. It must be the pressure or stress or low blood sugar. The start of a cold, lack of sleep, a million different sensible and more logical reasons than evil spirits or a troublesome schoolgirl.

One thing was true: his cast and crew were letting him down. What did he expect from a bunch of kids? They had no commitment, no discipline. His chance to redeem himself in front of Alan Wolf was ruined.

Ravenswood jerked upright and glared around the theatrette. 'Where is everyone?'

'Well, Angelika and Lila are missing. Holly's gone to look for Violet. Jez is in the hospital. Wayne's washing the blood off his tunic,'

Jacinta said, counting on her fingers. 'Lionel stormed off and Kon is around here somewhere. But we're here.'

Ravenswood dropped his head again.

It was three years since his second year at uni and the night of the final performance of his Directing course. He had chosen *Endgame*, another challenging piece but one of Alan Wolf's known favourites. All of his lecturers and his classmates were going to be in the audience and his final marks depended on the performance's success. With a small cast of four, it should've been easy. But once again, he'd been lumped with slackers. They chatted amongst themselves and ignored him unless they had something to whinge about. When Ravenswood insisted they needed one more run-through, they practically rioted. It had only been one in the morning. Who needed sleep? The performance was more important.

All four actors stormed out on him, and on that day, exactly like today, Ravenswood had been left pacing up and down backstage and tearing at his hair as the minutes ticked down until the curtain rose.

Ravenswood had needed every single mark. The lecturers hadn't understood his assignment that compared Chekhov's *Uncle Vanya* to *Cat on a Hot Tin Roof*. His analysis was had obviously been too intellectually challenging for this backwater university. He had protested but the lecturers had claimed he didn't answer the questions. Yet again, the academics had stifled his ingenuity with their bureaucratic nonsense. Eventually he brushed it off, convinced that he would ace the final performance. But now, without actors or a play, he faced an F. His whole career, his whole future was at risk. His Plan B had been to play all the roles himself. After all he knew every line and at least there was one person he could rely on.

He had been making up his face when the cast turned up fifteen minutes before curtain rise. He almost collapsed with relief when they arrived—but then he realised they were rolling drunk.

They went on, giggling and slurring. They swayed across the stage, bumped into sets and missed their cues. One of the cast belted out a dirty rugby song when he couldn't remember his lines.

Endgame became a comedy. and Ravenswood stood in the wings, open-mouthed and watched them crush his future under their drunken feet.

Three years later at Beacon Hill High School, it was happening all over again and he was just as powerless to stop it.

He rubbed his hands up and down his forearms. Under his clothes, his healed scars itched. Hiram, the red-combed rooster was back, putting him to shame. Ravenswood had never learned. Here he was trying to prove he was better than everyone else and failing publicly again. The impending flop of his Macbeth was a reminder of what he already knew in his heart. He was nothing.

Useless.

Get up now, he told himself, leave. He could start afresh, far away from Beacon Hill, the home of the Nathair, the place where they stripped convicts of their skin to appease their God. Mrs Petrakis was wrong. Fiona was wrong. It's no allegory. He'd seen them in his dreams: trussed-up bodies swinging from the ceiling, red-raw flesh glistening in the firelight, the helpless screams of grown men.

Ravenswood jumped to his feet. The seat shut behind him with a clang and he clutched his forehead. The images wouldn't leave his mind.

The disciples were butchers, their meat still conscious as they peeled the skin from the muscle while the onlookers chanted the name of God, over and over again, without compassion. Their cheeks were flushed and their eyes were glassy as they invited Satan into their hearts under the guise of God, just as Josie warned. But even she was not immune. She had been just as infected and blind to his insidiousness. The Nathair, the original Kindred, became Satan's vessel and together they contaminated the ground of Beacon Hill.

He slumped back down into the theatre seat.

A splash of holy water and a few hymns was never going to be enough. Evil was clever, it hid dormant in the soil until the time was right to return.

'Mr Ravenswood?' Jacinta tapped his shoulder gently.

'Leave them alone, Josie,' he blathered.

'I think he's lost it,' said another voice said. It sounded so far away, as if echoing down a long tunnel.

Ravenswood shook his head and blinked. He looked up to see the concerned faces of his cast crowded around him.

'Have the girls come back?' he asked weakly.

'No,' said Jacinta. 'Remember. Holly went to look for them. Remember?'

He slumped and muttered. 'Useless.'

Was it his fault? Had he brought the evil with him? Deep down he knew he was bad. He was tarnished, and life and God never let him forget. So far, he'd been good. He'd stopped himself but the pull was so strong, sometimes it ached like an empty belly. If only he could start all over, make himself pure again.

God created these hurdles for him, opportunities to put the past behind him, yet time after time he repaid Him with selfishness and failure. He wanted to make Alan Wolf recognise his true talent. He needed to redeem the F he received for Directing 201, the biggest blackest mark on his already tarnished soul.

His ego had ushered in the darkness, brought the shadows and a famous cursed play to an already rotten place. Just as Josie had warned.

He shuddered. He should have listened to Holly. They were all in danger and he was responsible.

He moaned aloud and wished the ground would swallow him up, return him to nothingness. It was the only fate he deserved.

VIOLET

Miss Quinlin curiously disappeared into the semi-darkness. The fluorescent tubes fizzled overhead, flickering like a fitful Morse code.

Violet approached the next corner with damp palms. There were so many closed doors and empty spaces, so many places to hide.

A power tool whirred into action. The sound coming from somewhere further down the corridor. Violet swallowed hard. Images from horror videos flooded into her mind.

She followed the sound to the social studies wing, her heartbeat fluttering in time with the erratic lights. She paused outside the double glass doors and peered through the glass to a short corridor which branched off into four classrooms.

In the dim light, she spotted the silhouette of three bald heads in the classroom on the left. The maintenance men. Violet gulped again. Three men had been left to wander freely around an empty school and two teenage girls were missing.

As soon as the maintenance men had arrived at Beacon Hill High School, the stories had spread: they were criminals, paedophiles, mental patients. Violet had never listened. Sure, they were weird, but they had seemed harmless enough. And anyway, the school wouldn't let ex-offenders near children. They did background checks, didn't they?

Violet eased the door open and slipped into the social studies wing. Apparently, the men were from some kind of religious order: something about thorns. Violet didn't know much about religion and her mum only believed in hard work, clean houses and low-fat yoghurt. If they were religious, what would they want with Lila and Angelika anyway? Weren't monks supposed to be celibate? Violet shivered as she ticked off the recent strange events inside her head. The power on the blink, the falling set, the fire alarm. These men had the means and probably some perverted motive. She winced and wished she had a proper plan. And a weapon.

She snuck closer towards them.

The three men had their backs to the door as they stroked beige paint up and down the classroom wall in unison like a dance. Horizontal rain splattered against the window.

She loitered in the doorway and searched the room. There were no signs of Lila or Angelika: only paint brushes, trays and tins, drop sheets on the carpet, and an electric drill with a paint mixer attachment.

Violet checked her watch. How long had Lila been missing? There had been plenty of time for the men to hide her away and return to work. Or maybe there were others roaming the corridors.

She sucked in a breath. There were three of them and one of her. She steeled herself and stepped into the room.

'Hello,' she said in a surprisingly nonchalant voice. 'I'm looking for two of my friends. Have you seen them?'

The three men slowly turned their heads in unison and stared at her with blank faces. Lightning crackled outside and light reflected off their bald heads. One of the men, his eyes bulbous and staring, shrugged.

'A girl with burgundy hair and another tall blonde one?' Violet said as she stepped closer, careful to stay out of reach.

The man with the bulging eyes shook his head. His face, even his eyebrows, were completely free of all hair. The other two, one short, one chubby, stood with their arms flat by their sides and stared without blinking.

'You're really not allowed to speak?' Violet frowned. The man nodded and Violet pursed her lips. Sometimes schoolyard stories were true.

She studied their faces, unable to tear her eyes away. The three men gazed back at her. Their blank expressions gradually softened and her own frown melted away as a wordless understanding passed between them. A warm feeling trickled up through her body, her nerves replaced by a placid calm. All her doubts about them dropped away and the room hummed with a sense of gentleness. Later on, she'd swear the three men glowed.

Violet didn't know how long she stood there but her eyelids grew so heavy, she longed to lay her head down on the carpet, just for a few moments. It had been such a long day.

Thunder rumbled outside and she blinked. The noise pushed the clouds from her head. She remembered why she was here.

'If you see either of them, give them a message,' she said, her voice feeling strange in her mouth. 'We're looking for them. Tell them to come back to the theatrette.'

The boggle-eyed man nodded.

'But you can't tell them, can you?' She chuckled. 'Maybe you could point or something. I'll keep looking.'

Violet's body seemed more graceful as she headed out of the room. The men were strange but not sinister. It had to be someone else. She turned and waved to them and tripped on the drop sheet, which bunched up to reveal the carpet underneath and the corner of a black hardcover notebook. Just like Lila's journal.

She righted herself and snatched up the book. Her hands trembled as she opened the front cover to see 'Lila McFarlane' scribbled on the inside in her tiny spidery handwriting.

Her stomach plunged.

'What are you doing with this?' she said, brandishing the notebook.

Lila always kept her journal close. This was the first time Violet had even touched it.

The men, of course, said nothing.

'Why is this here?'

A wave of nausea hit her and her body wilted. They'd tricked her with hypnosis or something. Darkness was all around.

'What have you done with them, you perverts?'

The leader shook his head. The other two stood blankly like robots once again.

'Where have you put them?' Violet said, still waving the book at them. The short man and the fat man put down their paint brushes, slowly and deliberately. She tightened her grip on the book. 'What have you done with Lila?'

The leader turned back to the wall with his paintbrush in hand and continued with his work. Violet scoured the room for a better weapon than the sharp cornered book. A paint-splattered chisel lay on the drop sheet underneath a window, but it was too far away.

Violet tensed. 'Tell me where they are,' she said, gritting her teeth while her legs trembled.

The other two men stared back expressionless and silent.

The man who had been painting turned around and pointed. He'd written a message in beige paint on the wall. He nodded feverishly as Violet read the words aloud.

'*Not us,*' she said. 'Well, who then?'

The painting man picked up his brush again but stopped with a strangled squeal. Violet's eyes widened when she realised why.

His message was fading away before her eyes. The wall sucked up the words until there was nothing left. The other men dropped to their knees and bowed their heads, frantically crossing their chests.

With a shaky hand, the man turned and painted again. This time, the word on the wall was '*evil.*'

Violet swallowed as the temperature in the room plummeted.

'Who?' she said with chattering teeth. 'Tell me what you know.'

Slaps of red paint appeared from nowhere in angry splashes across the wall, covering his message. Violet's eyes and mouth widened, her panicked breaths were visible in the frozen air.

The painting monk lifted his brush again, even from this distance Violet could see the tremble in his hands. The kneeling men silently murmured, their lips moving in sync. As they prayed, more jagged stripes of blood-red paint materialised on the walls.

'Tell me!'

The painting man's shoulders hiked as he took a deep breath and touched the tip of his brush to the wall.

At the back of the room, an electric motor buzzed into action. Violet spun around. The drill sat upright on the drop sheet, the red stirring attachment whirring like a ceiling fan. But there was no one there.

The monk painted a single beige stroke but it was instantly devoured by the red wall. He bent over and dipped his brush into the paint tin, ready to try again.

An object whistled through the air past Violet. The metallic blur was too quick to make out, but it flew like a spear across the room.

The chisel.

The sharp-edged tool chisel stabbed the painting man. The blade lodging deep into the nape of his neck.

The man gasped and swayed but he didn't scream. His head lolled as he dropped the brush and gripped the chisel, the handle stuck out of his neck like one of Frankenstein's bolts. His knees buckled as blood seeped through his fingers.

Violet gaped open-mouthed as the other maintenance monks jumped up from their prayers. The short one held the injured man firmly while his fat companion took hold of the chisel handle and tugged hard. The painting man's body spasmed as the chisel came free. His face twisted and his lips snarled but he didn't make a sound.

He collapsed onto the carpet. Fresh blood oozed from the wound and dribbled down his neck, a dark stain growing at the collar of his coveralls.

The chubby man threw the blood-smeared chisel across the room. It thumped against the wall and landed on the carpet near the buzzing drill. Violet stared at the chisel. It was an ordinary tool, aside from the blood. It lay motionless and there was no sign of the evil.

But her attention shifted to the drill, which was still buzzing like an irritating blow fly. Violet inched towards it, fascinated but frightened.

The evil was there. She sucked in a lungful of courage, clenched her jaw and stamped on the whirring attachment with her chunky-soled boots. She stomped and kicked until the red plastic shattered into a hundred small pieces on the drop sheet.

She smiled.

Briefly.

Violet's stomach churned as the motor continued to hum. She was an idiot. As if the evil could be so easily defeated.

She backed away and turned to the men.

The small monk and the plump monk sunk to their knees, continuing to pray while their friend lay on the floor on his side.

'You can't leave him. We have to do something.'

But they paid no attention to her.

'Someone tell me what the hell is going on!' Violet stamped her foot.

The PA system hissed into life and a blast of piercing static blared out of the speakers. Violet flinched.

'Help me,' said a weak voice, barely audible through the pops and splutters.

'Lila?' Violet whispered as she slumped towards the wall, her thighs like jelly. She strained to hear. 'Is that you?'

'Please. Hurry.'

'Lila? I'm coming for you!' Violet swallowed her fear. 'Where are you?'

The speaker crackled and then the classroom was silent again. There were no more slashes of red paint on the wall, the drill stopped buzzing and Violet was alone with the three maintenance monks.

'Get up. We have to rescue her.'

Violet stood over them but they continued their prayers, their eyes firmly closed. She stamped her foot.

'How can you just sit there.'

But their eyes were shut like vaults.

'I need to know what I'm up against!' Violet yelled and kicked at a can of paint. 'What should I do?'

The painting man opened his eyes and scrawled on the wall in his own blood: red on red. '*Pray*' was barely decipherable.

'What good will that do?' Violet flung her hands in the air.

The three men ignored her and returned to their prayers. Violet slumped. 'Thanks for nothing.'

She trudged down the corridor and through the double doors on shaky legs. She didn't have a plan or a clear idea of what, or who, she was up against.

But she had to find Lila.

CHAPTER 15

RAVENSWOOD

RAVENSWOOD SLAMMED THE LIGHTING BOX DOOR AND FLOPPED down on the padded office chair inside. He leaned his elbows on the lighting desk and buried his thumping head in his hands.

The door opened and closed again.

'Finished?' he muttered through his hands.

There was no reply.

'You done, Toby?'

Ravenswood glanced up but there was no one there. The lighting box was still dark as it should be, the only light came from the glowing knobs and dials on the console. He looked out the wide viewing window and saw Toby was on stage, climbing down the ladder in plain sight. Ravenswood's breath snagged in his throat.

In the far corner of the small room, something lingered by the door. It was a darkness, a jet-black shadow blacker than the black surrounding it. For some unknown reason, the ill-defined presence felt female.

'Angelika?' Ravenswood said. 'Is that you?' His heart beat like a warning bell under his shirt.

The scent of clean bedsheets and roses drifted over him, and his mouth went dry. He would never forget this perfume as his nose pressed against her shirt and she grappled him into a headlock and dragged him across the yard.

'No,' he stuttered. 'It can't be.'

A harsh bark of laughter came from the corner. 'Useless boy,' the shadow hissed.

Ravenswood scrambled to his feet. 'You're not real.'

He flinched and shielded his eyes as the stage below blasted with an intense white light.

'Who is not real?' the voice cackled.

'Mr Ravenswood! Can you turn it down?' Toby yelled. 'You're blinding us down here.'

Ravenswood grabbed the fader and dimmed the lighting.

He inhaled and faced the corner. 'I won't let you ruin it,' he said as he tried to swallow the tremble in his voice.

The murky presence in the corner melted into a dark pool and inched towards him like black lava along the floor and walls.

'You don't need my help. You are ruining it all on your own,' the voice whispered directly into his ear. 'Useless.'

He clutched his head. 'You're supposed to be dead.'

The door handle rattled and Ravenswood scuttled into the corner, away from the shadowy creeping oil slick. He barricaded himself behind a chair.

The voice followed him. 'I only want to help you. You know what you need to do.'

He shook his head. 'I don't. I don't. I never did.'

'But you do. I've told you a thousand times. Beg forgiveness. Atone for your sins. All of them.'

'I have. Believe me, I have.'

'Liar! Nothing has changed.'

Ravenswood squeezed his eyes shut.

'Why single me out?' he wailed. 'Why can't I have what I want? Why do you make me suffer?'

'You never learn. I am trying to help you. Do you want to embarrass your father and God again? Don't you want to be pure?'

Ravenswood covered his eyes. 'Leave me alone. You're not real. I'm overworked, or something.' His breath rasped in his throat. 'This is impossible. Dr Leishman said...'

The door handle jolted again.

'Enough. Face your punishment like a man.'

'You're not real. You can't touch me.'

Out of the darkness, the blurry shadow grew claws and loomed ten feet tall. Ravenswood covered his nose as another familiar smell invaded the room: the eye-watering reek of chicken manure and corn pellets.

Hiram.

Ravenswood froze. He was a kid again, cowering against the chicken wire fence. The black shadow claws lunged at him. Ravenswood yelped and protected his eyes. One. Two. The razor-sharp spurs slashed his cheeks.

'Stop,' he spluttered.

But Hiram kept coming.

Ravenswood flinched and moaned, his arms like jelly, useless against the clawed attack. How could this be happening? It made no sense but the pain was real, and deep down he knew every word Josie said was true. There was only one way to make them go away. He gulped and cleared his throat. 'You're right. I wanted to be the centre of attention. The one they all looked up to.'

Hiram struck again. *Slash*.

Ravenswood squealed but kept going. 'I wanted their praise, and their admiration and respect. I thought I deserved it.' He licked his dry lips. 'But I was wrong.'

Slash.

'Isn't this what you want?' he said, shrilly. 'What else do you want from me?'

'You're not finished.'

He sucked a jagged breath in through his teeth. 'I have impure thoughts. But I haven't done anything. Believe me. I've been too ashamed to act. But the thoughts are there. I can't help it. I can't be like the others.'

As he said the words, the shadow of Hiram melted back into the gloom. Ravenswood breathed out and wiped his cheek.

The shadow laughed. The sound bounced off the walls and rang inside his head, and a new set of shivers rippled down his spine. Ravenswood chewed his lip. The laugh was unfamiliar. Or was it? His eyes widened as he stared into the raven-coloured cloud at the other end of the room, his mouth opening and closing.

The laugh sounded younger, playful, yet hard. Josie had never laughed like that, she barely laughed at all, except when fluttering her eyelashes at his dad.

'Who are you?' he stuttered.

The laughter changed from female to male.

This was a very familiar voice.

It was his own.

'You know exactly who I am,' the shadow said in his own voice.

VIOLET

Violet's mind churned with thoughts of evil and red paint. The hooded man with the black dog, the green-faced witch and the garbled plea for help over the PA system. And it all began with the words of the bus driver. Darkness and one will never return.

What had she stepped into?

She focused on the sound of her boots, the squeak of leather and the comforting normal noise of her own footsteps on the ground. Left. Right. Left. Right. Floors and shoes were reliable things. But in the distance she caught a new noise, a squeaking. Had the maintenance monks changed their minds? It didn't sound like men. It sounded like...

Violet turned and gasped.

Rats, hundreds of them.

Bile squirted up the back of Violet's throat.

Sleek, black and Chihuahua-sized with big yellow teeth, the wave of rodents scurried along the corridor towards her.

She squealed and picked up her pace, her pulse thumping in her throat. The writhing crowd of rats rushed down the corridor, clambering over each other and skidding up the walls. Their scraping claws and squeaks came closer and closer.

Violet burst into a sprint but her legs and lungs were quick to complain, thanks to all her smoking. She panted up the corridor towards a weak light coming from the metal workshop. She ran full pelt towards the door and tumbled inside, frantically slamming the doors behind her. Violet leaned her full body weight against the doors and wheezed. For once she was glad of those her few extra kilos.

The scratching at the door started before she had a chance to catch her breath. She pushed back and grunted, anchoring her feet into the floor as the door buckled inwards.

But then the scratching stopped.

Her heartbeat hammered in her eardrums as Violet listened hard against the door. The plague of rats seemed to be heading away in the opposite direction. But she braced herself against the door until their claws and squeaks were completely gone. She sagged against the door, only the pipes rumbled softly overhead.

There were stories of a wave of rats streaming down Liverpool Street after they demolished the old hospital but she'd always thought it was a myth. Was this yet another example of the darkness in the school walls?

As her breathing returned to normal, Violet glanced around. It had been two years since she'd last stepped inside the workshop but nothing had changed. Like Phys Ed, metal work and woodwork were the first subjects she dropped when she could choose electives. She had been happy to escape the sour beery breath and tangy B.O. of the tech teachers.

The room looked the same, except for one thing, a splash of something red on the scuffed lino floor. A wet red stripe led all the way into the dim workshop. She checked her shoes. Her soles were painted with blood.

Lila?

The workshop was dark except for a single square skylight. Violet squinted over the dented and graffitied wooden benches, past the looming shapes of industrial lathes and drills and all the way to the chainmail gates at the back where the dangerous tools lived.

The tech teacher's office on the right was lit up, with its glass windows all round like a fishbowl. It was perfect for the lazy teachers, the ones who pretended to supervise without actually leaving their desk, while down the back, kids sniffed glue and welded ninja stars. There was no one inside the office, only a desk and an empty chair in front of piles of papers.

Standing in front of the main source of light, Violet realised she was on display, that anyone hiding in the dark would be able to see her clearly.

Another noise came from deep inside the dark workshop.

Violet froze.

She heard a sniffle.

'Violet,' said a voice, ever so quietly from the same direction as the path of blood.

Was it Lila? Violet craned forward to listen but her heartbeat was too loud. She couldn't tell for sure.

'Violet.' The voice spoke again, this time a little louder.

She squinted into the dark, her head tilted but she didn't move.

'Violet!' screamed the voice.

This time Violet was certain.

'Lila! I'm coming!' She rushed into the darkness towards the scream.

~⁀~

HOLLY

Holly ran past the closed doors of the science block and the library. She didn't look back until she reached reception. She stopped at the main office and listened but there were no footsteps following her. Had she imagined the hand on her shoulder? Holly shuddered, picturing Violet with wild eyes and a maniacal grin. Her straggly mousy hair half-hiding her face and a revving chainsaw in her hands.

She cupped her hands and peered through the rectangular sliding reception window, where the sour-faced school secretary Miss Fischer usually sat. A weak light was shining from the back: possibly a lamp in the out-of-bounds teachers' lounge or Mrs Petrakis's office.

Something or someone shifted in the half light.

'Open up.' Holly battered on the glass. 'I can see you in there. Mr Booth?' She scowled at the telephone sitting out of reach behind the locked window on the reception desk. 'Where are they?' She growled. 'Slack arses.'

Shapes shifted in the shadows and Holly's heart wrenched. She pulled her face back from the window. She wished her cousin had never dared her to watch those videos, with the evil dolls and masked men. 'Calm down. There's nothing to be frightened of. Everything's completely normal.'

She took a deep breath and focused. She wasn't afraid of the dark. She wasn't. It had only been a dream on Monday night and it was daytime right now. Although with the storm and the dodgy lights, it was barely daylight. But there was no need to be afraid.

'I need to use the phone.' She knocked again. 'Somebody? Anybody?'

But no one answered.

She grit her teeth as she turned. Should she go back to Ravenswood's office and use his phone? Or follow the trail of blood?

A chemical stink smell floated past her. Holly scrunched-up her nose. The sweet-sour stench intensified. Holly coughed as the foul smell turned acrid and burned the insides of her nostrils. She covered her mouth and nose with her sleeve. Was it paint or varnish? A gas leak?

With her free hand, she beat on the reception window again. 'Mr Booth!'

The brick walls wobbled at the edges of her eyes and the floor shimmered underneath her. Dark blotches swarmed in her vision. Unseen hands clutched her chest and squeezed the air from her, like the shadowy figure from her dream.

'This can't be real,' she murmured to the empty corridor.

Her knees buckled and she slid to the ground, her ears ringing. The walls around her undulated with menacing faces and the air filled with hysterical laughter.

Is this black magic? Or was she the one losing her grip on reality?

Holly gasped for fresh air, the smell like a noose around her throat. Holly lay her cheek down on the cool linoleum. She was drowning. As she struggled to keep her head above consciousness, she thought of the black and white candles, the spool of white ribbon and the scrunched-up spell. If only she'd had the guts. If only she'd listened to Dahlia, she could have stopped all this.

The cackling died away and the corridor was quiet again but the floor hummed. Something was coming. Then Holly heard it, subtle at first, masked under her own laboured breaths, but the scurrying grew louder. Holly squinted into the dim light, her ears straining towards the coming noise. She gasped.

Rats.

Like burst floodwaters from a dam, hundreds of slick greasy-furred rodents hurtled towards her, snarling with their yellowed teeth bared. The corridor echoed with squeals as the germ-ridden horde rushed closer.

Holly screamed.

This was no dream.

VIOLET

Violet's pulse hammered as she headed towards Lila's scream.

The rain was pelting down on the skylight like gunfire, and the afternoon sky was as dark as night. Violet was left with only her eyes to guide her in the deafening rain. She checked left and right and then smiled.

She leaned over a graffiti-etched work bench and grabbed a hammer from the wall. The tool was heavy and comforting in her hand but not enough to stop her shaking. As the rain dwindled to a steady drizzle on the roof, she crept further into the dim workshop.

The industrial-sized machines loomed over her. She rested her hand on the cold textured surface of a lathe. Each machine was wide enough to hide a person, or a body.

The knot in her stomach tightened, her every instinct urged her to get out but she couldn't stop now. Lila was here somewhere and this was the only way Violet could make things right. She winced, thinking back to the terrible things she'd said and the pain on Lila's face.

Violet couldn't blame a curse or a play or black magic. There was no conspiracy. It was Violet and Violet alone. Her dreams had transformed her into a monster. Is that what Holly had been talking about all along? Violet cringed again. Holly was the next person on the list after Lila, but first things first. She set her jaw and walked towards the locked gates at the back, hammer held high.

The lathe roared into action. Violet jumped back, almost dropping her hammer as the engine revved up to full speed.

Something sharp hit her in the back of the head. She grabbed at her hair and spun around quickly enough to see a screwdriver clatter to the concrete floor behind her.

'Real funny,' she yelled over the rumble of the machine, her eyes narrowed. Her hammer ready, she swivelled in all directions.

The lathe switched itself off and the whirring died down until the room grew quiet again.

A giggle echoed from the far side of the room.

The hairs on Violet's arms bristled as the room turned icy cold. It was exactly the same feeling as in the red-painted classroom. The evil was here. Violet exhaled long and low through her teeth.

'Violet,' a teasing voice whispered in her ear.

Violet spun to her left. The voice was so close, a puff of breath tickled the skin of her neck. But there was no one there.

'Violet...' called the female voice again, familiar yet unfamiliar. 'Violet...'

'Show yourself,' Violet demanded, using the full power of her theatre voice.

Someone gasped close by.

Her eyes widened and her stomach flipped.

Lila.

Violet rushed behind the six-foot drill press machine to her right.

But it wasn't Lila.

Angelika stood with her hands hoisted above her head, tied to the machine. Blood dribbled out her nose and her hair was plastered against her face. She looked up at Violet with a trembling lip.

'Violet,' said another voice behind her.

Violet whirred around. Like Angelika, Lila was tied to a bandsaw bench, lying flat on her back.

'Lila,' Violet exhaled.

'No,' croaked Angelika.

Violet rushed over to Lila. Her burgundy hair was wild and messy and there were five thin scratches like claw marks down her cheek.

'Are you alright?'

'You're here,' Lila sighed through dry lips. 'I knew you'd come. I knew you wouldn't forsake me.'

'I'm sorry.' Violet reached around to untie Lila's hands. 'I've been such a bitch.'

'You don't need to apologise.'

'But I do. Oh, you're not tied up.'

'Don't,' said Angelika again. 'Please.'

Violet scowled. 'Wait a sec. I'll untie you next.'

'I think she's in shock,' Lila said, her eyes gleaming as she sat up.

'Everyone seems to react differently to stuff like this.' Violet helped Lila off the bench. 'Tell me. Who did this?'

'I knew you'd come,' Lila said

Violet sighed. 'When I heard you were missing, I had to do something. I'm so sorry.'

'You were just upset.'

'No. I was awful. Can you forgive me? I can understand if you won't.'

'Of course,' Lila laughed, her hand on Violet's shoulder. 'I never blamed you. I only wanted to help. That's why I did this. I did it for you.'

'What?' Violet frowned. 'What do you mean?'

'This,' Lila said.

Lila strode forward and slapped Angelika across the face hard. Angelika cried out and collapsed into gulping sobs.

'I got rid of her exactly like you wanted. Now the role is yours.'

Lila's pupils were huge like shiny black marbles. She moistened her lips with a grin. 'What shall we do with her?'

CHAPTER 16

'*O*UT, OUT, BRIEF CANDLE!*'*
    A voice boomed in the lighting box. A new voice. Ravenswood flinched. What now?

It was Macbeth's, or rather, Lionel's clear voice amplified by the microphone on stage, his words drowning out the other voice in the lighting box.

'Life's but a walking shadow, a poor player
That struts and frets his hour upon the stage
And then is heard no more: it is a tale
Told by an idiot, full of sound and fury,
Signifying nothing.'

Shakespeare's words rang in Ravenswood's ears. He parted his fingers and looked up. He nodded and clutched his head once more. Suddenly it all made sense.

The door rattled again but this time it swung open. Ravenswood gasped and huddled into the safety of his corner.

'Mr Ravenswood? Mr Ravenswood? Are you alright?' Toby said, jangling a set of keys.

Ravenswood spluttered and shielded his face. 'Leave me alone.'

Toby flicked a switch and the small room was flooded with harsh white light. Ravenswood blinked and the haze eventually lifted from his eyes. There was no one else there. No Josie, no Hiram, not even a shadow.

'You're bleeding!? What happened?'

He stared at his hands, there was blood caked under his fingernails. His shoulders slumped.

'Should I call someone?'

Ravenswood stumbled to his feet, and Toby rushed forward to take his arm, but Ravenswood fobbed him off with a wave.

'Everything's in place,' Toby said, backing away from him with his palms outstretched. 'When Violet comes back with the others, we can start straight away.'

'Thank you, Toby.' Ravenswood wiped his face with his blue plaid handkerchief. He should have felt buoyant after his confession. He'd released all the lies sitting like silt in his chest. Instead, he felt deboned.

His epiphany was worse than the years of blaming Josie and the Kindred. He should've listened to Fiona. His tormentors were long gone. He had been the only one keeping them alive.

Ravenswood swallowed. He'd make the call to Dr Leishmann first thing tomorrow.

'Are you sure you're alright?' Toby said.

Ravenswood stared through the glass down to the stage. Lionel and Jacinta were doing the Nutbush in their medieval costumes, while the other boys kicked a hacky sack into the air.

'Let's get on with the show,' Ravenswood said with a pained smile.

The production was the only thing he had left. At least that was real.

'Where are those girls?'

VIOLET

Slap.

'Stop!' Violet's eyes bulged so wide, they almost popped out of their sockets.

'Isn't this what you wanted?' Lila grabbed Angelika's hair and wrenched her chin up high.

'No,' Angelika muttered, blood bubbling on her split lip.

'Let her go. What's wrong with you?'

'She's out of the way now.' Lila dropped her grip and Angelika's head slumped. 'The stage will be yours. Like it should've been all along.'

'Not like this. You're hurting her.' Violet inched forward.

'You wanted to hurt her.' Lila's eyes were wide and innocent, but at the same time savage. 'You said so yourself.'

Violet tensed. She wanted to run. Again. Go home, climb under the covers and hide forever. She'd said these things. She'd dreamed about smashing in Angelika's face, watching her squirm, doing exactly what Lila was doing. But her belly squelched with nausea, instead of satisfaction, at seeing the defeat on Angelika's face.

Violet shook her head.

Lila scoffed. 'I thought you were stronger than this.'

Violet narrowed her eyes. 'What's got into you?'

This was her closest friend, standing in front of her. The same freckled face she saw every day on the bus, at recess, in her bedroom where they sat cross-legged and listened to her crappy cassette player. Together they swooned over the posters of Corey Haim and River Phoenix posters and planned the day they'd finally get off this stupid island.

But this wasn't Lila. This Lila stood straighter, her skinny, flat chest puffed out like a pigeon. Her head was tilted back to show her white throat. Her nervous voice sounded suddenly like steel.

Lila raised an eyebrow and laughed. 'Yes. What indeed,' she cackled as she paced up and down in front of Angelika and jabbed her in the ribs like a cat toying with a mouse.

Violet tightened her grip on the hammer. 'What are you doing?'

Lila stopped and spun around with a sigh. 'You disappoint me, Violet. I thought you were one of us.'

'Us?' Violet gulped, checking the darkness around her.

'I thought we could have such fun together. But I was wrong.' Lila smiled sadly. 'You are just as stupid as the rest of them.'

Violet gasped. It hit her with a flash. 'You're not Lila,' she whispered.

'Bingo. You're right but you're also wrong. I'm here to help Lila. And you. But you're very ungrateful. I don't like when people are ungrateful. I've put in a lot of hard work to be here. But as usual, nobody cares.'

'What have you done with her?' Violet stammered.

'Lila's around here somewhere.' She waved her hand. 'She does love you. She asked me to do this especially for you, and she promised you'd join us. But she was wrong. How unfortunate.'

'Unfortunate?'

'Yes. For you. I'll have to get rid of you. Like the other ones.'

Violet raised her hammer. Lila laughed and calmly smoothed down her burgundy hair as four pairs of black hands emerged from the shadows.

'What the…?'

The fingers wrenched the hammer out of Violet's grip and flung the weapon to the ground. Violet stared open-mouthed at her empty hand.

'You're not dabbling with a few black candles now, Violet. This is the real stuff. Not like those pagan try-hards.'

The black strong hands grabbed Violet by the shoulders and arms and dragged her on her heels towards a hulking drill.

'You don't deserve Lila. She did everything for you. But you could never see beyond your own selfishness. You failed her just like all the others.'

'I know, Lila. That's why I'm here. I'm sorry.' Violet wriggled helplessly. 'Get these off me and we can talk properly.'

'Talking time is over. It's your turn to suffer. Like she's suffered. You have no idea the pain she's been through.'

'I'm sorry, Lila. I'm here for you now. Tell me everything.'

Lila scoffed. 'Lila's not in control anymore. You're talking to her anger and fear. Aren't they so much more fun?'

The hands shoved her Violet down flat on the bench, squeezing the breath from her lungs. With her head pressed against cool metal, Violet stared up into the hard-cutting edge of an industrial-sized drill bit. She tried to thrash her arms and legs but the strong fingers held her tight.

How had she missed the change in Lila? Violet trawled back through every one of their conversations since Monday looking for hints. She even replayed the cringe-worthy scenes where she was played the monster. Lila had been jumpy, chewing at her fingers and rarely sitting still, but Lila was always like that. And then there were her nose bleeds? And her insistence about curses? All the strangeness—the dreams, the accidents, the shadows—had it been Lila all along?

'Lila, please wake up,' Violet pleaded.

Lila laughed, her eyes blazing red. 'Save your energy.'

'Why are you here?'

'You drew me here.'

'Me?' Violet chewed her lip.

'All of you. There is so much delicious dark energy in this place. I've been waiting so long for the right moment to come out and play. Lila here kindly let me in. It took a little coaxing but she eventually saw the light.'

'Who are you?'

'No one. Everyone.'

'What do you want?'

'Now, that is an interesting question.' Lila rubbed her chin. 'I've pondered this for millennia. There has been so much written about my motives, mainly by small-minded people with even smaller imaginations, but I don't want to rule the world. I much prefer to stir the pot and watch what happens when everything goes awry. It's such fun.'

Lila spun around with a chisel in her hand and lunged at Angelika, gouging at her creamy face. Angelika mewled. A trickle of red ran down her cheek and neck.

Lila prowled back and forth, giggling. Her laughter morphed and buckled, mutating into a bellowing cackle that scraped over Violet's teeth, while the shadowy hands pinned her shoulders down hard against the metal.

'You hate this, don't you?' Lila spat into Angelika's face. 'Damage to your precious face? I've seen inside your head. Wow. What a messed up place you've got in there. I could have easily chosen you instead of her.'

Angelika squirmed half-heartedly, her eyes downcast.

'This place is a real smorgasbord. So many choices,' Lila giggled.

'Lila. No,' Violet said.

Lila yanked Angelika's hair. 'Who's the one in control now? You can't manipulate me like you can the others. Is this helplessness worse than damage to your face? This is all new to you, isn't it? Now you know how the rest of them feel.'

Angelika's shoulders trembled and tears joined the blood running down her face.

'How boring,' Lila sighed. 'I thought you put up more of a fight. I was wrong.' She turned to Violet. 'Your go.'

The black hands pushed Violet's head down even harder onto the platform. The machine roared into action, and the drill bit span above her head.

'Lila doesn't like this,' Lila said, raising her voice over the grinding motor. 'But I'm beyond caring. Lila is weak but I'm not. I'll make you pay for what you did to her.'

The drill rumbled. Violet swallowed hard. The spinning drill slowly descended towards her forehead.

'I haven't done a good trepanning in ages. They say drilling a hole in the forehead frees the evil spirits from the mind. Ha.'

'Lila,' Violet said. 'You must be still in there somewhere? Please. Stop this.'

As Violet held her breath, her eyes fixated on the rotating drill bit, her teeth clenched as she anticipated the sear of pain.

One of them *had* taken darkness into her breast. But what about the other two predictions? Was Violet the one who would disappear for ever?

'Lila. Lila. You don't need to do this,' Violet begged.

'Lila can't come to the phone right now,' Lila laughed.

Violet grimaced. The air prickled over her skin as the drill bit came closer. With her arms and legs restrained, she only had one option. Luckily her mouth was free.

'Why are you doing this to her? To Lila. Didn't you say you were helping her?'

Lila furrowed her forehead. 'This is what I do. Isn't it, girls? I give people what they want. Sometimes, when I deliver on my promises and my new friends get to experience what they truly want, they change their mind. People are fickle like that.' She shrugged.

'Girls?' Violet frowned.

With a snigger, Lila slipped out of earshot and into the dark. Violet clenched her whole body and waited, her breaths shallow.

The shadowy fingers loosened their hold as feet shuffled nearby. Violet turned her head and Lila stepped back into the light. But she was not alone.

Lila thrust a body onto the concrete floor. The person dressed in black landed with a thud, a mop of dark curls covering her face.

'Rowan?' Violet gasped.

HOLLY

On the ground, Holly braced herself. She covered her face with her hands as the stampede of claws and squeaks neared.

Something small slammed into her head and sharp toenails clambered through her hair. Holly squealed and shook her arms, flinging the rat up against the wall, but a second rat took its place and scuttled over her forearm. A third jumped up on her shoulder and scurried down her back. Its claws scratched her skin through her thin witch costume. A fourth rat, and a fifth, scraped and gnawed. Holly stopped counting after that. She cowered wishing for the Pied Piper.

Years ago, at a Grand Final party in her street, while the parents had drunk Moselle and danced embarrassingly, Bernadette from next door, who was older with a perm and smoked menthols, had told all the kids the tale of a rat plague. When the council had demolished the remaining buildings on the future school site, rats had flooded Beacon Hill. They'd infested the houses for months, chewing through power lines, raiding pantries and setting up nests in cupboards. At the time Holly thought it was just another freaky Beacon Hill story. She frowned. That had been thirty years ago at least, if it happened at all. But the scratches of claws on her skin were very real. Where had they all come from?

'Help. Someone,' she shrieked.

An endless stream of rats clambered over her. Holly curled into the foetal position and tucked her arms underneath her. Saliva flooded her mouth as gusts of hot breath ruffled against her neck and fur rubbed against her skin.

She retched.

The taste of vomit sharpened her senses. What was she doing lying here expecting someone else to save her? The rodents were big but she was ten times their size.

Her adrenaline surged and her mind cleared. She stopped shaking with fear and shook with anger instead.

'Get off me!' she screeched and tore a rat from her neck and pelted it against the brick wall. It squealed as it bounced and scurried away.

Tiny claws pierced her scalp and she grabbed a handful of matted fur. But she was too slow to stop the sharp teeth gouging a chunk of flesh out of her face. Holly wailed and clutched at her cheek, her hand filling with warm blood as the triumphant rat leaped off and scampered away.

'You little bastards.'

Holly pulled herself to her knees and then her feet as she flailed her arms. She sent a few more rats skidding across the linoleum with a swift kick.

She waded through the stream of rodents surging past her as she limped towards the door. The strange gas smell lingered and Holly pressed her hand pressed firmly against the leaking rat bite on her face.

She reached the double fire doors and leaned on them but they, too were locked.

'What is going on?' she roared, fists clenched. 'This is a fire hazard.'

As she grimaced, a scream pierced the air. Holly's stomach twisted. She peered through the small rectangular windows. Lights blazed up ahead, coming from the stairs leading to the metal and wood workshop. She pressed her ear against the hairline crack between the doors.

'Lila.' She rattled at the doors. 'Lila!' She yanked them with all her strength.

Another scream rang out.

'Violet! Stop!'

But the doors were locked tight. Holly groaned and slumped against the wood, her own breath loud in her ears.

'Holly, Holly,' a voice cried.

Holly glanced around the empty corridor. The voice sounded close, but suddenly she was all alone. Even the rats were gone.

'Lila?' she said.

'Holly!' the voice screamed. 'Hurry!'

'Lila! I'm coming.'

Her chest thumped as she ripped the fire extinguisher from the wall and slammed the hard butt into the small windows. Glass splintered with a satisfying crack.

'I'm coming!'

VIOLET

Lila tugged at Rowan's tangled hair and revealed a grey-skinned face mottled with bruises. Violet whimpered. She tried to look away but the shadow hands pried open her eyelids.

'Our runaway has come home. Well, she never actually left the school grounds in the first place. Getting rid of the understudy was step one. She was Lila's first. Lila was so nervous but I was so proud.'

'Is she?' Violet said but she already knew the answer. Rowan's lips were blue, and her eyes were blank.

Lila snorted. 'You people. You're blind to what's going on right under your noses…'

'You…you didn't?' Violet stared open-mouthed. She blinked, wishing Rowan would move, wishing it wasn't true.

'…so wrapped up in your own petty little dramas. "Does he like me?", "Do I look fat?", "What did she mean by that?" Blah blah blah. Lila and I could whisk someone away without anyone noticing, not even the police. Fools. Not that I'm complaining. It makes the whole game much easier for me.'

Lila let go of Rowan's curls and her face hit the concrete with a thump.

'Lila? How could you?'

'We're only doing what you wanted, little friend. What you were too gutless to do. I just helped. And as you'll learn, I deliver on my promises.'

'I never asked…' Shame squeezed Violet's throat closed again. Rowan's corpse was stone cold evidence of all stupid reckless things she'd said.

'Oh, but you did. Everyone heard you.'

Violet's eyes misted over but she gritted her teeth and sucked back the tears.

'Rowan. I am so sorry.'

'Too late now.'

Violet's stomach was rock hard but this time she didn't look away from Rowan's dead body. It didn't matter whether she meant it or not. Her hands were as guilty as Lila's.

Think.

She had to do something.

Think.

Her mind was as murky as a churned-up creek bed.

Lila cackled again.

The drill whirred, the metal caught in the half light as the strong black fingers gripped her shoulders.

Think!

There had to be a way.

'I know you're still there, Lila,' Violet said, gently biting her lip. 'Please come back. You have to be strong. Don't let this thing take you over.'

'Oh, so now you're concerned about your friend?'

'Don't listen, Lila. I know I've been a cow. I'll make it up to you. I'm your real friend. Not this *thing*. Remember my thirteenth birthday when you secretly baked that cake. We hid it away in my bedroom but we forgot to get a knife and had to eat it with our hands. Remember? Big fistfuls of cake. We gorged ourselves until we felt sick and rolled around on the carpet, moaning. I had chocolate icing under my fingernails for days.'

Lila patrolled up and down but her mouth stayed closed. Violet breathed a little easier and kept going.

'And the time at Mid-City when the ushers threw us out of that soppy romance movie for laughing too much.'

Lila stayed quiet.

'And the time we dyed your hair with the supermarket dye and it went green instead of blonde. We thought we were going to get in so much trouble.'

'Oh, give up,' Lila said. 'Stop glossing over the past. I can taste your fear. It tastes like treacle.'

'And the first day we met in Grade seven homeroom?' Violet persisted. 'Remember Miss Smolik with the big lump on her face? You said you liked my sweatshirt. The one with Mickey Mouse on the front. How embarrassing. We were such kids.' Violet forced out a light-hearted laugh.

Lila stood with hands on narrow hips. 'This is all very nice, but where were you when Lila really needed you?' Lila's eyes were as hard as the drill bit revolving above Violet's head. 'Didn't you notice the bags under her eyes? How she was wasting away? Didn't you wonder why she never wanted to go home? You never asked what was troubling her.'

Violet lay open mouthed. She had noticed these things but this was just Lila. Everyone had their quirks. She would have asked if she suspected something was truly wrong.

'Didn't you know what was going on? What her stepfather was doing to her?'

'No,' Violet choked out. Was it true? Had her best friend had been suffering every day and she hadn't even noticed?

'Let's hear some more stories about what a great friend you are.'

'Why didn't you tell me?' Violet spluttered. Her voice cracked as she pictured Lila's stepfather's rough hands touching her, forcing her. How alone she must have felt. Violet vomited into her mouth.

'Oh, she tried.'

'I'm so sorry,' Violet snivelled. 'Please forgive me.'

'Me. Me. Me.' Lila tossed her head and laughed. 'It's still all about you, isn't it? Jeanette. Violet. Whatever you call yourself. You're still the same selfish little brat.'

Violet sucked in a shallow breath. She was the worst friend ever. She didn't need the black hands to hold her down anymore. She didn't even bother to struggle.

'Oh, your self-loathing tastes like liquorice,' Lila tittered.

Then Lila's laughing stopped abruptly. She frowned and turned her head.

Violet followed Lila's gaze.

A silver ball rolled out of the darkness and along the floor and stopped under Angelika's feet. The ball hissed and fizzed, and burst open into segments like an orange. Smoke poured out of its centre and sent pink-grey clouds billowing into the air.

Lila cleared her throat.

Once.

Twice.

The plumes of smoke curled and twisted towards the ceiling. Lila coughed and pressed her fist over her mouth. The shadowy hands loosened their grip around Violet's shoulders.

Tendrils of the pink-grey smoke flitted across the room and circled Lila. She doubled over, her hands on her thighs as she gasped and coughed.

Violet narrowed her eyes. She was breathing easily while Lila choked. Angelika also seemed unaffected. She was as listless as a rag doll but not coughing. And Rowan's corpse didn't move, of course.

Violet sniffed the air, trying to identify the caustic smell wafting in the smoke, but she'd spent most of Year Ten Chemistry daydreaming about her first Hollywood movie deal.

Above her head, the twirling drill slowed to a standstill.

The smoke swirled around Lila's body, wrapped around her legs, arms and neck and secured her with a vaporous rope.

Thump.

Scrape.

A familiar shape emerged from the shadows. Violet's eyes widened. 'Stop. I command you.'

A plump woman in a pink cardigan lumbered forward, her eyes on Lila. 'Stop. I command you.'

'Miss Quinlin?' Violet shook her head.

'You are not welcome here. Retreat. Back to whence you came.'

Lila lifted her head. She opened her mouth and spoke in a voice which was both syrupy and brittle, both masculine and feminine. It was coarse with experience and bright with youth. The voice was familiar and yet the strangest thing Violet had ever heard.

'You think you can stop me.'

The shadow hands pulled Violet down fast against the metal bench.

Lila straightened up to her full height and tossed aside the smoke restraints. She barked out a laugh. 'You? Science teacher?'

'We have done it before and we will do it again,' Miss Quinlin said and flung a handful of white sand into Lila's face.

Lila swatted away the grains. 'It'll take more than salt to get rid of me, you silly old woman.'

A person in a black hood carrying a bow stepped silently into the light.

Violet gasped. It was the man with the big black dog from the bush track, the one lurking around Beacon Hill in the dark. What had he said to her again? *Beware.* He must be Lila's accomplice.

'Watch out, Miss Q,' Violet called. 'Behind you.'

Miss Quinlin smirked.

'You are not welcome here. Retreat. Back to whence you came.' The man revealed short silver hair as he pulled down his hood.

But it was not a man at all. The woman's cold blue eyes stared straight ahead, her pupils white and cloudy. She was blind.

A third woman emerged from the shadows on the left.

'You are not welcome here. Retreat. Back to whence you came,' she said in her lilting foreign accent.

It was the curly-haired bus driver in her forest green uniform.

Violet spluttered with relief.

'You are not welcome here. Retreat. Back to whence you came,' all three women said in unison.

The dark room lit up with an orange flash as the blind woman struck a lighter and fired off a flaming arrow.

Bullseye.

The arrow pierced the centre of Lila's chest. Flames radiated across her body and ate away at her long black witch's costume. But Lila didn't even flinch. She laughed, hands on hips.

'Oh, ladies. Such amateurs,' she sneered. 'This is only my current form. You are only hurting the girl.'

Lila dropped her chin to her chest and blew hard. She whistled like a gale and snuffed out the flames as if they were candles on a birthday cake.

The bus driver lunged forward with a glass vial and sprayed water at Lila. It sizzled as it splashed against her skin.

'Holy water?' Lila arched an eyebrow, but angry welts flared up on her cheeks. 'Come on, children.'

'Peridot water is much stronger.' The bus driver smirked and showered Lila with more liquid.

Lila narrowed her eyes. Her pale skin rippled and bubbled like melted cheese under a grill. Her face bulged with blisters.

'By the power of three, we command you.'

Miss Quinlin bowled another smoke bomb. The ball unfurled at Lila's feet. The smoke ropes snaked upwards, and restrained her limbs. The blind woman shot another flaming arrow. This time, the tip ploughed into Lila's left shoulder. The bus driver slapped more water across Lila's face and Miss Quinlin followed up with a handful of salt.

'Air, fire, water, earth,' they said with one voice, commanding and confident, their heads held high.

Uneven on her feet, Lila grimaced. 'Pathetic. You need more than folk magic to defeat me.' But her voice wasn't as strong as her words.

The women ignored her. They launched their weapons: smoke, flaming arrows, infused water and salt flew in all directions. Lila covered her head with her arms as the three women closed in and circled around her.

'By the power of the Warden, we command you. Water to drown, fire to burn, air to smother, earth to bury.'

Lila dropped to her knees as an arrow stuck straight through her torso and flames licked at her from both sides.

'Water to drown, fire to burn, air to smother, earth to bury.'

Lila swatted weakly as showers of salt bounced off her body.

'Water to drown, fire to burn, air to smother, earth to bury.'

Lila's face and neck were scorched in sections like pork crackling. The air was cloudy with smoke and the smell of cloying chemicals and roasted flesh.

'Leave this body. Leave this child and return to whence you came.'

Lila crumpled into a heap on the concrete, howling and screeching. Her high-pitched cries scratched at Violet's eardrums.

The shadow hands loosened their grip around her body.

'Leave this body and return to whence you came.'

The three women circled Lila as the smoke billowed and thickened covering Lila's head like a sack.

'Leave this body and return to whence you came.'

Lila folded in on herself, like a slug in salt.

The lights blasted on. The room was as bright as a relentless summer day. The temperature sky-rocketed and within seconds sweat trickled down Violet's spine. In the harsh white light, the shadow hands completely evaporated and Violet leaped off the drill bench. She hurried towards Angelika, who was slumped against the saw bench, her eyes stretched open but unseeing.

'Help,' said a little voice.

Violet stopped.

Lila. The real Lila.

Lila looked up through messy hair, her face criss-crossed with weeping sores and jagged red welts. With a trembling lip, she reached out for Violet.

'Leave this body and return to whence you came.' The women continued their chant.

'Stop,' Violet cried and rushed to the circle of women with her arms outstretched. 'It's Lila. Can't you hear her?'

'It's not complete,' said the blind woman. 'We have not defeated it. Leave this to us.'

'Violet, please? Make them stop,' Lila sniffed. 'I'm sorry. I only wanted to help you.'

'By the power of the Warden, we command you. Water to drown, fire to burn, air to smother, earth to bury.'

'You're hurting her!'

'Don't listen to what she says,' the bus driver said. 'It is not your friend.'

'You don't understand. It's gone from her. Can't you see?'

'No,' said Miss Quinlin, grasping at Violet's wrist. 'We're not finished. Trust us.'

Violet pushed aside the three women and wrapped her arms around Lila's neck, and drew her into her chest.

Lila rested her head against Violet's shoulder and sobbed. 'I'm sorry.'

'I know. I'm sorry, too.'

The friends embraced, laughing and crying at the same time, their tears dampening their black witch costumes.

'It's all over now.' Violet smiled.

CHAPTER 17

VIOLET

Lila's shoulders heaved with heavy sobs. Violet held her tight. 'It's gone. You're safe now.'

'Be careful,' the bus driver warned.

The three women loomed over the girls, their faces wrinkled with concern. Bombs, arrows, water and salt at the ready.

Lila bit down on her shaking lip. 'Make them go away.'

'You're upsetting her,' Violet said. 'You can go now.'

'Violet. Listen to us. We can't go yet,' Miss Quinlin said.

'Thank you for getting rid of it, but we don't need you anymore. Can't you see? She's all better.'

'The entity is strong. Don't be fooled,' said the blind woman.

'I'm not an idiot. I know my friend when I see her.'

'Do you?' said the bus driver.

'Leave us alone. It's over.' Violet pointed towards the door. 'Thanks for your help. But it's time for you to go.'

The three women did not move.

Lila sobbed again.

'Go.' Violet got to her feet, her nostrils flaring.

Miss Quinlin and the bus driver glanced over at the blind woman standing firm. They copied her.

Lila covered her face with her chewed fingers. Violet crouched beside her, rubbing her back.

Little by little, Lila's crying changed.

Gradual and faint at first, her sobs softened into giggles.

Violet recoiled with a sharp inhale.

Lila's laugh grew louder, more malevolent and amplified into a high-pitched shriek as a manic grin spread across her scalded face.

'Too easy,' Lila laughed and shook her head. 'You never did listen, did you, Violet?'

Miss Quinlin, the blind woman and the bus driver moaned and clutched at their stomachs.

'You think you can defeat me with a few chemicals and water?' Lila stood up. She rolled her shoulders and cracked her neck. She smoothed her hands over her face and when she looked up, her face was clear, skin good as new.

The three women slumped to the concrete floor. Miss Quinlin whimpered.

'Now I have some new friends to play with. What fun.' Lila kicked Miss Quinlin in the face. She flicked off her glasses and crushed the lenses under her boot. Miss Quinlin rolled on the ground like an upturned turtle.

'I command you...' The blind woman spluttered but stopped and writhed as another convulsion tore at her body.

'Leave them alone,' Violet said. This time, her hands were free but her hammer was somewhere on the other side of the room.

If Miss Quinlin and the bus driver could not defeat the evil, what chance did Violet have? If only Anthea or Yaya or even Dahlia were here. Violet scrubbed her fingers through her hair.

Lila paraded around the three women, moving from one to another. 'Eeny. Meeny. Miney. Mo...'

Violet pressed her lips together and launched off the floor onto her feet. 'Take me,' she said, her chin thrust in the air. 'Leave Lila and take me instead.'

'You?' Lila turned, her head tilted to one side. 'I don't think so. It's really quite comfortable here. Once I'm bored with you lot, I'm going out to the theatre to play with the others. No one'll suspect a thing. Weird little Lila is the perfect disguise.'

'You say you've been inside my head.' Violet inched forward.

'Oh, yes.' Lila bounced on her toes. 'A wonderful soup of neuroses and grudges.'

'You know what I'm capable of. I'm much meaner than Lila. It's in-built already. Imagine the extra fun you'd have inside me.'

Lila grabbed the blind woman's head and gripped her by her short grey hair. The woman's face was tight with anger and Lila released her grip, letting her head drop onto the floor with a crack against the concrete. The blind woman stopped moving.

Violet swallowed.

'Go on.' Lila turned back. 'You were saying.'

Violet cleared her throat. 'You've seen the hate I have within me. Wouldn't I make a better host than Lila? Deep down, Lila is good. Not rotten like me.'

'Boo hoo. Poor you,' Lila cackled. 'But you may have a point.'

'Don't!' Miss Quinlin squealed, a stream of blood running down her forehead and between her eyes. 'You don't know what you're doing.'

'Shut up.' Lila stamped on Miss Quinlin's fingers and laughed as the science teacher howled.

'We could burn off their fingernails with blowtorches and then slice them into pieces. With that saw over there,' Violet said, nauseated by her own suggestions.

'Oh.' Lila stopped short and looked over at Violet with a raised eyebrow and a smirk. 'Perhaps I did underestimate you.'

Violet drew in big lungfuls of air and pasted on a smile. 'Leave Lila and come to me,' she said.

'You know what you are saying?'

'I want you to.'

'You all do. Sooner or later.'

'Stop. No,' said the bus driver with a croak. She crawled on her knees across the concrete, and reached out her fingers. 'Stop.'

Lila walked over and stood toe to toe with Violet. Violet's breaths were shallow as Lila studied her face and eyes intensely. Violet's pulse thundered in her ears.

Lila clutched Violet by the throat.

'You asked for this.'

Violet's vision blurred, and the room spun and shimmered. The lights flashed on and off. Lila's fingers squeezed Violet's larynx, her grip so tight that veins were visible on the inside of Violet's eyeballs.

'Ready or not, here I come,' Lila said with a trill.

Violet forced her eyes open. Lila let go of her throat and grabbed a handful of her hair instead. She wrenched back Violet's head and exposed her throat. Lila opened her jaws wide like a snake.

A black shadow emerged from her mouth and curled into the air. The shadow shifted and contorted, from inky clouds of air into the form of a howling man, then a screeching woman and finally into a snarling monster with pointed horns.

The shadow swarmed around Violet's head like a black balaclava and blinded her while a rancid stench invaded her nostrils.

The three women pleaded but their voices seemed so far away as the shadow penetrated her mouth. Violet choked as the blackness trickled down her throat and rushed into her body, freezing her from the inside out. Her heartbeat dwindled to the slow beat of a battle drum. She slipped into the darkness.

Wails of pain rang in her ears, scores of unfamiliar voices. Visions of pools of blood, snapped bones, white gristle and flayed skin passed before her eyes. She saw a man trussed up above a fire, yowling in pain, as a crowd of onlookers chanted and a man in a leather apron carved away his skin with a knife.

Violet writhed and gasped for breath. The shadow was showing her the truth of what happened here in Beacon Hill. The black memories were still fresh in the soil and the school walls played the images back to her.

Violet tumbled further into the darkness and clambered through new footage. She witnessed gun fire, stonings and white-knuckled strangulations. She saw broken teeth, torn dresses and bloodstained underwear.

Then she heard their voices. Young and old, male and female, in every language on earth and yet they all wailed with the same pain.

You won't reject me. Not this time.

I deserve it.

He never loved me.

No, I won't let you go.

It's not my problem.

She shouldn't be walking by herself at night.

They're not even human.

No one will ever love me.

Like punches to the face, Violet was bombarded with new images, new voices. But as the moments ticked by, her initial shock and revulsion quickly faded away. She looked closer and listened harder, this time with curiosity as the scenes of horror skimmed over her.

Before she could stop it, a smile curled across Violet's lips.

She looped back to the original scene, and the sacrifice on Beacon Hill. The way the man's eyes bulged in pain was almost funny, it was so pathetic. Stupid little man. He deserved everything he got.

A new rush surged through Violet's body like a bolt of lightning. The cold was gone; Violet now hummed with a red-hot power. She giggled to herself and glanced around the workshop, her head singing with thousands of years of wisdom and memories, of violence, of betrayal and lies.

Violet understood now. She was not the originator or the instigator. These dark impulses existed naturally in every person. She was only the amplifier.

New images streamed into her mind. A red-combed rooster pecking at childish skin. A man groping a young girl, ignoring her protests and the terror in her eyes. Snakes writhing and hissing, fangs glistening with poison. Spiders crawling. A laughing doll's face. A broken mirror. The punch in the ribs.

Violet tasted and smelled all their fears, both the victims and the perpetrators. She knew everything, what everyone was thinking and worrying about and what they plotted. She saw the longing, the craving for revenge, the wounds underneath that never healed. She sucked in the pain and anguish that radiated from the women and girls lying on the floor. It was delicious. She wanted more.

Then she heard her own laugh. She was cackling exactly as Lila had before her. But Lila was on the ground now, hugging her knees to her chest with wide frightened eyes. This time it was the real Lila staring back.

Violet wanted to call out to her, to explain what she'd done and why, but she couldn't speak for herself anymore, the darkness would not allow it.

VIOLET

Violet was a stranger in her own body.

She grinned at the three women as they helped each other up on unsteady feet, their faces bruised and bloodied.

The power was stronger than she had ever expected, the real Violet was squeezed into the far back corner of her mind.

Violet turned her head and spied the cabinet running along the back wall. The ordinarily locked gates were wide open. She reached inside and lifted out Mr Neilsen's pride and joy: a long sword, its hilt carved with runes in copper and silver. It was fresh and new but an imitation of an ancient style. Violet bounced the sword in her hand to test the weight.

She took a few wide swipes, enjoying the singing of the sword as it cut through the air. There was no residue of death within the steel, not yet.

The bus driver, the blind woman and Miss Quinlin joined hands in a circle and resumed their chanting. Their voices were low, but of course, Violet could understand them. She heard everything and everyone, both internal and external. The way their fear intermingled with the spell was delicious. Their efforts were futile, their words meaningless and weak, and yet her fingers and toes began to itch.

'Is that all you have?' Violet laughed as she sauntered towards them, swinging the Viking sword. She pondered over which woman should lose her head first and imagined the splatter of blood onto the concrete. But the tickling irritation continued like a buzzing mosquito she couldn't swat.

'I haven't got all day. Give me your best shot, ladies,' Violet said. 'There's a whole cast of messed up children waiting for me.'

The scratching intensified and spread into her skull. Her head gnawed with a dull ache. Behind the pain, the real Violet sensed a gap, an opening within her mind, and she stretched out and crept into the vacant space. Whatever the three strange women were doing, it was working. Violet felt her own hand grip the sword.

She opened her fingers and the sword dropped to the floor with a clang. The power growled inside her but Violet smiled back sweetly.

'It's too late,' the darkness said through her own mouth. 'I have you.'

'That's what you think.' Violet grimaced, each word a struggle ejected forcefully through her lips. She clutched tightly at the space within her own head. There could be no retreat.

But without her bidding, her hand reached down for the sword. She tried to pull her arm back but her fingers were wrapped around the hilt before she could stop herself. Then she was upright with the sword confidently in her right hand.

'Who's in control?'

Violet tried to scowl but the dark visitor kept a smile plastered on her face. She forced her lips open and stammered, 'I want you to leave. Leave this place now. Leave us.'

'I belong here. There is so much ego and angst within these school grounds, I could stay full for years.'

'Leave.'

'She invited me.' Violet's finger pointed at Lila.

'If I'd known what...' Lila cowered and swallowed hard. 'I am so sorry.'

'Your invitation has been withdrawn,' the real Violet replied. 'Leave.'

'I command you to leave. I command you to leave.' The three women chanted under their breath and looked at Violet with light gleaming in their eyes and smirks on their lips. The temperature of the workshop plunged and their breath rose into the air in puffs of white smoke.

'You don't dare,' said the darkness through Violet's mouth.

'I command you to leave,' Violet joined in, repeating the words along with the three women.

'I command you to leave.' This time Lila's voice joined them.

'I don't listen to schoolgirls.'

'You will listen to me.'

'Oh, will I?'

Three pairs of shadowy hands materialised above Miss Quinlin's head. Violet gasped and the science teacher gulped but she maintained her mantra, even as the hands descended over her face.

One dark hand clapped over Miss Quinlin's mouth while another hand pulled back her curly head, revealing her pink chubby throat. The bus driver whimpered and the blind woman frowned with confusion, unable to see what was happening but unable to break the chant to ask.

Miss Quinlin spluttered under the gag of the shadowy hand. Another pair of hands grabbed her ankles and swept her off her feet. She landed heavily, her elbows and hips hitting the concrete hard, white salt spilling from her bag onto the floor.

'Let her go,' Violet said weakly but she could feel the incantation waning. Once again, the delicious cold power vibrated deep inside her and radiated from the marrow of her bones.

An image appeared inside Violet's mind, a glimpse of the entity's next move.

'No,' Violet stuttered.

But the shadowy hands paid no attention to her.

A hand hovered over Miss Quinlin's chest and like a blade, it plunged deep inside. The shadowy fingers pierced through the science teacher's clothes, her skin, her ribs. Her eyes bulged as she screeched.

'Stop,' Violet cried.

The others stopped their chanting and stared.

Miss Quinlin thrashed and babbled, her eyes rolling as the hand dug deep inside her chest. She moaned and convulsed on the floor.

'I'll show you who is in control,' Violet's lips said.

The black hand re-emerged from Miss Quinlin's chest, gripping a mass of blood and flesh in its fingers.

Violet's eyes widened.

The bus driver screamed as the shadow hand thrust the glistening red heart triumphantly into the air. Blood dripped through the black fingers onto the oil-stained concrete.

Miss Quinlin's body shuddered and jerked. Red tears ran down her pale cheeks and dribbled from her ears. Her chest was clean. Not a single drop of blood stained Miss Quinlin's pink fluffy cardigan.

'Neat, huh?' The entity said. 'I too can move in mysterious ways.'

Miss Quinlin's convulsions stopped. Her body lay limp and still. The bus driver choked out a sob and rushed over to her.

'Someone tell me what's happening?' cried the blind woman.

'And then there were two. How does the saying go? Two is for mirth.'

The hand, brandishing the stolen heart, glided through the air towards Violet.

'No,' Violet said.

'Oh yes,' her own lips replied.

The hand came closer and closer. Violet could smell the raw meat, the stink of a butcher's shop.

'Open wide.'

Violet clenched her jaw hard but her body was not her own and her mouth opened obediently.

'No,' she tried to say but the words were only inside her head, and even then they were faint and weak.

She gagged as the first drop of blood hit her tongue and the dark hand shoved the wet organ into her mouth. She shuddered, her mouth overflowing with the taste of blood and uncooked flesh. Her cheeks bulged and bile shot up her windpipe like a flame. Despite her protests, she started to chew.

Her back teeth worked hard, grinding up the rubbery valves and ventricles. Her jaw muscles cried out with the strain but the hand pushed more into her mouth, forcing her to gulp down the half-chewed lumps. A tear trickled down her face as she munched on her science teacher's heart.

But then the cloying taste of iron and tough texture disappeared and Violet's mouth was filled with sweet whipped cream, ripe mango, raspberries dusted with sugar and pink marshmallows. This was the most glorious delicacy she'd ever tasted. She wanted it and she wanted more.

Violet gobbled it down, groaning with delight.

Until she was interrupted.

'What the hell?' said a voice.

Holly stepped into the light, her hand clamped her mouth.

Violet wiped the wetness from her mouth with her back of her hand. She looked down and saw the smears of blood on her skin. Miss Quinlin's blood. The illusion and the taste of ambrosia vanished in an instant and her mouth was filled with the foul taste of rotting meat. Realising what she was doing, she retched.

HOLLY

'Violet?' Holly's eyes widened.

Violet stood hunched like an animal, her teeth and lips wet with blood.

'What is going on?' Holly stammered, her arms shaking as she held the fire extinguisher higher. It was worse than she ever could have imagined. 'What are you eating?'

'It's not how as it appears.'

Holly spun around to face the woman bus driver, the woman with the strange predictions.

'You?' Holly said. 'Why are you here?'

'She's right, Holly,' Lila murmured. Holly squinted into the shadows and saw her friend slouching against one of the standing drills, her freckled face ghostly white. 'Violet is trying to save us.'

'Lila!' Holly put down the extinguisher and rushed to her side. 'Are you okay?'

'I think so. But I'm not the one who needs your help right now.'

'I knew it was her all along. Why wouldn't anyone listen to me?' Holly said, her mouth tightening.

'No. You've got it wrong. It was me. I invited the demon in.'

'Demon?' Holly recoiled. She blinked rapidly, her eyes darting between Lila and Violet.

Violet grinned as she licked blood from her fingers. 'Welcome Witchy-poo,' she called out across the workshop. 'How nice of you to join us. Have you met the science teacher? Oh, and the lovely Rowan of course.'

Violet gestured to the two corpses on the concrete: Rowan face down and Miss Quinlin on her back with red rivulets down her face.

'Are they...?' Holly clutched at her throat. 'Did you?'

She stared open-mouthed as she tried to untangle what she saw.

'Your friend is right. We need your help. Join us,' said a new voice. A stranger, a woman with milky blue eyes. 'Together we can defeat her.'

'You and your nursery rhymes,' said Violet. 'Don't waste your time.'

'She invited the demon inside her,' the bus driver continued.

'To save me,' Lila said.

Violet paraded up and down, swinging a sword. The blade glinted in the light and sang through the air.

Holly tilted her head. 'Are you absolutely sure it's not Violet?'

'Believe me,' Lila whispered.

From the outside, there was nothing different about her, aside from the blood-smeared mouth, of course. Demon or no demon, she was still the centre of all this chaos. Had Violet drawn Lila into her delusion?

Yet somehow the air in the room seemed filled with a cold dread that dragged at her heart. As though all her nightmares had gathered in one place. Was this what evil felt like?

Holly sucked in a shaky breath. Nothing made any sense but at the very least, the bus driver and the other woman had a plan.

She wiped her damp palms on her witch's costume. 'What do I need to do?'

'Take over from Bridget,' the blue-eyed woman said. 'We need a third.'

'Miss Quinlin?' Holly gulped as she looked again at her teacher's dead body. 'What happened to her?'

'Best you don't know.' The bus driver grimaced. 'First we need to get to her bag. Help me.' She pointed to a calico library bag strapped diagonally across Miss Quinlin's chest.

Holly winced but followed the bus driver's instructions. The bus driver led the blind woman to the corpse and placed her hands on the dead woman's shoulders.

'On my count?' The bus driver said.

Holly slipped her hands underneath the fuzzy pink cardigan. She swallowed. The body was still warm.

'One. Two. Three. Lift.'

She and the blind woman groaned with effort. Miss Quinlin was not a small woman in life. In death, she weighed a ton.

'Need some help over there, girls?' mocked Violet.

They managed to lift the body just high enough for the bus driver to slip the strap off Miss Quinlin's shoulder. The bus driver handed the calico bag to Holly.

'Inside you'll find salt and smoke bombs. Once the spell has begun, follow—'

'Spell?' gulped Holly.

The bus driver nodded and Holly thrust the bag back at her, shaking her head. 'No. Sorry.'

'But we need your help,' the bus driver said. 'Together we can drive the entity out of her. Two is not enough.'

'Lila. You do it.'

'We don't know if there are any remnants of the demon still inside her. We cannot take the risk. You are clean.'

'Have you seen this bite on my face. I don't feel so clean,' Holly said. She tried to chuckle but the bus driver frowned back at her.

She swallowed. Not witchcraft. She'd promised herself in kindergarten. This was the one promise she was determined to keep. A single word would undo all the years of denial. Giving in now would make her the Witch Girl after all.

Holly folded her arms tightly across her chest.

She didn't have to follow her family path. She wasn't Dahlia.

'Please,' Lila begged as she tugged at her arm. 'You have to help.'

Violet paced and swung her sword, her face twitching as she muttered. Her face seemed to be split in two halves, her lips curled on the left, then the right, it was as though she was arguing with herself.

'Look. See what the demon has done already.' Lila pointed to the carcasses on the floor. 'What it made me do.' Lila swallowed and scrubbed her hand across her forehead. 'I can still see her eyes, pleading as I squeezed her throat. I wish I could help and make amends. But the ladies are right. I'm tainted. Please. We need you.'

Holly's chest tightened. She dropped her head to avoid their eyes and remembered Dahlia's advice. *'Listen to your gut'.*

Her gut spoke loud and clear.

She sucked in a deep breath.

'I'm sorry. I can't. You have to understand. Anything but that.'

'But we need three,' the bus driver said.

'Is there something else I can help with? I'll get the police?'

'Holly?' cried Lila.

She shook her head. 'I can't.'

'Young lady. This is gravely important,' the blind woman scolded.

'Please, Holly,' said Lila said again.

''Never,' Holly said, knowing they wouldn't understand. She closed her eyes to block out their faces. She knew they wouldn't understand.

Then a new voice spoke, a small frightened voice spoke.

'Please,' the voice said.

Holly's eyes flicked open and she stumbled backwards. 'Violet?' she muttered. 'Jeanette?'

Violet's face was an expressionless mask but her voice was weak and desperate. 'Please, Holly. Help me.'

VIOLET

'Enough!' the voice in Violet's head commanded. It reasserted control and locked her jaw, preventing her from saying anything more.

Violet wished Holly could see past her jailer. Had she shoved Holly away too many times? After everything she'd done, Violet didn't feel she even deserved to be saved. Did Holly?

Holly slumped with a sigh. She wiped her face with her hand. 'You have to understand. I said I'd never do it.' Her eyes welled with tears as she looked at Violet.

It was Violet's turn to sigh.

'No one will save you,' the entity laughed. 'You are mine!'

Violet whimpered but the sound was only audible inside her own head. She let go like a drowning swimmer surrendering to the ocean. She'd saved Lila. At least that was one thing.

Violet noticed Holly bend over. She picked up the calico library bag and slipped it over her head. 'What do you want me to do?'

Violet screamed for joy from the inside of her body.

'Follow our lead,' said the blind woman and the bus driver produced another vial of peridot water. They started to chant again.

'I command you to leave. I command you to leave.' Their eyes gleamed with fresh fervour and on the third round, Holly joined in. 'I command you to leave.'

The women encircled Violet and the itch returned to her hands and feet as the chant growing grew louder.

It was working.

'You wouldn't dare,' the entity snarled from her mouth.

Violet lifted the sword up high. The sharp blade glinted as she brandished it above her head.

'I command you to leave,' the three women repeated. This time Lila joined in, and even Angelika murmured from her slumped position in the corner.

Violet took a deep breath and braced herself. The chant rattled inside her head like an unrelenting car alarm.

'No one wants you here.'

'I command you to leave.'

'There is only one way to banish me and you don't have the guts, Jeanette Black. Or should I say, Violet.' Violet laughed. 'You think you're special. You believe you're better than the others, but you're as broken as anyone here. Such a selfish little brat. I know. I see everything.'

'I command you to leave.'

'You're right. I'm selfish. I'm no one special,' the real Violet said.

'I command you to leave.'

'But you're wrong about one thing. I have the guts. Now!'

Violet plunged the blade in under her own rib cage. The cold metal penetrated through skin and flesh. The blind woman released a burning arrow, the bus driver splashed her with sizzling peridot water, and Holly flung a handful of salt then tossed a smoke ball.

The room went dark, but this time it was not the electricity malfunctioning. Violet's eyes were clouded with pain. She spluttered. The agony was like an operatic chorus, deafening and blinding, more intense than she could ever imagine, each second of pain seemed to last ten.

She doubled over. The sword fell from her fingers in slow motion and landed on the ground with a clang.

'I command you to leave.' The five women continued their chanting, their voices waxing and waning.

'What have you done?' the power said, using her lips.

The real Violet pulled the flaming arrow from her chest and threw it to the ground alongside the sword. She clutched at the hole in her waist as her warm rich blood soaked through her witch costume and pooled in her hand.

'Metal was the missing element,' Violet whispered. 'We were one. I could hear your thoughts like you could hear mine. You told me exactly how to get rid of you.'

A wailing spewed from her mouth, preternatural and ear-splitting.

'Be gone,' the real Violet muttered, her eyes slits.

Her knees buckled and she slid to the ground and lay in a pool of her own blood. She convulsed and a slimy black shadow slipped out of her open mouth.

'Violet!' Lila and Holly rushed over.

As she writhed, Violet thought back to their fateful bus ride home on Monday. The bus driver had been right but Violet wasn't the shining star, she was the one who would depart forever.

Voices and faces swirled above her, and then the workshop and the whole world went black.

CHAPTER 18

VIOLET
A week later

RAVENSWOOD STEPPED ON STAGE IN FRONT OF THE RED CURTAIN. He wore a red chrysanthemum in his buttonhole and a smile on his tired face. The scratches had almost healed.

The audience hushed.

'Ladies and Gentlemen, welcome to our production of William Shakespeare's *Macbeth*.'

The full house applauded.

'This holiday program was a little experiment. A production of Shakespeare in less than a week? In hindsight, what was I thinking? But I believed in my cast and as you will see, they have all risen to the challenge.' Ravenswood adjusted his tie. 'I must thank you all for your patience, given the little postponement of our performance. On a sombre note, tonight's performance is in memory of our beloved science teacher, Miss Quinlin. Not only was she a great educator, but also a great supporter of our theatre program at Beacon Hill High School. I think you'll agree we would have her blessing tonight. So, in memory of Miss Quinlin, 'let's go on with the show' as they say.'

Ravenswood ducked away and the red curtain rose. Dry ice rolled across the stage as the witches stepped into the light.

'*When shall we three meet again,*' said the First Witch.

Toby gave Violet a little nod through the window from his place at the lighting desk as she positioned the spotlight onto Jacinta's green face from her place at the back of the theatrette.

'*When shall we three meet again?*' Jacinta's first words were a little shaky but passable.

Violet knew she would have performed the role better, obviously, but after everything, she'd chosen to step aside and help Toby with the lighting instead.

She stared at the sea of heads and wondered which one was Alan Wolf. She recognised one curly head in the audience. Mathilde, the strange bus driver had popped into the theatrette before the performance started, and pulled Violet aside.

'I am so glad to see you up and about again. It was quite an ordeal you had.' She placed her hand on Violet's shoulder and grinned. 'You are a brave warrior, young lady.'

'I have so many questions,' Violet had said. 'What are you? Soldiers in some kind of army?'

'We're merely a group of concerned citizens.' Mathilde chuckled. 'We have a sacred duty to watch over Beacon Hill and keep the troubles at bay. All the signs told us something was coming but we didn't know exactly where it would manifest. Or with who.' Mathilde sighed, a painful smile on her lips. 'I should have examined my visions more closely. Poor Bridget.'

Violet shook her head. 'You were right. In one way.'

'Regardless, it won't bring her back.'

'But we won.'

Mathilde pursed her lips. 'For now.'

The theatrette, the corridors, the whole school seemed different with no cold pockets and bright reliable lights, even the pipes had stopped their thumping.

When Lila spoke her lines, an honest truth echoed underneath her words:

When the hurly-burly's done,
When the battle's lost and won.

She'd moved out of home to live with her older sister and she seemed to be her old self again. But even under her green witches' make-up, black bags hung under her eyes. To all outside appearances, the dark entity had left her without a trace, there was only Lila behind those eyes, but Violet wasn't so sure whether she was as lucky. Was she left untouched?

Holly spoke next:

That will be ere the set of sun.

She had come to the hospital and sat by Violet's side.

'I'm so sorry,' Violet had said. 'The way I behaved. I was such a… but thank you. I know how hard it was for you.'

'I thought the worst of you.' Holly patted her hand as Violet swallowed a sob. 'I feel terrible. I should have trusted you.'

'It was completely mental. It's still such a blur.'

'Like a weird dream.'

Violet checked the ward for nurses and lowered her voice. 'But what I don't understand is what happened to Rowan? She was there, wasn't she?'

Holly shuddered and leaned closer. 'When the demon left you, it came out of your mouth like black smoke coming out of a chimney. You passed out but then the smoke floated across the room. Over to Rowan and wrapped itself around her neck. Like a leash.'

Violet gasped.

'And then somehow Rowan got up to her feet. She walked out of the workshop with the smoke around her.'

'Where'd she go?' Violet's eyebrows soared.

'No idea.'

They had sat in silence for a moment as Violet pictured the undead Rowan wandering the bushland around the school. Another legend of Beacon Hill was born.

Violet had pushed the thought aside and grabbed for Holly's hand. 'Let's forget about it. All of it. Go back to the way it was. You and me and Lila. Best friends forever?'

Holly cleared her throat and averted her eyes.

'I've got something to tell you. My mum got a new job. In Queensland. We're leaving next week so I can start the new term. Mum says there's heaps more opportunities for me up there.'

'Queensland?' Violet laughed weakly and wiped away a tear. 'How will you cope with all that sun?'

Holly shrugged.

'I can't thank you enough. Thank you,' Angelika said. She was the next person to visit Violet on the ward.

'Don't worry about it.'

'Who knows what would have …' The lump on Angelika's forehead was turning yellow, and her split lip had a healing scab down the centre. 'After what happened to Rowan…'

'Did you see her, too?'

Angelika gulped. 'I thought it was my concussion.'

'None of it makes any sense. But it's over now.'

Angelika leaned over Violet's bed. 'I've been thinking. I want to thank you. Properly.'

Violet shook her head.

'But I want to. I'm not sure I'm up to it. After everything.'

'You'll be fine. You'll be great.'

'Are you sure? You realise what you're saying? You wanted it so badly.'

'And where did it get me?' Violet laughed but winced in pain as she clutched at the stitches in her side.

Lady Macbeth had completely lost her lustre.

The day before the performance, all four girls and their mothers were summonsed to Mrs Petrakis's office. Ravenswood was the only man in the room. He stood at the front of the room beside the headmistress facing eight women with their arms folded.

'While the death of Miss Quinlin is deeply saddening, it was not wholly unexpected,' Mrs Petrakis said. 'Bridget Quinlin was not in the best of health. This was traumatic for the girls to witness but unfortunately, as we all know, our lives are fleeting. We wish we could shield our children but sadly we cannot protect them from the randomness of death.'

Violet frowned.

'But regarding the other *claims*, we've investigated and uncovered that the source of the other complaints was the new paint. Our advisors suspect that certain chemicals inside the paint combined with the stress of the play, lack of sleep and the effect of influencing each other with silly stories about evil spirits…' Mrs Petrakis arched a dark eyebrow at Holly. '…led to their headaches and hallucinations.'

Ravenswood said nothing. He glanced at his shoes as he bit down on his lower lip.

Violet's mum narrowed her eyes. 'So, this is all the school's fault?'

'Please be assured the paint was perfectly safe, Mrs Black. It met all required Australian standards. We would never knowingly put our students in danger.'

'Right,' scoffed Holly's mum.

'There have been multiple recorded cases of schoolgirl hysteria all over the world. I've been reading one particular...'

'With all due respect, Mrs Petrakis, hysteria diagnoses went out with bustles. There is obviously another explanation,' Angelika's mother spat. 'I want the Education Department to undertake a full investigation.'

The other mothers mumbled in agreement.

'If you think this is the best approach, you're perfectly within your rights. Bear in mind, it might make for an *interesting* inquiry. But if you're willing?'

Violet listened with her head bowed. She exchanged a shrug with Holly and Lila but they didn't say a word. Violet was sick of talking. She knew the truth no matter what the adults said.

Violet never imagined she'd enjoy being in the background, but there were other ways to shine like a star. She twisted her body, cautiously avoiding the bulky bandage at her side, and swung the round bright light onto Wayne.

So well thy words become thee, as thy wounds...

THE DARK HAND

Don't be fooled.

You did not defeat me.

The five elements merely pushed me from your body.

Believe me, I left of my own accord.

I went back into the shadows to lie and wait until next time.

I can wait. I know how to wait.

But I'll be back.

Maybe not in Beacon Hill. Perhaps not among the cast.

But have no doubt, I will re-emerge somewhere.

There are billions of you out there, riddled with guilt, pride and despair.

All you need to do is invite me in.

I can help you.

I can help you all.

What fun we could have.

You never know, if you're lucky, our paths may cross again someday.

THE END

*Thank you for reading **The Flower and The Serpent**.*

If you enjoyed this book,
please leave a review or tell a friend and share the word.

ABOUT THE AUTHOR

 Madeleine D'Este grew up in Tasmania and is now based in Melbourne. After studying law (but never practising) and travelling the world, Madeleine now lives a double life, working in corporate Australia by day and writing female-led speculative fiction by night. Madeleine also hosts a writing interview podcast *Write Through The Roof* and a weekly book review show on www.artdistrict-radio.com.

Keep in touch with Madeleine for news, reviews and pictures of cake at www.madeleinedeste.com or on Twitter at @madeleine_deste.

PUBLISHED TITLES

ACKNOWLEDGMENTS

This book is dedicated to Karen and Annie.

As always, I have many people to thank for helping me bring *The Flower and The Serpent* to the page.

My early readers; Martin McConnell, Taj McCoy and Martin Rothaemel, and to Mark Morris for his encouragement and advice to amplify the gore. Thank you as always to my sounding board, Scott McAteer and for his additional theatre knowledge. Thanks to other members of the D'Este Advisory Board including my mum on Tasmanian owls, David Valsorda on fire trucks and Aaron Smith on machinery and all things engineering.

Huge thank you to my editors Jo Burnell and Rebecca Pay, and to Jake Knight for his blurb critiques.

And thanks once again to Deranged Doctor Design for their wonderful cover art and formatting assistance.

THE ANTICS OF EVANGELINE - EPISODE 1

EVANGELINE
AND THE
ALCHEMIST
MADELEINE D'ESTE

CHAPTER ONE

IT ALL STARTED WITH A RAT-A-TAT-TAT ON THE PROFESSOR'S laboratory-workshop door. Evangeline and the Professor looked up from their inventing to see Miss Plockton in the doorway.

"Chief Inspector Pensnett ta see you, sir?" she said.

Evangeline perked up on her stool. A policeman here at 56 Collins Street? Something exciting was surely about to happen.

"Ah, yes. I plum forgot."

Evangeline's father stopped adjusting his new, improved auto-chariot and walked over to the wooden bench, placing his trusty brass screwdriver with the ivory handle down beside neat stacks of brass cogs, wheels and pins. Her father, Professor Montague Caldicott, the pre-eminent horological-engineer in all the Colonies, smoothed down his humongous moustache with his real hand.

"Your lesson is over for today, m'dear. Follow Miss Plockton upstairs and continue with your embroidery."

"But Father..." Evangeline groaned. "I could be of some assistance."

"Police matters are not for the ears of impressionable young ladies. All those dead bodies and smugglers and swarthy criminals. Far too sordid."

"I never get to do anything interesting," Evangeline grumbled as she stowed away her rosewood-handled screwdriver in the pocket of her dress, along with a handful of brass pins. The smaller and more delicate screwdriver was a recent gift from her father, an encouragement to pursue her own inventions.

Evangeline's plain bottle-green day dress, buttoned to the neck, was not the latest fashion but it was better than she had ever imagined in her previous life on the grey foggy streets of London, when her toes poked through holes in her boots. Cold was something she had yet to worry about since she arrived three months ago on the dirigible from Singapore. She wondered whether Melbourne could be anything less than sweltering.

"Out. Out."

The Professor shooed Evangeline and Miss Plockton from the laboratory-workshop, before carefully locking the door behind him.

There was a time when a visit from the police would have frightened Evangeline. She would have hurried to hide her loot, but not today. Today she was a reformed character, setting aside her urchin ways and learning to be a proper young lady. But being good all the time was a bit dull.

Evangeline sulked all the way up the stairs, clumping her feet and dawdling. Her father passed her, continuing up the oriental carpeted hallway into his study, closing the door behind him. The conversation of men was muffled by the closed oak door.

Evangeline loitered in the hallway, waiting for Miss Plockton to drag her into the sitting room to complete her crudely stitched handkerchief. Whilst Evangeline was proficient in many skills, needlecraft was not one of them.

Rather than bustling Evangeline away, Miss Plockton did something curious. Her father's personal secretary produced a large brass key from her pocket and opened the small closet adjoining the Professor's study. The room where all the house linen was stored.

The house on Collins Street, where Evangeline now lived with her new extended family, had many secrets. Built by a gold prospector with some alleged unsavoury tastes, there were many hidden passages and nooks within the walls and floors. Evangeline was yet to be trusted with a set of keys, her attempts to explore the house thoroughly hindered.

Inside the small room smelling of lavender and camphor, Miss Plockton pushed aside a stack of damask curtains, revealing a pencil-sized hole in the wall. An audito-projector, one of the Professor's best-selling patented inventions, appeared from under another stack of bedsheets. Miss Plockton wound the key, placed the brass tube over the hole and the audito-projector sprung into action. The sounds of male voices emerged through the horn, as clear as the Melbourne summer sky outside.

"Eavesdropping, Miss Plockton?" Evangeline gasped.

"On occasion, a secretary needs ta take initiative," Miss Plockton said.

Impressed by Miss Plockton's rebellious act, Evangeline squeezed into the tiny room beside her. There was little room in the linen cupboard with the two women's fulsome skirts.

"Thank you for seeing me, Professor," Pensnett said. His voice was gruff with a tinge of the Black Country.

"My pleasure, Chief Inspector. Anything to help the Constabulary."

"I understand you are responsible for inventing the auto-chariot, sir?"

"Oh, yes. One of my many tinkerings."

"Actually, we've had a few problems with auto chariots. Reckless young gentlemen racing along Flinders Street."

"Oh, I know nothing about that…"

"Not to worry, sir. I am here for your assistance with another matter entirely. I have rather a curious case on my hands."

Evangeline's skin tingled. She knew there was something exciting in the wind today.

"We have reports of new unusual shipments of gold hitting the market of Melbourne."

"I am a humble horological-engineer, sir. Although I occasionally branch out into other experimentations, I know nothing of rocks and minerals from the ground. Why is this gold 'unusual'?"

"There have been reports of strange activity. It does not behave as gold should. Apparently gold purchased from a reputable merchant in Goldsmiths Lane has blackened. Overnight."

Evangeline heard a familiar clicking sound. It was the brass fingers of her father's clockwork hand. He was probably stroking his proud whiskers as he often did when he pondered.

"Allegedly, on Monday, the gold was bright and yellow, and yesterday, the nuggets looked more like iron. Dull and grey."

"Of course. Alchemy. Fool's gold."

From her hiding place in the cupboard, Evangeline's eyes widened. But before a gasp of surprise could emerge, Miss Plockton deftly placed a ladylike hand over her mouth. On first inspection, with her tight steely bun and pinched face, Miss Plockton appeared pure hell or high-water Highland Presbyterian, but Evangeline wondered whether she owed some of her efficiency to a touch of the fey.

"We understand you dealt with similar occurrences in London, Professor."

"I assisted the Goldsmiths Guild by developing a device to identify the offending alchemical material. I can't remember whether I brought it with me. I'll have to rummage through my trunks."

"Was the perpetrator apprehended?"

"The device was a success…But alas, we were too late to catch the fiend on that occasion."

Evangeline listened greedily to the details of the Professor's colourful past. Perhaps he was not as boring as he appeared. They had only been reunited for three months, and there was so much she did not know about her long-lost father. She had not even heard the full story of his missing arm. She vowed to grill him at the next available moment.

"Do you have any clues to the identity of this scoundrel, Chief Inspector?"

"Unfortunately not. The heights of the gold rush are over but Melbourne is still a transitory town. It is hard to keep up with all the comings and goings."

"And there is still plenty of money to be made by unscrupulous characters."

"Indeed. I thought I'd come out to the Colonies for a quiet life."

The Chief Inspector and the Professor chuckled.

"Clues are scarce, I'm afraid," Pensnett continued. "When we spoke with the goldsmith in question, he claimed he could not remember the person who sold it to him. The poor fellow was very flustered by his shoddy memory."

"As though his mind had been erased?"

"Quite. He blamed some type of phantasm."

"A ghost? And you believe him?"

"I'm not a man of science. It might sound ridiculous to you…"

"Not entirely…"

"But I have seen enough unexplainable things in my time to keep an open mind. The goldsmith is a reputable businessman."

"Hmm…intriguing."

"And the case gets even more peculiar."

"Do tell."

"The goldsmith surrendered the remaining gold, but when my Constables checked the evidence again this morning, the whole lot had turned grey. Not a speck of gold left."

"Transitory augmentation. How devious."

The linen cupboard door burst open.

"Hallo. What is going on here?"

It was Uncle Augie.

Evangeline and Miss Plockton both blushed red, caught in the ungenteel act of eavesdropping.

"A game of sardines? How fun. Move over." Augie's voice boomed as he pressed his generous frame into the cupboard. Evangeline cried out as a heeled boot squished her delicate toes.

"Uncle Augie. You do have big clod-hoppers."

"Miss Evangeline." Miss Plockton scowled. "Language, please. This is not a fish market."

"Ssh," Augie hissed. "You are both terrible at this game. I would have expected better from you, Miss Plockton."

The door swung open again.

The Professor and Inspector Pensnett stood in the doorway, frowns etched into their foreheads.

"Oh drat. They found us. Squeeze on over, Miss Plockton. We must make room," Augie said.

"What is going on here?" The Professor stood with hands on hips.

"Sardines, my old chum. Join in."

The Professor spied the audito-projector clamped against the wall and roared.

"You have been spying on me."

"Please forgive me, Father…" was all Evangeline could say. Miss Plockton was white as the damask sheets beside her. "I only wanted to…"

"Why is everyone in the linen cupboard?" Uncle Edmund appeared in the hallway, dabbing a handkerchief at his damp forehead, glistening from the outdoor heat. "Is it time for tea?"

"I must be off, Professor," Chief Inspector Pensnett said. "I am grateful for your time and advice."

"Yes. Yes. Let me show you out. Please excuse my impertinent daughter and my secretary. I shall dismiss her at once."

Evangeline gasped again.

"Don't worry, Miss Evangeline. He gives me my notice at least once a week. Usually on Thursdays," Miss Plockton said as she bustled away to fetch the tea.

Evangeline's stomach rumbled loudly. Augie glanced at her, horrified.

"What a beastly noise from a young lady. How can I present you to the Normanbys if your bodily functions speak so loudly?"

"I can't help it," Evangeline retorted.

"You take after your Uncle. Always hungry."

Augie looked fondly over at his best friend. Edmund and Augie had accompanied Evangeline to Melbourne on the long dirigible journey from London to Rome, Rome to Delhi, Delhi to Singapore and then finally

Singapore to Melbourne. The Professor's younger brother, Edmund, was an accomplished architect. He was called to Melbourne to design many of the modern sandstone buildings springing up on every street corner, in preparation for the World Exhibition in 1888. Edmund and Augie were constant companions, they shared a room on the dirigible and even had adjoining rooms here in the house.

Augie, or August Beauchamp, wasn't Evangeline's real uncle. He had recently taken over the Prince Albert Theatre on Lonsdale Street and knew all the fashionable people in town. When he wasn't managing the theatrical types of Melbourne, he was Evangeline's strict etiquette master.

A triangle chimed down the wooden hallway.

"Goody. Tea. I'm famished," said Edmund as they all emptied the linen cupboard and traipsed down the hall to the conservatory.

Evangeline smiled to herself. She hoped there would be more talk of the mysterious alchemist over tea. It would be awfully exciting if the Professor would let her help.

To read more of *Evangeline and the Alchemist*, go to Amazon, Kobo, Apple Books and many other ebook platforms.